DRINKS WITH DEAD POETS

Glyn Maxwell

Drinks With Dead Poets

The Autumn Term

OBERON BOOKS
LONDON

WWW.OBERONBOOKS.COM

First published in 2016 by Oberon Books Ltd
521 Caledonian Road, London N7 9RH
Tel: +44 (0) 20 7607 3637 / Fax: +44 (0) 20 7607 3629
e-mail: info@oberonbooks.com
www.oberonbooks.com

A catalogue record for this book is available from the British Library.

HB ISBN: 9781783197415
E ISBN: 9781783197422

Printed and bound by CPI Group (UK) Ltd, Croydon, CR0 4YY.
eBook conversion by Lapiz Digital Services, India.

Visit www.oberonbooks.com to read more about all our books
and to buy them. You will also find features, author interviews and news
of any author events, and you can sign up for e-newsletters so that
you're always first to hear about our new releases.

for Anna Leader

Preface

Every word, phrase or sentence spoken by the literary figures in this book is drawn *verbatim* from their letters, diaries, journals or essays.

Words have been elided here and there, or slightly edited, the better to resemble speech of the passing moment, but I have at every point sought to preserve the tone and meaning – if not the immediate context – of the written words. For the sketches are not intended to be biographically accurate with regard to appearance, accent, attire or manner. Nor do they imply any personal hierarchy of poetic importance. They are animations of how it felt to encounter particular bodies of work, each of which has had a significant influence, whether aesthetic, intellectual, or even dreamlike, on my life as a reader and writer – in fact on my life as a life. As such, they are drawn in a spirit of reverence and good humour. They, like the village and the students and their mystified professor, are works of make-believe.

Week One – September 26th

I am walking along a village lane with no earthly idea why.

I mean it, it's raining, left foot, right foot, left foot miss that puddle, I know it's a village lane because the sky is plentiful, albeit white – *it all be white* – and the cottages peter out a short way up ahead. Tiny front gardens for this pot and that pot, some tasteful wrought-iron lampposts till they end in the trees. Very few cars – actually none, not one. Looking back the way I came I have no clue where I just came from.

I know it's a village because a little corner-shop for anything's coming up right now, the cluttered glass bay window seems to bulge out over the pavement as I pass it and am noticed by two conversing figures within and now I spy a grand little pub across the road. It has a crooked chimney and a red-and-gold sign. I'm at the four-ways, I suppose, the junction, the heart of the place. The grand little pub is called the Cross Keys, and it's open, or its side door is, opening into grey-green light but I'm evidently dreaming so I may not need a drink at all.

To my right the road curves away gently uphill towards trees, brown scruffy woodland, I can't see all that far that way. To my left, now I look, the opposite way, I see a wide kind of boulevard marching off tree-lined, a broad oval green along its centre, plenty of large houses, white and pink and yellow and pale blue. A couple of hundred yards away there's the black-and-white striped awning of some kind of *inn*. So there's a pub, and there's an inn.

I breathe. I consider it to be afternoon, early afternoon. I consider it – probably – to be autumn. I consider myself to be dreaming, my clothes to be – a quick look – *on*, my mind to be sound. I wait for the place to disappear, go away, be batted away, for my dreams will never long allow me that glee of knowing the game – think what I'd get up to, I did that once! – but I'm just standing here in the drizzle.

What would you do?

*

It's a free house, a warm dark empty pub with a saloon bar and a public bar. I stop inside: it's *today*, I note with weird relief, it's *nowadays*, not a day I saw coming but nevertheless it's *nowadays*. That means everyone I know is somewhere. I cross the floor of the saloon bar where a fruit-machine is flashing all alone by the wall, fruits hurtle, fruits arrive, nobody wins, nobody dies. The carpet reeks with old beer. There are green lanterns in alcoves in the walls. There's a fire look, someone cares.

I hear a peal of laughter around the side of the bar and some youngish people are clustered round pints and half-pints. I'm not dead then. They have bags and coats and suitcases around them, they're arriving or departing. They turn and stare at me or grin and look away as I near the bar, and it seems to me it's all gone quiet. Am I meant to be saying something?

Well I don't say hello because I'm not that sure they're real. Maybe that's why I seldom do.

At the God-given haven of *any bar on earth* I smile though no one's there. No one's – tending. So I admire the bewildering citadels of optics and my mirror-self's there too in his black coat look, he seems rather more at home, not unsatisfied with arrangements.

I will wait here till I know. Wait here till things change, till I remember where I've got to, till this bright white interlude makes sense and I can go. I scan the glossy okay menu avidly as a stocky man in green trudges up the steps from a stone realm below the floor.

'What can I get you squire.'
White wine please white wine.
'Small or large.'
Large, it's raining. Also, do you have the papers?
'No.'
Right. No worries.
'Look at 'em all just drinking in the day.'
I'm – drinking in the day.
'Students I mean.'

Right.

'£4.30.'

Right, so... students. There's a college here?

'Yeah tell me about it.'

I rather wanted him to tell *me* about it, but I liked the idea of pretending I belonged – if I *did*, maybe I *would* – so I nodded like I knew and took my large wine to a little wiped table in the corner, at the other end of a series of tables, the last of which was the students. They weren't all young over there. There was an older woman with a gentle look and hair mildly tinted lavender, leaning forward to see, and a solemn lad with a bristly face, not a lad a bloke, throwing me a watchful look. The others, twenties, thirties, a group of – colleagues? A thin hunched boy with dark hair drooping over an eye. A tall pretty brunette with a big white woollen scarf she is turning round to look at me who cares they're all departing. I would follow them to the station. If there's a station.

One of the younger ones had cropped scarlet hair, she raised a good-as-drained pint in my direction.

'Just got here?' she demanded, both charming and accusing.

Just got here, I said, which was true, actually, and somehow sweet to say.

'Don't mind us, we're getting acquainted,' she loudly confided from the midst of them and went right back to doing just that. After which a couple of them kept clocking me and glancing away when I looked. I wondered what they were thinking, assuming they were real.

I was thinking I don't have my phone, I don't have my shoulder-bag, I don't have a place to sleep. I think I need to find a hospital and ask for help – 'Miss, sir, ma'am, doctor, I have a daughter and a life and two parents and two brothers, I was married, I'm a writer, I write books and plays, I do all sorts, my name is – I'll come back to that I live in a long peaceful flat by a canal in Angel will you call someone?'

I'll do that, I think, say those words to someone soon, so I swig my wine and head out through the door, hearing one of the non-existent people say *Nice to meet you too, professor.*

*

It's not raining any more, it's bright and cloudy with the puddles here and there, and off towards – work it out – the north-west there's a patch of blue to be seen through the grey, white, and mauve clouds, some three whole differing races of cloud.

Down here below, where I've no earthly idea, the four corners of the junction are occupied by the pub (north-east), the local shop (south-east), and a little square church (north-west). Diagonally across from me on the last corner is a business, an office of some kind, with a smart sign I can't read from here and a lit room. The person working in there – it's a young smartly-dressed woman I can see and the sign says Student Services – must have put the lights on when it was dark and rainy, she doesn't need them now, but she goes on at her keyboard in there, typing obliviously, tilting her head to read something she needs. I just about make up my mind to make her acquaintance when I'm aware of other movement, to my right, up the way leading north.

Along that lane that leads off between the church of St what does that say Anne's? and the Cross Keys, and a little way up to the right side, there's a long gap between houses. I assume it'll be allotments or a sports ground, it would be where I come from, but there's more of it than that as I near it, much more, in fact it's a fairly huge ploughed field stretching away from a low wooden fence. This is rather a small village, there's an end to it right here. The field rises gently, rolls and reaches the vague brown woodlands quite a way away, far enough to be misty, and at the fence a dark-haired boy in a costume – a *brunet*, I suppose – is just standing there watching.

Because he looks so ludicrous in his tall white collar and lilac cravat, so focused on the view of sweet nothing in particular, so haplessly wrong in this place at this time, I feel an instant connection, and – I don't exactly approach him, I just stop some twenty yards or so away but also leaning on the fence and I too look at the great ploughed field for a while. The fence is strangely warm in my hands as if with heat he's generating. Then I check I'm not dressed like he is. No my dreams don't run to costumes.

4

By the time I reach the boy he's looking at the fields again and frowning. I find this a bit stagey, but fair do's, he's in costume, perhaps he's sort of *being someone*.

'Atkins the coachman,' he says, 'Bartlet the surgeon, Simmons the barber, and the girls over at the bonnet shop say we'll now have a month of seasonable weather.'

Then he turns to me, this panel of experts having had its say.

Right (I go) there's a bonnet shop?

He nods as if of course there is. Sniffs and looks back at the fields, which clearly impress him more than I do.

'I'll tell you what,' he says, a little softer and more to himself: 'a man might pass a very pleasant life in this manner: on a certain day, read a certain page of full poetry or, or – distilled prose…'

Distilled, yes,

'Wander with it, muse on it, reflect on it, bring home to it, prophesy on it, dream on it till it becomes *stale*… when will it do so?'

When? I – don't know.

'Never.'

I guess not. Have you, um, are *you* doing that today, Master – ?

'Keats.'

Right. Right, obviously, good, so are you doing that today, the thing with the page of poetry? Musing on it? Like you say? Is good to do? John? Sorry *is* it John?

He takes out a handkerchief and wipes his nose, sniffs, makes a pouting shape with his mouth but is also nodding, until he gathers to a sneeze and explodes and recovers, 'Fifth canto of Dante. That one.'

That one. Yep, it's a good'un.

I try to remember what's in that one, while nevertheless nodding in awe at the magnificence of that one, and the boy who's trying to be Keats looks out across the fields again.

'In the midst of the world I live like a hermit.'

Okay, because I'm dreaming I may as well go for it, as the high distant trees are tipped with sunlight – though I lose my nerve almost straight away –

Season of mists and, mellow,

(He looks at me sharply) 'I can't be admired. I'm not a thing to be admired.'

Well. Me neither, man. Have a nice day.

I nod politely and back away down the lane. I'm not a little hurt. I could have rather done with making a friend by the wooden fence there.

Heigh-ho, I muse, I shall have a nice day regardless.

And I *do* have friends here, there's the barman who doesn't like students for one, there's that sceptical angel in the woollen scarf and there's the lavender lady, the pale boy in the corner, and oh there's the figure of the typist through the window in the room called Student Services. Slim pickings perhaps, but it's not a normal day. I don't need to be the pal of some frock-coated emo with his tousled head full of lines and limousines and Oscar speeches. I go striding to the office of Student Services, I am healthy, I sniff the cold fresh mulchy air and my pale old limbs are pumping, I am the captain of the afternoon, let's say, I am at least *involved* with my fate.

*

Because every day of my life it's the same.

I begin at any dawn, have done nothing at all, known no one, thought nothing, written less, left no print. I light candles at my dark window, sit amazed on earth.

I end way after midnight furred and groaning with acquaintance, banner headlines to forget, old stories, fond habits, love if there's love.

Then it all begins again.

This is not the first day in my deck of fifty-two years when I've been puzzled as to where I stood and my best guess was heaven.

*

Student Services was probably in her thirties, had quite sensible fair hair in a ponytail, had a white blouse and a neat blue jacket. She was slightly plump, and frowning. As it's a dream I could marry you, I was thinking. She stopped typing.

'Better late than never!'

I'm not late, I'm dreaming.

'Traffic was it?'

Yes. I – dreamed there was traffic.

'It's still traffic,' she said, getting up from her desk and going to a drawer she slid outward and peered in. The sign on the desk said KERRI BEDWARD.

Then I can't help asking as she stoops to leaf through some file, her blue dolphin pendant jumping free,

Your surname is Bedward, is it Welsh I'm Welsh, kind of.

'It means son of Edward.'

By blood I am, mostly.

'Pardon? This is you.'

READING LIST for Elective Poetry Module
3pm, Thurs, V.H.B.   Prof: Maxwell.

26th Sept.	Keats.
3rd Oct.	Dickinson.
10th Oct.	Hopkins.
17th Oct.	Brontës.
24th Oct.	Coleridge.
31st Oct.	Poe.
7th Nov.	
14th Nov.	Clare.
21st Nov.	Yeats.
28th Nov.	Whitman.
5th Dec.	Browning.
12th Dec.	Byron.

There doesn't seem to be much rhyme or reason in the sequence (I said) which Brontës? Which Browning? Why's there nothing on my birthday?

She was sitting down again drinking juice from a green bottle.

'I wouldn't know.'

You wouldn't?

'It's what you sent us.'

Yeah right. Do you – know – there's kind of an annoying kid dressed as Keats out there on the road by the big field, is it a sort of Keats festival you're having this week?

'I'm not having anything, just my vitamin blast.'

I mean it really helps when you're teaching someone to have his zombie lookalike wandering round the place. Will there be lookalikes every week?

'You had a difficult journey.'

No. No I didn't. It was – easy. Thank you.

'Seen your digs yet?'

Ah!

'Would you like me to show you them.'

Very much. Kerri.

'You've just time before the class.'

The – class.

'It's in your hand.'

READING LIST for Elective Poetry Module
3pm, Thurs, V.H.B.   Prof: Maxwell.

It says elective, I'm going to the pub.

'Elective for them, not you.'

What's VHB mean?

'You're in the village hall. Just over the road.'

VH. What's B?

'It means you're not in the hall, you're in the side room. There's a kettle. And the heater works. There's tea and coffee and there was actually a Twix but I took it and ate it about an hour ago. I'm regretting that now.'

I'm. I'm – teaching Keats in the side-room. To whom?

When she didn't reply I looked at her and she was making her finger go in circles, which I took to mean turn the white page over

H. Bannen
L. Bronzo
O. Faraday
C. Jellicoe
I. McNair
N. Prester
S. Sharma
B. Wilby

'You don't seem very prepared in a way.'

I'm always this prepared.

Upon which a young man came into the office from outside, working his wet blue anorak hood away from his beaming face.

'Professor Maxwell! Raining raining, it's me Orlando! Ollie, Ollie Faraday, remember? Remember from the class?'

Ye-es. Yes I *do*... very much so.

'I haven't seen you since that wedding, I'm in your class again!'

Yes. Why? Didn't I teach you everything?

'What? God no! Christ! (mind my French)'

But I've nothing else to tell you. I was so much older then, you got it all, I retired, I went to heaven look, I met Kerri Bedward.

'Don't mind him,' said Kerri, 'he had a difficult journey.'

*

I live in a – no I don't – I am staying in a very pleasant bright attic room with the sloping ceiling and the cute slanting shelves of dark wood and a desk and a little tartan-blanketed bed and everything! A kitchenette, a tiny bathroom! I reach it – or have done, once so far – up a whitewashed spiral staircase, three floors. There's a bedroom on the first floor, with the door open: it doesn't look like anyone's staying there. The next flight leads to me.

This is perfect.

'Seriously?'

It's down a little lane. From the Cross at the heart of the village you walk a little way north, you leave the church with the village hall behind on your left, the pub behind on your right. The field where the kid was dressed like Keats will come up soon on your right but before you get that far you take a little lane left, not a lane a path, with grass growing through the stones, you keep to this, okay, and mine's the white house at the end, overgrown, where you can't go any further – look I don't know who on earth *YOU* is, I'm just saying there is a place I stay, and if this *YOU* were here, this is what I'd be telling this *YOU,* do you follow me?

'Are you alright, you're staring.'

Sorry. Kerri. I'm getting used to things. I'll look, you know, out of the window.

The view is westward, there's a patch of light behind the clouds, where the sun *would* be hiding mid-afternoon in autumn. Out beyond the village is that long grey lake in the distance. It's got a little wooded island, I wonder if I can get there. There are some larger light-brown buildings in a row before the lake, square and squat, three or four storeys. Before those there's a clear gap where that central green must be, and the inn and the coloured houses. Nearer still, the small spire of the church at the Cross.

It's still raining, but it's brighter now and I think blue sky is coming, if what's over there is coming over here.

Is what's over there coming over here?

'What's he say now,' murmurs Kerri, trying to twist the key off the ring of keys without breaking her nails.

Where's – *everything*. Restaurants, shops, everything. The bonnet shop.

'What? there's no bonnet shop.'

Keats says there is.

'He doesn't live here. You're teaching in ten minutes. After that you can do what you like.'

*

Teaching in a dream isn't that different from teaching in real life. I don't feel ready and I don't feel old enough. I won't remember their names, I'll upset someone. I want to be exonerated. I want to go home to my toys, I'm in the middle of a game with them.

Anyway there they all are in the porch of the village hall, Ollie Faraday and white-scarf woman, there's lavender lady and solemn bristly bloke, pale thin lad, scarlet dye girl and a maybe Indian woman in a pink silk headscarf who's got an e-cigarette with the weird blue tip. I look at my white sheet.

That's only seven.

None of them know who's missing, they all met in the pub or the office or this morning on the train and they've all become fast friends like folk will do in these situations. They've got three in-jokes going and what else do you need.

Finally there's a big beaming fellow in overalls lumbering up the lane. He grins apologetically, like he'd run if he could run, 'Wilby here!' he exclaims, 'Wilby here and always will!'

The clock is striking three in the little bell-tower.

'Barry Wilby!' doesn't look like he belongs with us, and he's too late for the in-jokes, but here he is among us as they all bustle forwards around me, forming a grinning or muttering crew, through the dusty village hall to a cold decrepit side-room I believe we'll be calling home.

*

First did anyone else see the kid out there in the cravat? No?

'Professor, it's – '

Well I did and he said he's Keats. Perhaps he's a teaching material. No one saw him? Okay, perhaps he's a delusion. Either way.

Dyed-scarlet girl has got her hand up.

Yes what.

'Can't we all say our names?'

They have names and they're from places, what an excellent dream this is. I write them down as they say, and ask them to sit in the same seats next week. Though as I'm only dreaming there won't *be* a next week. I draw a little chart to keep from falling to bits with laughter.

Heath (☹)   Samira (ind)

Iona (scarf)   Lily (red)

Barry (big)   Ollie (☺)

Niall (ssh)   Caroline (eld)

moi

I finish off my chart and laugh anyway, trying to make it a cough.

'What's up?' Ollie wonders. He looks sympathetic, like he knows me, can look after me in a way the others can't.

Oh I. I just had déjà vu.

'I get that,' say most of them.

Okay Keats.

'Yay we're back!' Orlando revels to himself.

The thing about Keats is. Or one thing about Keats is. His real name wasn't Keats. (Some of them start making notes.) No his real name was Bains. Johnny Bains.

(Ollie pauses before making this note, is I think looking at me with a tilt of the head for a moment, then bows to these strange tidings, and makes the note in his brand-new book with a floral cover that appears to be made of metal.)

The problem with Keats is *Keats*. The word *Keats, John Keats, Keatsian.* Say it, go on, say it to yourselves (two will, six won't) till you leach all meaning from it.

'Keats,' says Ollie: 'Keats.'

'*Keats…*' Caroline Jellicoe samples it thoughtfully… '*Keats.*'

Because it comes at us just groaning with *poetry, beauty, adieu,* mists of *adieu* and *what ye know on earth,* it's high, it's beyond, it's untouchable, it's *Keats.* I don't think we can hear much else when somebody says *Keats.* So remember: his real name was Bains. Johnny Bains from Norf London…

(I wait for the scribbling to stop.)

Look. It wasn't, cross it out, I'm saying *imagine it was,* I'm saying imagine that's how it struck the ear, because – that's what they thought of him, the circles, the coteries, the tall posh diffident not-needing-a-job literati. And the lad is trying to make it as a doctor, he's gotta make it as *something* or he'll starve, right? His folks are dead and gone, dad at nine, mum at fifteen, his sick doomed brother needs looking after, his little sister does, his other brother's soon to sod off to the New World forever, and the Bains dosh is tied up with some solicitor who never lets them near it. Poor Johnny, coughing little spluttering med student. He doesn't want that life. He turns away from anatomy books by candlelight and tries his hand at this:

New Morning from her orient chamber came,
And her first footsteps touched a verdant hill...

We all started somewhere. I in my aunt's living-room in a house outside Geneva. Fifteen one afternoon, sitting alone by a grand piano, wrote on a piece of paper against the long black polished lid – 'It's spring and the flowers haven't opened/ There's one too many stars in the sky.' Look we all start somewhere. Eight years later I got a poem accepted for some leaflet. I literally jumped for joy. (A quarter-century later I sent six poems to the *London Review of Books* and got one accepted. My first reaction was to wonder *what's wrong with these other five?* Don't become me.)

Anyway it was quicker for Johnny Bains, and it needed to be. Johnny mate you've got a poem in *The Examiner!*

O Solitude! if I must with thee dwell,
Let it not be among the jumbled heap
Of murky buildings; climb with me the steep –

Meanwhile in a nicer part of London: *I say chaps, have a look at this 'Johnny Bains', he's not just apprenticed to a sawbones, look he's got verses in here! I say, have a read, Johnny wishes to be alone, but not just any old way. He feels the buildings are looking jolly murky today, oh you do, do you Johnny? So what he's going to do is climb, shall we all climb with Johnny?*

They called him one of the *Cockney School,* spat it out like gentlemen, but little Johnny Bains is hiking on the slopes of Parnassus! He's going to be a poet! He has less than five years left.

*

In a dream you can teach anything, no one's watching, no one's here.

I thought maybe I'd teach poetry like I write it, try and engage anything, books, jokes and make-believe, show where it is I'm standing when I think, what the view is as I feel things, what the light's like while I breathe, because nothing I can do or say takes anything from anywhere. I'm only giving back in the light of how it came.

*

So, in contrast to Johnny Bains, you all have the capability to vanish right out of poetry right now. Feel free to do so. You do that by taking an almost conscious decision to cease hearing. You do that by filing John Keats and his murky buildings and his mellow autumn and his drowsy numbness away in a file marked Old Immortal Poetry – *adieu, adieu* – and filing away with it every physical *bodily* element that make his work indestructible, unkillable, *not leaving before you do.*

Then you go back to writing like you think the thing is done now. Like the thing is done since one day, phew, someone figured out life is ugly, has no beauty, needs no music, is simply *not to be risen to.*

Example: *I feel like shit, feel like I've been drugged old-school. That bird's kinda like me, making its one noise. That's all I want to do, that or maybe die. I dunno. Probably dreaming anyway.*

Just a normal day in dreamland, we can access that. But how does that feeling arrive *at the body*, when you slow time down, when you put a hand on it as it marches by in its uniform, and you bemuse it with *this*?

> My heart aches, and a drowsy numbness pains
> 　　My sense, as if of hemlock I had drunk,
> Or emptied some dull opiate to the drains
> 　　One minute past, and Lethe-wards had sunk:
> 'Tis not through envy of thy happy lot,
> 　　But being too happy in thine happiness, –
> 　　That thou, light-wingéd Dryad of the trees,
> 　　　　In some melodious plot
> Of beechen green, and shadows numberless,
> 　　Singest of summer in full-throated ease...

In saying this to yourself you take it very slowly, and you try to be aware what your throat, tongue, and lips are doing. Which means heeding the vowel-lengths, the consonant-clusters, because some words take a huge great while to say, they lie longer on the body, seem in no haste to leave you.

And you feel the movement of the frown on your forehead, the wrinkles and eyebrows, the bouncers at the gate – 'what's it like man it's like *hemlock* – how long ago shit was it *one minute???* – plot of green what green very green kinda *beechen* green, *that* green!' – the hairs of your eyebrows act like the hairs up your nose, class, absorbing what comes in at you through the senses, whether it's one of the senses or all five or all seven.

Poems that stay stay because the body feels them.

I said: *Poems that stay stay because the body feels them.*

Because the body doesn't *want* to move at the pace of time. It *wants to be slowed down.* That's pretty much its only wish. *Singest of summer in full-throated ease…* Never end, never end, I am ending, never end…

The body desires to be slowed down and to be graced, adorned, with language.

It wishes, fair creatures of an hour, it wishes all its life to be at standstill.

And when I feel, fair creature of an hour,
    That I shall never look upon thee more,
Never have relish in the faery power
    Of unreflecting love; – then on the shore
Of the wide world I stand alone, and think
Till love and fame to nothingness do sink.

Two years left.

So Johnny Bains writes poems to a season, to a month, to sadness, to a vase, to sleep, to stones, to *laziness* for Christ's sake, to fame, to Milton's hair, Mrs Reynolds's cat and the Elgin sodding Marbles, he addresses things, he apostrophizes, O this, O that, O, O, O is awe, the maw, the craw, the oral, O is the open mouth, astonishment, horror, wonder, and it is the stamp and seal of Old Poetry to be filed away where you file Old Folks, but think of it another way…

Johnny Bains, for his seven years of work, is telling the world *I love you*. He's ill half the time, he coughs and hauls his breath back up, so his poems can gasp *I love you*. By the time he's coughing blood on the cotton sheet he's in love with *actual* Fanny Brawne

– bright star, would I were steadfast as thou art – so he just goes on saying *I love you* till there's no you, and no I, and no years left at all.

See, you're blushing by now. It's *oh* these days, not O.

*

But I'm dreaming, I'll say anything. I'm dreaming I said anything. I think I like Iona, she's Scots, Iona McNair, am I this old in the dream? And big Barry's got his hand up.

Big Barry. I mean Barry. (I get away with things in dreams.)

'What is it you mean when you say he's got two years left?'

I step back to absorb this question, and you know it never does get answered, never would and never will, as right then the sun comes in, O – man alive does the sun come spreading in, fair floods our little room with gold, the low last autumn sunlight finally making it to my class. They have bronze in their hair, Ollie, Caroline, Iona, and their clean new pencil-cases glint in it and their water-bottles gleam with it, and the pages all turn yellow and some sighs and yays and murmurs mark the pleasure of having sun for the last, late, only time today. We move gently towards, like waterlife under the waves. Because soon it's gone again, wrong side of clouds or houses, and we're left with the blue-grey embers of afternoon, and eight strangers to get used to, and all these scrawled-on yellow pages suddenly everywhere.

'What is it you mean when you say he's got two years left?'

Class… people… why is the paper yellow?

'What's that?'

All these sheets of paper were white. And now they're yellow, yellow-gold…

Lily Bronzo opens her mouth: 'Is it off hemlock you haff drunk?' and they all laugh and chuckle and wait for me to. But:

No I'm serious, look, I got them from the office, from Kerri Bedward in the office it was a big sheaf of white paper it came from a box in the corner!

Ollie addresses everyone: 'He's had a bit of a rough journey, apparently right professor?'

'Is it important, the colour?' Iona McNair wonders with concern.

Yes no it's the – reading list. I gave it out at the start, did I not?

'You did!' says Barry Wilby, lifting his own yellow sheet and flapping it in the air, 'got it handy. *Reading Series!*'

Reading List.

'Reading Series,' says Barry, mournful like it's his fault.

Reading – ?

'Series,' confirms Samira, sitting back and looking out of the window.

'It really is *quite* a series,' Caroline bucks me up.

'Cool game this sir,' says Lily Bronzo.

'Why don't you look at it, mate,' the bloke called Heath murmurs from the far end of the table as he doodles over his.

Yes. Why don't I.

So I look at my yellow page with the Reading List.

READING SERIES.

Elective 711: Poetry/Maxwell   *Thursday, Village Hall, times TBC.*

26th Sept.	Mr. J. Keats.
3rd Oct.	Miss. E. Dickinson.
10th Oct.	Fr. Hopkins SJ.
17th Oct.	The Misses Brontë.
24th Oct.	Mr. S. T. Coleridge.
31st Oct.	Mr. E. A. Poe.
7th Nov.	Field Trip.
14th Nov.	Mr. J. Clare.
21st Nov.	Mr. W. B. Yeats.
28th Nov.	Mr. W. Whitman.
5th Dec.	Mrs. E. B. Browning and Mr. R. Browning.
12th Dec.	Lord Byron.

Just testing, I knew that, guys. Of course it says Reading Series. Poe on Halloween, I get it, a Field Trip on my birthday yay, of *course* the page is yellow…

'Sir.'

Yes, um, Lily.

'Why do you keep saying you're dreaming?'

Do I?

'I like it,' says Niall softly on my left, the only thing he's said.

I don't know, Lily. I think I'm going to stop now.

'Also it's like, we've *paid?*'

I make appointments with most everyone, three next week, three the week after, three forever I shall look at their poems, that's why they're here, to meet me one-to-one and learn how to be poets, I shall no longer say I'm dreaming as it seems more likely I'm in some sort of long-term coma, between you and me and the gatepost with which I have evidently collided, and off go all my poets through the gloomy village hall again, out to the chilly daylight and away in twos and threes.

*

'Wasn't so difficult was it.'

Kerri Bedward's in a light brown coat, she's locking up her office.

How do you know it wasn't difficult, it was difficult.

'It's not difficult now, it's over now.'

I suppose. Where's, um.

'What?'

Where's.

'What's the matter. Say.'

Where's. Um… Oh for chrissake where's Keats.

'Who the visiting poet?'

Yes the visiting poet.

'He went past the window about an hour ago, towards where you were.'

The village hall?

'That's where he's reading. Look at the yellow sheet.'

It was white when you gave it to me, Kerri.

'Pardon? No it wasn't.'

I took it from that pile of – oh. They're yellow. Very yellow. Long day.

'Two hours, sure, exhausting. I was here at eight-thirty.'

I didn't exist then. Sorry – look I'm just thinking, Kerri, if he's

Keats – of course he's Keats, *I* knew that – it's just I didn't remind the students, I handed out the Reading Series, do you think they'll come and hear him? He's Keats.

'Well you know, students. Also there's a Meet'n'Greet tonight, like a big Orientation? All the writing students, all the professors.'

There's what?

'A little party at the halls, white wine, sort of thing, get-to-know-you. Quiche. You should go if you're not busy. There'll be lots of folks there, it's in Cartwright 202.'

Fucking Keats is doing a reading.

'Pardon?'

Sorry.

'You know what students are like, um, *Glyn*, they've got lots of options, they're customers these days.'

*

I find him sitting on the stage in the village hall, we must have all walked right past him. He has a little blue hardback volume face down on the stage and his eyes are shut. It's a low and dusty stage but then he's not a very tall chap so his legs don't reach the floor. I test the fluorescent lights a bit, good grief we're doing this here, then I go and sit down next to Keats. My legs do reach the floor.

Look John I should have asked you to the class, now I think, I'm a moron, what've you been doing?

He picked up the little book, looked at it, and closed it.

'Reading, writing, fretting. The last I intend to give up and stick to the other two.'

That's a plan. You – wrote this afternoon?

He beheld his dangling legs in their grey velvet, frowned, and gathered them up beneath him until he sat cross-legged on the edge of the stage, swaying side to side with the effort. Then he broke into something like a little grin: 'I say to the Muses what the maid says to the man: take me while the fit's on me.'

Ha ha ha! (I roared with laughter) ha ha ha ho yes ho ho brilliant John I like it he he he it won't be a *huge* crowd tonight, more of a select sort of quality crowd it's, you know, the start of term.

'I never expect anything.'

Usually wise in this line of work. Would you take some questions after the reading? Then maybe we could get a beer in the, you know. There's a tavern in the town.

His eyes light up and he raises his hand as if to remember something he heard lately: 'Stopping at a tavern they call – *hanging out.*'

They do, yes!

'*Where do you sup?* is *Where do you hang out?*'

It still is, these days! We still say – I mean it just – it is.

'Hanging out… with a cherry brandy.'

Quite possible! Anything else you'd drink if they don't have…?

'I enjoy claret, to a degree.'

Better, d'you like – whisky?

'Very smart stuff. Very pretty drink, much praised by Burns.'

Very true, that's –

'Twill make a man forget his woe; twill heighten all his joy; twill make the widow's heart to sing, tho' the tear were in her eye…'

Tear were in her eye, that's – indeed what it will do, great stuff!

The day was looking up. John's mood was buoyed by his little Burns recital, and he decided to go for a walk in the cool October twilight, though he seemed unsure of where to be quite when. I said start walking back when you hear the bells chime the three-quarters, and off he ambled up the road in the northerly direction, stopping almost straight away. He turned a full circle as if to take in everything and then confided cheerily, 'The setting sun will always set me to rights!'

*

'Small or large.'

Huge.

'Y'know the bottle's better value.'

Give me value, Norman.

'Look at 'em all just drinkin'.'

The pub's more crowded now. There are too many people to be given nicknames or epithets, I'm really just interested in boozing for a spell, but Ollie rocks up beside me, beaming as usual:

'Getting stuck in!'

Beside him is bristly Heath in a leather jacket, guy's not yet cracked a grin.

Help me out, Ollie, no one's gonna show up to this reading and it's *Keats*.

'I know, it's the meet'n'greet in Cartwright, it's really bad planning.'

Sod the meet'n'greet, you've all met, you've all gret, come and hear Keats.

'We've not met the novelists or playwrights,' says Ollie.

What novelists, what playwrights.

Ollie acknowledges my uselessness with a smile, 'The *other* writing classes?'

Am – *I* teaching them?

'No! They're at the Uni!'

Aren't you at the Uni? You're always at some uni.

'We all are! You're like, an elective, Glyn, an option. We don't get credits. I spread the word! If you build it they will come, or something, who's the second glass for?'

Me again. I need to sit.

Soon we're joined at what's already The Poets' Table (give me strength) by Caroline the lavender lady, and Iona the Scots girl who says *aye*, we all say where we come from, we get through that bottle then Caroline picks one better. The women say they'll come to Keats. Ollie says he'll do his best, Heath makes a roll-up.

That's how I come to be standing in the chilly dark outside the village hall on the deserted lane in the village of Lord Knows, at roughly seven-fifty shouting out to no one:

Reading here tonight! John Keats! *The* John Keats! In person!

Well I *say* to no one, but I don't forget to raise my lone plaintive cry to the black and newly starry heavens, which I do think ought to hear this, plus the man himself is sauntering up the lane to make my lunatic rant come true.

*

'When old age shall this generation waste,
    Thou shalt remain, in midst of other woe
Than ours, a friend to man, to whom thou say'st,
    Beauty is truth, truth beauty, – that is all
        Ye know on earth, and all ye need to know.'

Twelve hands make the sound of ten hands clapping, because Heath doesn't deign to clap from his chair three rows back, he just nods alone in the dark a bit as if that helps. Then again at least he showed up, to show his tough-guy approval of the gifted little chap. No sign of bloody Orlando or Barry or Lily Bronzo. On the front row the angels clap ferociously, Iona McNair, Mrs Caroline Jellicoe, and a tall girl called Isabella I believe I know. And shy wordless Niall is clapping for all his worth, as am I, as I sit down next to John on the edge of the stage again, but that's ten hands and that's your lot.

Wonderful, John, you said you'd be happy to take some questions?

(He looks at me and shrugs and Caroline's already raised her hand)

'That was so beautiful, John. Can you tell us something about your influences?'

Influences John?

(He looks at me as if this wasn't quite what he had in mind, but he seems to make up his mind to be agreeable)

'I – never quite despair if I read Shakespeare.'

(The three women are all nodding in approval, and he goes on)

'I'm very near agreeing with Hazlitt that Shakespeare's enough for us.'

Hazlitt, yes, earlier John we met earlier remember, you talked about Dante... that amazing Canto Five of *Inferno*? (I haven't had time to look it up but at least I got the number.)

John smiles wider than ever before, his legs give a little dangling kick, and he leans back with his hands spread behind him on the dusty stage: 'Paulo and Francesca... I dreamt of – I'd passed many days in rather a low state of mind and I – I dreamt of being in that region of hell... one of the most delightful enjoyments I ever had... I floated about the whirling atmosphere with – with a beautiful figure to whose lips mine were joined – it seemed for an age – I was warm… flowery tree-tops sprung up and we – we rested on them with the lightness of a cloud… I tried a sonnet but – nothing.'

Did you cry to dream again, John?

He clocks my Caliban, applauds me with a bully-for-you, and says 'I could dream it every night.'

This obviously earns a short adoring silence, which Isabella breaks by asking 'Do you think a poet is born? Or can you learn to be one.'

I glance at her approvingly but she's gazing on him like a moon at a planet. I'm being cold-shouldered in my own coma.

'In the first place,' saith the poet, 'Sancho will invent a journey heavenward as well as anybody.'

From *Don Quixote* there (inserts their teacher)

'No… the poetical character,' goes John, 'it's not itself…' Isabella's already seriously nodding and scribbling, 'it – *has* no self. It's everything and nothing. It has no character. It enjoys light and shade, it lives in – *gusto*, be it foul or fair, high or low, rich or poor. It has – it has as much delight in conceiving an Iago as an Imogen. A poet is the most *unpoetical* thing in existence, because he has – he has no identity. He's continually *in for* – filling some other body…'

Are you talking in terms of the poet as playwright, John?

To which he pays no heed: 'I think poetry should – surprise by a – a fine excess, not by singularity. It should strike the reader as a – a wording of his highest thoughts – appear almost a remembrance… its touches of beauty should never be halfway – the rise, the progress, the setting of imagery should – like the sun – come natural to him, shine over him and set soberly, in the – luxury of twilight…' He grins and looks for his water-bottle, 'but it's easier to think what poetry should be than to write it.'

Iona has a question: 'Do you have a favourite way to work?'

He's still concluding his thought: 'If poetry comes not as naturally as the leaves to the tree… it'd better not come at all.'

(I say after a silence) Iona's asking if you have a way you tend to work, John.

'Where you sit,' she smiles, 'like a nice view of something? Do you write at dawn? After midnight?'

A lark or an owl, John (I go helpfully) I'm a lark myself if anyone's interested,

'I read and write about eight hours a day…' at which Iona's mouthing to Isabella *oh my Lord…* 'I went day by day at a poem for a month – at the end of which time I found my brain so overwrought I'd neither rhyme nor reason in it – yet… It'd be a great delight to know in what position Shakespeare sat when he began *To be or not to be…*'

He chuckles and points at himself with both forefingers, as if to say How about cross-legged like me? pretends to inscribe verses on the air and we all laugh, then he goes back to the question, indicating an imaginary room of his dreams, setting out walls and all his special places:

'My books in a snug corner… Mary Queen of Scots… Milton with his daughters in a row… a head of Shakespeare… I should like the window to open onto Lake Geneva, and there I'd sit and read all day like the picture of somebody reading…'

'Can we come and visit?' Caroline Jellicoe beams for England.

'Fine weather, and health, and books, and a fine country,' the young poet sighs, 'a contented mind, a diligent habit of reading and thinking – and an amulet against the ennui, please heaven, a little claret-wine cool out of a cellar a mile-deep, a rocky basin to bathe in, a strawberry bed to say your prayers in, a nag to go you ten miles or so,' then he gestures to his tiny little audience, 'two or three sensible people to chat with,' then at me with a wink for dramatic counterpoint – 'two or three spiteful folks to spar with, two or three odd fishes to laugh at and two or three numbskulls to argue with!'

John that's so –

'*And – and –* a little music outdoors played by somebody I don't know… a little chance music…'

He starts engraving on the air again, mouthing the exaggerated shapes of 'To Be Or Not To Be That Is The Question…' when the sweet quiet is abruptly broken by a loud voice from the side of the hall. I look there in time to see big Barry Wilby silhouetted by the light of the porch, only just arriving having missed the whole of the reading. He repeats himself but louder again:

24

'Where d'you get your ideas, Mr Bains.'

(oh for fuck's sake) You know what? Let's walk twenty yards with John Keats and bloody well get him his claret-wine and his numbskulls! Ladies and gentlemen I give you John Keats!

*

We hit the Cross Keys just before it fills up with the Orientated from the Meet'n'Greet, so we're able to colonize a little snug with some big plum-leather chairs. Those who heard him read – plus Barry Wilby, who came too late – settle thereabouts, throw coats and bags over seats to possess them, and Isabella and I go and buy the first round.

How's the writing, Isabella.

'After that I just feel like stopping.'

Don't, though. I walked to class with my old teacher once on Bay State Road in Boston. He said he'd just read four lines of Ovid and *he* felt like stopping. And he's him. If you stop, you *should*.

'I'm writing a novel.'

Oh. I said *that* to my old teacher and he called me a whore. Here comes our wine.

*

When we get back with our red and our white, a lemonade for Barry (the lummox) and yes, why not, a shapely glass of De Kuyper's cherry brandy, John's in full flow:

'Negative Capability,' he's saying (as it happens) accepting with a nod his beaker full of the warm Netherlands, 'that is, when a man's capable of being in uncertainties – mysteries, doubts, without any irritable reaching after fact or reason. Coleridge, for instance – *incapable* of remaining content with half-knowledge!'

What's Coleridge like, I ask as I pour the white.

John downs half his brandy in response – I send Niall off with a twenty to get two more – and our poet grins into his glass.

'Coleridge… I walked with him at his alderman-after-dinner pace for near two miles I suppose… In those two miles he broached a thousand things… see if I can give you a list…'

We all gather closer, and I wonder if any of them know who Coleridge is, know he's dead, know he's alive, know Keats is dead or alive, know where we are, why we're here, what's happening to me, I think you could possibly say I dwell in Negative Capability, anyway, our Visiting Poet is talking: 'Nightingales, poetry – on poetical sensation – metaphysics – different genera and species of dreams – nightmare – a dream accompanied by a sense of touch – single and double touch – first and second consciousness – the Kraken, mermaids, a ghost story… I heard his voice as he came towards me, I heard it as he moved away, I'd heard it all the interval! He was civil enough to ask me to call on him at Highgate.'

'Do you know Lord Byron?' breathes enraptured Isabella.

John sits back and considers.

'There's this great difference between us. He describes what he sees – I describe what I imagine. Mine's the hardest task.'

I hear Heath say 'Hang on, though,' and I step in:

Wordsworth?

'Wordsworth… sometimes – in a fine way – gives us sentences in the style of school-exercises. *The lake doth glitter/Small birds twitter!*'

He creases up at this gibe of his, then sighs and clears the air between them: 'He has epic passion… martyrs himself to the human heart… I don't mean to deny his grandeur – I mean to say we needn't be teased with grandeur… a great poet if not a philosopher. Let's have the old poets.'

It seems appropriate to drink to that and we do, and here come the rest of my students to stand around us, and some novelists and playwrights no doubt, it's getting pretty crowded in the Cross Keys, as a girl dressed all in black snakes through, deposits a double-shot of something clear by my right hand, says: ''sup Max,' and goes away again.

Hey Mimi? (I summon up too late, as Barry Wilby asks his question again) 'Just askin' about your *Ideas*, Mr Bains,' and Keats, who is fair plastered by this time – 'I should've been a rebel angel…' – 'young ladies that wear watches're always looking at them!' – 'I think I'll be among the English poets after my death…' – suddenly *delights* in being called 'Johnny Bains' and reels this thing off in his best cod-cockney voice:

'Two or three cats
And two or three mice –
Two or three sprats
At a very great price –
Two or three smiles
And two or three frowns –
Two or three miles
To two or three towns –
Two or three pegs
For two or three bonnets
Two or three dove's eggs
To hatch into sonnets!'

*

At the end of the day John Keats was young, and slight, and he couldn't really hold his drink – who *can* hold that much cherry brandy? – so having thrown up pure crimson down a drain he was now propped between myself and Heath Bannen as we waited on the lane by the light of a half-moon. Lots of other people were there, it was a raucous night by now, but no one had any clear idea what we were waiting for except, oddly, John himself, who kept saying this was the place.

He confided in the two of us one by one, to this shoulder then that, confided in his gentleman supporters, out of the earshot of the mostly female crowd. To Heath I believe he said, 'See what it is to be under six foot and not a lord,' and to me, with his eyes ranging across the shrieking and bonding women all around, he said: 'I do think better of womankind than to s'pose they care whether Mister John Keats – five feet height – likes 'em or not…'

After midnight struck we heard hoof-beats and a small horse-drawn carriage came clopping in from the east, a shade late for Cinderella. The hooded coachman said nothing, the windows were black. John vaguely waved at everything from me to the moon and stars, and we helped him step up. At the door he simply slurred to the world with his eyes bright: 'Ignorant! Monstrous! I's forced lately… to make use of the term *MINX*…' And then he tumbled inside and as the hinged door swung shut with a whiff of perfume, there did seem to be someone rising in time to catch him.

*

I sit in my digs and watch the moonlight on the lake out to the west. My head's still ringing and clanging with the time I've had. It had to break up quickly, I felt I was waking up, so I said my quick *adieux* and was off. But I didn't wake up, I walked back home and here I am at my window, dreaming, dead, comatose, mad, or wide wide bloody awake. Wherever I am it's term-time.

*   *   *

Week Two – October 3rd

I woke up and it was all a dream.

I filled with relief and joy and disappointment, then soon some grand acceleration of thankfulness came shuddering through, resolving itself into the heartfelt words *To whom do I write a cheque?* now I'm back in the Angel with everyone to tell everything to, where will I start with it all, so many little details, I better get back to the banquet what banquet the banquet in the circus-tent what circus-tent?

And I'm staring at the ceiling, it is surprisingly close by.

I met Keats.

I never closed my curtains last night and the world outside is bright grey.

I am completely without a hangover, which in normal circumstances means I didn't drink, or I drink so much I'm doomed, but in this case means nothing.

Now I'm kneeling on my bed like a boy, is this some memory of prayer, some bookending of sleep – or bookending of – what? I do like my room. Tartan blanket which I needed, I gather it towards me, it's cold air beyond it, and the matting on the wooden floor, and the slanting windows out on the world, whatever world, three windows, mine, and the things I had with me when I came here are propped up there and there. My boots, they know what's what. I stumble and stride about, good god I'd started my unpacking. Somehow I had a suitcase and my wash-bag's gone where it knows to go. All these empty drawers to fill! Books open on the small desk, some closed, some open, one open at a page.

A Thought went up my mind today –
That I have had before –
But did not finish – some way back –
I could not fix the Year –

Nor where it went – nor why it came –
The second time to me –
Nor definitely, what it was –
Have I the Art to say –

But somewhere – in my Soul – I know –
I've met the Thing before –
It just reminded me – 'twas all –
And came my way no more –

Oh it's all a dream again, I knew as I deflated, standing there, and how did I know? Because I taught Keats on a Thursday, and I don't have to teach till next Thursday, so this can be only Friday, and never *in my entire life* have I prepared a class six whole days early, as I clearly have in this case. QED. Quod Emily D.

Until it's a dream, or not a dream, I gaze out through the nearest window, over the rooftops of the cold quiet place out to the strip of lake in the distance, the only bloke on earth as usual, I am at my address.

And so: my – *Address – What are you telling me? What did I do wrong where I was? What did I need telling?*

You are telling me something. I've seen things like this, I end up a better person. Do I? How? Will the same things keep happening and I understand them more? Or different things keep happening and I somehow learn to love it? What work are we engaged on here?

Then I feel a lightness, as if the beloved of my life are reachable, close, as if they know I'm off somewhere, at my work in some strange way, know I'll be back from where I'm gone.

So this day's like every other. It feels like I can call them all – but my bird-yellow phone is dead now, and I didn't bring a charger, it slipped my mind to be omniscient.

I have to work, but I can't. I never do my work when I feel I can. Work starts helplessly, I find myself *At It*, the body leads me there. Not this time.

The books are open, I open the windows, the wind will turn their pages. I need to eat instead. Having mastered the physics and acknowledged the biology I shall go out alone and explore – and it's this preposterous Faustian *hubris* that makes some terrible person start battering on the door downstairs.

Maybe it's not battering, maybe they're not terrible, maybe it just strikes me like battering because I do not feel like talking. I tiptoe to the window and peer down.

I see the path, a needless zigzag through the tiny garden, am relieved there's no one on it, wait too long thinking that, which lets a lady back right into view, stare up and clock me before I can hide. *Shit shit shit* runs my little birdsong.

I hear nothing, I stay gone. I sidle through the long little room, leaning inches to see till I do see – who, *Caroline* of the tinted hair walking away off my domain. I didn't want to be wanted for anything. I will see off invaders. I will run away, to show I can, there's money in my pocket somehow, there always is these days – comes of saying yes and working fast and saying *right what's next?* – there is money, I'll be back in time to eat a triumphal breakfast.

*

'Teacherman! Señor!'

That went well.

The big man in overalls is calling up the lane. I was heading north away from the Cross, to where the great field stretches from the fence where I met Keats but I didn't get that far, there was Barry Wilby, drinking milk beside a milk float.

Hey there. Barry.

'Taking a walk eh, *were we.*'

We, no, I was yes, wondering where *that* leads…

'Oh it's a super quality stroll, that one.'

Yeah pretty much why I was taking it (but, you know, standing by a milk float's good too) what are you up to on this grey day Barry.

'Doing my rounds.'

You're a milkman.

'No,' as a sleeved hand waves from the driver's window and Barry nods his big head, 'she's the milkman, I'm her pal. I'll be seeing you later.'

You will?

'Professor!'

Pincer movement, my pursuer Caroline, emerging from Student Services with a wave and a puzzled look as she marches on my world.

Catch you later Barry… *Caroline is it Caroline?*

'We had a ten, did we not have a ten?'

Did we not what did we what (oh I vant to be alone)

'One-to-one at ten! You didn't come so I went to your place! Kerri Beds told me where you are! I saw you in the window.'

Was that me.

'Eh?'

Yes that was me, I was, sorry, difficult phone-call.

'You have a signal? No one has a signal on a Thursday. How do you have a signal?'

I – it's gone. (Note to self: can't fib in a village)

'Kerri Beds said she had *no clue* about your plans.'

I look over at Student Services and there's Kerri in her office, talking to a young man in an anorak.

Caroline says 'Schedules are posted in her office.'

Sorry did you just say it was Thursday?

'The Academy tutors do that – what's that? Yes you teach at three. I know it's three because on Tuesday at three I have Material Poetics with Gough Slurman he's tremendous.'

(I really hate this coma now, what Academy)

'Eh?'

What happened to the damn week.

'Oh, I see, well yes, good damn question.'

*

We walk west along the verge of the oval village green. So I stood her up – but she's not *real*, I don't have to teach her. But evidently she *thinks* she's real, so I really did stand her up, so I really do have to teach her. But it won't affect the world in the end so it's not worth my time. But it will affect how I feel right now so in fact it damn well is. It's no contest. My philosophical default has always been not to offend, which is maybe why you don't know who I am or haven't noticed I've vanished.

'This is my first time, you know, so be kind! But don't go pulling any punches please, I want to know what you think, but how about you go easy on a rookie.'

(I haven't read her poems, I haven't got her poems, I'm not here)

'I've made duplicates, in case you mislaid them, I can see you're a typical chaotic poet. But before we *do* sit down, what do you reckon to 'em?'

They're – you know what Caroline they're forceful poems. They're full of… force.

'Are they.'

But they also have a – a sweetness.

'You think? And there's me thinking they were brutal.'

Oh don't worry they're brutal, but somehow the sweetness – *offsets* that.

'Offsets it, I should be writing this down, shall we wait till the caff it's right here…'

(Caff? Caff won't cut it, do you know who I am? I see the heavenly sign of an Inn, my sign, about fifty yards further, it is called The Saddlers Inn, I shall join the Union of the Saddlers, I shall fight in their ranks) You know what, Caroline, I'm going to Buy You Brunch! (makes up for this morning, I can speed-read her poems while I *down some dry white anything*) and I won't take no for an answer!

*

SOUTH HADLEY SEMINARY
Nov 2nd, 1847

Bill of Fare

Roast Veal
Potatoes
Squash
Gravy
Wheat and Brown Bread
Butter
Pepper and Salt

Dessert
Apple Dumpling
Sauce

Water

Isn't that a dinner fit to set before a king?

*

'Are you all right?'

Yes. Miles away. Something I read. Back here and now (I read six sheets of poems in the time it takes to say so) I'm remembering these yes yes there's clearly an anger.

'Yes there's a bloody anger mind my German.'

(Forlornly I await my eggs florentine) It's like the speaker can't see beyond this *You* figure who betrayed her.

'You mean me and my ex-husband. The betrayer is called Ronald. The speaker is me. I'm the speaker.'

There's a language we have to use (I shuffle her six pages) we never assume identities ha! sounds like a spy movie.

'Of course, I know the game.'

If anger doesn't sing it's just anger.

'And what if I don't feel like singing?'

Then no one will hear her – I mean you. Least of all this man called You – I mean him.

'Ronald.'

Ronald.

'Why would I want him to hear it?'

No reason.

'He doesn't deserve to.'

No. Ronald doesn't deserve to. Here comes your croque monsieur…

Like most poets of the day and age when we set about teaching, I am haplessly cast as counsellor, shrink, trainer, mate, provocateur, Fool in the Lear sense and fool in the fool sense, and I see Caroline, having paid her money and taken her choice, might deploy me in any combination at will. I find that if I keep my eye on her line-breaks (for the play of nerves) her vowels (for the swell of emotions) and the scope of her vocabulary (keep it small and tight if you're pacing round your garden) I can help her find the sound she wants. In this game I've been calmly, hopefully passed first-hand accounts of rape, war, grief, schizophrenia, child abuse and terminal illness, I can handle a rough divorce. The duty is to the poem, I have to address it almost *independent* of the poet, gently bypass the suffering human and talk straight to the creature, like a dog-lover might do in the park. Now I'm telling it: *Help her. You and I can help her.*

Caroline sees some young students go by outside the window.

'Kids and their shiny faces. They'll learn.'

And I remember that in this life, as in life, I have no idea how old I look. I don't think they're kids at all, or if they are I'm one too. Maybe Caroline wants me for her generation. She has a point but I will stand my ground. My soul is thirty-seven, I'll be a-sitting on that gate when I'm the aged, aged man.

The Inn door opens with a jingle and it's Kerri Bedward. Great, a coma with recurring cast, everyone cheer. A side of the bar is also the Reception, she's heading there when she sees me.

'Just the man. Can you meet her at the station?'

What? Yes. The station (and let us state it while we may) you mean can I meet the nineteenth-century poet Emily Dickinson of Amherst Massachusetts at the railway station?

Kerri pauses by our banquette waiting to see if there's anything funny or wrong about that, but according to her clipboard there isn't: 'Ms – *Dickinson*, yes, she's on the 18.30.'

1830, of course she is. Where's she coming from, Kerri?

Kerri looks at me. My habitual cluelessness was funny the first four times.

'The agent didn't say. She's staying the night though.'

(Caroline's scribbling on her poems: *offset the brutality???*)

Are you coming to hear her read her work? (but they both hope I'm addressing the other one and Kerri's moved on to Reception. I face Caroline) You could write like our visitor.

'Eh what now?'

Find a single form forever. Write no other way.

'Would that not be monotonous?'

You *are* a single form forever, Caroline, arms legs head heart hands feet etc. So write in a single form forever. Full-throated like a bird.

'Yes. Well. Glyn. Dealing with what I'm dealing with? Sheer malice of Ronald. Mother who thinks I'm *her* mother. Son who doesn't give a damn who I am. Right now I'm too – full of what I need to say.'

Yes. Of course you are. You need a thousand forms, that's just what the monotonous blackbird tweeted me this morning, he needs horns and scales and udders and a mane and a tail and a sting and to really improve his English.

*

This is later, of course, I mutter that alone, when I'm walking back to the Cross, when my posh brunch has been paid for, and I've been told I can get it next time, as if there was a next time ha!

To stop in the Cross Keys is obviously foolhardy, as my usual practice for one-to-ones is to set them up in threes, so I'm banking on a double ambush, and I don't even reach the bar before they catch me, first of course Orlando.

'Overdid it last night, did we?' he goes, beaming like it was all his Plan.

Don't really know, mate (which is nice to say, being true)

'It's actually Lillian Bronzo next, not me, so…'

We reschedule. I offer several days on which I don't expect this realm to exist or at least I won't be corporeally present, but he means twenty minutes from now, 'we can squash it in before class!'

Oh yes. Class.

'What you got for us today?'

We're. We're going to play a game called Hots For God.

'Ha! Like it!'

I don't mean game I mean exercise.

'Totally. Bring it.'

Up comes Lily of the scarlet pixie hair. 'Oi, listen you: I heard a fly buzz when I died, right. The stillness in the room was – hang on, I know it – '

'*In the air?*' prompts Ollie,

'*Shut it* – like the stillness in the air before the heaves of storm. *Yesss.* Learned it. You said to.'

I did? I did. All of it? Or just – just the one stanza.

'Jesus, slave-driver or wot.'

Ollie says: 'Superb stuff, but it's *between* not *before.*' He sags with regret and continues: 'The eyes around had wrung them dry – '

I feel such tenderness towards Lily, Lillian, as if she's the first person ever to have memorized lines of Emily – she may believe she is – that I thoroughly tell a lie:

Depends on the edition, Orlando. There's a version with *before*.

'Oh there is? Fair enough. It's a folio thing.'

Totally, man, it's a folio thing, it's a folio thing, Lily.

*

Lily's thing is she's homesick. You'd never catch her using the word, but it's there in her scratchy voice. We're sat down at a corner table and she has to top the lunchtime hubbub.

'In Camden I'm like on the scene, right,' she coughs, 'I got mates, the shit we write is *about* each other, it reacts, it's like it's, mess with me I'll mess with you, or sometimes you're the bomb no *you're* the bomb, I dunno, what the crap do I write about here?'

Don't write about here.

'It's the space here, man, it's too far *between* shit.'

Don't write about here. Write about where you come from. Map it in your mind. Don't write down anything. Map the evening you want, how you get there, where it is, who's there, what happens, map how drunk you get, map it by the second, bus by night bus, map it so strongly it can't be forgotten. Rhyme and rhythm and shit and don't write down *anything*.

'Cool. Seriously?'

If it sticks in your memory it gets in the club. If it doesn't too bad. Your ears are doormen – door-persons.'

'No they're doormen. They're called *Saul* and *Gregor* actually, they're evil.'

*

Ollie wants to know if I think he should write poems to his girlfriend:

Depends who's your girlfriend. No, probably.

'You know. Mimi, from the ol' class.'

Mimi. You're in a thing with Mimi (I knew that)

'I know! Part of me thinks – result! It's full on, though. Or also not at all sometimes. She's such a. We got together at that wedding.'

That's what people get at a wedding. So why isn't Mimi in this class now?

'She's on the acting module.'

The Academy.

'Yeah.'

So she's not doing any poetry class?

'Not doing any writing class. *I* am, I'm doing Textualities of Now with Suzi Judas, she rocks, but no the problem is – my work's got kind of, a bit more, y'know, *now*-ish, like I don't so much do that moonlight and roses thing any more like I used to?'

Chocolate boxes.

'Totally! I've gone more, like, like postmodern? Arguably postpost.'

No more heroes, all gold, black magic, so you want to tell her sweet things but you don't *do* sweet things any more.

'I totally don't in a way.'

You don't know how to say *You're lovely like a rose, Mimi.*

'Finger down throat or what!'

Let me think about it, squire.

'Or more like a black rose? She might go for that do you think? I'm struggling here. Thing is, I already sent one, it's gone.'

You already sent her a poem?

'I wanted to ask you first, I couldn't find you, I didn't think of a black rose, I went with a starlight/ocean vibe.'

Nice. Yes I think you should send her love-poems, Orlando.

'You do?'

Obviously don't say you asked me. Then you'd look like a –

'God no! What happens in the Cross Keys stays in the Cross Keys!'

Drink your drink, man. Let's play Hots For God.

*

I died for Beauty – but was scarce
Adjusted in the Tomb
When One who died for Truth, was lain
In an adjoining Room –

He questioned softly 'Why I failed'?
'For Beauty', I replied –
'And I – for Truth – Themself are One –
We Brethren, are', He said –

And so, as Kinsmen, met a Night –
We talked between the Rooms –
Until the Moss had reached our lips –
And covered up – our names –

*

Heath	Samira
Lily	Ollie
Barry	Caroline
Niall	Iona

moi

Why can't you all sit in the same damn places every week?

'*I* can't *all* do anything,' Lily points out like some stroppy punk Alice.

Okay let's not use cards, let's use dice. Write down the numbers 1 to 6. Five of the faces are people in this room, you can include me if you want to, also yourself. And the 6 is God. You include Him whatever. What? Yes. Or Her. Or Them. Or It. Look the sixth face is something beyond these walls, you name it yourself. Fate, time, the stars, the weather.

So let's go round the room. Say 1 is me, 2 is Niall, 3 is Barry, 4 is Lily, 5 is Heath, 6 is whatever God is to You, okay?

That's my version, do your own.

Now write another 1 to 6.

1 is *Love For.* 2 is *Hatred Of.* 3 is *Pity For.* 4 is *Envy Of.* 5 is *Fear Of.* 6 is *Hots For.* Are you getting the picture?

As these dice are enough for the game, these four walls and floor and ceiling are enough for the world. This is all there is. The black-dots-on-white die: people. White-dots-on-black die: emotion.

Samira raises her hand and asks: 'Are these going to be poems, professor?'

Of course. They're going to be four-line poems, rhymed ABAB.

(A communal groan)

'Nursery rhymes,' Heath says.

Yeah for nursery slopes (I say because he's getting on my nerves)

Samira puts her hand up again: 'It's hard enough having to falsify an emotion about someone you don't want to write about, but – formal constraints as well?'

You're right. Let's make it harder. Mention only what's in this room.

Consternation: 'Nothing's in the room!'

Nine chairs, table, kettle, mugs, fridge, clock, windows, pen and paper and the trace-memory of a Twix wrapper. Oh, and not forgetting that Nothing's in the room.

I weather the groans like a port in a storm. You can't teach the poet I'm teaching.

*

Exactly one hundred years before I lived, a woman in a small Massachusetts town came across an article in *The Atlantic Monthly* and realized that it was, in theory, addressed to her.

It was asking her for poems.

LETTER TO A YOUNG CONTRIBUTOR.

My dear young gentleman or young lady, – for many are the Cecil Dreemes of literature who superscribe their offered manuscripts with very masculine names in very feminine handwriting, – it seems wrong not to meet your accumulated and urgent epistles with one comprehensive reply, thus condensing many private letters into a printed one. And so large a proportion of "Atlantic" readers either might, would, could, or should be "Atlantic" contributors also...

At considerable length, a literary critic named Thomas Wentworth Higginson sought to explain to all the aspiring writers out there – you, me, and so forth – what kind of poetry might make it into the pages of *The Atlantic Monthly*. He urged the young hopefuls to 'charge your style with life' and weeks later there came in the mail, from that same woman in Massachusetts, four odd little poems and a note: 'Mr Higginson, are you too deeply occupied to say if my Verse is alive?'

*

You can't teach Emily Dickinson, you can't write like her either. You no more have to write in her stanzas than you have to write limericks or clerihews. But you do have to absorb that she wrote about *everything she could think of* – herself, others, life, death, God, Time, being here, being gone – in little quatrains shaped like hymns, rhymed or half-rhymed, mostly four beats then three beats, four, three, stanza-break, and she barely left her bedroom.

She finished her chores, had lunch, went upstairs and sat down at a desk about the size of a tea-tray. She had two windows overlooking the one town she lived in. That was pretty much it, give or take a term in South Hadley and a short trip to Philly. Her only niece, Mattie, had a childhood memory of entering that room with her. Aunt Emily closed the door behind them, mimed the act of locking it, and said: 'Mattie, here's freedom'.

What you should be asking yourself is this: what is there so mighty and demanding in *you* – by which I also mean *me* – that calls for such a vast plenitude of forms? Are you more complex, do you see from wider angles, have you solved her questions?

What you owe to such a poet is a true pause for thought.

Face the wonder of her narrow choice before you run bewildered from it. For it's narrow like a ray of the sun.

And when you've finished running, from rhyme, from form, from repetition, from silence or stillness or the abstract nouns that some vague sense of the Modern has told you you can't use any more – as if your use of concrete nouns is the last word in exactitude – when you've finished running from all that and are panting with your freedom, or sweating from the demands of your so complicated life-scape, at least sit down at your own tea-tray and try writing *the present second* –

I heard a Fly buzz – when I died –
The Stillness in the Room
Was like the Stillness in the Air –
Between the Heaves of Storm –

The Eyes around – had wrung them dry –
And Breaths were gathering firm
For that last Onset – when the King
Be witnessed – in the Room –

I willed my Keepsakes – Signed away
What portion of me be
Assignable – and then it was
There interposed a Fly –

With Blue – uncertain stumbling Buzz –
Between the light – and me –
And then the Windows failed – and then
I could not see to see –

Yes we can note the glories – do it – her infinite narrow way of *I* along which all things travel – evoking the Wonderchild *to whom it occurs to write* 'when I died' – the vast O in *Onset* as the mouth's one option when the last breaths are gathering – the words that forlornly spread themselves, entreating the moment to slow: *Keepsakes, Assignable, interposed* – the use of *Be* in 'King/Be witnessed', which falls outside of mortal Time – try 'Was' or 'Is' to see what I mean – those last brave shots at aural infinity: *Flyyy, Buzzzzz, meeee, faaaaailed* – and, above all, the profound humility of the dashes – removing from the poet the grand assuming cloak of power to begin or end *anything* – stick a full-stop at the end and you've shot the thing like the Fly who killed Cock-Robin.

So much for the glories. Higginson, shaken, wrote her back with guarded encouragement but found it hard to see 'what place ought to be assigned in literature to what is so remarkable, yet so elusive of criticism.' He couldn't make her out at all. Eventually he had to go to Amherst just to look her in the eye, for she wouldn't travel. At the door she gave him two lilies and said: *These are my introduction. Forgive me if I am frightened; I never see strangers, and hardly know what I say.*

He knew he was in the presence of the unique. Later he would say he'd never met 'with any one who drained my nerve power so much. Without touching her, she drew from me. I am glad not to live near her.'

And yet to Mattie, the niece, 'Aunt Emily stood for *indulgence.*'

Despite Higginson's interest she had virtually nothing published. That which was was altered for the worse to match conventions of the day. Bullet-hole full-stops. You can still find those versions, it's like trooping to the churchyard to stand by her grave, as I did with my Amherst students in the small hours on her birthday. But read her as she meant you to and she's standing right beside you.

She left her bedroom for good in 1886. Her sister Lavinia found eighteen hundred little poems locked away in a chest.

*

Let's lock *you* in a room with your freedom.

Like in all my games and exercises, cards or dice stand in for fate and circumstance, and you play the role of Human Item Stuck on a Shred of Time.

So go on, shake. Shake.

Niall: Hatred of Caroline.	('Got it.')
Barry: Envy of Glyn.	('How now, brown cow?')
Lily: Pity for Samira.	('*Really?*')
Heath: Love for Caroline.	('Oh jesus…')
Samira: Hots for Lily.	('Mm-*hm*. I see.')
Ollie: Fear of God.	('Woo, terrified!')
Caroline: Hatred of Lily.	('Oh no must I?')
Iona: Pity for Ollie.	(smiles, starts writing)

Is everybody happy? You bet your life you are. Express that one emotion using the form I gave you and the things inside the room. Amaze yourself. Bother me. Leave them in my box in Kerri's office. I won't share them with anyone, this is you against a dice-throw. In all my exercises the benefit is half in your resentment and three-quarters in your effort, it doesn't matter how I think you did. If you do it you win, if you don't the – Windows – fail –

And with that I'm off to the station.

*

It's at the south end of the village. I've always assumed I came by railway because I was walking north from it when I began here. It's a very small station, an old green stone building by the line. There's no name on the name-sign, just room for it. There are benches on some paving-stones and that'll do for a platform. There's a path on the rails to the other side, then a wild-flower meadow sloping away and some little patterned cows far off against the autumn mist. Sunlight never came today, the lightest clouds are low and dull in the sky to my right. I can just make out the lakeshore in the distance. To the left the ground rises into wooded hills, and I see a tunnel entrance over yonder in the distance, blue on the grey hillside. I sigh and then in silence a tiny train appears.

I like to see it lap the Miles –
And lick the Valleys up –
And stop to feed itself at Tanks –
And then – prodigious step

Around a Pile of Mountains –
And supercilious peer
In Shanties – by the sides of Roads –
And then a Quarry pare

To fit its sides
And crawl between
Complaining all the while
In horrid – hooting stanza –
Then chase itself down Hill –

And neigh like Boanerges –
Then – prompter than a Star
Stop – docile and omnipotent
At its own stable door –

I await a small frail lady in white as the train slows down and grinds and stops. Then when no one descends at all, why would they – *one* does, slender and straight, from the very last carriage in a dark blue shawl and with her hair tied up. Once on the platform, some forty yards along, she goes on looking at the train, and then watches it pull away and leave her all alone. She seems so intent on doing this I stop walking, and we wait until the train has quite curved out of sight behind me, as if we can't begin until we've ceased to dwell on how we came.

I resume walking towards her, and am suddenly proud to be dead, or in a coma, or in a dream, and must resist saying so, must resist saying so,

Miss Dickinson it's a dream to make your acquaintance!

She is pointing at her little feet: 'I resolved to be sensible, so I wore thick shoes,' and I burst out like an idiot:

I lived five years in Amherst! I lived on Dana Street! I taught in Johnson Chapel!

She raises her eyes from her shoes, not quite so far as to catch my eye, and says: 'Old Time wags on pretty much as usual at Amherst.'

The pleasantries I spout next I'm embarrassed to relate even here, but I manage to remember to take her little round suitcase, and enquire about her journey on the train.

'The folk looked very funny. Dim and faded, like folks passed away.'

Weird that.

We're walking along the lane, myself and Emily Dickinson, who focuses mainly on her walking feet in their sensible shoes, with occasional glances up ahead.

'The world's full of people travelling everywhere.'

Tell me about it!

'Until it occurs to you that you'll send an errand, then by hook or crook you can't find any traveller to carry the package.'

Totally. I mean I know.

'It's a very selfish age, that's all I can say about it.'

There's a spark in her voice that suggests she might be kidding, and I steal a glance at her but don't receive one back.

You're staying at the Saddlers Inn, Miss Dickinson. They do a good eggs florentine I mean they do eventually.

While I resolve to jump in the lake later, she sighs: 'I could keep house very comfortably if I knew how to cook!'

I know. Me too. Totally. You can see the inn in the distance there…

We reach the Cross and she stops, turns and looks all four ways like I would.

'October's a mighty month,' she says. Then she asks where there's a library.

(I don't know where there's a library) Let's get you checked in, yes, then I'll see if the Library's open. The reading's at eight, in the village hall. There's some other stuff going on tonight, usual things on a Thursday, but my poetry group will be there, heigh-ho, so a small keen high-class crowd!

*

We jingle through the door of the Saddlers Inn, whereupon Kerri stands up smartly from a table to escort our Guest to Reception. I get to sit down for a second, stare clean out of my mind through the windows and find life's splendours too bright to bear. I actually do this in Angel too, and the Garden City and New York City, not just in dreams and comas.

My vacant stare can't help but fill up with strangers, and a group of several walk by the Inn, interesting faces, various ages, a rag-tag bunch, and one who stops, frowns, peels off from the gang and here she comes, Mimi, in her black suede jacket with tassels, a death-stare to the closing door for jingling in her wake.

'Why aren't you teaching, Max, Orlando's at your class.'

Collected our visitor, look.

Mimi sits down opposite and glances over at the small woman stooping to sign the register: 'Woo. Legend.'

You remember her?

'You taught me, didn't you. *Zero at the bone.* When's her reading?'

Eight. Can I ask you, why don't people drink in here? it's nice and peaceful.

'Answer supplied with question,' she goes.

Cross Keys is a bit grim.

'We like upsetting Norman. He hates students and he hates drinking so we pile in and order cocktails on account.'

Fair enough. Who were all them?

'*Who were all them?* Glad I took a course with *you* Max. They're the actors from my course. I don't mean actors, they're just freaks doing what I do.'

Why don't you take *my* course again? Killer reading series, look.

'Nah I want to try acting. Anyway I can always come to your stuff, it's not like it's official, we don't get credits.'

You *can* come, are you *going to*?

'To her? Hell yes. Moneypenny wants you.'

Over at Reception, Kerri's quietly beckoning. The boy at the bar is querying something, while Emily has drifted off to peer at the cheap prints on the walls.

She's signed herself in *Mrs Adam, Amherst*, which got the desk-boy confused.

It's fine, (I say) she can say she's who she likes. Right, Miss Dickinson?

We wrongly assumed she'd heard none of this, instead of all, and she turns again with that downward smile not quite meeting our eyes: 'I've lately come to the conclusion that I'm Eve, alias Mrs Adam.'

Neither Kerri nor the boy understand why she'd say that, but Mimi snorts with appreciation from across the room, so Emily waves this cheerfully her way: 'You know there's no account of her death in the Bible. Why am I not Eve?'

Mimi grins in support, while Kerri offers to show our Guest upstairs to the Bluebell Room. As they're ascending out of earshot I slide in opposite my former student rolling her roll-up.

Not going to smoke that in here, are you?

'Not going to say that in here, are you, so look I have this problem,' and she takes out a piece of pale blue paper, flattens it face up. 'Been sent this valentine that's just a fail in three ways. First I don't do valentines, second it's October, three it blows.'

(I read it and well yes) Why do you think it's a valentine, it doesn't say it is.

'Alright it's just a poem, but still Max, come on, it's got *love* in it look.'

Is it from Orlando?

'Yeah alright four ways.'

Why don't you ask him to stop?

She licks along her liquorice rizla, 'I want him to know he ought to.'

How will he if you don't tell him?

'If I tell him it's too late.'

Like you say, you have a problem. What can I do?

'Not your circus, not your monkeys. Can I smoke this out in the world?'

Sure Mimi. You smoke it out in the world.

*

I forgot to ask Mimi where the library was – like she'd know – but it didn't matter for when Kerri brought our Guest, now all in white and looking much more like herself, treading down from upstairs, round about the tables and out through the jingling door, the Library's where we were heading.

Kerri asked polite questions on the way:

'How long have you been away from home, Miss Dickinson?'

'Been nearly six weeks,' she said briskly, then I felt her voice begin to clot with sorrow, 'a longer time than I was ever away. Kind of *gone-to-Kansas* feeling.'

Not over the rainbow then (say I).

We're walking east we three, over the Cross, leaving the pub behind on the left, and then upward on a slight gradient, curving into trees. It's getting quite gloomy by now, more blue than grey, and I'm pretending I know there'll come a library soon – but everything else is real, and the small voice I hear is even running with my thoughts.

'I was very homesick for a few days, but I'm now quite happy. If I can be happy when absent from my... I have a very dear home. Love for them sets the blister in my throat.'

That'll do it for sure.

We seem to have passed the outskirts of the village now, the last houses, a barn or two, and I'm wondering where this library is, where the signs are, what the time is, when we reach a little collection of stalls set back in a leafy space all carpeted with coloured mats. There are old books on every stall, twelve stalls, volumes and volumes, and great swathes of canvas thrown back behind the hardwood frames as if to protect them when needed. They'll be needed soon, the day is ending and there's dampness in the air.

This is all the library is.

I mean to say that aloud but don't know if it's a question, or a horrified question, or a sad statement, or a sigh of the times. The reaction of our visitor sends all those four packing, for she just stares, palms raised, in on a miracle, quoting in delight: '*And I saw the Heavens opened...*'

She advances on the first stall and starts to trace her finger along the spines, as Kerri murmurs to me discreetly 'Keep an eye on the clock...'

We've got a good hour, I say cheerily, we've got a *wondrous* hour.

'Wondrous forty minutes,' goes Kerri, doing up her coat.

'An hour for books,' says Emily, absorbed.

She starts finding things of interest: eight big black volumes of Shakespeare – 'why clasp any hand but this?' – a battered blue book she takes and weighs in her palm – 'of Poe I know too little to think' – a tattered Byron with the spine gone – 'I've heard it argued that the poet's genius lay in his foot, as the bee's prong and his song... are you stronger than these?' – right at me, making me stronger from foot to forehead – then a dozen hefty red titles – 'Father gave me quite a trimming about Charles Dickens and these modern literati' – which of course we all three smile at for different reasons, especially when she wags her finger and sounds an old soul's Yankee voice: 'nothing compared to past generations that flourished when *I* was a boy!'

She reads for a while and I try not to stare at her reading. Kerri shuffles her feet a bit to show it's cold and time's troops are marching by. I ask Emily if her parents encouraged her to read, and she closes the book she was reading. 'My mother doesn't care for thought, and father…' She sets the book back neatly where it was. 'Too busy with his briefs to notice what we do. He buys me many books but begs me not to read them, he fears they joggle the mind.'

The wind gets up and dark leaves blow about her ankles. She watches till they settle.

'No one taught me,' she says.

I feel a drop of rain. It's too dark to read a thing now.

She asks how one may borrow from this library and we both simply spread our hands to say *do what on earth you please*, so she chooses a dense little brown volume from the shelf, comes over and drops it straight into Kerri's coat pocket. I could see the name on the spine in golden, GEORGE ELIOT, but not which one it was, and I'd forget to ever ask. But 'a little granite book to lean on,' was what she said to Kerri. Then she insisted on joining in with us pulling the covers over the stalls, and tying them in place with all these frayed black ropes.

*

'My life closed twice before its close –
It yet remains to see
If Immortality unveil
A third event to me.

So huge, so hopeless to conceive
As these that twice befell.
Parting is all we know of heaven,
And all we need of hell.'

Her voice doesn't so much cease as disappear and she sits down between the tall lit candles in the chilly hall. We burst into acclaim, I start musing on whether it's possible to rig up applause on a loop, which I could maybe control from a switch at my seat. For this will never bloody suffice. I make do with clapping like a loon, nobly supported by my tiny class (or most of them, Barry's not turned up again, nor has Samira, nor Ollie) along with two or three *Academy* girls at the front including long fair Isabella my one-time student. The desk-boy from the Inn came, bless him, but I see him creeping out now the reading's over. And a portly bearded man in a hat I noticed earlier in the pub. Mimi slid in at the back about halfway through, the worse for wear I thought, and loudly requested 'that one with the fly' to which request the poet politely acceded.

I'm afraid the applause will stop if I stop, so I twine my arm through a chair-back to carry it to the stage and keep clumsily clapping away. When I lower the chair down nearby the poet I'm still at it, last man standing, then I sit.

A quite incredible reading, Miss Dickinson! I'm sure you all have questions before we adjourn to the Saddlers Inn? So, any questions…

This, as in all poetry readings, silences Creation.

How about I start us off… Um, Miss Dickinson, this maybe sounds silly, well it does now – ha! – but what do you like to have *around* you when you write?

'For companions?'

I nod and she smiles downward as if she'll say nothing… Then:

'Hills, and the sundown, and a dog as large as myself, that my father bought me.'

The audience love this, and she looks right at them. 'They're better than beings, because they know but don't tell.'

A dog person not a cat person then (I play safe to the pet lobby) and Emily shudders to confirm the impression: 'My ideal cat has a huge rat in its mouth, just going out of sight.'

Some dog-lovers sway with vindication as she adds: 'though going out of sight in itself has a peculiar charm,' which leaves everyone blankly smiling. 'Carl would please you,' she tells the front row, 'he's dumb, and brave.'

One of the Academy girls asks with biro poised: 'Miss Dickinson whom would you regard as your main influences.'

She smiles: 'For poets I have Keats, and Mr and Mrs Browning' (and Lily happily hisses '*Keats!*' along the chairs to show them she remembers life a week ago) 'for prose, Mr Ruskin, Sir Thomas Browne, and the *Revelations.*'

'What about Whitman?' Heath asks flatly, as if she had it coming.

She puts her hands together in her lap. 'Mr Whitman, Mr Whitman…' she ponders, only to reveal with quite a fierce little smile to no one, 'I never read his book but was told it was *disgraceful!*'

Her new devotees laugh who've not read him either, but Heath has, and sits there. She notices his stillness:

'Perhaps you smile at me. I had no monarch in my life, and can't rule myself.'

Heath looks uncomfortable and nods by way of support.

'Could you tell me how to grow?' she asks him, innocent of mischief.

Blindsided, he looks grave, stares away, quits the field.

'Or is it unconveyed,' she says, looking up at the rafters, 'like melody or witchcraft… I've no tribunal.'

All smile amiably as she passeth understanding.

Breezily I ask if she follows world affairs, and she makes that clear as day: 'Won't you please tell me who the candidate for President is?'

We all mention names you know and the candles cringe with shame.

'I don't know anything more about the affairs in the world than if I were in a trance. Do you know of any nation about to besiege South Hadley? If so, do inform me – I'd be glad of a chance to escape, if we're to be stormed.'

Out of the laughter Caroline ventures: 'Emily, if I may, when you say your soul selects its own society, do you mean you rather prefer your own company to, well, to company? Do you think you have a tendency to avoid people?'

I don't expect her to agree quite but what do I know? 'They talk of hallowed things, aloud, and embarrass my dog. He and I don't object to them, if they'll exist their side.'

WEEK TWO - OCTOBER 3RD

Lily digs it and ventures 'How d'you like *know* good poetry when you see it?'

Emily shakes her head slowly, then breathes in sharply – 'If I – read a book and it makes my whole body so cold no fire can ever warm me, I know that's poetry. If I feel physically as if – the top of my head were taken off! I know that's poetry. These are the only ways I know it. Is there any other way?'

The consensus murmurs there is not, and then she closes her eyes and sighs from memory: 'Though earth and man were gone, and suns and universes ceased to be, and Thou wert left alone, every existence would exist in Thee.'

(There's a space for mooing in awe which is duly filled, while I find some recklessness to hand) Is that a new poem, Miss Dickinson?

She smiles sadly, and it hits me too late, not hers at all –

'Gigantic Emily Brontë…' (We all nod, we knew that) 'Of whom Charlotte said: *Full of ruth for others, on herself she had no mercy.*'

Caroline is nodding wisely, and Lily pipes up: 'Bit random but: when you say about hearing a fly when you died right? which is *mentally* good, and about life closing twice and that? like, what is it you *mean* if that's not moronic.'

Emily frowned, then thought, then said she'd tell a little story, of a woman who came to her door in Amherst one morning, 'an Indian woman with gay baskets and a – dazzling baby, at the kitchen door. Her little boy *once died,* she said, death to her – *dispelling* him. I asked her what the baby liked, and she said – *to step…*'

Lily devilishly shivers, when a husky voice from the back inquires: 'You ever send a valentine?'

The audience frowns and giggles and turns, enjoying that question, and I notice both Caroline and Heath staring back curiously at unbothered Mimi for longer than they need to. I assumed everyone knew everyone, as we do when we know no one.

Sure she sent a valentine:

'Put down the apple, Adam,
And come away with me;
So shalt thou have a pippin
From off my father's tree…'

She may not have meant to but she says this straight at Niall, who visibly freezes in the beam. His eyes are wider than I've seen them. His shy paralysis seems to slow the atmosphere, and though she's no longer looking at him, the expression on his face is *you and me in the dark together* – out of which she mines a gem for him and him only: 'I work to drive the awe away. Yet – awe – impels the work.'

*

On the short walk to the Saddlers from the village hall – Emily suggested we prolong it by walking the long way clockwise round the lamp-lit oval green – several of her listeners made their private move towards her side, but I noticed that the one she sought out and found was Heath. By the time I reached them, rather fearing he might be indelicate or rude in some way, they were parting most politely: 'I've read nothing of Turgenev's,' I heard her say, 'but thank you for telling me – I will seek him immediately.'

She then walked some slow yards with Iona McNair, who said she liked that bracelet very much, and the poet, having touched Iona's white scarf and wondered at the material, said gaily: 'Santa Claus was *very* polite to me last Christmas. I hung up my stocking on the bedpost as usual – I had a perfume bag, a bottle of otto-of-rose to go with it, a sheet of music, a china mug with *Forget me not* upon it, a watch case...' she couldn't remember for a moment and now everyone was listening... 'Abundance of candy! Also two hearts at the bottom of it all, which I thought looked rather ominous.'

Lily came up explaining why last Christmas in Camden Town was a *total mare*, then asked her, before I could do anything, how she went about being published, to which Emily cheerfully pronounced: 'Two editors of journals came to my father's house and asked me for my mind, and when I asked them *why* – they said they'd use it for the world.'

She chuckled at this sufficing answer, so Lily did, actually I did, then one of the Academy girls quickened her pace and asked if Emily enjoyed a bit of – we couldn't catch what – to which she said: 'To live is so startling, it leaves little room for other occupations!' and all wondered and jested as to what had been asked, and all jingled and jangled into the inn so pleased they'd chosen to attend.

*

We'd lost a few by now. Niall, who had shied away – *shying* was Niall's active verb – Heath, who parted from the poet with a stiff male bow from some bygone century in his mind, the Academy girls who'd got all their answers, and Mimi, who'd had her fun. Lily, Bella, Iona and Caroline sat down around a table set for tomorrow's breakfast. The desk-boy listened from Reception as he doodled in a ledger. Our company was briefly augmented by Barry Wilby, who dropped by to make his apologies – 'duties, Teacherman, beaucoup de duties' – and wanted to ask 'Mrs Dixon where she gets her ideas' – but at that point I called a halt, for the lady looked fatigued and on our time not hers.

All four women rose to escort her upstairs, and Barry cried 'Another day!' and though I summoned up the speech to tell her how I felt, by the time those words came in their nervous Sunday best I stood alone, in the cold on the lamp-lit village green, watching her one amber square of light go on in the wooden roof of the inn. I'd done all I could do with a smile. I didn't expect to be here in the morning. I waited till her room went dark.

*

On the way back I swing by Student Services – Kerri's given me a key now and I can pick up what's there. These are.

Samira Sharma: 'I Have the "Hots" for Lily'*

If we all spent a night in here
I would stay awake until you sleep
and then I would overcome my fear
and cut a red hair for me to keep.

(*I do NOT have the hots for Lily.)

Pity for Orlando (I. McNair, Poetry/Maxwell)

I don't think – I can risk it –
It is not – my Place to say –
But I want to give that boy – a Biscuit –
And tell him – Things will be okay –

I collect them, as if I'll need them, if I'm dead I may well need them, and I lock the office behind me.

*

At the end of his _Letter to a Young Contributor_ Thomas Higginson wrote the following, and I thought I'd tape it to my bedroom wall before turning in for the night. He couldn't figure out anything either – and with his one great Young Contributor he both grasped and missed his chance – but he sensed there was a place where it would matter to have tried. He was a famous abolitionist.

War or peace, fame or forgetfulness, can bring no real injury to one who has formed the fixed purpose to live nobly day by day. I fancy that in some other realm of existence we may look back with some kind interest on this scene of our earlier life, and say to one another, – 'Do you remember yonder planet, where once we went to school?'

*　　　*　　　*

Week Three – October 10th

I'm wondering why the sky is blue.

I always know why it isn't when it isn't but I've woken and it is, I'm looking at it.

Or I was looking at it, now I'm *gazing into* it, sky did that to the verb, blue did that to the preposition, bequeathed it time and sweetness and reach, not bad going for empty space. I'm gazing into blue sky.

With the deep breaths I concede: it's October, autumn, fall, falling, landing, landed. Thursday again. I'm alive in the sense of being where I was, I'm still contracted, *hired* in some shape or form – there'll be a class to teach.

But since something brought me here, thought why to, chose when to, there must be a reason it was cloudy before and now it's perfectly fine. What chose me for this – didn't it choose the weather too? Now *there's* a way in. Tap the void on the shoulder, see what turns around.

The void has personality or not, is present or not. Give it a capital V and it's *The Void!* that V lights out for the visible horizon, the *oid* is deep enough for aliens to swim in, see? on speaking terms already –

But small v, the void? doesn't want to be talked to.

Here I am, perched on the bed upon my tartan coverlet, my trusty flying carpet that sailed me here through the galaxy. I pat it like my dog. I give *everything there is* a personality, I decide to meet them all, I place them all along a zodiac of character and yet the void's a void? *My own heart let me have more pity on…*

Everything is someone. Colours, cutlery, capital letters. A's complacent, B indignant, C tricky, D worthy, I can't help this, never could. The hot tap thinks the cold tap's common, the cold tap thinks the hot tap's precious. I back out of my small bathroom peacemaking – *you're both right* for pete's sake – my fingers are clannish brothers with a secret, my toes a mum and her babies, my slippers hush me: *pipe down they're trying to sleep*, and yet the void's a void? Perhaps that's all that humans do, fill the space with folks to meet... *My own heart let me have more pity on...*

Something brought me here. Or an accident befell me and while I wait to be *well* – well what? – something keeps me here. While it keeps me here I do this work. Why should I do it? Do I grow old if I don't? Do I grow old if I do?

The sky is blue. If it stays like this all day I will have to respond, lead my students out of doors, start walking and not stop, breast the horizon like a tape and keep running, seek and find the trail of what brought me here, ask questions till it's black and even *I've* been left behind.

I have to start considering how one departs this place. Ah:

My own heart let me have more pity on; let
Me live to my sad self hereafter kind,
Charitable; not live this tormented mind
With this tormented mind tormenting yet...

Look whose books are open on my desk in the grand old sunlight. Father Gerard Manley Hopkins, of the Society of Jesus. He is coming here today, *Hopkins*, which he furthermore can't be, so I had better prepare some questions.

I cast for comfort I can no more get
By groping round my comfortless, than blind
Eyes in their dark can day or thirst can find
Thirst's all-in-all in all a world of wet...

Where I'm from I don't believe a *word* the little priest believed. Not a word, not *The* Word. And yet to subtract *what that was* from his work leaves the poems still immensely standing, gold, white-gold cathedrals in splendour, numberless cathedrals throng an infinite sunny common. There I worship daily, hurrying through shadow. How do I believe?

I remember, from where I'm from, sitting in a bedroom while my small child was trying to sleep. It was Christmas Eve in England at the turn of the century. She believed what children do. Make-believe, made to believe. A great old red-and-silver stocking was draped at the bottom of the bed. Her mouth was open on the pillow, her breaths trembling, mine were steady, eyes shut. *I must organize the magic in an hour or so, stay awake to sort the miracle, get in costume, play the part…*

I am Father Christmas, and so is Father Christmas. She and I knew different worlds, worlds that *couldn't both be so.* Between them something poured and streamed – *belief* one way, *compassion* the other, and now they both flow both ways, poor believer, poor nothing…

Soul, self; come, poor Jackself, I do advise
You, jaded, let be; call off thoughts awhile
Elsewhere; leave comfort root-room; let joy size
At God knows when to God knows what; whose smile
's not wrung, see you; unforeseen times rather – as skies
Betweenpie mountains – lights a lovely mile.

These words are still surrounded by what surrounded them. It surrounds me too, and it wore blue this morning, cloudless, all its mountains moved, I need coffee, I need orange juice – I want my *betweenpie* – I have three appointments, I am not where you still are, I have quietly shut the door and am off on my zigzag path.

*

The Saddlers is busy with breakfasters, I see the clock says eleven-twenty, these are brunchers brunching. I take a little table in the midst of it all. There are two couples, one with a child, three young men in anoraks, a grave old chap my age who smiles, ha! the old ones are the best, it's only me in a gilded mirror. All except he and I are busy and chatty with the clement weather, its – clemency? Its mercy? If it's mercy, what had we done?

I find myself at the Reception desk, leafing through the Book.

Mrs Adam   Amherst Massachusetts   October Third.

So she *was* here, I knew that.
'That's not her real name, sir,' points out the desk-boy.
Oh is it not.

'Doom is the house without the door, it enters from the sun,' he adds, evidently changed for life in his black ring-neck sweater.

Very much so (I say). Dust is the only secret.

'Parting is all we need of hell.'

I guess. If you work on Reception. (He looks hurt and I smile to heal) Your own self you should have more pity on.

'I've not learned that one, sir.'

That was me. I'm a poet too.

'Sounds good. At the Academy?'

No, I teach in a room off the village hall. There's a kettle, d'you have a Father Hopkins staying here tonight?

'I'm checking that, sir… no, sir. Actually there's no one.'

*

Samira meets me at the Cross Keys. I suggest we sit in the garden but she has allergies, so I watch the blessed morning through a porthole window, then turn as she's unclicking a poem from a ring-binder. She's wearing a turquoise headscarf. She sits back, enlaces her fingers in conference, and waits till she herself says:

'It's a sonnet.'

Which is its problem.

'Explain?'

A sonnet doesn't have to know *exactly* where it's going, Samira, but it's aware it's a sonnet. It's put its good shoes on, has stood up in them. Whereas in this – emotions crash in, thoughts crash in – you didn't *mean* them to – there should be white space they come to fill, and gaps of bites they leave behind. The creature of this poem is being buffeted, assailed, it's not in control of matters. It didn't *choose* to write this, it got *chosen to by you*. I'd break it up into couplets or three-liners, you can keep it bound with your rhymes and that, they can reach across the drops. Whoever it's about –

'It's not about anyone.'

Then, the, *You* in it – the *You* in it doesn't know or care it's a sonnet and shouldn't be helping it to set like –

'It's not about anyone.'

– cake. Fine. Good.

'There isn't anyone.'

Then – *be afraid there's no one* (I do the scary voice)

'There isn't no one either.'

Fine. So *show* me no one. Can I meet him? (whoops)

'Who says it's a him? Not that it matters, it's not.' She takes the poem back: 'Can I ask when you will return our last assignments?'

What.

'When we were made to hate someone, or pity them, or have *the hots*.'

It's just an exercise, you don't need it back. Jump a hurdle, tone a muscle.

'I don't have the hots.'

Did you like that exercise?

'I don't trust dice. I can't write things I don't feel. I don't want things out there that may be used against me.'

*

Heath doesn't want to sit outside either so he slides in where she was. He already has a beer but didn't bring any poems.

'Working on something major.'

I look forward to it.

'Not for you, for format.'

Oh right. What's Format.

'Rupture equals structure. Monday afternoons. Me and Bronzo take it.'

Lily, I'm with you, The Academy. Rupture equals what?

'The equals is an equals sign, it doesn't *say* equals, it's *rupture = structure*.'

And Format is – the subject?

'*format*'s the professor. Small f, italics. He's cool. He doesn't self-identify as female or male or anything. He says he has a first name but we have to solve it, he's left clues all round the village.'

I think you'll find it's Wayne.

'Excuse me?'

Nothing. Why are you taking my course if it doesn't get you any credits.

'Why? *format* said you're old school. Good to know what I'm up against.'

Up against? You're not up against me, Heath.

'That's not your decision, is it.'

Guess not. What else did *format* say.

'He said you only know three things but you really fucking know them.'

Way to go, *format*. That does sound like me.

*

Niall sat watching us through his fringe for a while, leaning by the bar, then when Heath stood up he came over. The two of them did some three-part fist thing, 'sup…sup,' men have to do nowadays, and then Heath moved off and Niall sat.

What *is* up? I wonder.

'I like it here,' he mutters, surprising us both.

It's hard to tell if you do.

'No, because if I didn't I'd leave, I'd go somewhere where I did.'

Somewhere where, where would you go, Niall.

'Away.'

Away… (I have to ask, and you have to blame the blue sky) Niall I don't want you to take this the wrong way but I don't know where I am or how I got here.

'Oh I know.'

You *know* where we are and how we got here?

'No I know you *don't* know. I know that about everyone.'

Sure. Do you know when we can leave?

'At the end of term, I suppose.'

So will we be home for Christmas, Niall?

'I thought you'd know, at your age.'

I thought I'd know at my age.

'Also,' he falters, 'I don't – much want to be home for Christmas.'

Oh. Okay. Okay if *I* am? Feel free to join us. Mulled wine, trimmings, Monopoly, Triv.

At a loss, he rubs his chin as if testing for stubble. There isn't any, I back off the poor soul:

Guess you don't know anything either.

'I know every picture on the walls of this pub and could tell you them if you asked me.' Though I don't, he shuts his eyes. 'Left of the door: horses streaming over a hedge. Next a lady in Edwardian costume. Then a high mountain scene painted by a local. Behind me a map of the clans of Scotland. A white cow with three brown patches – '

Show me a poem eh man.

He sighs like he'd hoped I'd forgotten. Digs two out, stares, disowns them as he passes them over.

But they're damn good. Short lines trying to be free, blown back in on themselves, blown back at line's end to fail and fray and try again, with the white space crying *stop there little sailor* till Niall hears it and has to.

I am about to tell him I think he's really good at this *lark*.

And I tried not to, for as long as ever. There's no going back once someone's told you you're good at this *lark*. I looked right in his eyes through his fringe and still wouldn't tell him, I was grieving at my power.

*

Jackself will do this class outside. This may be the last blue day of the year, the last blue day of my life or the world's, we are going to find a field for it, a tree to shelter by, and the poets of all time can come and find us, maybe tell us where we are.

*

July 22 [1872]. Very hot, though the wind, which was south, dappled very sweetly on one's face and when I came out I seemed to put it on like a gown as a man puts on the shadow he walks into and hoods or hats himself with the shelter of a roof, a penthouse, or a copse of trees, I mean it rippled and fluttered like light linen, one could feel the folds and braids of it – and indeed a floating flag is like wind visible and what weeds are in a current; it gives it thew and fires it and bloods it in.

Hopkins' journals are rich and painterly – he painted – they bubble with his vivid scrutiny. In the spontaneity of the prose – the 'I seemed', 'I mean', 'indeed' – you hear the creature striving to set it all down *especially*, there's not usually much time for reflection, very little 'how this makes me feel', not even that much God – except when Wales looks so amazing from a hill he feels the need to convert it – anyway all his breath is taken up transporting beauty into words.

It was a lovely day: shires-long of pearled cloud under cloud, with a grey stroke underneath marking each row; beautiful blushing yellow in the straw of the uncut rye-fields, the wheat looking white and all the ears making a delicate and very true crisping along the top and with just enough air stirring for them to come and go gently...

This isn't today's exercise, do it when I'm away, but you should stop right where you are and stare at something, not move until it's turned to words. Until it's turned to words so truly the thing itself floats home to heaven. You'll be crouching there forever but I *will* give you an A.

'An A means nothing these days,' Ollie calls out from where he's stretched in the grass.

An A *star* then.

'Got four of them already,' says Lily equally sadly.

An *actual* star then. I dunno, Polaris. Alpha Centauri.

'Keep talking,' and I do: Look, how bluebells make you *feel* isn't part of describing bluebells. Praising God isn't either. This is:

In the clough / through the light / they came in falls of sky-colour washing the brows and slacks of the ground with vein-blue, thickening at the double, vertical themselves and the young grass and brake fern combed vertical, but the brake struck the upright of all this with light winged transomes. It was a lovely sight. – The bluebells in your hand baffle you with their inscape, made to every sense –

Samira has her hand up.

We're sitting in a yellow-black meadow, by an oak tree. We walked twenty minutes south-east from the village to get here, Iona said she'd lead us like a nursery class, in a crocodile, she smiled and took the register, here miss, here miss, some of them held hands. On the way we passed a complex of sandy-coloured buildings, grassy squares and water features, which she saw me peering at.

'The Academy,' she said. 'No dawdling.'

We left it behind us and walked over and over the meadow through the longer and longer grass to the greatest of seven trees. From here if you look back you see the long bored roofs of the student halls, the indignant tower of the church. To the east on the hillside I can see the far tunnel where the train appeared that time. The landscape is yellowy bright and peaceful, an autumn surprise.

I and Niall and Heath are in the shade of the oak, the rest spread out in the afternoon sun like they couldn't go another step. Ollie's lying face down and is not his cheerful self. I presume Samira is about to mention allergies again.

Yes Samira.

'Hopkin says *It was a lovely sight.* That *is* how it makes Hopkin feel. That's not pure description, which you implied it was.'

Good. Yes. Well. He's taking a breath. Is Hopkins.

Lily looks up from her infinite daisy-chain: 'You always have an answer.'

Yeah weird that.

'And what does he mean by *inscape*?' says someone, obviously.

I was waiting for someone to ask that.

So I find my place in a book I've had since school and boom out like a bird reminding all souls what we've come for:

I caught this morning morning's minion, king-
    dom of daylight's dauphin, dapple-dawn-drawn Falcon, in his riding
    Of the rolling level underneath him steady air, and striding
High there, how he rung upon the rein of a wimpling wing
In his ecstasy! then off, off forth on swing,
    As a skate's heel sweeps smooth on a bow-bend: the hurl and gliding
    Rebuffed the big wind. My heart in hiding
Stirred for a bird, – the achieve of, the mastery of the thing!

'A-B-B-A-A-B-B-A,' Niall notes to himself: 'the rhyme scheme.'

'You're havin a laugh,' says Lily.

'He's right,' says Ollie.

'Who asked you,' asks Lily Bronzo, and Heath says 'what's inscape.'

I was sitting on the grass to read, now I'm kneeling and alert. This is where poetry brings me, *upward* to my knees:

So three brand-new things you'll meet when you meet Hopkins. *Inscape! Instress! Sprung Rhythm!* You can ask him about the first two, they're his own words, or if you're shy go and look in the books in the wood. I'm more interested in the third.

'Should we be taking notes?' wonders Caroline from behind great Jackie-O shades.

'It doesn't feel like class,' says Lily, poking a straw in her juice-carton, 'it feels like coming outside for a story. It's too nice to take notes guys.'

She's right. I tell them:

Newsflash, it's not October it's July! It's not autumn it's still summer! I forbid any mention of coldness or darkness, the colours *brown* and *orange* are not to be entertained!

'At least say those *in*-thing words again,' Caroline pleads, 'I have *no* idea what they are.'

No!

Brute beauty and valour and act, oh, air, pride, plume, here
     Buckle! AND the fire that breaks from thee then, a billion
Times told lovelier, more dangerous, O my chevalier!

     No wonder of it: shéer plód makes plough down sillion
Shine, and blue-bleak embers, ah my dear,
     Fall, gall themselves, and gash gold-vermilion.

The accents are for stress. They differ between editions, and he's not consistent with them, but we keep Emily's dashes so we keep Gerard's accents. Odd punctuation's always a signpost that something's not bedded down in the culture, something's bristling, woken up. For you don't have to read much Hopkins to see that – as with Emily, sixteen years older and three thousand miles away – the style stood in almost total isolation from the traditions and conventions of the time.

They went unknown. Emily left barely a mark on her day. Gerard wrote poems at Oxford, burned them all, trained to be and became a Jesuit, and after seven years' abnegation started writing poems again. But, apart from the odd glimpse in little journals, Father Hopkins S.J. saw nothing in print. His great friend Robert Bridges is now perhaps as well known for getting a volume of Hopkins published as he is for being one of the Poet Laureates. Poets Laureate. Whatever.

By then it's 1918, twenty-nine years after Hopkins. At last his lamp could shine as it should and now he stands where he stands.

'How's he getting here, do we know?' asks Caroline, and I don't. I haven't checked anything with Kerri, for damn the village hall I just wanted to be in the sunshine while it lasted.

Prosody lecture. Short. What I just read you, the first half of 'The Windhover', is clearly not iambic (da-DUM) or trochaic (DAD-um) or dactylic (DA-da-dum) or anapestic (da-da-DUM) – which brings us to the end of my Prosody Lecture – but at various times it's any of these. It just deploys them where it needs to.

Hopkins – like me, as it happens – thought Greek rules of prosody were useless for English. What he wrote in he called Sprung Rhythm, the sources of which were alliterative Old English and rhyme-rich Old Welsh. Each stress is followed by one un-stress ('MOR-ning') or two un-stresses ('MAS-te-ry'), or three un-stresses ('RUNG up-on the'). These endlessly varying forms are deployed wherever Hopkins feels them or finds them.

Another word for this is, arguably, *prose*.

If you – like me again, as it happens – find it physically uncomfortable, literally nauseating – to apply rules of prosody to poetry, you can at least hear that the inner rhythms of a Hopkins poem change incessantly *like prose*.

And yet there's no major poet in English who sounds *less* like prose:

Summer ends now; now, barbarous in beauty, the stooks rise
    Around; up above, what wind-walks! what lovely behavior
    Of silk-sack clouds! has wilder, wilful-wavier
Meal-drift moulded ever and melted across skies?

I walk, I lift up, I lift up heart, eyes,
    Down all that glory in the heavens to glean our Saviour;
    And, éyes, heárt, what looks, what lips yet gave you a
Rapturous love's greeting of realer, of rounder replies?

Not prose. Well spotted. Stanzaic patterns, outrageous rhymes –
how about *behaviour/wavier/Saviour/gave you a?* in your face, Byron
– the alliteration, assonance – all these are strung too tight for that
– but it's the *rhythm* we're looking at. Trying to make a *thing* of
Sprung Rhythm, God forbid trying to write in it – feels like missing
the point. Some poets want to know *how* they're doing what they're
doing. I don't, Hopkins did, he was a skilled draughtsman.

Here's the creature turning its head, scratching and gasping as its
scribbles in a journal:

(Hey look) **Summer ends now; now, barbarous in beauty, the
stooks rise around;** (look up there) **up above, what wind-walks!** (oh
my) **what lovely behavior of silk-sack clouds!** (I wonder) **has wilder,
willful-wavier** (what's it like?) **meal-drift moulded ever and melted
across skies?**

That seems to me like his journal *on fire*. As if he retrospectively
named something that burst from him like water from, well, a
spring – ecstatic heightened *prose* that he shaped into verse-forms.

What would a poet look like if he or she wrote in ecstatic
heightened prose that *wasn't* shaped into verse-forms?

For the lands, and for these passionate days, and for myself,
Now I awhile return to thee, O soil of Autumn fields,
Reclining on thy breast, giving myself to thee,
Answering the pulses of thy sane and equable heart,
Tuning a verse for thee…

I wait a bit. When the wind blows and chills us I remember it's
October, but am damned if I'll be cold. The sun is shining and I'm
listening.

Heath is sitting there cross-legged, head down, head up:
'Whitman.'

Go, Mr Bannen. The most interesting poet to compare Hopkins with isn't Alfred Lord Tennyson, or Master Robert Browning, the garlanded superstars of his day – or Dylan Thomas, an echo down the valley – but Long Island's Walter Whitman, another spring, arguably the wellspring of American free verse, and ours too.

Most of the canonical poets I grew up on set their souls to verse, in forms that existed already – sonnets, songs, ballads, pentameters. They stripped and breathed and stepped in a wide running river. Not Hopkins and not Whitman. Hopkins' forms are strained into existence to bear the force of his spiritual joys and miseries, Whitman's to carry the surge of his awe at earthly plenty. One verse is highly formal, the other seems in flight from any form at all, but they strike me as kindred powers.

For neither poet are the resources of the poetry of his day *enough*.

When I read the best free verse I hear eddies of this feeling, declined perhaps, but echoes of its force – *I need this fresh form of mine to carry what I feel alone.* This is why so many of the great free verse writers, the originators, seem gnarled and unique, often hard to fathom as people. It's not a small thing to cry this into the Void – let alone the void – *there is nothing YET BEEN MADE to carry my goddamned song!*

People are staring.

Of course Hopkins is not a writer of free verse, come on, and only I would claim him as one of its forebears (and only when teaching outside in a field in a dream in a coma) but while you listen to some more – he may not want to read us any poems, he may be shy, he may not come at all – maybe bear in mind *these* things: rap, performance, hip-hop, their ingenuity, their bravado, the babble of close sounds, one word helplessly hatching its neighbour, see if anything strikes you as cousin to this work.

And before that will someone please open the Pimms, we are here to pretend it's summer.

And they do, and Iona's sending round cloudy plastic beakers blue pink and green, and Lily's pouring the Pimms in a jug, and Caroline's adding the chalky lemonade, the fruit dropping in in a clump with a splash, and everyone moves from one posture to the next to accept the gift in the long dry grass, though Barry Wilby mumbles, frowning at some private mishap, 'Got me dandelion'n'burdock,' and the breeze comes, leaves flutter and fall and no one says so, and I can't stay here forever, I'll be off soon, I will find out where I am and be off soon, get back to my dear life but in the meantime...

> How to keep – is there ány any, is there none such, nowhere
>> known some, bow or brooch or braid or brace, láce, latch
>> or catch or key to keep
> Back beauty, keep it, beauty, beauty, beauty, ... from vanishing away?
> O is there no frowning of these wrinkles, rankéd wrinkles deep,
> Dówn? no waving off of these most mournful messengers, still
>> messengers, sad and stealing messengers of grey?
> No there's none, there's none, O no there's none,
> Nor can you long be, what you now are, called fair...

There is a pressure from above – the direction from which a believer feels a Presence – a divine downward pressure on the language. This is why the words can't move far, or change much, it's like the Presence forcing time into stone into minerals into jewels – *bow brooch braid brace lace latch catch key keep* – bursting chrysalises into butterflies – *lace latch catch key keep back BEAUTY BEAUTY BEAUTY* – there is a religious gladness in succumbing to this pressure, a bliss in *undergoing* it, *undertaking* it, I shall inch from word to word like an insect, feeling every one though it pleases me or pains me, I shall let each word be heated by the Light as it passes, glow red and glow no more, harm and hurt and heal and help me!

After seven years of poetic silence, when he thought verse incompatible with his calling as a priest, two things happened to Hopkins. He dwelt on the work of the medieval scholar Duns Scotus, which made him think again, then the drowning of five nuns in a Thames estuary shipwreck forced *this* from the dark –

> Thou mastering me
> God! giver of breath and bread;
> World's strand, sway of the sea;

Lord of living and dead;
Thou hast bound bones and veins in me, fastened me flesh,
And after it almost unmade, what with dread,
        Thy doing; and dost thou touch me afresh?
Over again I feel thy finger and find thee.

                I did say yes
            O at lightning and lashed rod;
        Thou heardst me truer than tongue confess
                Thy terror, O Christ, O God;
Thou knowest the walls, altar and hour and night:
The swoon of a heart that the sweep and the hurl of thee trod
            Hard down with a horror of height:
And the midriff astrain with leaning of, laced with fire of stress.

            The frown of his face
        Before me, the hurtle of hell
    Behind, where, where was a, where was a place?
            I whirled out wings that spell
And fled with a fling of the heart to the heart of the Host.
My heart, but you were dovewinged, I can tell,
        Carrier-witted, I am bold to boast,
To flash from the flame to the flame then, tower from the grace
    to the grace.

            I am soft sift
        In an hourglass

So am *I*, grace or not, and I will attest in purgatory, in hell –
failing these when I make it home to Angel – that the reason this
poem is 280 lines long, far longer than anything else of his and way
longer than it needs to be, is his boundless joy at *making verse again*.
Any true poet will tell you that, the believers and the non: it's the
joy of mastery fused with the bliss of being mastered, and if not by
God by language, by the creditors of oxygen, by time that's stopped
to listen.

*

'As kingfishers catch fire, dragonflies draw flame;
As tumbled over rim in roundy wells
Stones ring; like each tucked string tells, each hung bell's
Bow swung finds tongue to fling out broad its name;
Each mortal thing does one thing and the same:
Deals out that being indoors each one dwells;
Selves — goes itself; *myself* it speaks and spells,
Crying *Whát I dó is me: for that I came…*'

He didn't come by train or carriage, he was suddenly there far-off on the hillside, a slight figure resolving as we chatted and watched into a short fair-haired gent approaching in the trim, fastened clothes of his day. By that time Kerri Bedward had hurried here from the village, from the opposite direction, escorted by the beaming stranger in his anorak, saying nothing. Kerri was wondering where on earth we'd got to, so of course I said:

On earth we got to here.

'The reading's in the village hall.'

No it isn't, it's right here in the village field (I told her with the late-summer freedom of the dream I'm having).

Then the beaming guy in the anorak saying nothing said politely: 'Academy property, this meadow as it goes, but you're more than welcome to use it, Mr Maxwell, just inform us next time.'

I'm informing you by being here. And there is no next time, there's only time. Here comes Father Hopkins.

The beaming guy mislaid his beam, reset it, then turned to face wherever it was needed next. Kerri walked forward in a sulk to meet our arriving guest, and Iona, a better lady than me, passed me lemonade to offer him.

*

'I say móre: the just man justices;
Keeps grace: thát keeps all his goings graces;
Acts in God's eye what in God's eye he is —
Chríst — for Christ plays in ten thousand places,

Lovely in limbs, and lovely in eyes not his
To the Father through the features of men's faces.'

He lowered his book down and we clapped. He'd said he'd read
for ten minutes but he read for almost twenty. Barry unzipped a big
blue sports-bag that turned out to be full of rolls and fruits in paper
bags, and we sat around all lunching, *dining*, the sun was lower now
than summer, it's autumn, *fall*, it was trying to say it kindly.

I didn't know how to address him, so I plunged in at the height:
Father Hopkins, would it be all right if my students asked some
questions?

Of course he'd just taken a big bite of a roll so we all laughed as he
nodded and waved with a muffled yes, and Iona started out with the
understatement of the ages: 'It's so lovely to hear you read your work.'

He'd sat down in the shade but his eyes were in the late sun now
and he shielded them as he sought her in the blaze:

'My verse is less to be read than heard,' he began politely,

See? (I hissed to Lily who was nearby) he's a *performance poet*…

'It's oratorical, the rhythm. I don't write for the public…'

'Their loss, eh!' Barry chortled, and I cut in before he could ask
Dr Hoskins where he gets his ideas –

Wouldn't you *like* people to read you?

He smiled and shrugged, 'It's the holier lot, to be unknown.' He
meant to leave it at that but couldn't quite: 'it always seems to me
that poetry's unprofessional,'

You mean it isn't a profession?

Far off towards the village I glimpsed the Academy chap crossing
the field with Kerri. To do what instead of *this*?

Hopkins went on:

'That's what I've said to myself, not others to me. No doubt if I
kept producing I should have to ask myself what I meant to *do* with
it all – but I've long been at a standstill, and so the things lie.'

Samira had her hand up, but Lily advanced, blocking his view of
her, and wagging grapes at him: '*After* you've had some grapes, can
you say about what it was like to burn all your poems that time cos
I could never do that even when they're rubbish I do like burning
things just not my own shit right?'

73

He lowered a branch of grapes to his palm, and said nothing for a moment.

There's nothing you have to answer, I said: Samira what's your question?

Lily glanced round with scorn and Samira's eyes flashed back in retort:

'*I* want to know what Sprung Rhythm is, it's not been properly explained at all.'

At this the poet looked up, put a grape in his mouth and thought a little, said this, as if trying to remember, as if trying to piece together, 'Winter of '75... the *Deutschland*, in the mouth of the Thames... My rector said he wished someone would write a poem on the subject. I'd – long had, haunting my ear – the echo of a new rhythm. Which now I realized on paper.'

Samira scribbled in shorthand, looked up, ready for more.

'It consists in – scanning by accents or stresses alone – without any account of the number of syllables. A foot may be one strong syllable, or many light and one strong. I don't say the idea's new – there are hints of it in music, in nursery rhymes. *Ding, dong, bell; Pussy's in the well, Who put her in? Little Johnny Thin.*'

Someone snickered and he broke off shyly. I rushed to his aid: Got that, everyone? *Now* it's explained.

But it wasn't, for he added:

'It's the nearest to the – native, natural rhythm of speech, the least forced – the most rhetorical and emphatic.'

Ollie spoke: 'Where did you sort of – get it from, Brother Gerard?' ('*Get it from,*' Lily scoffed, 'like on eBay')

'So far as I know,' said Hopkins, reaching for his lemonade, 'it existed in full force in Anglo Saxon verse... in great beauty. In *Piers Ploughman* – '

A fine work (I told them) I studied it at Oxford –

'– in a degraded and doggerel shape.'

Oh. He ploughed on as the students giggled and he brushed away old Langland: 'I'm coming to the conclusion that it's not worth reading.'

'There's *you* told, chief,' Lily gleefully whispered, and Gerard, sensing, said kindly to me: 'Of Oxford I was very fond. I became a Catholic there.'

You were Balliol (I ventured) I was Worcester (as we do) hey we were neighbours!

Heath couldn't give a shit: 'What d'you reckon to Whitman.'

'How about Dylan Thomas?' piped up Ollie and I said stick with Whitman.

'He don't *know* about Dylan Thomas,' said Barry Wilby out of the blue.

Whitman (I said again), what do you think *he's* up to?

Gerard sighed at length and got comfortable on the rug.

'I can't have read more than half a dozen pieces. Enough.'

'Enough for what,' said Heath the way Heath does.

'To give a strong impression of – his marked, original manner. In particular his rhythm.'

Do you think it resembles yours? (I wondered.)

He had the last of his grapes and threw the sprig off in the meadow.

'I always knew in my heart Walt Whitman's mind to be – more like my own than any other man living.'

He let that take its course. Then he smiled around our rapt assembly: 'As he's a very great scoundrel this isn't a pleasant confession. Also makes me more desirous to read him – and more determined that I won't.'

'Ha! Why's he a *scoundrel?*' Lily wanted to know, and Hopkins shook his head as if he'd gone too far and let's not stray from the work. He leaned and took a piece of Dutch cheese Iona had cut for him and held out on the cheeseboard.

'There's something in my long lines like his. That the one would remind people of the other. Both are irregular rhythms. There the likeness ends.'

'D'you *rate* it though,' Heath pressed him.

'His – his *savage* style has advantages, and he's chosen it, he says so. But you can't eat your cake and keep it. He eats his offhand, I keep mine. I notice a preference for the alexandrine.'

Long line, six stresses –

He nodded: 'I've the same preference. I came to it by degrees, I didn't take it from him.'

(Enough on Whitman) You know, Father Hopkins, *I* once found a form I couldn't stop with, like you, I mean, with sprung rhythm, for me it was terza rima – it seemed infinite to me.

He looked puzzled.

'English terza rima is – so far as I've seen it – badly made and tedious.'

Well (I said, nettled into the following nonsense) it maybe was, then, before, I mean but that was before, I mean, who knows, I've not done it yet oh and Shelley, Ode to the West Wind! (everyone's looking at me) Caroline.

'Yes… yes I love your poems, Reverend Father,' she said, resuming slicing a peach, 'but I wonder do you think they are hard to understand? Sometimes, just a tad?'

'No doubt my poetry errs on the side of oddness,' he said crisply.

'Oh I don't *mind* that at all,'

'Obscurity I do try to avoid… but as melody is what strikes me most of all in music – and design in painting – so design, *pattern* – or what I'm in the habit of calling *inscape* – is what I aim at in poetry.'

In the silence I pray skywards no one asks about inscape, and they don't, because they're tiring, but Hopkins, gazing off towards the nearest neighbour-oak to ours, says quietly, of it, piece by piece: 'To be determined and distinctive is – a *perfection*, either self-bestowed – or – bestowed from without.'

I drink to that. (And I drink to that.)

Lily pipes up, 'I've got a question but I forgot it, so just hang on Brother Father Your Graceful Holiness, hang on while I remember?'

He smiles, presents his palms to say of *course*, and meanwhile Heath steps in, no truck with the honorifics: 'What d'you reckon to Wordsworth, mate?'

'Inimitable. Unapproachable.'

'Yes!' Lily cries in delight, '*That's* what it was, my question, *Keats!* We *know* him, he was cool he threw up, do you rate him?'

Gerard lifts a hand, takes a breath, and Lily gapes in expectation of success, with which the priest now handsomely provides her:

'Astonishing,' is the verdict, 'unequalled at his age. Scarcely surpassed at any. One may – surmise whether – if he'd lived – he'd not have rivaled Shakespeare.'

'*Yesss,*' Lily hisses, fists clenched in victory, 'and also, also, more like a personal question, and not being funny right, but how d'you *know* a good poem, does like your head come off and stuff?'

Hopkins is smiling, maybe trying to catch up, so –

How do you know a good poem? (I translate for the good fellow).

He ponders and says: 'Lines and stanzas should be left in the memory... I'm sure I've read and enjoyed pages of poetry that way. Sometimes one enjoys and admires the very lines one can't understand. *If it were done when 'tis done* – is all obscure and disputed, though how fine it is everybody sees and nobody disputes.'

Nobody disputed. The wind blew quite chill now and I heard someone shiver aloud. And I murmured as I uprose and staggered, knowing where Hamlet was going with that: *The be-all and the end-all...*

*

What else was there... We were standing for a while, I remember, for when I rose they rose for the onset of leave-taking, and someone saw the first star, was it Ollie? though Samira said it's Venus and Lily muttered is it bowlocks.

And Gerard took some wine, I recall, some red I think, I see him standing there with us, jolly in our group in the dusky meadow, it was as if our picnic went on informally, upright, and I think at that point Samira asked a question about the Classics. She knew them well, tended to bring them up, and wondered why he didn't allude to them more often.

'Are you doing that to be different?'

He snorted at this and had a bit of a rant, I remember: 'The Greek Gods!'

'They're not in your poems at all, are they,'

'Totally unworkable material – '

'What? How can you *say* that?' she shrieked, thrilled to have set him off –

'– which chill and kill every work of art they're brought into,'

'Oh my god this man is a crazy man!'

'Not gentlemen or ladies!' he cried, 'cowards, without majesty, without awe, foresight, character!'

'He's just written off most of English literature,' she informed us, 'What did Athene do after leaving Ulysses?'

'She – wait,'

'Lounged back to Olympus to afternoon nectar! Nothing can be made of it!'

Lily put her arm on his shoulder: 'Do you drink wine often, father?'

He loved that and laughed to me in a loud aside: 'This is to ply the lash and be unpardonable…'

Later – a half-moon was up by now – I told him we'd been pretending it was summer, we'd had such a warm unseasonable day, and someone mentioned climate change, someone could not forbear to, and then there was quiet but he nodded like he knew.

'Some geologists say – the last end of all continents – and dry land altogether – is to be washed into the sea. And that when all are gone, *water will be the world.*'

'Fools'll still be saying it's got nothing to do with Mankind,' Samira said drily.

'Yeah while they're friggin *drowning*,' said Lily.

This brought the stars out in earnest for the saying of farewells. Some of the gang had stuff to do and were on their way already. Away across the dark meadow glittered the lamps of the student halls. Little silhouettes – Caroline in her wide hat, two people arm-in-arm, then Heath – went stepping through the lights with shoulder-bags and baskets.

'It's October, chief, get over it,' Lily told me as she turned to go.

Samira called: 'Lillian are you going to Cartwright?' and when Lily didn't turn or respond, she said anyway 'We're all going to Cartwright,' and followed her through the field.

Some twenty yards away Barry was a-rummaging in his sports-bag. I was expecting him to ask his usual daft question, so I called out:

Got your cricket pads in there mate?

But Hopkins turned at that – broke off from extolling Thomas Hardy to Niall: 'The sword-exercise scene in the Madding Crowd! – the wife-sale in The Mayor of Casterbridge!' – to suddenly wonder brightly 'D'you *play* cricket here at all?'

Not me (I said) I'm football, me!

But he was lost in an old joke of his about his time in Ireland: 'A Tipperary lad… lately from his noviceship, at the wicket – another bowling to him. He thought there was no one within hearing – but from behind the wicket he's overheard – after a good stroke – to cry out: *Arrah! Sweet myself!*'

He roared, we roared – and in the din there roared the ghost of an Irish poet I knew who'd be loving that joke somewhere – and elsewhere deep in all that Niall bade his shy goodbye, passed the little man something and was gone, and what with Barry Wilby still checking his sports-bag some way off, I was alone a short while with our visitor.

'*Sweet myself…*' he grinned, subsiding.

For some reason I was dumbstruck without the others around me, so we scanned the constellations till one of us could speak. *He* did.

'Out of much much more, out of little not much, out of nothing nothing.'

Yes.

Then I was suddenly going to ask him –

I am suddenly going to ask him – I ask him –
Father.

He turns.
Where are we.

Inevitably, to my dismay, this brings Barry to his feet over there and here he comes setting off towards us with all sorts of coats and blankets. I feel the moment's lost but the next one proves me wrong –

'In careful hands,' says Hopkins, and he said that for sure, and then I'm sure I hear him murmur 'I'm so happy, so happy,' and then I *think* I hear him say: 'I loved my life.'

'Plotting something, are we?' booms big Barry Wilby as he reaches us, looming over the little priest in his suit of cloth, 'Coats, Father, jumpers and coats, gloves and what-have-you, provided by the village!'

Barry is indeed encumbered with warm clothes – he was the only one of us to think of it – but gently Gerard passes on this gracious offer, save for one dark woollen scarf he loops around his neck. It's hours till it will strike me that's what Niall gave him.

It feels like our conversation is over, but then he enquires softly whether we've ever set eyes on the Northern Lights. What follows I took, shall always take, to have been meant for me.

'Beams of light and dark, like the crown of rays the sun makes behind a cloud. Independent of the earth. A strain of time not reckoned by our days and years, but – simpler – as if – correcting the preoccupation of the world.'

Neither of us had seen them.

'Northern Lights…' Barry Wilby mused: 'Lights… but of the *North*…'

Two thorough handshakes and the priest was gone, treading away in the grass, the way he came, soon swallowed up in the gloom of the east. The air smelt of soil and smoke, muddy football boots, mulled wine. Time flared and flashed with seasons coming, for it too could *fall and gash gold-vermilion…*

'Northern Lights,' said Barry.

I couldn't stop myself saying:

He – Father Hopkins – just – told me he *loved his life.*

I glanced at Barry alongside me, he was looking straight into the dark.

'Ho now,' said Barry, 'why shouldn't he love his life.'

Not *love*, Barry, *loved,* past tense – he said he *loved* his life. As in, his life is over now. I think he did, I'll swear he did.

'Now now, señor, no swearing… Don't reckon ya caught that right.'

The wind blew cold.

Do you – *know* something, Mr Wilby?

'Me? Ho no. I know he likes his Greeks.'

He said he *didn't* like the Greeks.

'Did he? Oh. Heigh-ho. Well I know the Northern Lights. Crown of rays, he goes, I'd like to catch that someday. Shall we walk?'

*

O wild West Wind, thou breath of Autumn's being,
Thou, from whose unseen presence the leaves dead
Are driven, like ghosts from an enchanter fleeing,

Yellow, and black, and pale, and hectic red,
Pestilence-stricken multitudes: O thou,
Who chariotest to their dark wintry bed

The winged seeds, where they lie cold and low,
Each like a corpse within its grave, until
Thine azure sister of the Spring shall blow

Her clarion o'er the dreaming earth, and fill
(Driving sweet buds like flocks to feed in air)
With living hues and odours plain and hill:

Wild Spirit, which art moving everywhere;
Destroyer and preserver; hear, oh hear!

'Hey that's not your usual style there, is it señor.'
How would you know my usual style, Barry.
'You usually go on a bit, sort of thing.'
That isn't the whole poem.
'Oh well. Another time, I got a date down this here lane here.'
You do? Okay then. Later.
'Off I go then.'
Right. Bye, Barry. It was Shelley, by the way!
'Come again?'
IT'S ENGLISH TERZA RIMA!
'COME AGAIN?'
Never mind.

*

The Keys is buzzing, but none of my class are there, and I remember they had an event of some kind – why do their events always clash with my reading nights? I squeeze against the bar, and Norman spots me with a gloomy nod. I see he's making with intense annoyance some devilish cocktail out of all sorts of pricey liquids.

Hey Norman. What you making there.

'Beats me, it's her again, she wrote it down, look.'

A – Fat Like Buddha. Rum… Cointreau… Benedictine?

'Bloody annoyance is what it is.'

There's Mimi round the short side of the bar, cackling to some soulful young guy with ice-white hair.

'Hey Max. You made my drink yet Norman?'

Norman darkens into his catchphrase, 'Bloody students and their bloody drinking…'

'Oi Max this is Jakey!'

Yo: Jakey.

'He's famous.'

'I'm so totally not! Don't listen to her!'

'Don't listen to him, Max.'

Shall I just not listen to anyone?

'No change there,' says Mimi, turning.

'Nice to meet you, professor,' says the ice-white kid, politely enough, following Mimi away.

She only does it to annoy you Norman.

'Do what she damn well likes, but it ain't just me who's getting annoyed is it, it's my whole clientele and that includes you.'

I'm not annoyed. I spent my afternoon in the summer.

'Eh? What's this say, *Dubonnet*, now I have to trot downstairs for *Dubonnet* – nobody benefits from this madness, no one!'

*

'The circle is complete,' says Wayne as I slump down opposite.

Evening, *format*.

'It's a small f, Glyn.'

I *said* a small f, pay attention. How did you get a job here, Wayne?

'You know. Channels. You taught me everything you taught me.'

How long ago did I teach you?

'Wanna know exactly?'

Not really. I'm thinking of taking your class.

'Good man.'

Not really. Why don't *I* teach at the Academy?

'Have you applied? … Well there you go.'

I don't even know what I'm doing here, Wayne.

'You're talking to me.'

Jesus what are you drinking?

'A Redheaded Slut. Jägermeister, schnapps, cranberry juice. Mimi Bevan bought it and left it there.'

What's it like. (*Bevan?*)

'It's like Jägermeister and schnapps, but with cranberry juice.'

Rupture equals structure. Hm. You, I don't suppose you know where we are, do you? In the universe, this is.

'This is the saloon bar. That's the public bar. It's full of playwrights. I hear I missed Hopkins. He was soft sift in an hourglass. By the way what's inscape.'

Shut up.

'Who've you got next week?'

I won't be here next week. I'll be awake, I'll be alive, I'll be home.

'See you then then glyn.'

Likewise. *format*.

*

i hate caroline by n prester (g maxwell)

9 chairs at peace all night
have not a word 2 say
about who did u wrong or right
this time yesterday

*

Fear of "God"
Maxwell: 'Poetry' Elective, week 2

Only the rolling dice of Chance
    say FEAR MYTHOLOGY!
Poetry rises for the dance
    the Truth sits silently

    Orlando Faraday

*

Riddle for Caroline

crops up a lot in *Love Me Do*
but not in *Let It Be*
a little word you're welcome to
that's fuck-all use to me

Heath Bannen

(Hots for God assignment.
Prof Maxwell. Week 2)

*

Hating Lily for the Sake of Poetry

For four lines I must 'hate your guts'
    in ABAB rhymes;
poetry exercises do not half
    get on my t**s sometimes!

Caroline Jellicoe, Flat 5, Marlin House

*

I leave the curtains open so I can look the sky in the face. It's clouded over now, all the moon and stars are gone. It has its reasons. *You have your reasons.* I can hear the distant noise of a party from the student halls. Shall I go? Best dream ever. I drag my sheets the other way, bounce and sigh and stretch for comfort, try to sleep, can't sleep, recall these lines I learned for my class, my dad used to incant them too, remembered them from school he did, the rhythm ought to send me off…

So be beginning, be beginning to despair.
O there's none; no no no there's none:
Be beginning to despair, to despair,
Despair, despair, despair, despair.
                                        Spare!

I wake up, sit bolt upright – rain's torrential on my windows.
I have no idea where I am.
And then I remember – *I have no idea where I am.* Restored, I lay my head down calmly and not remotely sleepy. It dawns on me with a gasp that I'm smiling like my skull.

*   *   *

Week Four – October 17th

Morning. Outside it's wet, it's *violet*, it's absolutely pouring with rain and I take it personally.

Of course I do, of course, when all it is is the balance being restored, the delusion corrected, all it is is the thorough-going reminder one doesn't have a say.

The rain rain rain drums on the skylight, blusters at the windows. I feel I should close the curtains and have done with it but I can't, it would feel like my interment, I'm already choosing hymns.

Abide with me; fast falls the eventide… The darkness deepens; Lord with me abide… When other helpers fail and comforts flee look I've a class to teach. Probably only in my mind, but still.

I curl away from the hammering rain, I remember the following dream.

*

I was walking along a sandy beach in a coastal town. In my mind it was the east coast of England… There was a pier in the hazy distance. My brother was with me, we were due to appear in a play that evening and it would soon be time to get into costume.

Then that wild awareness came that seldom comes, that I was dreaming and I knew it.

I halted on the sand, and grinned and said Look. We don't have to do the show.

'I'm sorry?'

We don't have to do the show.

There was a pause in the dream which only angels know the length of.

Then he said: 'We can't let everyone down.'

I said: We can, because you know what? I've realized I'm dreaming.

And on we walked, with our two short shadows rippling over the white sand, and he seemed to be considering the weight of these words: that he was in a dream, and not even his own dream. Except, what he said was this:

'I still think we should make an effort.'

We walked on in silence over the sand. I was proud of his strength of character, and proud of having dreamed this.

*

I look in the cavernous wardrobe that yawns beside the door. Lamplight? yes I did try it for the passage home through a snowy wonderland of fauns and queens and Turkish Delight, but I just banged my head on the back, mothballs orbited my head and it hurt, okay? this is not a magic world. Things don't just happen.

That aside, the wardrobe has the things I need: raincoat, waterproofs, umbrella, hipflask. When the class is done and the reading's done, and I've one last crazy ghost-tale to tell the living clustered round the juke-box yawning *What?* I will pass right through them, I will leave tonight, not sleep, start walking, rain or shine, be some ancient washed-up mariner by the very furthest lamppost: Hey who the hell is that, you alright mate? *There was a ship.* Excuse me?

Bloody waterproofs, look at me, dressed for the weather, the opposite of sadder, the opposite of wiser, already rocking the morrow morn.

*

The zigzag path is of pink and yellow stone, red and brown in the heavy downfall. Everything I wear is crinkling and squeaking, I'm sucking rain off my philtrum. The road up ahead is brimming with puddles, the rain goes sweeping by in sheets, there's no one about – save a downcast hooded little kid at a bus-stop – there's a bus-stop?

Hey there what time's the bus? I don't see any timetable…

(The kid nestles into his hood as if yearning to take no space) Where does it go when it comes?

He says nothing and it keeps on raining. *Where does it go when it comes*, for pete's sake, how *would* you answer that? Seems I'd rather craft a cool line than get my questions answered, but we knew that.

The bus-stop has its back to the trees that fuss and flail in the downpour. It looks more likely they will swallow the village back to ancient forest than that a bus will come for him. Ah well, his business.

Then again, no one likes to be ignored. Something comes to mind, and I call out jovially through the bucketing rain:

There was no possibility of taking a walk that day!

Just came to mind somehow. It gets the deafening, cosmic silence it deserves, the kid sits still like loss in a coat and don't worry I'm on my way.

*

The Keys looks shut at first, then I see a light inside, but no one through the window, an unattended functioning bar, the fruit-machine flashing like it will when we've quit the planet: WIN WIN WIN. Norman must be down the ladder in his underworld, Vulcan taking it out on things. I walk on. It feels like mid-morning. The Saddlers it is, there's sure to be a crowd, but just as I'm about to take that route I see Kerri Bedward in Student Services over the road, lit up at her desk, hair in a bow, typing away by some colossal potted plant. Women hold up half the sky, all the sky, are the sky.

I splash towards the office with this suddenly in my head:

There is a spot 'mid barren hills
Where winter howls, and driving rain;
But, if the dreary tempest chills,
There is a light that warms again…

Which I must have learned for something – which reminds me who I'm teaching. *Whom* I'm teaching, get a grip. What I called out to the bus-stop kid is how *Jane Eyre* begins, my mum used to say it on rainy days. Wrong sister, though, heigh ho. Now *Emily* would have taken a walk, Emily would be out there bare-skulled if it were *hailing*.

*

'Before you ask.'

Ask what.

'I've not heard from them.'

From – you've not.

'Not a word since we booked them. These sisters of yours.'

Don't they just – usually show up? People have so far.

'The agent generally confirms but I keep going straight to voicemail.'

Voicemail? I just get a hiss, Kerri.

'The signal comes and goes. Goes, mainly. We get a signal on Tuesdays.'

I'm never here on Tuesdays.

'That solves that then. Have the rest of my almond croissant, you look hungry.'

(I take it. Kerri stops typing) 'And you know I'm not even, really, meant to be doing this.'

No (through croissant) why's that then.

'Crumbs on the carpet.'

Sorry what do you mean not *meant* to be doing it.

'They're a bit like, don't take this the wrong way, but you're not, you know, affiliated. Students can take your class, but only if it doesn't clash and they don't get any credits. You're dripping all over my magazine. Stand by the plant, it needs it.'

(I walk and drip and munch my almond croissant) This something to do with that bloke in the anorak?

'It's not complicated. You want to teach on Academy property there's a *form*, it's not a tax return. We gave you the village hall.'

The room off the village hall.

'We don't mind what you teach. Well, *I* don't.'

What.

'Things are tightening up a tad. These calls to the agency, little posters I run up for you guys, chairs arranged, it's all on my own time sort of?'

Right. Because I'm not official. What do I do to be official?

'Don't mention it. Well, you take one of the mauve forms from under the map there, fill it out, yes that one, and make an appointment at the Academy, ask for Tina Yeager.'

Map. There's a map.

'Hello? D'you not have maps in your world?'

There's a map there's a map there's a MAP! To the north it ends in white, to the east it ends in sort of green, to the south it's just all symbols, to the west it just goes blue…?

'I think you'll find that's water.'

There's – nothing in any direction. The railway line just disappears.

'Where do I start – that's how maps are made, Glyn, it looks elegant like that. It's *called* A Map of the Village and it's *showing* you the village. You can see what you need to see.'

When does the bus go, *where* does it go when it comes?

'What bus is this then?'

There's – a little guy in a hood sitting waiting for a bus in the rain. Round the corner from my digs.

'Oh. That's sad. Someone should have a word. How are your digs?'

The digs are fine. Except I *did* ask for a wardrobe that leads to a wintry fairyland full of posh kids and magic beavers,

'Did you? oh. There's a problem with today.'

What? hang on where's my pigeonhole. For my stuff, it was right here, I was right here, between *BARBARA MACE* and *JEFF OLOROSO.*

'Barbara won't share, Jeff says he needs the width. I told the students to use your letterbox.'

They'll all know where I live. I mean stay.

'They do anyway, so what?'

Forget it. What was the other thing, hit me.

'It's just there's been a *bit* of a double-booking…'

Actually don't hit me.

*

As I thought, the Saddlers Inn is rammed, forty fools in a steaming line for their Full English. I see Heath and Lily in the queue together counting out some money, behind them I see Ice-white boy and Mimi and the theatre gang, pale ginger girl, skinny oaf in shades. Their faces are grey-pink as if they stayed up all night, idiots think they're a day ahead now. Over there at her corner table Caroline's glancing up from a book, my old Hopkins book she goes back to reading. The portly bearded man is wondering may he share the table: she nods, and he shuffles into place. I see Bella and her Academy girls in a huddle over huge green smoothies, checking which is which. By the window a fierce concentrating blonde with dark-lashed eyes. In a red top with shoulders. Is staring right at me.

Well I really don't queue, I'm dead, but just this once maybe and I actually make it through the door, ta-daa! *tinkle tinkle* but six more faces turn to see and I back out, sorry, my mistake, I'm weird, back into the monsoon.

> Where wilt thou go, my harassed heart?
> Full many a land invites thee now;
> And places near, and far apart
> Have rest for thee, my weary brow –
>
> There is a spot mid barren hills
> Where winter howls and driving rain
> But if the dreary tempest chills
> There is a light that warms again…

I say that last stanza back in my bed under beloved sheets, *that's* how fast I ran, called a false start on that subaqueous grey Thursday.

*

One morning when we all were young, and the three of us shared a bedroom, and it must have been a Saturday and it must have been raining, we decided to take all of our toys and divide them up between us into three Forces. Alun, the eldest, chose all his favourites and arranged them on the bedclothes. These would be the Thompsons, and they would form the Air Force. Mine were to be the Davises, and we would be the Navy. That left the Army for David, the youngest of us, and he called his people the Walkers. Everybody had the surnames of our classmates. The Navy had a meeting by the pillow, in the light of the bedside lamp, with my off-white timeworn teddy bear Trevor Desmond presiding. In my mind the day outside is almost *orange* with rain but hell, Desmond's seen it all. He remembers when there was only him, not all these action figures and puppets, these cheap toys and souvenirs, but you know that old trooper doesn't *do* ill-feeling.

> The house is old, the trees are bare
> And moonless bends the misty dome
> But what on earth is half so dear –
> So longed-for as the hearth of home?

*

I woke up again at two or so, and hurried through what was now a filthy drizzle to meet Iona McNair at the Keys.

It's quiet in here, where's everyone.

(She's brought us tall red Maries, Bloody for me, Virgin for her, celery regardless) Can I switch these when your back's turned?

'Well you could, but now you've told me!'

Yep, blew it, where are you from, Iona.

'The Kingdom of Fife.'

You dwell in a *Kingdom?* Is it under a spell?

'Aye, it is, we've done this.'

We have?

'I think the group are all doing an assignment. I did mine already. Sláinte.'

I set an assignment? Blimey. Sláinte.

'Not for you, for Roger Batchett, he's lovely.'

Is he. What does Roger Batchett teach.

'Poetries of Dissociation.'

Delightful. Delovely.

'It would be, but it clashes with the reading tonight. I mean it's seven to nine.'

What, come on, don't go. Please, really. It's the – it's the Brontë sisters.

'I – well. Okay.'

Show me a poem. These Academy people they're – putting events on top of my events, they're – show me a poem.

'They're doing what?'

Nothing, probably nothing, show me a poem, show me a poem –

(She does, and I like them, they're not bad, they're about a lighthouse and a holiday, the line-breaks need work) Do you say them aloud, Iona?

'Sorry?'

Say them aloud, exaggerate the line-break space – wait longer. If the line-break's right something will *justify* the silence. If it's wrong then nothing *can* and the light will snap and you lose the patient.

She frowns while smiling, which only good people do, trying to understand, she says: 'You really should have switched the drinks.'

Because I'm making no sense?

'I am looking away right now,' she says, theatrically turning to look askance, and I switch the Maries on her.

We raise our glasses, nod, get our faces poked by celery, quaff.

'Go on then.'

Okay (I grab two beermats as one does to explain things, then can't think what they're for, put them back, and say) – Say the last thing you said again.

'I said *Go on then.* This is quite spicy.'

Before that.

'I have no idea, because you switched the drinks. These are not the actions of a responsible professor.'

Ah but I'm not affiliated. I'm a clown in a village hall.

'They'll get you in the end. They'll surround the place.'

I know what you said, you said *You really should have switched the drinks.*

'Can you prove that?'

Weirdly yes. Imagine it's a line of verse. It has seven words, so if you're breaking between words you have six possible places to break. After *You*, after *really*, after *should*,

'I get the concept,'

Or you don't break at all.

'Some poets break in the middles of words.'

Some poets can get lost. So, seven options:

1 *You really should have switched the drinks*

2 *You*
   really should have switched the drinks

3 *You really*
   should have switched the drinks

4 *You really should*
   have switched the drinks

5 *You really should have*
   switched the drinks

6 *You really should have switched*
   the drinks

7 *You really should have switched the*
   drinks

Exaggerate the spaces, see what happens to the scene: sense or nonsense.

'It's turned into a mad cocktail party.'

Yes they're all Noël Coward, but go past that. Here's what I hear: 1 is confident, planned from the start, 2 is *Brief Encounter*, can't take his eyes off her, in 3 something's just happened to them, he knows her better in 3 than he does in 2.

4 is a fail. You don't resume after a break with the tail end of *should've*, 5 has cheap rom-com timing, 6 isn't even good enough for *Carry On Switching*, 7 only works if the fellow is hallucinating in the space, right? Maybe *Carry On Switching* directed by Hitchcock,

'Can I write this down?'

No, do it with your poem. This one works, this one doesn't. So on and/or so forth. What will you do when you're home in the Kingdom of Fife, Iona?

'Och, we've done this.'

You did just say *och*, didn't you.

'I did, and now I'm saying och aye, I'll marry Alastair.'

Aye. You'll marry Alastair. You'll… marry Alastair. You'll marry… Alastair.

'You've had enough celery, you have.'
Ha! I switched it! Not even my celery.

*

MAIDEN in a white flowing cloak, long blonde hair, holding a plant.
KING, bearded, wry smile, hand raised, interested.
Poor FARMGIRL in a smock, carries a bowl of something rural.
Tall arrogant PRINCE in blue, high black boots, hands locked behind.
DARK LADY in a black flowing cloak, dark hair, sad face, same face.
SKELETON that won't stand up, very bendy, very useful.
MONKEY, one of three. See evil, hear it, speak it.
Smooth young GENT in a coat and tails, quizzical face, palms to the sky.
FAIRY child, pink wings, pink things, pink everything.
WIZARD holding a frozen fire, his own spell cast on himself, fly you fools!
CRUSADER crouched in battle, blindly slashing for his Lord.
ELIZABETH, the chilly old ginga, in a great white jewelled dress.

Not bad for a village shop. How many's that, Mrs Gantry?
'You have twelve there, professor, you don't want the cowboy?'
No I don't want the cowboy, I'm putting him back.
'Are they for your children?'
Not these days, Mrs Gantry. They're for my students.
'Really. Right you are. £47.88. What a horrid day.'

*

Heath

Lily

Caroline

moi

Is this it? Hands up who's not here… Hm, no hands. So no one's
not here. So we're fine.
(It's pouring down outside, it has literally not stopped. Literally
cats and dogs. Literally stair-rods on my literal parade.)
Seriously, a minute, tell me something. Who *is* Barry?

Heath very slightly unslouches his position: 'He's one out-there dude.'

It's just that – he missed his one-to-one today, *obviously*, but he also skips the readings. He only came to Hopkins because we did it in a meadow and he was stuck there eating a pie. Why does he even do this course?

'Love,' says Lily deadpan, 'like all of us, chief, for love.'

'Well we don't do it for credit,' says Caroline. 'She's right, we do it for love of books and poets.'

(I look at her) Thank you Caroline. Nothing slant about the truth. That's the worst line in Dickinson. Where are the rest? Iona, Ollie, Samira. The other one.

'Niall.'

Niall.

'They had to register,' says Heath.

Register for what?

'The UE course.'

What's the UE course?

'Dunno.'

'Oh my lord,' says Caroline Jellicoe now fussing her things together, 'it's on my calendar. I am frightfully sorry, I don't think it will take long.'

Lily's leafing in a glossy leaflet, 'It's a set course for writing students. They make us take it. Here look: *Understanding Employability.* It's in Cartwright 504.'

'I hate that room,' says Heath.

'Yeah well,' says Lily, 'I ain't going right, cos I don't want a job, and I sure as fuck don't want a job I can understand.'

'You know, Lily,' Caroline says as she rises, 'every time you use that word it has the teeniest little bit less meaning.'

'Is that right, Jelly? And does a fairy die somewhere?'

'Very witty, I'll be back,' says the courteous lady closing the door behind her, 'I want to hear about the Brontës.'

So. We happy three.

'Chief…'

Uh-huh.

'Not being funny right…'

Mm-hm.

'Why's your bag full of kids' toys?'

Is it?

'There's like, look, a fairy, a wizard, a knight in armour…'

Well. They were the lesson.

'That is just so cool. Go on then, teach us.'

Really? Okay… *MAIDEN in a white flowing cloak, long blonde hair, holding a plant. KING, bearded, wry smile, hand raised, interested. Poor FARMGIRL in a smock, carries* Nah. Not feeling it.

'Oh go on chief, can I be this *Lady*, no this *Skeleton* guy, look Heath!'

'I bags the monkey,' mutters Heath, pretending he cares.

'Cool! You're Baggs the Monkey. Go on chief, who are you choosing?'

Not in the mood, sorry. *There was no possibility of taking a class that day.* Look there's two of you. Two's not a workshop, two's a – shotgun wedding.

'You'd need another witness,' Heath points out, and makes Baggs the Monkey nod in solemn accord.

They're figurines. I used to use my daughter Alfie's, but, well, I'm away from home. So I bought these at Mrs Gantry's. You would pick two at random…

'Dark Lady and Skeleton!'

You'd write a poem from the perspective of the first – okay, say it's Dark Lady – you would write words Dark Lady speaks…

'What, you'd make up what she's like an' that?'

No, you stick with what you see. Face, clothes, the stem in her hand. Position of arms and legs, folds of dress. Start with that and grow outwards.

(Lily frowns at the painted figure) 'I think she's a bit of a raver but not till you get to know her.'

Then go there, get there, but start with what you see. Next you write words for the Skeleton: first him, what he's like, *hi I'm boney*, then what he thinks of *her, crikey what's she wearing.* You do *Alone-on-Earth.* You do *Good-grief-there's-Someone-Else.* Just – grow flowers in the cracks between them. *Form* them.

'Where you off to, loser?'

(Heath has packed up and his chair screeches as he goes)

'To find the Bouncy Castle.'

(He's gone, the door's left open. Lily picks up Baggs the Monkey.)

'He's a cunt, isn't he Baggs. *Yosh he ish Lily, yosh he ish.*'

Anyway, that's the exercise. Reduces your infinite options of self-expression to four cold inches of moulded plastic in the same kit forever. Focus on a creature who is frozen in a moment, on its ownsome with its things, with only *its* fixed expression, only *its* view to view, only *its* lines to say. Because, btw, fyi, that's how you look to the rest of Creation.

'I'm sad we couldn't play it, chief.'

I'm always playing it, Lily.

*

That was almost it for the Brontë class. Class couldn't be bothered. No word from the stars. It rained and rained.

Lily being now a little friend for life, I passed her a poem by 'Ellis Bell'. She sat up alertly, stared, and started announcing in her husky cockney,

'Cold in the earth, and the deep snow piled above thee!
Far, far removed, cold in the dreary grave,
Have I forgot, my Only Love, to love thee,
Severed at last by Time's all-wearing wave?'

Because I would, I set the Dark Lady on the table in front of her and placed beside it the Skeleton who can't stand up.

'Cool, *Yorick* in the house! Stand up! Stand up... fine, lie down.
– Now, when alone, do my thoughts no longer hover
Over the mountains on – eh?'

Angora. A place the sisters made up in childhood. Like Gondal and Gaaldine and Angria and Glasstown. Paracosms, write that down. They lived in a lonely house with a graveyard on two sides. There were six Brontë children, and their dad outlived them all. But because they had toys they grew stories, the stories grew people, the people grew poems, the poems turned novels. You find this poem in some books as 'Remembrance', but when she wrote it she called it 'R. Alcona to J. Brenzaida', that is, the bereft Rosina to the deceased Julius. Make-believe. An organic growth from child's play. She did nothing else, few weeks of school in Belgium, caught TB at her brother's funeral, died at thirty. She makes Dickinson look like Dr Livingstone. What am I saying here? Very little. Just that anyone – parent, guardian, government minister – who does *anything* to curtail or devalue or confine child's play, imaginary games, music, art or drama class, *anything at all* – is a fool and a scumbag and a slaughterer of promise and it's when they do *that*, Lillian, that a fairy dies, alright? That's all I planned to say. Go on.

'Cor.'

Over the mountains.

'Over the mountains on Angora's shore;
Resting their leaves where heath and fern-leaves cover
That noble heart for ever, ever more?
Cold in the earth, and fifteen wild Decembers – '

'Don't mind me! Press on with yer recitals!'

Barry lumbered into the room beneath a tower of yellow anorak: 'Ho now, just a little sprinkling eh!' he beamed, sweeping water from his sleeves, 'I'd like to show you something.'

You'd like to show me something.

'Yes. Somebody's waiting.'

Are they. Is that *me* waiting for *you* at the pub just now? For our one-to-one? Is that *me* waiting for *you* to show up to hear the great poets I invite here, *Barry.*

'Me culpa, me culpa, señor, I do get knotted up in me duties!'

I know you do, you go ahead, you show me whoever you – oh, oh, do you mean the boy at the bus-stop waiting for a bus that never comes because there isn't a bus because there isn't a road because there isn't anywhere beyond here, Barry, d'ya mean *that* boy?

'You come along too, Lily Bronzo.'

'Say what?'

'In answer to that, teacherman, I do mean that boy. I do mean that boy there waiting.'

He's – not waiting for a bus.

'No, señor.'

He's waiting – for what. He's. For us, he's waiting for *us*.

'Rhyme included, bus/us, I notice!'

Alright. Alright, Barry. Let's go and see what's what. Lily?

*

As we left the village hall we met Caroline hurrying back, registered, in her plastic poncho. Across the road four or five smokers huddled in the green-lit porch of the Keys. There was almost mist between us the rain was so relentless. The Ice-white actor was getting a light, and the slouching figure with him straightened up, 'Get back inside there Max, there's still an hour to go!'

'Silly girl,' said Caroline.

'Shall I smite her with my f-word?' offered Lily Bronzo. 'Or actually… get a smoke off Jakey.'

Lily hurried off through the puddles in her gold Doc Martens.

Caroline sighed with scorn, waited for me to agree with her what *children* they all are. Which tends to produce the opposite effect:

We're going on a bear hunt.

'We're doing what?'

Ask Barry.

'Barry, what's happening?'

'Going to see the fellow yonder,' he said, gesturing down the lane to the distant shelter with its lone hooded tenant, and, when Lily was back, fighting for the life of a damp tiny roll-up, and with Mimi too, and Ice-white Jake with his hands in pockets, we were assembled, off we set.

The rain seemed to intensify as if to warn us off this course, but we were infused and weathered now, we'd cancelled the day for this. The boy in the hood, now the focus of all attention, stayed still as before while he grew in our vision.

About ten yards from the shelter I stopped them:

Look I made a dick of myself earlier with this chap, can someone else say, um, *initiate?*

The two who moved quickest cared least or cared most, so I said Let Caroline do it, and Mimi said whatever.

Then I saw what happened clearly. Once in the dry air of the shelter Caroline stooped gently to inquire if the boy was all right. When he turned his face in our direction his hood came loose and we were all wrong.

'Oh good lord!' cried Caroline.

'Don't be startled,' pleads a small pale woman, 'don't be. You're all safe from Currer Bell.'

And she rises and leaves the shelter, leaves the lane along a barely trodden path into the trees, and we all but wade after her, helpless, speechless, into the gloom.

*

Wha ya may go t'bed.
I'd rather do anything than that. And Charlotte you're so glum tonight.
Well suppose we each had an island…

If we had I would choose the Island of Man.
And I would choose Isle of Wight.
The Isle of Arran for me.
And mine should be Guernsey.
The Duke of Wellington should be my Chief Man.
Herries should be mine.
Walter Scott should be mine.
I should have Bentinck.

*

Well suppose, well suppose. If you're in the woodland with me, then you come from Well Suppose. If you're not you don't know where I am, and good luck with your studies.

Caroline followed first, sprightly, cheerily, dressed for all weathers, Lily next, blithe and drenched, dye running, city kid turned water-pixie, then me in my dream, my death, my sleep, stark naked what do I care, then worse-for-wear blond Jacob, diffident smoking Mimi, 'is this how you teach these days Maxwell,' and Barry lumbering in last place. How did he know she was waiting for us?

We went through copses and beside them, then between them and *below* them, and soon there were no more fields or views, we were treading through the sodden mulch, mud-creatures in our habitat. Then our leader stopped for a moment, we all came to our squelching halts in the wood, she'd pulled her hood back on and was whispering to Caroline.

Caroline nodded, then sucked the air in briskly as she got the message. She turned back to face us, pointed at Lily then Mimi, and beckoned them up the line. She pointed at me, at Jacob, at Barry, and waved us further back. We got the picture too, girls and boys, and complied, and Charlotte went on walking.

*

She was the oldest of them who survived childhood (I'd say later in the Keys, where I must have looked a sight, sodden and exhilarated, drumming on the bar as I raved of my adventure!) it was Charlotte started them in their made-up worlds, you see, on that actual night, when the housekeeper said *Go t'bed* and instead they dreamed up whole freakin worlds man. Charlotte bags the Duke of Wellington to be chief, Emily bags Walter Scott. But then like, time goes by, Charlotte leaves them there, playing, puts childish things behind her. Point is, they carried on, her little sisters did, made new realms, went on with their creations…

'Right you are,' says Norman, pulling a pint of the local bitter.

Yeah our brother did the same to us, they should do, elder brothers. He got his own room, and left his toys in ours. But we went on too. He called our made-up world *Gime* – like, mimicking *'Shall we ply our gime?'* in the lazy London tones we had – and our toys were now the *Tuss*. These names were meant as insults, but they stuck and were worn proudly – you know, like 'Whig', 'Tory' – and his Air Force, the Thompsons – well they had no captain now, right, they were out of control, they turned to hard boys from the east of town, menacing cool kids who did things we couldn't do, stayed out late, had adventures. Gimeworld got wider, there were countries to have wars with, Knotland, Batland!

'Had a fun day in the woods did we,' a woman asks beside me.

*

The ladies walked ahead through the trees. Of the three male creatures shambling in their wake, only I was trying to listen. Jacob mooched along as if asleep, Barry punctuated our sodden progress with the likes of 'Rain rain, go away' and 'Nice weather for ducks', comments Jacob met with sniffs of nothing and I met with *hm* or *uh-huh* or *yep* or any of the other insuppressible tics that get me through the daylight hours.

Caroline was the closest to Charlotte and asked her quiet things politely.

'I'm very well,' she replied, 'I wag on as usual.'

The next question I didn't catch, but it made both Lily and Mimi look round at us with a common smirk, and I heard Charlotte say quite loudly:

'Do I think men are *strange*?' and they all laughed at *all of us ever*, 'I do indeed, I've often thought so,' and I grinned as widely as I could so she'd say more about us and I'd hear more about us, though she didn't turn to look. I could hear her plainly each time she nodded towards Caroline to her left, or the girls to her right, but her words were muffled when she looked ahead. Her thoughts on my weaker sex elicited frantic yelling and yaying in accord.

'The mode of bringing them up is strange, they're not – guarded from temptation…'

This turned Mimi round to wag a finger of blame at *me* for some reason as our little guest went on:

'Girls are protected – as if they were something very frail and silly, while boys are turned loose on the world!'

'You getting all this, Max?'

'Their letters are proverbially uninteresting…'

Way harsh! (I gaily protested)

Lily asked her what she always asks because she's always homesick:

'London?' said Miss Brontë, 'yes and no. I sometimes fancied myself in a dream...'

'Yeah tell me about it,' said Lily, and Charlotte, not knowing the idiom, began to: 'I've been to the theatre, seen Macready in *Macbeth*. The Crystal Palace is a wonderful sight – I thought more of it the second time than the first, it's hard work going over it. After some three or four hours you come out broken in bits.'

'That's like me in all museums,' said Lily.

'I've seen the pictures in the National Gallery. I've seen Turner's paintings and I saw Mr Thackeray.'

(I plunged forward) What's Thackeray like, Miss Brontë?

I'd tested the line between women and men, and for a terrible while our soaking footfall was the earth's tense heartbeat. I had resigned to being ignored, beyond the pale, when she responded loud and clear without turning, as if it was Caroline who'd asked about William Makepeace Thackeray.

'He wasn't told who I was, but I saw him looking at me through his spectacles. When we all rose to go down to dinner he just – stepped quietly up and said – Shake hands – so I shook hands.'

I dropped back in my sodden bliss, she'd spoken words to a question of mine. She added these for her new sisterhood:

'He's unjust to women, quite unjust.'

Said Lily Bronzo, 'I fu – I flippin' love London,' and I saw Caroline lean behind and smile gratefully for that small mercy.

Mimi had halted to light a cigarette, now the forest cover was filtering back the rain, so we three reached her.

'Where we off to Maxwell.'

Do you *honestly* think I know that.

'I think you know everything,' she said through smoke, 'this cretin thing's all an act.'

Jacob stopped with Mimi, so I went on with Barry, stuck with his wheezy breath, watched his big wellies sloshing along at my side. I needed to ask him things but I was trying to hear the women speak, so all I did was look at him once. He beamed right back, his large face a fairground mirror, and, as if fielding my unsaid thought, sang that trench-song to the tune of *Auld Lang Syne*:

'We're 'ere because we're 'ere because we're 'ere because we're 'ere…'

(I bloody hollered my next question) CHARLOTTE, MISS BRONTË, sorry Charlotte, Miss Brontë, these are my poetry students, can you tell us how you and your sisters started writing poetry?

I deftly accelerated in case she was going to answer, with Caroline both waving me forward and pressing me back, measuring the appropriate distance, settling on five yards or so. I could hear she was asking the question herself, properly, mildly, gently, and this elicited an answer.

'Once I was *very* poetical, when I was sixteen, seventeen, eighteen… We'd very early cherished the dream of – one day becoming authors.'

Yes, yes! You pretended you were men, you were Currer Bell, Ellis Bell, Acton Bell! (I bleated, a teacher, throwing off all dignity.)

'Ding Dong Bell,' Barry chuckled to himself, putting the red nose on it.

The earth rolled its eyes, the earth stopped, the earth turned: *Speak, Currer Bell…*

Charlotte stopped and the women drew up around her. When she resumed the walk she was reading aloud from a pale shred of paper she'd unfolded: '*It is long since we have enjoyed a volume of such genuine poetry as this. Amid the heaps of trash and trumpery which lumber the table of the literary journalist, this small book has come like a ray of sunshine.* The Critic.'

I nodded in approval at the taste of The Critic's critic, and Lily asked her:

'D'you read all your reviews then do you cos I'll *so* not do that.'

A short scornful laugh: '*The Economist…*' she cackled, as if some case was closed. She didn't need to read this one, she had it off by heart: 'the literary critic praised the book if written by a man. Pronounced it *odious* if the work of a woman…'

Lily and Caroline, gleefully appalled, closed in around her as I trod the manful trail of shame. She was folding away the paper: 'I don't like my own share of the work. Juvenile productions, crude, rhapsodical. I've not written poetry for a long while.'

'Who are your *favourites*,' Caroline prompted at her side with a nudge which made Charlotte stare, shocked, 'whom should we be reading in poetry?'

She recovered, went on walking and thinking.

'Let it be first-rate,' she said, 'Milton, Shakespeare, Thomson, Goldsmith. Pope – if you will though *I* don't admire him – Scott, Byron, Campbell, Wordsworth, Southey. I like Southey. Southey was happy at home and made his home happy.'

I was happy at home (I said softly, and out of the corner of my eye I saw Barry nodding for me gravely) as Charlotte continued,

'Not only loved his wife and children *though* he was a poet – loved them the better *because* he was a poet. I like Southey.'

On we went, all sweetened by her thoughtful words. It was going to be really very dark any minute. I could still make out the silhouettes of Caroline, Charlotte, Lily together. When I glanced behind to see Mimi and Jacob I saw sodden misty woodland, they were gone, had tailed off, called it a day. Now Barry Wilby clicked on his trusty camping torch and night fell.

*

Joining me for a drink are you.

'I have one, thank you,' and she did, the neat smart lady standing at the bar, in the red top with shoulders, she had some kind of pineapple juice, 'you know you could claim for them, don't you.'

What?

'Your toys you bought for your class. You could claim they are teaching materials.'

(I downed my vodka so another would come) They're not teaching materials, they're for my personal use.

'Did they enjoy your jaunt through the local woodland.'

What.

'Did they enjoy your jaunt through the local woodland.'

Are you Tina Yeager?

'Yes.'

From the Academy.

'In the daytime I am.'

Pleased to meet you (I shook her little hand in its fawn suede glove and Norman brought me my drink) *Everyone* enjoyed our day. You should have come too.

'I wasn't invited. No one was invited. Most of your class weren't invited.'

It wasn't a class. It wasn't a party. It was a jaunt through local woodland.

'Can I ask to what end, in pouring rain in the hours of darkness?'

You can ask what the hell you like, you have a heavenly face and you've no idea. And I'm dreaming, cheers, and there ain't no place in this cosmos where you are the boss of me.

She lifted her glass and shook it so the ice spoke.

'Is that right.'

That's right, Tina.

'There's a better pub than this one.'

*

Barry advanced with his excellent torch, remaining behind the women but pointing the beam at the undergrowth where they'd have to be walking soon, like some big fat doomed Sir Walter. I lagged behind alone. It seemed the land was descending, but it was curiously drier as if it hadn't rained here at all. The beam of torchlight bounced and jiggled ahead, a fox went through it, or something did, the trees were ancient dead-men.

Charlotte stopped in a misty space. She looked to the women on either side, finally turned and looked at we man-monsters behind. The torch-beam shone on the ground – Barry once again surprising me with his manners – so it was too dark to make much of her face. We all just breathed and waited. From the movement of her head and shoulders it seemed she was wondering where the other two had gone. Perhaps this is why she said what she now says, to those of us still here:

'Don't desert me.'

And as we start to cry *Of course we won't*, she says 'One by one, one by one, I watched them fall asleep on my arm.'

Then she hushes us completely.

We listen, then she does it again, as if to hush our breath itself.

Caroline hisses to Barry to kill the torchlight.
'Si señora.' Click.

And we're in total darkness.

No we're not in total darkness.
There's a light up ahead, a tiny firelight kindling and cracking a hundred yards away in the trees. Five inhalations praise it for being, four breathe out when it seems to be gone, but it's just that *someone's moving past it*. A dark little dwarfish shape went before it, around it, behind it and there it is again. Someone's made a lonesome fire in the trees.

And we wait for our visitor to tell us why she brought us.

*

Two stools drawn up against the bar, and Tina's black-stockinged knees press awkwardly on the panels to avoid the touch of mine. She reaches for the menu.

'So did you find anything in your jaunt through local woodland.'

God I didn't even know this pub was *here* (it's dim and plush and cosy, down a side-road near the station, couples murmuring in booths, we've bought red wine and are sat at the bar) no one's ever mentioned The Coach House.

'It costs too much for students. That's what I like. What did you go to the woods for?'

What did I go to the woods for, what did I go to the woods for...

'I can claim this on the Academy.'

What did I go to the woods for... Well. Tina. When I was about fourteen, and my brother about twelve I think, we were still playing Gime, our Action Men were giving a rock-concert. Gimeworld had started to mimic the real one, it was being sort of swallowed up...

'Are you exceptionally drunk, Mr Maxwell?'

Being sort of folded back into reality, and they were in mid-song, the Action Men, and the coloured lights were flashing on their faces, when downstairs the doorbell boomed, and soon came the sound of my mum traipsing upstairs to knock on our bedroom door. Cos it was my mates from school, right, and for the first time of nine hundred times they were asking me to come out with them, walk the streets of Welwyn Garden drinking cider under lampposts till we were drunk enough to explain ourselves in depth.

'You were playing with dolls at fourteen.'

So I had this momentous choice. Go on with the game in the World of Gime, or abandon it forever and start being a teenager…

'The suspense.'

I know. I abandoned it forever. And I guess once I'd gone my brother did too, in fact I know he did, he's fifty and I'm fifty-two, like a deck of cards but you know… we left our Supergroup still playing that song.

'This place shuts at two by the way.'

Nothing happened in the woods.

'Why did you go then, help me out here.'

Because I'm dreaming. We saw nothing. We found our way home. I *say* home. I found my way here.

*

Charlotte stands alone, the rain seethes in the branches.

And then she says quite suddenly: 'Papa bought Branwell some soldiers at Leeds. When Papa came home it was night and we were in bed, so next morning Branwell came to our door…'

Our eyes are becoming accustomed, there are two small children doing something by the fire in the circling tiger light, one is darker, one fairer, they are working on something, there are things strewn all around them. Thrilled to recall the morning, Charlotte cries: 'Emily and I jumped out of bed and I snatched up one and exclaimed *This is the Duke of Wellington!* Emily likewise took one and said it should be hers. When Annie came down she took one also. Mine was the prettiest, perfect in every part…'

The children are playing with hundreds of toys, toy soldiers, castles, palaces, galleons, cliffs, by the light of their thundering fire.

'Emily's was a grave-looking fellow, we called him *Gravey*. Anne's was a queer little thing – very much like herself – he was called *Waiting Boy*. Branwell chose *Bonaparte*.'

Charlotte's standing ahead of us, some ten yards off, clasping the trunk of a tree like a friend, silhouetted, moving only to the effort of these words. I glance at Caroline, with Lily backed against her, the elder has her arms around the shivering younger, the fireglow's on their faces. Right behind me Barry shines his torch below his big chin, grinning like a scary pumpkin, I say maybe not do that?

I want to ask a question, but I sense it will bring an end to this. Then I ask the damn thing anyway, for the rotten race of men.

Where is your brother, ma'am?

(It doesn't bring an end, it brings this after a silence…)

'Nothing remains… errors and sufferings. Life had no happiness for him.'

There's happiness *here*, look (and for the first time she quarter-turns, I tremble to have caused it.)

'My sister would never go into society,' she says, and it's the darker child who's in her eyeline, 'she'd say *What's the use? Charlotte will bring it all home to me…*'

She tenderly detaches the tree from her embrace and advances on the flickering glade. When she's very close she kneels down. Behind her, we all fall slowly earthwards too, as if cut down by a spell for even venturing into earshot.

The fairer, slighter girl is curled up on the leafy earth with a book, writing intricately in it, as if listing all the dignitaries she's set in ranks before her, turning a page, sighing, hard at work in her delight.

Whereas the dark girl in her dirty dress just stares at us.

Maybe not at us, maybe just stares. I hear the rustling of paper, and, again, Charlotte has drawn something from her cape. As she reads it out, the tall dark child peers forward and frowns, as if trying to make out birdsongs. Charlotte drives on anyway: '*There are passages in* Wuthering Heights *of which any novelist, past or present, might be proud. The thinking-out of some of these pages is*' – her small voice clots and thickens – '*the masterpiece of a poet.*'

She seems to sag there, folding the paper, weak with pride.

The child just pouts, I think she's missing her game.

'*The Palladium*,' Charlotte mutters to us, 'late justice, too late.'

'Oh dear, oh dear, oh dear,' sings the child, turning away from the darkness and back to look at all that's lit by the fire. She points at what the fairer girl's been doing, assembling several dignitaries she's still noting and underlining.

'The Gondals,' Emily states, and Annie looks up from her book.

Emily solemnly beholds the scene: 'The Emperors and Empresses of Gondal preparing to depart. For the coronation, which will be on the twelfth of July.'

Now Annie rises in rapture, her work curated, and explains into the dark woods to anybody out there: 'Emily's engaged in writing Emperor Julius's life. I'm engaged in the fourth volume of Solala Vernon's. She's read some of it.'

Charlotte quietly asks them something I don't catch, and as if in answer they both start going about the clearing, checking, picking up things, pondering and placing.

'Emily and I have a great deal of work to do,' says Annie, 'We've not yet finished our Gondal chronicles,' at which Emily tops her – 'There's no open rupture as yet – all the princes and princesses are at the Palace of Instruction – ' (and we spot the tiny figures assembled on a green plinth as Annie joins her, twin giantesses towering over the Palace walls): 'The young sovereigns with their brothers and sisters...' (The idea of it almost makes them resume, as if there were no ghostly sister out there to report to – let alone strangers – then Annie hurries to the left side of the clearing, to some fallen kings on a pile of dead leaves) 'The Unique Society were wrecked on a desert island returning from Gaaldine. They're still there,' (she gestures sadly to their sorry plight) 'but we've not played them much yet. I've many schemes in my head.'

'Oh dear,' Emily says again, having trod on a troop of horsemen, 'oh dear, oh dear...'

'She's writing some poetry too,' says Annie, and Emily hides her face in the game.

Annie contemplates this for a moment, then lowers herself to her knees beside her sister, brushing leaves from her back, then gathers the figures she wants in her hands and says strongly and deliberately, without looking up again, 'Take courage, Charlotte, take courage. I've the same faults I had.'

At which she joined in where they'd got to in the game. Charlotte rose, turned quickly and walked away right through us, not *through* us, slipped between us, I heard her ragged breathing do its best. The instant our eyes followed her all was extinguished, the woods went dark, there was no fire, no glow, no light in a clearing, and when Barry clicked his torch back on there was no one to follow either. What with his venture-scout know-how and Caroline Jellicoe's common sense we soon found our way to a road again, saw the lamplights of the village a half-mile off down the dale and did the one thing left to do. All together now, Lily and Barry and Jelly and me, to the tune of *Auld Lang Syne*:

We're 'ere because we're 'ere because we're 'ere because we're 'ere,
We're 'ere because we're 'ere because we're 'ere because we're 'ere…

It was as if nothing had happened, which made it easy to say so.

*

We wove a web in childhood,
    A web of sunny air;
We dug a spring in infancy
    Of water pure and fair;

We sowed in youth a mustard seed,
    We cut an almond rod;
We are now grown up to riper age –
    Are they withered in the sod?

Are they blighted, failed and faded,
    Are they mouldered back to clay?
For life is darkly shaded;
    And its joys fleet fast away…

'Are you done?'
Uh-huh.
'Are you teaching that?'
I dunno, are you learning it?
'I mean teaching it to the students. It doesn't sound very. Anyway.'

I wasn't teaching that. I know it, it's Charlotte Brontë remembering her childhood.

'Is everything you teach sort of *old*?'

Everything I've learned is.

'Not a mover with the times, then.'

A shaker with the times.

She finished signing for the drinks, and we left The Coach House so the owner Claude could get his beauty sleep. The night was foggy and damp, the lane was dark and narrow, far away at its end I could see the lamplight of the village green, four lanterns haloed misty bronze. Claude's footsteps clacked away on the cobblestones. I asked if she wanted to come back to my digs and her mouth fell pretty much Open.

'I'll pretend I didn't hear that.'

I'll pretend I didn't say it.

'You know, you can't just – do what you're doing. The students find you funny, but you can't do what you're doing. The meadow last week, the woods, the,'

Knowing this is all a dream and so on,

'Well. Yes. Case in point.'

I'm not affiliated Tina.

'You can be. If you want to be. Make an appointment. I'll give you the form.'

I've got the form, it's mauve.

'Fill it in then. Come to the office on Monday.'

I only exist on Thursdays.

'Oh ha-ha. How about we start fresh next week?'

Does Thursday work?

'See Kerri. I'm going this way. You're going that way. That way. No. Go that way. Good. Left right left right, there, you can do it...'

*

There was a limp sodden envelope on the mat inside my door. It said H. BANNEN on the outside in smudged blue ink. I assumed Heath was quitting the class so in the middle of the night and fair lost to reality the phantoms hear me say *Sod off then why don't you.* Then a rustling of typed paper, and they say *Wrong again,* the phantoms, they say *Wrong again, professor.*

*

From J. J. Bones to the King of Somewhere

Looks like I'm grinning at you. I look open-eyed.
The day's dirt sticks between my ribs, my foot's a foot-
long stave of toes. They can do what they like with me.
I bend anywhichway. My fists are cups that hold
jack shit. My pelvis is a heart-shape with a stake
through it aka my backbone. You got crown hair
beard boots & tunic breeches bracelets sword scabbard
you hold your hand out making your point must be you're
king of somewhere cos there's nothing to be done
with you, can't move or change, you just snap back into
shit you were born into. I'm watching from inside
you cos you're made of the selfsame crap I'm made of.

Heath Bannen. (Figurine assignment. Prof Maxwell.
Week 4)

*   *   *

Week Five – October 24th

Sometimes I'm telling this to my daughter as a child. Sometimes I'm telling it to my folks in middle age. Sometimes I'm speaking to total strangers in a queue, sometimes to you on a balcony, and on a rosy blaring morning I tell it to my three chums outside Double History, peering down the corridor, guys, guys, no *listen*...

I found myself in this place where I didn't know a soul. But they were all in their ways familiar and they wanted to know what I knew. I didn't think I knew jack *self* but somehow sitting there at a great big table all sorts of matters came to mind in the middle of the afternoon and the thing made total sense? Then in the evenings it grew weird and wild. Great amazing writers came, and I tried to do them honour, guys, no listen, *listen*...

I crashed out at night and when I woke up it seemed a day, a week, a month, a year and a life had all gone by together lately, hand in hand. A village, town, city, country, island, realm, an empire, lately, arm in arm together, over the hill and away they went. I lit candles when I wrote. I had ideas for classes I forgot when I taught classes. There was this local boozer quite a lot was wrong with. I met a short blonde woman I couldn't help disliking. And students were everywhere. And it was always Thursday... Don't know where the other days went. You?

You tell me in your own time.

I loved my little room. I loved my view from here. Loved to be far away yonder and spot my place from there: those three lit windows slanting in the roof, no one's in right now. Loved my walk to breakfast even while it rained like hell.

I didn't know who was running things, I didn't know why the weather changed, I didn't know the way home. I suspected I might *be* home. I didn't know where anything led, where the trains and buses came from, let alone why they never came. I could never get a signal.

I'd go to the woods for books sometimes, that was never a wasted journey. I'd go to the edge of the lagoon, gaze out at the little wooded island.

I couldn't make sense of Time at all.

So I nested in its care and right here is where you'll find me.

I believe I'll be home for Christmas.

I believe in *Father* Christmas but he doesn't need to call on me when the time comes, he already got me everything I hoped for. Either I've been good, or I've been bad and it didn't matter. Either way he's coming, probably dressed like me.

O Wedding-Guest! This soul hath been
Alone on a wide wide sea:
So lonely 'twas, that God himself
Scarce seemèd there to be...

Alfie, mum and dad, ladies and gentlemen; pals from Double History, golden lads and girls, chimney-sweepers, Father Christmas, Wedding-Guest – I am trying to tell you all a most fantastical story. Only nothing ever comes that's any different from my life.

*

My one-to-ones that morning were more couple-therapy than lit-crit. Caroline had decided there'd be no more poems about her ex-husband Ronald. She unduffled her coat and dumped the sheaf down on our usual brunch table at the Saddlers and said that was that, that's the collection, take it or leave it.

I didn't feel like picking over line-breaks with this facet of Caroline, and was damn sure she didn't, so I asked what order the collection was in and she said 'Order? chronological.'

I said free them from that. What he did to you is man-shaped. He hurts She at zero, leaves She to heal by numbers. Don't respond by the clock. Make your response in your own shape. *I'm healed already, mother-lover, feel free to sing along.* So order them by form. You have these fractured free-verse poems, lines floating over the page in a mood – or you have full rhymes in quatrains, or you have all sorts in-between.

'I'm getting better at form, they rather creak a bit.'

Let them. Creaking's bones, creaking's stretching, creaking's honest. The accomplished formless poem falls dead silent, oiled with choice. Nothing's straining: *we're* supposed to. But Form is Time singing about itself. Stretching, creaking, singing. Its ABCDEFG is *music* – the notes that play seconds-minutes-hours-days-weeks-months-years are all jiving on the staves.

Start with the best rhymed songs you have. Not the oldest or the newest but the best. What do you mean by it? *I can now sing what happened, because time has (a) absorbed the shock and (b) made me better at this.*

Then do some free ones. What do you mean by them? *Here's how I was once hurt, though you know I'm not hurt now (see pages 1, 2, 3, 6, 8 and 13).* Then gradually introduce more form, metre, rhyme. What do you mean by these? *Song became more dear to me than anything you left behind. The effect of your leaving was song. Song and I say stay away. Song and I say don't come back.*

'Who says I want him back? *God* no!'

Make the poems scoff like that. Music liberates you from the clock, the calendar, the schedule, Caroline. Rhyme, form, metre, it's the language reaching out to you: *we've got this, we've done this, we were there before, we can help.* They even say it when they can't, which makes them just like you.

Free-verse is always now. History went by and smashed your window on the way. Fragments bleed and bleeding's of the moment. Fine, you want to show the hurt, the harm. Just don't – *timetable* it. Don't answer He's question. Don't balance He's equation. Can we talk about the woods now?

I got nowhere with that. She just kept saying how much she liked their poems, 'the Yorkshire girls.' Look I *do* ask all the questions you would, I *try* to understand – but my students don't think anything's strange, so they're not the ones to ask.

She asked me round for shepherd's pie at her digs. I said I can do Monday and she said the hell you can.

'We both know that,' she said, duffling up her coat and leaving the table, 'I'm not an idiot.'

Ollie didn't want to talk about poems at all. Except to say he'd stopped writing them to Mimi – 'It was a good call, man, but it's not working for either of us. She hangs with her drama crowd, she says they're all gay, they don't look gay.'

Gay's not a thing you look, Ollie.

'I know, and it's great and stuff, but you know… now that Jake Polar-Jones turns out to be… you know.'

Turns out to be what. The white-haired guy?

'Hot, *hot,* they're like a double-act, everyone wants in on them.'

That guy never says a word, what the hell's hot about *him*?

'He was the Chocalux Man.'

Again?

'The Chocalux Man, turns out that was JPJ. That's why he dyed his hair. So no one here would clock him.'

JPJ? I want a drink.

'It's twenty past eleven.'

A drink, man, not a time-check.

We walked each other to the Keys, where I left him with Iona, who was pouring green tea and sharing poems with Niall Prester. She'd be bright and motherly, and Niall's melancholy air would give Ollie some cheering up to do, he always rose to that kind of thing and he went right to it, yo K-man and so on.

Then, just as I was bearing my small-or-large-large pinot grigio from the bar Samira swept in surprisingly late and flustered.

'Lillian Bronzo said to say in a note she sent that she's unwell at the moment and I can take her place for tutorial today.' She pointed to one of the quiet booths, where we now spend a peculiar half-hour on stanza-breaks and vulpine behaviour.

In Samira's poem 'Vixen' the speaker – 'it isn't me, obviously' – appears to dream about a fox. It strikes me as outright sexual – 'I've used alliteration, look' – not to say unsettlingly, seat-shiftingly sexy – 'it's also about poetry, like for example The Thought-Fox by Hughes' – and I share an e-cig with her, the green tip passing to and fro like a thing we shan't mention, as I arrow and star and underline her words like the best confessor ever. The one time I catch her eyes I almost reel at the shock and joy in them. It's like *Lily's* staring out as well. Then she grabs her poem and leaves looking weirdly proud, with not a word to her classmates.

Weave a circle round her thrice, I said softly as I joined them, but regretted it and went silent for a while without explaining further.

*

Mrs Gantry peered at the thirty-two fluorescent plastic highlighters I clattered onto the counter of her village stores. Garish green, manic magenta, obvious orange and bilious blue. Eight sets.

'Are these for your students, professor?'

We're going to do some colouring.

'We've a lot more action figures, you know, we've got a pirate in.'

Just the pens today, Mrs Gantry, I have a class to teach.

*

Heath	Iona
Peter	Caroline
Samira	Barry
Niall	Ollie

moi

Take it away, moi:

The Frost performs its secret ministry,
Unhelped by any wind. The owlet's cry
Came loud—and hark, again! loud as before.
The inmates of my cottage, all at rest,
Have left me to that solitude, which suits   5
Abstruser musings: save that at my side
My cradled infant who the crap is *Peter*?

'Here, sir.'

The man who wore the anorak that afternoon in the meadow is wearing a shirt and tie and pale blue jersey and sitting between we know where he's sitting, why is he, why are you there?

'Well it's an elective. I've, elected to take it.'

(I look around my elective class and somehow expect them all to be as riled as me but they're not which is itself annoying) Why didn't you take it before?

'I didn't know about it.'

You saw us in the south meadow. That was Gerard Manley Hopkins there.

'I didn't know it was elective then. Last week you didn't hold a class.'

Yes because your Academy pals made it clash with something, so we went for a walk in the woods instead. She sent you, didn't she. She sent you. Who's visiting today? Which poet.

'It's, well, oh, Mr. S. T. Coleridge.'

You looked. What does S. T. stand for.

'Samuel... Turner.'

Taylor, what school of poetry is he part of.

'Oh he's a Romantic, sir.'

Oh is he. What stopped him from finishing 'Kubla Khan'.

What prevented Coleridge from finishing 'Kubla Khan'.

Peter looks at me, then out to the window with its brief view of the weed-clad wall of the electric shed, then down at the table. Moves his blue pencil-sharpener. (Who brings a pencil-sharpener to a writing class? He's also got a ruler, a *protractor* for crying out loud)

'I don't know that,' he concedes, 'sir, I don't know all that much about him. That's why I've come to your class.'

Right. Okay. We'll sort this out later. Take one and hand them round...

'The gentleman from Porlock,' Ollie informs the newcomer, 'disturbed him on his opium trip,' and Peter asks: 'Would you spell that for me, friend?'

Hush.

My cradled infant slumbers peacefully.
'Tis calm indeed! so calm, that it disturbs
And vexes meditation with its strange
And extreme silentness. Sea, hill, and wood,   10
This populous village!

This is 'Frost at Midnight' by Samuel Trevor Coleridge, it goes on for fifty sixty more lines, you can find it in the trees. Read it, it's one of the most beautiful things there ever was. Listen to thoughts *dawning* on him. He hasn't planned it out. He's not reaching high like Keats, he's *receiving*. He plants 'Sea, hill, and wood' then he harvests them, 'Sea, *and* hill, *and* wood…' whatever they may yield, then he writes an *empty* line – 'With all the numberless goings-on of life' – who since Shakespeare had tried an *empty* line?

> Sea, hill, and wood, 10
> This populous village! Sea, and hill, and wood,
> With all the numberless goings-on of life,
> Inaudible as dreams! the thin blue flame
> Lies on my low-burnt fire, and quivers not…

Read it yet? Good (out comes my clobbering regiment, the Thirty-two Brave Highlighters) Peter you'll have to share the pens with Heath that's Heath right there. Take one of each colour and pass them on.

'Mi casa es su casa,' Heath mutters, reading the handout.

'I could have got you hundreds o' these fellers from the bulk store,' mentions Barry Wilby.

'No one has to share,' Caroline points out: 'Lillian is absent.'

'No shit,' says Heath.

'Fairy down!' I say brightly but Caroline isn't smiling.

'She's unwell with a cold,' Samira announces, 'which she's asked me to say.'

'Really?' Heath looks at Samira, 'shame.'

Highlight in GREEN every syllable with the long *EE*. So line 1 has the sound *tree* from *ministry*, then *me* in line 5. Highlight in PINK every syllable with the long *OW*. So *owlet* on line 2, *loud* twice on line 3 and so on. The ORANGE pen is for long *AY* – *Came* on line 3, *mates* from *inmates* on line 4. And the BLUE pen is for its own sound long *OO* in *blue* and you find that in *solitude* and *suits* in line 5, *Abstruser musings* scores two in line 6.

EE, OW, AY, OO. Do the whole poem.

'That *is* going to be colourful,' from Caroline, and Ollie, hopefully: 'When do we do that, now?'

'Way ahead of you, campers,' says Heath, snatching a green one from him.

*

Who or what is Peter.

(Kerri Bedward doesn't stop typing for me these days) 'Peter Grain, did he find you?' (clack clack)

Yes yes he found me, he's in there *now*! Doing my colouring game!

'Your – colouring game.'

It's my class, there's eight of them, not *nine*, there should be eight!

'Would you like another chair' (clack clack)

No! There are chairs! There are many many chairs!

'Would you like more students then for your – colouring game.'

No! Less! Fewer! One fewer. One *Peter* fewer.

'He has very good manners,' (she says, reaching over to the photocopier and tapping commands on it with android rapidity) 'he's nicer than Heath Bannen.'

I don't care, I don't care, he's something to do with the Academy, he's been told to spy on me, it's *her*, it's *her* – look I *know* that sounds paranoid.

'I'm glad you know.'

Eight is the limit. I only teach eight. It was in the stuff I sent you.

'I thought this was all a dream of yours, it's hard to keep up really.'

It was in the stuff. You must have lost it, what are you photocopying?

The Academy Proudly Presents

JACOB POLAR-JONES

(aka "The Chocalux Man") reading

RYHMES OF THE ANCIENT MARINER

by Mr. S. T. Colridge

(to be performed in the presence of the original author)

TONITE!!!
in **THE VILLAGE HALL**

8pm, October 24th   Refreshments

This isn't happening.

'Yes at eight look it's confirmed.'

This is – Coleridge *agreed* to this.

'The agent says it's fine.'

The agent says it's fine. Anyway well done Kerri, you spelt Chocalux right.

'I know! I double-checked it. But it was too late to order any!'

You think Samuel Coleridge wants to sit there and hear a kid who's famous for being in a chocolate-drink commercial *performing* his most famous poem?

'Apparently he's tired of reading that one, he'd rather read some new work. It was all Tina Yeager's idea.'

You don't say.

'The old and the new, sort of thing, past meets future. Look it's sold out! That's a hundred and twenty tickets Glyn *and* a waiting list! How many did you get for your other readings? come on, ten?'

We are not measuring friggin poetry by sales of friggin tickets.

'I thought you'd be more pleased. Jake's such a brilliant actor he comes in here he's sweet, he's so shy! he'll bring the poem to life. Sometimes poets aren't the greatest readers apparently. But an actor can really put in all the hidden emotions.'

Uh… uh…

'Glyn don't do that to your head. Oh dear, are we people in your dream again? Are all these visiting poets actually ghosts and only you know this? There-there, long day… Oh but would you hand out these eight amber flyers to your class? Actually *nine* flyers! I forgot about Peter!'

*

Put the flyers away. Burn the amber flyers. Look at the poem.

There are four points to make, one for each colour, one for each vowel. Let's start with the green. Long *ee* is a very common vowel and it's dotted throughout, but where does it cluster?

No one? Follow the green… How about lines 7–14? *peacefully, extreme, sea, sea, dreams.* A long vowel is gifting you time, you dwell on it: *sea* and *dreams* and *peace* are all in their way vast, right? Both *sleep* and *dreams* come back a lot – remember Coleridge is alone sitting by moonlight, beside his baby son in a cradle – also *breathings* is coming later, not *breath,* he chooses *breathings*… Samira what.

'Are you saying that when he writes an *ee*-word he always means sleep or dreams?' which two words set her off on a yawn she barely stifles.

No. Watch where the sounds cluster. It's not that any one vowel tends to mean any one thing – it's that if you cluster them around a meaning, then you've chosen that colour, which means you *have it to work with later.* Think painter, think palette. Something in the poet's brain, and by extension ours as listeners, now associates *ee* with a sense of peacefulness and carefulness that emanates from the sleeping infant.

> So gazed I, till the soothing things, I dreamt,
> Lulled me to sleep, and sleep prolonged my dreams!   35
> And so I brooded all the following morn,
> Awed by the stern preceptor's face, mine eye
> Fixed with mock study on my swimming book:
> Save if the door half opened, and I snatched
> A hasty glance, and still my heart leaped up,   40
> For still I hoped to see the stranger's face…

What matters here is not that *sleep* and *dreams* happen to share a long *ee*, it's that having deployed them on line 35, Coleridge doesn't *touch* long *ee* for the next five lines. And what are the next five lines? Where are the next five lines *set* Ollie.

'They're set in a school.'

Unwillingly, right and when does *ee* come back? Anyone, Niall?

'*Leaped* and *see*. Oh and *hasty* – *hasty, leaped, see.*'

Well done, a cluster of meaning about the schoolboy's dreamy joy at the thought of someone from his childhood magically intervening in the misery of the classroom. Like most of us right now, ho-ho.

'What about *study* on 38?' asks Samira, 'stud-*ee*.'

Oh yeah. Well. It's not stressed, is it.

'Always an answer,' says Caroline.

It's what you pay for. Last word on the green *ee*-vowel: the last ten lines of the poem. These ten lines contain, say, a hundred syllables. How much pink *ow* have you marked? *None*. Right. Orange long *ay*? Not one. Amazing. In *a hundred syllables*. How much blue *oo*? One. Just one. The very last word of the poem:

> Therefore all seasons shall be sweet to thee,   65
> Whether the summer clothe the general earth
> With greenness, or the redbreast sit and sing
> Betwixt the tufts of snow on the bare branch
> Of mossy apple-tree, while the nigh thatch
> Smokes in the sun-thaw; whether the eave-drops fall   70
> Heard only in the trances of the blast,
> Or if the secret ministry of frost
> Shall hang them up in silent icicles,
> Quietly shining to the quiet Moon.

And how many green *ee's*? Eleven: *seasons, sweet, thee, greenness, mossy, tree, eave, only, secret, ministry, quietly.* They weave a circle round him, he ends the poem nestled in whatever sense of peace he's drawing from the sleeping child. Whatever *ow, ay* and *oo* mean here – *in this poem specifically* – he steers almost completely clear of them for the last ten lines. He mixes a colour and paints in it. *It*, and not those. Or *these*, and not that.

'Are you saying it's planned that way?' Samira frowns.

'Not convinced,' says Caroline.

I'm not saying it's planned at all. I'm saying his early choices inform his later choices, it doesn't mean he's consciously making them. He's a poet, hard work, dumb luck, read forty books, God, DNA, who knows, Sam can make a human sound (where *sound* is a noun) and Sam can make a human sound (where *sound* is a verb.) That was said about me too and it's true if you bother to look. Or bother to read aloud. *OW*, the pink. What you got?

> The Frost performs its secret ministry,
> Unhelped by any wind. The owlet's cry
> Came loud—and hark, again! loud as before.

'Here at the start!' Ollie finds them: '*owlet, loud, loud!*'

Good. Simple: *ow* is the owlet's cry, *ow* is a vowel that doesn't half move your throat and lips if you do it justice. There's effort in it. How many *lines go by* until the next pink *ow* vowel? Shall I tell you? It's twenty-three. Which is roughly *two hundred and thirty* possible syllables, *not one of which is OW*. It next appears as *how*, twice, in a completely fresh turn of thought: 'But O! how oft,/How oft, at school…'

I'm not saying *ow* is *always* the owl, but because it is at the start, Coleridge now associates – subconsciously – that vowel with the distracting cry he heard. This isn't onomatopoeia, right – if he was playing that game he'd do which vowel? – 'oo,' 'oo!' – yes! – 'tuwit tuwoo!' – thanks for that Barry – but the *ow* is an association that, having been made, lamplights certain neurons dot dot dot…

The *AY* – orange – again, you can find clusters if you look: in lines 43-48 you have *play-mate, Babe, cradled, vacancies, babe…* all associated with either happy memories or the presence of the child – even *vacancies* seem bountiful in this company:

> Townsman, or aunt, or sister more beloved,
> My play-mate when we both were clothed alike!
>> Dear Babe, that sleepest cradled by my side,
> Whose gentle breathings, heard in this deep calm,   45

Fill up the interspersed vacancies
And momentary pauses of the thought!
My babe so beautiful!

Vowels well from the deep, vowels hail from regions of the brain, they will cluster in the Piccadilly of your cerebrum, they'll look out for each other on the tube. Consonants are what they wear to work.

See with the blue *OO* it's the clearest of all: a whole *brood* of 'em on lines 5–6: *solitude, suits, abstruser, musings...* the *oo*-sound clusters when he's *lost in thought*. Then they're thin on the ground, save the odd *blue* or *who*, and when do they cluster next? Lines 20–21, when again he's *lost in thought*: 'Whose puny flaps and freaks the idling Spirit/By its own moods interprets...'

What else? You can trace the theme through *whose, music, soothing, brooded, beautiful, who, universal...* then the field is ceded completely to serene blissful *ee* for all the last ten lines, until that little blue adieu: 'Quietly shining to the quiet Moon.'

There was indeed quiet then, they'd caught fatigue from me somehow, though the work had cheered me up. But then Caroline asked: 'Are you going to look at the underlying themes at all?' and I threw them the fuck out.

*

It wasn't her fault or theirs. It was giving out the stupid flyers and everything they stood for, it was Samira yawning and Peter existing. I said I was done for the day, if they had any questions about Samuel Coleridge they could ask Jake Polar-Jones.

They shuffled out in all their versions of disappointed. On his way past me Peter Grain asked if there were any assignments to catch up on and I said no.

So he kept moving and I told him:

Look. I'm afraid you can't come back. I'm afraid this course is full, it's a mistake they made in the office, I insist on just eight students, I'm sorry. If I'm still dead in the spring I'll come back and teach, I dunno, drama. Paradigms of Drama.

'I shall be sure to sign up,' Peter told me glumly at the doorway.

Yeah I'll pencil you in.

Ollie was the last out, his hand on the door-handle, quite a long look. Then:

'You all right there, man?' he said.

I'm good, mate. I'm good. It's the poem.

'I know. I thought so.'

The words.

'I know, home thoughts kind of thing.'

Yep. Good man. Go on. I'm fine.

*

My babe so beautiful! it thrills my heart
With tender gladness, thus to look at thee,
And think that thou shalt learn far other lore,
And in far other scenes...

There was something I'd wanted to tell them, something Coleridge said. I learned it at school. It was the most profound thing I'd ever read about writing. I sat in the sixth-form study room at lunchtime. The sense that I'd received this from him at the telescope-end of two centuries was dizzying.

I'm not going to tell them now. I'm going to read it to myself. It's this fragment from the famous distinction Coleridge made between Imagination and Fancy. It's in *Biographia Literaria*.

> This division is no less grounded in nature than that of delirium from mania, or Otway's *Lutes, lobsters, seas of milk, and ships of amber* from Shakespeare's *What! have his daughters brought him to this pass?*

I don't even know if I have this right, it's more about where it led me.

The Otway example makes a pig fly or says there are aliens. Fantasy, the magical, sci-fi, the surreal. *The thing is so because I say.* I move the pieces. Fancy: a 'mode of memory emancipated from the order of time and space, modified by the will.'

The Shakespeare example takes something *already in motion* (King Lear is mad and blames his daughters) and *rides it somewhere else* (Poor Tom looks mad so the mad Lear thinks he must have daughters too!) Nature moves the pieces, I just make my moves across them. Imagination.

I have no idea if this is what Coleridge means. It's what *I* mean now. I say it to myself in a cold and lonely room off a village hall.

I think it to myself in Café Maureen by the station, my latest bolt-hole. I look out through the window up at the distant hillside and that forlorn far black vowel of the railway tunnel.

I *fancy* I hear a horse-drawn carriage clip-clopping up the lane bringing Samuel Taylor Coleridge to the village.

I *imagine* my heart beats two-for-one because I'm about to meet him.

*

Incidental life intervenes. As I leave the Café and start walking back towards the Cross, I hear a loud brisk conversation in my wake and when I glance round it's blonde wind-blown Tina Yeager in blue jacket and matching skirt, talking to two young men in parkas.

She spies me and I won't slow down. If she wants to explain herself her footsteps will have to quicken, but I listen and they don't. On we go, their talk just out of earshot as I reach the Cross. I see Coleridge's little walnut-brown carriage bouncing down towards the Saddlers, and I follow, turning once to see Tina's party halting by Student Services. I would have ignored her, but she's holding one of Kerri's amber flyers for tonight, grinning and calling in my direction: 'Will we be seeing you later professor?'

I stride on irritated, only to find the carriage has stopped outside the Saddlers Inn, the coachman dismounted, no one emerges. I ready my fatuous query:

'Is this for Mr Coleridge?'

The coachman says: 'Dropped Sam at the tavern, sir. Where might I find the ostler? Horse is hot, I'm cold.'

*

It doesn't take Coleridge long. He's thoroughly ensconced by the fire in the snug of the Cross Keys in a haze of ancient smoke and – given he's only had about twenty minutes – a remarkable count of bottles and pints and listeners. Of the six or seven grouped around him I see there's Isabella and her classmates Kornelia (slim, awestruck) and Molly (boozy, bespectacled) come from Doug Spore's Is Fiction Fiction seminar, there's also Roy Ford, a Jamaican, one of the actors, who stood me a drink on my first night, he winks as I enter, and a couple of other fellows look round briefly and turn back to the story.

Coleridge, to the fascination of all, is trying to light a pipe: 'Sunday morning – Hamburg packet – set sail from Yarmouth…'

As I pull up a little stool at the corner, Bella is pleading through the smoke, 'Do you really enjoy that habit, Mr Coleridge?'

'God forbid, four times a day – breakfast, half an hour before dinner, afternoon at tea, just before bed-time – but I'll give it all up,' and he gets it piping blue smoke as Bella and her pals merrily fake coughing spluttering and dying. Roy Ford's pouring me some red, brings him back: 'You set sail from Yarmouth…'

'For the first time in my life,' Samuel tells us, 'beheld my native land *retiring* from me – all the kirks, chapels, meeting-houses – Now then, said I to a gentleman near me, we're out of our country. Not yet! he replied, and pointed to the sea: This too is a Briton's country…'

Ironic Britannic whoops as the smoke stole over the table, and the gang sat back and royally quaffed. I wondered when I'd get a chance to introduce myself, there was still pale light outside – are we far from the sea? I wondered, are we far from the land… I could see this ship had sailed and I needed to join the crew.

'We were eighteen in number,' said the poet, 'five Englishmen, an English lady, a French gentleman and his servant, a Hanoverian and his servant, a Prussian, a Swede, two Danes, a mulatto boy…' Here most of them glanced at Roy Ford to know how to play this, but his mild gesture and grin said *let it go, it's his story*, 'a German tailor and his wife – the smallest couple I ever beheld – and a Jew.'

I wanted to catch up: A packet is a boat, right?

And 'Did you hurl?' someone needed urgently to know.

He glanced my way: 'Far superior to a stage-coach – as a means of making men open out to each other.'

'Did you throw up?' Molly pestered.

'Faces assumed a doleful *frog*-colour – I was giddy but not sick. I found I'd – *interested* the Danes. I'd crept into the boat on the deck and fallen asleep, but was awaked by one of them about – three o'clock in the afternoon – told me they'd been seeking me in every hole and corner, insisted I should drink with them.'

Ha! *Danes*, I say, still catching up, as Coleridge chuckled 'Christened me *Doctor Teology* – dressed as I was!'

All in black, this day on land as that day at sea, and his hair is brown and dirty, his eyes so blazing-bright from the firelight and his wet lips never stop themselves, 'we drank and talked and sung – then we danced on the deck!' He lifts his pint to drink, but engrossed as he is in reliving details, soon sets it down again spilling: 'One came and seated himself by my side – his language, his accent were – so *singular!*'

Now he smiles, raises a hand as if to indicate he'll play the role, and plunges into crap comedy Danish – *'My dear friend, is I not very eloquent? Is I not speak English very fine?'* Then he clears his voice to be himself: 'Most admirably!' – and again the Dane – *'Vat an affection ve haf for each odher!'*

Coleridge is so very loud that most of the folks in the pub have by now congregated nearby. I see Heath, Niall, Iona at the far end of the group, probably wary of the bastard I'm being today, several drama students, the desk-boy from the Saddlers, Nathan, who now wears dark-glasses indoors, also *format* is present in a starling-glittery three-piece suit, he draws ringed planets as he listens.

'Seven o'clock,' says Coleridge, 'the sea rolled higher – and the Dane – eliminated enough of what he'd been swallowing to make room for more!'

'Yeeuuugggh,' say all of us.

Then he reaches towards Roy and puts a hand on his shoulder, press-gangs him for the yarn: 'His servant-boy, Jack, had a good-natured round face…'

Roy frames his grinning face with his hands for they're a double-act now and the company cheer them on. Coleridge drinks, 'the Dane now – talked like a madman – entreated me to accompany him to Denmark, he'd introduce me to the King etcetera, he declaimed the Rights of Man: *Ve are all Got's children! The poorest man haf the same rights with me. Jack! More brandy!*'

Still game, Roy lifts the poet's drink towards him, and Sam-as-the-Dane gulps and claps him on the back: *'Dhere is dhat fellow now! He's my equal! Ve are all Got's children…'*

God's kids all drank to that, and in the lull Coleridge, as himself, as if he hadn't touched a drop, said: 'I can hear him now…'

'Wow,' says Molly after consideration, while Isabella wonders from her heavenly lamp-lit corner: 'Where d'you come from, Mr Samuel Taylor Coleridge?'

Roy laughs: 'Poor guy just got here and you want the life-story?'

Of this, Sam catches only 'life-story' so of course he's off. I suppose by now it's crossed my mind that we could keep him here, hold him, keep him safe from tonight's 'performance' of his work…

'Family on my mother's side inherited a pig-sty in Exmoor – and nothing better since that time. Father's side… my grandfather was a woollen-draper in South Molton in Devon. He was reduced to poverty. My father walked off to seek his fortune, proceeded a few miles, sat down on the side of the road, overwhelmed, wept audibly.'

He pauses to drink a long draught, as if drinking in his history once more among the sorrowful young faces.

'A gentleman passed by, gentleman who knew him. Enquiring into his distress – took my father with him, settled him in a neighbouring town as a schoolmaster. He got money and knowledge, married his first wife, walked to Cambridge, entered Sidney College, distinguished himself for Hebrew and Mathematics.'

He drinks again, returned safely to his station in life, and is ready when I ask him what books he liked as a boy.

'I read incessantly. My father's sister kept an *everything* shop at Crediton – I read through all the gilt-cover little books that could be had – Tom Hickathrift, Jack the Giant-killer, I used to lie by the wall and *mope*. Robinson Crusoe, Arabian Nights… One tale made so deep an impression I was haunted by spectres…'

'Do you *believe* in ghosts?' says Bella after a silence.

'No, madam. Seen far too many myself.'

He looks grave, then snorts, then we all do at the unmistakable chime of wit, and at Bella being a *madam*, then he stops abruptly, looks around at us all as if groggy with waking: 'I'm not fit for public life.'

He sighs and stoops to sip his drink. A couple of conversations start up on the fringes. Roy Ford leans over to me: 'Heard you're teaching Drama in the spring, professor, is that so?'

What? Who told you that?

'But were ya happy?' Molly resumes interrogating.

'God forbid,' Sam answers. 'My father was very fond of me, and I was my mother's darling: in consequence I was very miserable,' – Molly laughs so hard she spurts cider – 'No, my father used to hold long conversations with me. Eight years old I walked with him one winter evening, from a farmer's house a mile from Ottery... He told me the names of the stars, how Jupiter was a thousand times larger than our world... That the twinkling stars were suns that had worlds rolling round them... And when I came home he showed me *how* they rolled round... Profound delight. But – from reading fairytales, my mind had been – habituated to the *Vast*. Children should read romances, giants and magicians. I know no other way of giving the mind – a love of the Great, the Whole...'

No one breaks the spell for a while, there are sighs and coughs and whispers. I notice Bella is fair trembling with questions, and now she leans in to ask, the only cure: 'Mr Coleridge, why do you write?'

'Because my life is short.'

'Not true!' but she has more: 'Will you ever, I'm sorry, I'll *die* if I don't ask – will you ever finish Kubla Khan?'

This gives him an old smile from the ages, and he reaches for his dormant pipe, knocks it, sits back against the plum leather and answers her: 'Tomorrow's yet to come.'

I look and it's night outside, it fell so fast, all the lamps on the Green are lit in the mist. I know what's coming, here it comes. Academy folks arrive in their parkas, range around the edges smiling, they'll be bringing him to the village hall.

In the lull of more drinks arriving at the table I move in, face to face:

It's an honour to meet you, Mr Coleridge (and he ponders in a strange voice as his hand and mine are shaking) 'Coleridge, *Coleridge*... Not so much harm in him. He's a whirl-brain, talks whatever comes uppermost.'

Are you happy here? (And all I meant was here right now, but he takes the long view out through the dark window) 'Another winter in England will *do for me.*'

Ha! I hear ya! I'm a poet myself, as it happens.

'Poets,' he goes vaguely (christ I hope no one's listening) 'gods of love. Gods of love who tame the chaos,' and he drinks to saying no more.

Mr Coleridge. It's. Do you. Do you really not mind if an actor reads your Ancient Mariner this evening? (The Academy guys stop dead with concern, their anoraks crinkle and uncrinkle. It's on the flyer, *it is printed what will be.)*

'It'll be happiness and honour enough,' he says, not remotely bothered, 'I've now seen all the rainbows.'

*

Kerri was right, the village hall is rammed. The rabble from the pub pretty much fill what seats are left. The air is jovial, carnival. I sit disapproving in the midst of much yelling. I've slid in near the back, as the Academy folks lead Sam towards the stage. I didn't set this up and I've told him so, my work is done. I see spotlights have been rigged, I see green gels, red gels, dry-ice machine, a rain-stick. I see Tina Yeager's down there on the front row with the people dressed smartly, doubtless basking in the light of a full house. I know everyone here somewhere, people who never come, Kerri, Wayne, Maureen from the café? Clyde Mapping. There's a bearded portly fellow I keep seeing, he's on his own as usual.

I see they've seated Coleridge in a throne-like blue velvet armchair on the stage-right side. I begged Roy Ford to see he was sorted for wine, and he's done that. I see Sam imbibing serenely: *a deposed king*, my mind clanks and rumbles...

The lights go down, there's cheering, then a spotlight and the actor saunters in, all in black, his dyed cream hair like froth on a Guinness, and he freezes. The great dark hall goes quiet. Nothing happens. I ever so slightly die.

He unfreezes. *I* freeze.

'So I heard this tale from my man Sam,
that there's this old-time sailor-man,
he's messin' with this gang of three
he says *You'll do* – guy says *Why me?*
yer mad old geezer, hear that sound?
that's music! time to party down
and I'm Best Man so DO ONE, squire!'

Past the lance of blue light in which the once-and-future Chocalux Man jives and jazzes the thing to dusty death, I see the gleam of a glass ascending to what must be Sam Coleridge's lips, and I pray to Whomsoever that he's too far gone to care but I don't see anything else because I walk out. It being that sort of day.

By the side of the village hall I sigh a cold cloud of steam and remember I meant to sit at the front so everyone could see me do this. Oh well. I'll let them know. As I quicken my steps west towards the green I hear the unearthly rumble of a sound effect, topped by the shriek of the actor – 'And now the storm-blast came and it was *mental*, it was *postal*' as the cheap mic howled feedback in its futile protest, and I never did learn which word was doomed to rhyme with *postal*.

*

I cross the village green and keep going west, past the large low student halls, the double-doors of Cartwright, the weathered crimson picnic tables at De Vere, the cool sculptures outside Benson, this is Ollie's hall and Heath's, I heard them say that's where they're off to. After the halls are the narrow lanes of terraced houses, dotted with lamps and trees, Caroline lives down one of these streets, she said she was too old for dorms, and it's here where Norman goes stomping home after a night of grumbling. There are bikes chained up in tiny gardens. A few lights in upstairs windows but no silhouettes, no shapes to test the heart.

I turn right into what seems a cul-de-sac. Four Victorian lampposts guide the way to a wall at the end that's black with ivy. From a house on the left there's movement and I'm seized with the urge to hide – and yet that dream-paste fills my thighs to the top and fixes me where I am, where I wait to see or be seen.

A man turns at the door of the house, is chortling to its tenant. The porch light goes on and off as he makes his way down the garden path. By the time he sees me I'm chuckling amiably:

What would it take for you to actually come to one of these readings?

'Riches, teacherman, beyond your wildest dreams.'

We meet by the front gate of the now-dark home, shake hands for who knows why:

I mean, the whole damn village is in the hall watching Celebrity Death-Gig, and you *still* find something else to do! Why did you take my class?

Barry looks at me.

'Whole dambustin' village is *not* in the hall.'

All right not the *whole* village.

Barry breathes the night air and takes in the nearest houses, pointing off and further off: 'Mrs Kerr. Bob Tomlin. The McCloud children. Jessie.'

(I don't know what to say) Well didn't they want to come? There's a Living Breathing Legend in the village hall right now, oh and some old poet showed up too (look I *know* Barry doesn't do sarcasm, but I do and I need my fix).

'No no, it's a bit too much for 'em.'

Too – much for them. So this is what you do. You visit.

'Always do so, always done so. Shall we walk?'

Anywhere Barry, it's your village.

'Now then. Could never abide the moth-light. The lamp you all flock to, see all them moths there, dead and alive? It drives me off, it does I suppose, I can't help but wonder, I never could help but wonder, how they all holding up?'

How is who holding up? You mean – everyone.

'Yes I suppose I do mean everyone.'

How is everyone holding up. So if, let me get this straight, if people are gathering somewhere, you, Barry, have to be somewhere else.

'The more people, the farther gone I suppose.'

Who are all these people?

'Old folks, señor, young folks, or sad folks, or anxious folks, all sorts really. People who don't go out much.'

Lonely people. You visit lonely people.

'They ain't lonely when the bell rings!'

No. I suppose. So… Why *did* you take my class? I'm not lonely, Barry. Am I?

'No one's lonely when the bell rings.'

Right. Right. No one's lonely when the bell rings. By the way, been meaning to ask this, *á propos* and all that, am I dead, mate?

(At the end of the little cul-de-sac we see the bright lights of Benson and De Vere. I don't feel dead at all and he has the broadest smile on his big face)

'You don't half talk some cobblers!'

(I laugh, I do) I do, I know. Can I ask you one more question? (He's still grinning at my nonsense, enjoying the night air) What do I do for Christmas?

'Now that,' he stops, 'I can't help you with. How do I know what you do for Christmas?'

I mean – *may* I – do what I always do? As in, as in, *go home.*

(Barry Wilby claps me on the shoulder) 'Do I look like the feller to stop you doing what you always do? No! So there, señor, so there.'

Look I – I ought to get back to the reading.

'Yes I better press on with me visits!'

So we cordially part, and he lumbers off towards a dark end-terrace when I suddenly think to ask him –

What do *you* do for Christmas, man?

He wheels his bulky frame round, stands there in the road and, without answering, starts rummaging in the capacious pockets of his overalls.

'As it happens I *have* a thing for you, drum-roll if you please…'

He holds up his fist, and I go across the road to see what gives. His soft big hand lowers and opens to reveal a small cube of dark plastic.

'Wilby to the rescue.'

Right. (I take it.) Right, and. What do you want me to do.

'What you wish to do,' says Barry, 'Do what you wish to do.'

*

I'd estimated that Jake's modern rendition of 'The Rime of the Ancient Mariner' – to restore it to its actual name – would take about forty minutes at a Polar-Jonesian pace, allowing me to slide back into my seat before the poet started, but I'd reckoned without certain *cuts* that Jake – or whomsoever had perpetrated this retelling – had made to the old ballad, as I was later drily informed. The poem had been sheared as well as simplified, so both that and Coleridge's own brief slurred recital were now over. The hall had been pretty much returned to its shabby timelessness: house-lights up, too bright and dusty, dozens of empty chairs and litter, twenty or so people left. Sam was deep in his armchair stage-right, they'd brought the microphone to him. His red wine had been replenished, and a little blue glass phial was now deposited beside it by his coachman, who trod back to his seat in the front row and slumped there job done. He was alone in Row A, the Academy group having sailed some time ago.

Sam was mumbling into the mic: 'I'd compare the human soul to a ship's crew cast on an unknown island... suppose the shipwrecked man stunned, for many weeks in a state of idiocy, loss of thought and memory... then gradually awakened. Mrs Barbauld once told me she admired the Ancient Mariner very much, but there were two faults in it.'

'No freakin way!' cried Molly, who must have asked the question, 'Mrs Barble you're *so* outta line you *bitch!*'

'It was – improbable, and had no moral...'

Bella and others tried to outgasp Molly with scorn and ridicule of Mrs Barble's perverted critical view, but Sam hadn't finished: 'As for the probability, that might admit some *questions*... but as to the want of a moral?' he scoffed, 'I told her the poem had too much. Too much!' He shook some drops from the phial into his wineglass and drank whatever drug it was. 'Too much. Ought to've had no more moral than the Arabian Nights – merchant sitting down to eat dates by the side of a well… throwing the shells aside… Genie starts up and says he must *kill* the merchant! Because, *because*, one of the shells put out the *eye* of the Genie's son…'

'Like the albatross, I see,' said Caroline to end that: 'Do you think of yourself as part of the Lake School, Mr Coleridge?'

He leaned forward steadily and glared at the floor, 'Utterly unfounded, that we – that we – God forbid – belonging to any common school…'

'You're often associated with William Wordsworth,' she pointed out, doing a good impression of being the only grown-up in the building.

Sam put a haughty posh voice on: 'the School of Whining and Hypochondriacal Poets that haunt the Lakes!'

'Can I ask my stimulants question?' oh jesus *Mimi*, all we need.

'If I should die,' said Coleridge softly, and the sounds of druggy sniggering fade abruptly with these words, 'and the booksellers will give you anything for my life… be sure to say… Wordsworth descended on him… from Heaven. By showing to him what true poetry was he made him know that *he, himself,* was no poet…'

You're a great poet, sir (I had stood up beyond caring, one myself right now) and your work will last forever, and we're going to let you go free now, so, Samuel Taylor Coleridge ladies and gentlemen!!!

As the feeble applause did its best to deafen the curious mice, I felt a tap on my shoulder, it was Lily Bronzo huddled in a great shawl.

'Had my hand up, chief!'

You're ill, you don't count.

'I's gonna ask him what it's like to be great mates with a Northern poet who's more famous than him.'

You're funny. Made a recovery have we.

'It's Coleridge, chief, come on!'

As I moved towards the stage, where the jubilant gang had surrounded the poet's armchair with books and beermats for him to sign, the coachman stopped me with a blue leather glove on my sleeve.

'I'll take him off your hands, sir.'

Oh. Would he like to have dinner maybe?

'Better take him off your hands, sir. Might I give you one of these?'

Right. You had *business cards*?

'Beg pardon?'

Nothing. Have we met?

'Ned Stowey. We have now, sir.'

I advanced to the low stage, bid my adieux to Coleridge, who blinked at me from far away and began to introduce himself, then I was heading back through the hall with only one thing left to do.

Peter Grain was stacking the old chairs because no one else was doing it and it probably needed doing. He lowered a stack of five to the floor and looked puzzled as I reached him.

Your pencil-sharpener, squire. Read some Edgar Allan Poe. See you Thursday.

*

The Cross Keys was packed with folks from the Academy. I made the mistake of going into the saloon and there they all were – Jacob Polar-Jones sat blithely enthroned among fans and actors and students and guys high-fiving in their parkas. Tina Yeager was giggling with Jake. She saw me at the door and straightened: 'Did you enjoy the show, professor?'

(I'm the same in heaven as I am on earth) Yeah well done Jake, nice job, very *now*.

(Jake glowed like his birthday, Tina nodded like his agent and said) 'I believe the poet went home happy.'

We always go home happy.

'Pardon? Professor we need to do this *every* week. Have you heard of a poem called The Raven? We're going to ask the author if Jacob can perform it.'

Yeah good luck with that.

'Are you going to join us?'

Nevermore. I ducked out and went round to the public bar, which was equally packed if slightly less annoying.

White wine, Norman.

'Small or large.'

Gigantic.

'He doesn't need that, Norman,' a voice heckled from the bar opposite, 'he needs a Climbing For Honeycomb, that's blackberries, basil, rum, cassis – '

'I ain't talking to you, miss.'

*

Some bloke left the only bar-stool and I reached it and sat down. I raised my great big piss-gold wine so the green lamps leered inside it, and peacefully I spoke these words I'd been hoping to hear all day, now their maker had departed: *Weave a circle round him thrice, and close your eyes with holy dread, for he on honey-dew hath fed, and* –

'sup Max.'

Nothing. Kubla Khan. It never ends.

'Jakey blew, didn't he.'

Scare me.

'You walked, I saw you, I'm gonna tell Miss Titmouse *what* did you just say?'

Scare me. Next week. It's Halloween. Scare me.

'Scare you how.'

You and your actor friends. Do something. Weave a circle round me thrice.

'You serious Max? Cos you know we *could.*'

Why do you think I'm asking.

'You had a weird day, who knows. Guess we can scare you.'

I want you to. I want you to scare me to death. So I can go home.

'Whatever.'

She sucks by straw from her blue cocktail, sets it on the bar, and stares down at me like I'm preposterous. Then she reaches, *lunges* for the back of my hair, looms down with her dark lips to mine and is suddenly drooling liquid in. It goes in and all over the bar and me and she's wiping her mouth with her black suede sleeve, 'That's called a Gun Metal Blue. Mezcal, brandy, lime, what else…'

Curaçao?

'Dur. Can you clear this up, Norman? Ha! Blood-bond, Max, deal's done, I'm going back to the party. See you on Fright Night.'

*   *   *

Week Six – October 31st

There was a man dwelt by a churchyard –

That's how far he gets, the little boy in *The Winter's Tale*, when his mother's asked him for a story – 'a sad tale's best for winter!' – but that's how far he gets before the King bursts in, in a rage, mistaken, and sunders them forever...

I was cast in it, as the King, at school, but that never happened either, the Clown dropped out of the play with a week to go, he was moving to another town. He cheerfully told the aghast director not to worry, he'd still buy a ticket to see it! Clown. They cancelled. I was left wandering the corridors and classrooms for months muttering *I have tremor cordis on me: my heart dances; but not for joy, not joy...*

No one knows where the little boy was going with the story. Maybe he didn't either. And soon he was dead too. And unlike his mother, whose statue would come alive in an hour or so, stayed dead.

*

It's foggy outside. *I* dwell by a churchyard but can't see it from these windows. We all dwell by a churchyard but can't see it from these windows. Unless we're the Brontës and can see it there and oh look there too, let's make up a story... I think of the shipwrecked little stalwarts of the Unique Society, out there in the green woods in the mist this morning. Will the sisters play with them today? Will someone check on our Action Men?

Today! I remember what day. I'm actually standing by my slanting window, visible to spectres out there, wrapped in my pale-blue duvet, applauding my friends the tormentors so that my duvet slides to the floor and I'm freezing naked. Fog! FOG! Good start. Good move.

And you know, now you say, there *was* a man dwelt by a churchyard...

*

Out I go, all dressed in brown, the light is cold, my breath's a genie, I can see some thirty yards. I feel my grin is widening, awaiting the first figure to loom of a sudden from this morning mist, I am ready for my first scare, Ms Bevan…

Clown, I see it's early. Not even the dead get up this soon. How do I know it's early? I turn at the sound of a creeping engine and here comes the milk-float moving through the cloud, overtaking me very slowly, with the figure of Barry's lady-friend mildly signalling at the wheel, mildly signalling not turning. Turn! Scare me! Have a frightful face! Have any face! In the mean time: Good morning!

Instead, with her little legs swinging from the back of the float is a silver-blonde child of nine? ten? looking oddly at me. Her legs stop swinging.

The milk-float buzzes onward, clinking into mist. I scent everything that's autumn – leaves, smoke, earth, cider, bygone books and inkpots, baked potatoes, fires burning, *fall, fall, over and ember…*

Lo! Death has reared himself a throne
In a strange city lying alone
Far down within the dim West,
Where the good and the bad and the worst and the best
Have gone to their eternal rest…

The Saddlers Inn is open, I'm the first, I take a window seat, spread out with my books and things beside the great white oblong nothing. Bliss! The desk-boy Nathan is dressed all in black but he's always dressed like that these days.

'Just toast at this point, professor, but I'll do you tea or coffee.'

Do me, do me coffee.

'Up early this morning, professor,' he says when he returns.

It's Halloween. I like Halloween.

'Oh man. I'm meant to wear a devil's hat. Hat? Horns, I guess I mean.'

Did she tell you to?

'Excuse me? No. Who?'

143

Never mind.

'Mr Ridley handed them out last night. He got them at Mrs Gantry's. We could choose. Witch's hat or devil's horns. I don't believe in it myself. Toast?'

I don't *believe* in it either. I'm just – something's going to happen. Toast yes, brown, no white, no brown!

'What's going to happen?'

That's what I don't know.

(Nathan pours milk into my coffee, the jug is in the form of a small cow, milk pours absurdly from its mouth, he lifts it away with a flourish.)

'Hm, something's going to happen, that's the same as every day, right?'

You know what I mean.

'I guess.'

He goes to fix my toast, and I realize he's American, or he is now. Was he before? I'm ready for my frights, you see. Be ready, be prepared! Never did join the cubs or scouts and it's too late now. I grin like a face and open my book up.

The skies they were ashen and sober;
    The leaves they were crisped and sere –
    The leaves they were withering and sere;
It was night in the lonesome October
    Of my most immemorial year,
It was hard by the dim lake of Auber,
    In the misty mid region of Weir –
It was down by the dark tarn of Auber,
    In the ghoul-haunted woodland of Weir.

After breakfast things get done: brisk walk to the wood for some books I need, stroll back dreaming up a class, clobber my cold pink hands together and swing by Student Services. Kerri has a little purple witch's cloak but she's put the conical hat on the floor.

'It's too big, it's not working with my fringe. And push the door, it's bitter.'

Where's your familiar?

(She switches her typewriter on and it hums) 'Where's my what?'
Your familiar.
'You mean I'm familiar – to you?'
Um… Is Mr Poe coming.
'Yes. He is.'
On the 18.09?
'I believe so.'
Did they ask him if JPJ could read his poem The Raven?
'I have that information, where is it, here, yes, they did ask
the agent that question and the agent answered *anyone* can read
Mr Poe's poem, *everyone* should read his client's poems there's no
charge, they are more than happy, I don't think he's understood the
question there. Anyway I got the template for the poster look and
it doesn't mention Jacob. It's Mr Poe reading and lecturing, then
refreshments.'
Good, get it printed before Miss Titmouse screws with it.
'Pardon?'
Nothing. Halloween thing. Do you really not need the hat?

*

It was many and many a year ago,
    In a kingdom by the sea,
That a maiden there lived who you may know
    By the name of Annabel Lee;
And this maiden she lived with no other thought
    Than to love and be loved by me…

Lily loves that I've a witch's hat on. She swanned into the Cross
Keys late for noon, in a black cape, the gold DMs, and blood trailing
from her mouth and eyes. I was busy reading a poem for class.
'Got an idea for you, chief, what you drinkin'?'
She goes to get bottles of beer, the place is quiet. There are toy
cobwebs and spiders and heads in all twelve corners. Norman seems
weirdly in the spirit of the thing. He's not gone as far as a costume,
but he does seem nuttily cheerful, joking with Lily at the bar.
Perhaps that's the old boy's take on Opposite Day.
Niall's in a booth alone, gazing at what appears to be a blank sheet

of paper. Quiet Kornelia from the Fiction Seminar is in another, making notes from a book. When she sees me she points above her head and smiles, meaning my hat.

Lily comes with the beers, 'So I had this great idea in the night, right,'

I assume this relates to poetry in some form?

'Got zero new poems, if that's what you mean, been up to me friggin' eyes!'

It's alright, ma, they're only bleeding.

'D'you like it, you should get some, Mrs Gantry's got all like slime? No, I been thinking about the shows, right,'

Yes let's get TV actors to do them *all*, because what on *earth* is interesting about great poets coming to town to recite their poems *many centuries after they've died?*

'Yeah I know, yeah,' she's pulling her witchy cloak around her, it has satin-look emerald lining, 'it's cool and shit, but students kind of need that little bit extra maybe in this day and age?'

You mean because you've paid.

'No well there's that, but it's not about the dosh, chief, it's more like getting us involved kind of thing? What's the word, you know,'

Interactive.

'Like hands-on, that's two words, cos otherwise it's kind of like elitist? but so my *idea* is, right, we like do a support slot.'

You do what.

'A support slot. We, the students yeah, read our work before the main event. But it's not like a boring reading yeah, like *Blah blah the moon this and my soul that* etc it's like a slam, like a contest!'

This is definitely scary but not in the way I hoped for.

'Eh? So maybe like three poets? E.g. Then there's like judges, like you even, you could be a judge, chief, and then there's like an interval yeah, then there's the, you know, who's next, *my love is like,* whatever, some flower or other.'

We drained our beers and she stared and waited for me to burst out cheering. I was trying to figure out how to kill it when she said: 'It would totally get Yeager off our back, cos everyone would come to support their mates an' that so the place would be rocking and I could totally organize it cos I do that shit in Camden for free.'

And I realized she was right, and I asked her to do just that.

'You're kidding.'

You can't be in it, Lillian, you're a performance poet, already I mean, it wouldn't be fair, but how about *you* set it up, and you and me can judge it? You judge on performance, me on the poem – '

'I keep forgetting you're a poet, mate!'

I… (gaiety the only option) yep, every day except Thursday I'm the finest poet in the village.

'Dunno chief, you read Jeff Oloroso?'

Shut up and anyway, I'll be dealing with the Guest, you and Jeff can judge it, and sometimes you can perform, but you can't compete, okay? There's no class scheduled next week. Have it ready for then.

She loved everything about what I just said. She sat back well impressed, as if I'd thought it all up myself. The first slam would be on Thursday 14th November. It would be called Night of the Living Living, and off she went to make it so, leaving this behind from weeks ago, with the words 'Love, mysterious ways, etc.'

<u>Pity for Samira</u>   <u>Maxwell exercise 3rd Oct</u>

Never seen a face that works
So hard to disapprove.
D'you know your lips make tiny jerks
When your eyes move?

*

Heath didn't come and wasn't going to. Niall stalked quietly over from his den in the booth: 'Heath said for me to bring this.'

From a large manila packet came ten pages of verse: THE HOLLOW PERSONS *(EXTRACT)* by HEATH BANNEN. I absorbed the contents page while Niall stood there being unsettling.

Sit the. Sit down, Niall.

'He's, Heath is, not coming in today.'

Why, cos he's writing these?

'That's what he said to say, but I think it's more – more *her*.'

Her. You mean Lillian.

'Yes, because she's got, involved with, you know…'

I don't need to,

'I know, it's Sami Sharma, you don't need to know.'

So why do you want to tell me?

'I – don't know. I want to – bless them. The two of them. The three of them, him too. By saying names.'

Fine. Consider them blessed. What do you have for me, man?

He passed me a sheet of paper, the blank sheet I'd seen him with. I didn't think anything of it, I leafed through my folder and jested:

Lily didn't bring anything, Heath didn't show at all, you gonna make me strike out here, man, nought-for-three?

'This is the rewrite.'

(I still didn't get it) I liked this short one from last time, it's mysterious –

'That's from before.'

Doesn't mean I can't like it (I said childishly, choosing pages) oh this one?

'That's old too, you're looking at the new one.'

This, this blank sheet is the new one.

You've cut everything.

'I didn't cut it, it cut itself.'

(I looked at his blank sheet like something might appear on it, *who by fire, who by lemon-juice*) Let me dwell on this a while.

When I was ready to speak, he spoke.

'I'm okay with it.'

Okay with there being nothing?

'It was a process. It was – . I didn't mean it to happen.'

Niall, you know what I said about white space, it's like,

'Can you, I know this is rude, say nothing for a short time, professor?'

I – yes. It's not rude, man… And I can. Long as you like. Within reason.

'You – did say about white space, the things it could be, the things it could do. Say. But to me it's just been, started being, *one* thing. But – this isn't like, d'you know, *lie down, tell me your dreams, time's up, thank you doctor* – this is like please, please, listen to me.'

'It would start on a line. Not always the first line. Just – lap at it somehow. Like the last word I'd put was no stronger than – than *it*. And once that word was gone the next began to be the same. Like it heard what happened, like the fever caught it. The word felt weighty, sort of – bloated, *plagued*, all wrong and with a laptop you can just – well. Then it started in on the fronts of lines. Why that word, why make that move, why take that breath, then both sides, same time, it didn't mean me harm. It – didn't mean me harm, it sought – is that a word – it *sought* to, save me from, sought-to-save-me-from, harm. Gently took sharp – edges – from me. And I'd be saying in my mind: so you want me to be true, and the truth says very little, so I'll leave very little but I felt it, *it*, very kind, very kindly, kindlily? go – *hush, let me – let you – let it – go*. And I was left, here, with this. Which to you looks like it resembles a sheet of paper maybe a blank – expanse of paper but to me looks old, and scribbled, and exhausted, and denied, and I need you to take it from me, Glyn if I may call you, because it needs cutting as it is, I just, it, it, needs cutting as it is.'

Niall –

'I'm making all my old mistakes – '

Niall, man –

*

There is a two-fold Silence – sea and shore –
    Body and soul. One dwells in lonely places,
    Newly with grass o'ergrown; some solemn graces,
Some human memories and tearful lore,
Render him terrorless: his name's 'No More'…

As I walked to class – having walked him back to Benson Hall, me floundering for answers to a question unprepared-for in this life, he giggly and cheerful now he'd cried out loud his struggles – there suddenly blazed-up the appalling thought that *they* had set him on me – *Scare Me* – Mimi had set him on me to be strange, does he even *know* Mimi? I could see how that might play out, though, that this was part of Fright Night and things weren't what they were…

And this blasphemous yet ultimately soothing notion was reinforced twenty minutes later by, well, seeing this in Village Hall B:

Samira (princess)	Barry (scarecrow)
Iona (cat)	Ollie (zombie)
Peter (horns)	Heath
Caroline (witch)	*Niall???*
Lily (Lily)	

How did *you* get here so fast?
'I changed my mind. I ran.'
But I walked straight here.
'You didn't,' went Samira, looking elsewhere combing limitless black hair, 'we saw you in Mrs Gantry's.'
Only cos Lily said she had slime but she'd sold out.
'I've got some spare,' said Niall, weighing green gunk in his hand as if nothing had ever happened.
I see that. Where do *I* sit, where does *Moi* sit?
'On your broomstick?' suggested Iona.
'Nowhere!' Lily cried, 'I've taken your place! You're the King of Fools!'

Who said that (I began lamely) I don't see anyone in my seat, reckon I'll just sit there (I pretended Lily was no one, began sitting on her, displaced her with her squealing and they scared me up an extra chair) seeing as I have my Magic Hat, now move up and shut up. Edgar Allan Poe.

Once upon a midnight dreary, while I pondered, weak and weary,
Over many a quaint and curious volume of forgotten lore –
While I nodded, nearly napping, suddenly there came a tapping,
As of some one gently rapping, rapping at my chamber door.
''Tis some visitor,' I muttered, 'tapping at my chamber door –
    Only this and nothing more.'

First stanza of 'The Raven'. 'The Raven' made him famous pretty much overnight. Like most of Poe's verse it's highly formal, kind of stagey, overwrought, gothic in a good way, romantic in a bad way. Poe was manically productive, compulsive, alcoholic, constantly broke, devoted to his wife, and his reputation's still recovering from the vengeful slanders of a horrid obituarist. I don't think Poe's a great poet. Great storyteller yes. 'The Raven' seems popular with folks who don't do poetry. And you're right Lily, they did it in *The Simpsons*.

'Why we doing him then,' says Heath, who's made no obvious concession to the witching season.

Why? Because it's Halloween and I'm the King of Fools.

Ah, distinctly I remember it was in the bleak December;
And each separate dying ember wrought its ghost upon the floor.
Eagerly I wished the morrow; – vainly I had sought to borrow
From my books surcease of sorrow – sorrow for the lost Lenore –
For the rare and radiant maiden whom the angels name Lenore –
    Nameless *here* for evermore.

'That line's from a Dylan song,' said Orlando, not looking up at all.

Exactly, ripped from Bob, like everything.

'I must say I'm enjoying this poem!' bursts out the Scarecrow Barry, whose every jolly gesture scatters straw over the table.

Good! 'The Raven' has *eighteen* stanzas just like those. The form is intricate, flamboyant, in-yer-bewhiskered-face. He swiped it from Elizabeth Barrett, whom we'll meet in a few weeks. She enjoyed his poem and graciously wrote him so from England. It's a mad hypnotic form. If you don't ride it when you read it you're in limelight babbling nonsense, oh! *talking of which,* anyone hear the *Mariner* last week?

'It was tremendous,' said Caroline.

'Very modern,' Peter Grain agreed.

Good (said the King of Fools) but someone said about Poe reciting 'The Raven' that his listeners were *afraid to breathe* in case they broke the spell. Your move, Polar-Jones.

The stanzas end with the following words: *nothing more, evermore, nothing more, nothing more, nothing more, nothing more!, nothing more, 'Nevermore', 'Nevermore', 'Nevermore', 'nevermore', 'Nevermore', ah nevermore, 'Nevermore', 'Nevermore', 'Nevermore', 'Nevermore', nevermore!*

The meaning of each one is ever-so-slightly different. Ten are spoken by the narrator, eight by a large black member of the genus *Corvus.*

'A raven!' Barry shares with us all, 'Bingo! Nevermore!'

Now you try doing that.

I said *Now you try doing that.* Find a word or phrase you can end nine stanzas with. Not eighteen, *nine,* I am half your friend. I don't care what shape or length your stanzas are, but they have to be formally the same, they have to be nine in number, and they have to end with your word or phrase. And your word or phrase has to mean something slightly different *every time.*

'Can it have like ghosts and shit?' questions Lily, writing this down.

It can, it's the season, take out your black highlighters, but it doesn't have to be gothic. Or funny, or silly, though I won't stop you going there. You know the word we have for *silly* was once the word we had for *blessed.* You do now. The point is it could be *real.* As in *realistic,* as in *realism.* You feel one way about something – and whatever you think or do or say in the daylight, your heart and soul – insert the words you use for these – slams back to that one way you feel, like gravity pulls it, magnets haul it, the freakin' moon is roping it in. Natural pull. Whatever you say in the stanzas *does not prevent it coming again.* Well this could be loving someone, refrains have plucked that lute forever. Missing someone, praising someone, hating someone. Or: *timor mortis conturbat me – the fear of death disturbs me* – William Dunbar, 'Lament for the Makars', find him in the wood, every fourth line, ghost from a dead language, *timor mortis conturbat me, timor mortis conturbat me, timor mortis conturbat me, timor mortis conturbat me, timor mortis conturbat me,* ad not quite infinitum. Pattern as dry realism. Rhyme as bone. Not AAA but A forever, not shadowed or repeated but *the same damn thing* oh, I dunno, you find it. By which I mean yes, Lily, ghosts and shit. But turn it, turn it, turn the meaning one degree, like your one and only power.

I'm going to walk out in the fog now, I may be six minutes.

*

I do do that. Leave the students stuff to do and need to leave the room. I always return with something, so it looks like I had a reason. But the reason I leave the room is I can't cope with the scuffling, sighing hush. Can't bear to have made silence. V Frankenstein would get it.

Anyhow not this time. This time I leave it to go and stand on the frozen lane, look six ways into the fog, come on scare me, where the hell, I'm here!

And I remember one of Poe's stories. It's about a man who is expecting something terrible to happen. But I can't recall what does.

*

So, to answer the excellent question of Mr Bannen: *Why we doing him.* Why we doing who we're doing. Search me. The office says I set it up but I can't remember *why we doing anything.*

Keats because it's autumn and we're here because we're here. Emily to wonder why. Hopkins just – to wonder. The Brontës to – remind us things *begin*. Sam TC for the soul, the voyage, this order enough for you? Time's not played fair with me, so I won't – or Time's played fair with me, so I will – either way we play all day in the sun, me and my shadow. *It* and *its* shadow. Poe because the sun sets?

The tales of E. A. Poe, my friends, have a considerable claim to have originated or pioneered or suggested detective fiction, the modern ghost story, the thriller, shlock horror, the whodunit, the gore-fest, *film noir* and freakin' sci-fi. He's why Hitchcock wanted you to wet yourself. He's why we're lumbered with Sherlock Holmes. But if you're any shakes as a storyteller you light candles for Mrs Christie as well as Dostoevsky. Where Poe sits on that spectrum is up to you, but he's got his own colour, he's a part of the rainbow. So respect the one who did that, buy his poems, help the poor soul scrape a living.

And something else. If you do as I just did and say, on technical grounds, this is not a great poet, first off you're not alone: Yeats called 'The Raven' 'insincere and vulgar', Aldous Huxley scoffed the poems wore 'a diamond ring on every finger', Emerson said 'oh you mean the jingle-man?' and so on. But to take any position is to make yourself a dot in the clouds: I see from here, I say from here. You can possess the finest critical mind, your dot may be one pure state-of-the-art Cyclopean platinum eyeball, but why place yourself at a *point*, where everyone sees around you? *Oh she says this because she thinks that! He* would *say that because he hails from there...*

Once you place yourself you're stuck with that. You can be read now, guessed-at, *extrapolated*. The lover of books is older than that, breathes deeper than that, shouldn't plant his flag, shouldn't get herself so comfy the cobwebs form. The lover of books keeps turning the page, it's all you can see us doing! Well I contradict myself (someone's going to tell you soon) we must dance, stomach opposites, we must puzzle and perplex, must be gone when they arrive. Be gone when I arrive! Where are you?

Alone in Café Maureen, waiting for his train, reliving my babble in my class that afternoon.

Make yourself at least a *line*, a line to travel, add that whole dimension. So you can swim up close and stare and bob your gaping fish-head at the incompetent or tasteless – but also, also, swim away, fly away to far away, from which vantage Edgar Poe is a glow, a phenomenon, *flash!* a St Elmo's Fire. Or, on the incandescent plane to which our language has ascended, he's a *thing!* Edgar Allan Poe is a *thing!* And he's striding out of a pea-souper fog on the platform where I stand. You with me?

*

'Why don't they pay with a good grace – and promptly? A young author, struggling with despair, in ghastly poverty, is politely requested to compose an article for which he'll be *handsomely paid…*'

(If you know me you'll know I'm trotting through the mist alongside Edgar Allan Poe, nodding in accord and saying 'yeah, I know' by way of affirmation)

'He neglects the *sole employment* which affords him the chance of a livelihood,'

Yeah, I know,

'– and having starved through the month completes the article!'

Is this *you* you mean, Mr Poe?

'A month – starving still – and no reply,'

I know, yeah,

'Another month, still none,'

Jesus *still* none? blimey

'Two months more, still none. At the expiration of six additional months, personal application at the editor's office,'

It's down here, Mr Poe, the Inn's not far now,

'Call again! Poor devil goes out, does not fail to call again. Three or four months more,'

Tssh, oh I know,

'The article is demanded. No he can't have it, call in *six months after the issue* and your money's ready for you,'

At last!

'And he would have waited if he could – but Death would not. He dies! by starvation. The fat editor is fatted henceforward and forever, to the amount of five and twenty dollars very cleverly saved – to be spent generously on champagne.'

Did I hear you say champagne?

He checked in, changed from light black to dark black, and we sauntered through the whitechapel mist to the cream-and-crimson Coach House, where, in a guilty response to my caveats above, I got us a bottle of Moët and beamed goodwill till my cheeks ached.

I studied in Boston, Mr Poe sir, studied poetry on Bay State Road!

'We like Boston. We were born there.'

Er, I know, that's why I said –

'The Bostonians are very well in their way. Their pumpkin-pies are delicious. Their Common is no common thing... Their poetry's not so good.'

Cheers! Did you tell them that?

(His glass rose up and he drank, and our eyes met for the first time) 'We shall never call a woman *a pretty little witch* again, as long as we live.'

Ha, witch, cheers, like it. So: there should be a crowd tonight, the fiction classes are all coming too, there's a nice Halloween vibe, are you going to read –

'Frogpondians...'

Yup

'We delivered them a "juvenile" poem, they received it with applause!'

Mm-hm

'Next thing was to abuse it in the papers. The poem, they say, is bad. We admit it, we insisted on the fact in our prefatory remarks, over and over.'

Yeah so what's their problem?

'The Frogpondian faction hire a thing they call the *Washington Reformer* – something of that kind – to insinuate we must have been "intoxicated" to "deliver" such a poem.'

Oh-ho! And were ya, man?

'Why can't these miserable hypocrites say *drunk* at once and be done with it?'

Yay! here's to that my friend,

'We shall get drunk when we please. The old Goths of Germany would have understood it. Used to debate matters of state twice, once drunk, once sober,'

Claude can I get the check –

'Sober that they mightn't be deficient in formality, drunk lest they should be destitute of vigour!'

Oh we're not destitute of vigour here, man –

'As for the editor of the *Jefferson Teetotaller*, or whatever it is, we advise her to get drunk too, as soon as possible, for when sober she's a disgrace to the sex, on account of being so awfully stupid.'

Well, yes, there we go (but now the Yankee fellow thwacks his hand on my shoulder, a friend for life for the evening) 'To be controlled is to be ruined!'

Hey let's hit the venue, shall we?

'I'll walk with you,' goes Edgar with a sniff, 'Lord help my poor soul.'

*

'*Prophet!* said I, *thing of evil – prophet still, if bird or devil! –*
By that Heaven that bends above us – by that God we both adore –
Tell this soul with sorrow laden if, within the distant Aidenn,
It shall clasp a sainted maiden whom the angels name Lenore –
Clasp a rare and radiant maiden whom the angels name Lenore.
  Quoth the Raven, *Nevermore.*

Be that word our sign of parting, bird or fiend! I shrieked, upstarting –
Get thee back into the tempest and the Night's Plutonian shore!
Leave no black plume as a token of that lie thy soul hath spoken!
Leave my loneliness unbroken! – quit the bust above my door!
Take thy beak from out my heart, and take thy form from off my door!
  Quoth the Raven, *Nevermore.*

And the Raven, never flitting, still is sitting, *still* is sitting
On the pallid bust of Pallas just above my chamber door;
And his eyes have all the seeming of a demon's that is dreaming,
And the lamp-light o'er him streaming throws his shadow on the floor;
And my soul from out that shadow that lies floating on the floor
  Shall be lifted – nevermore!'

He signed off with a flourish, blew out his taper, I heard girls whispering 'nevermore' in awestruck echo. Then began the loudest longest drummingest ovation of the autumn term. He bowed and gazed and bowed and stared, the mad old ham, the pissed old pro. Even the sceptics were nodding and grinning at his force and energy, indulging a child, as dead professors do living artists. I leaned out of my row and peered back at the whole crowd. Lots of black and red and orange, some horns and beaks and masks, but not remotely bloody frightening.

*

I was glad I'd caught that early drink with him, because as soon as the applause died down he was swamped with acolytes, and did his cause no harm by declaring the cold hall no place for literary talk. At the Keys I couldn't get close.

'I've made no money!' he proclaimed from his long packed table, 'I'm as poor now as ever I was in my life – except in hope, which is by no means bankable!' and his audience blared approval. Some dozen drama, literature and *genre-fiction* students were clustered along, while others knelt or leant or stood in his smoky aura. Some of my poetry students showed, some didn't, no surprises. The only other focus in the room was a little intense booth where *format* was reading Edgar's story *The Imp of the Perverse* to the ones who listen when *format* speaks:

'We stand upon the brink of a precipice,' he read from a large black volume: 'we peer into the abyss – we grow sick and dizzy. Our first impulse is to shrink from the danger. Unaccountably we remain. By slow degrees our sickness and dizziness and horror become merged in a cloud of unnamable feeling. By gradations, still more imperceptible, this cloud assumes shape, as did the vapor from the bottle out of which arose the genius in the Arabian Nights...'

Poe himself seemed unaware of his own words being intoned to a rapt audience a matter of yards away. He had his audience where he sat:

'What's Poetry?' he exclaimed and no one was quick enough – 'Poetry! Give me – I demanded of a scholar some time ago – give me a definition of poetry… He proceeded to his library, brought me a *Dr Johnson*, and overwhelmed me with a definition!'

Poe's brand-new circle duly trembled with contempt. 'Think of poetry – and then think of Dr Samuel Johnson!' Presumably knowing nothing at all, they saw what the words *Doctor Samuel Johnson* made them see – 'think of all that is fairy-like – and then all that's hideous and unwieldy – think of his huge bulk, the Elephant! And then think of Prospero – Oberon – Titania!'

And the voice of Wayne/*format* murmured on in the background:

'And because our reason violently deters us from the brink, therefore do we the most impetuously approach it. There is no passion in nature so demoniacally impatient, as that of him who, shuddering upon the edge of a precipice, thus meditates a plunge…'

Scare me. Next week. It's Halloween. Scare me.

'Scare you how.'

You and your actor friends. Do something. Weave a circle round me thrice.

'You serious Max? Cos you know we could.'

Why do you think I'm asking.

'You had a weird day, who knows. Guess we can scare you.'

I want you to. I want you to scare me to death. So I can go home.

'You okay there, Glyn?'

Ollie was at my table, pulling cellophane off a new notebook.

Yeah man, I'm good, I'm good (and then I hear Poe, mid-declaration –)

'Every plot worth the name must be – ' he had raised his hand for quiet and his finger on high for emphasis – 'must be elaborated – to its denouement – before anything be attempted with the pen.'

Hold your horses though (I murmured to myself) –

'It's only with the denouement constantly in view that we can give a plot its air of, of, of *consequence, causation*, by making the incidents – and especially the tone – tend to the development of the intention!'

Hold your horses though (I spoke under the noise, to no one in particular) why? *Life's* not like that, why should stories be? Why not grow the flower of a chapter from the soil of the last? (Something about me – or him – made Poe aware I'd said this, and nor was I quite done yet) If the ending's written, Edgar, none of us can breathe, and we *can* breathe, we *will* breathe!

Pointing right at me through the grinning of his devotees, with transatlantic *brio* he boomed: 'We *know* the British bear us ill-will!'

(I smiled at them all, a writer myself) But the denouement's not in view! We see some yards into a fog, that's all!

And Poe has raised his glass to what? to our all being there this ancient autumn night, to storytelling, to book-talk, to raising a glass itself, which he did and lowering it said this: 'I've often thought how interesting a magazine might be – written by any author who would detail, step by step, the, the, the *process* by which any of his compositions attained completion...'

That's a first-class idea, man (I called out, seeing where this was heading)

'Why such a paper's never been given to the world,' he wondered to his drained glass, 'I'm at a loss to say,' and the rest was drowned in voluble proposals from his blissful fanbase, including this from a vampire-girl all but contiguous to his cheek: 'Like, Mr Poe, how did you write The Raven for example?' and off he went, in clover, 'My first object was *originality*...' Done with it all, drunk and aware I am, I glance at Ollie, who's opened his new notebook and is titling its first blank page.

Hey how's old Mimi doing these days, man?

'Do I look like I would know that. Man.'

*

No one sees me leave the Keys, or not so as I notice. Last time I walked from here at night my shirt-front was blue with cocktail stain, my chin sticky from my blood-bond, my heartbeat silly, blessed but what? Where was she, where was anyone? Half the crowd at the reading had had animal masks, birds, foxes, cats, that could have been them, and they weren't in the pub, that could have been them, that could have been them *not being there*...

Are they scaring me by waiting? Are they scaring me with

wondering? With nothing? That would disappoint, I must say, I go walking, it's bloody freezing. If I wait for the fright will it never come at all? How can I *unknow* it?

How can I unknow death? (I keep walking) Is that how everyone lives this life? Did I miss the class when that course was advised? How do you unknow death?

There is a man stands by a churchyard.

Hold your horses, only me.

The names buried here are like names buried everywhere, weather-worn to monosyllables, defunct like war-dead surnames, carved and dated, gone together, and the children they raised grew dates themselves, have joined them on the journey. It's on the north side of St Anne's, the yard. Dead flowers for the recent. The dark-now locked-now village hall is a humble barn beside the church, a kennel to its cottage. I walk the path around to that shabby patch with its barred ticking sub-station titled *DANGER OF DEATH – I am trying to unknow you!* – on the scrap of land that serves as the garden to our Workshop.

Half the rooms I've taught poetry in spend half their lives as kindergartens. We read our Frost or Auden in the Red Room full of coat-hooks, or the Purple Room with big bold crayoned drawings on the walls, *Becca, Poppy, Calvin, Juan,* artwork turning and glittering in corners. I'm reminded of this when I see the long dark window of our workshop room, see a display of masks those children must have made – *what children, what kindergarten* – they are seven people's faces – *what children, what children –*

They are not masks they are faces. I am aware my hair's gone ash-white, is crackling, is on end, I note my heartbeat's skipped some pages –

They are six or seven people in a stance together, huddled in the window, looking out at me and they are not faces they are masks, wide plastic bearded faces, broad faces with broad grinning chins, Johnny Appleseed? Paul Bunyan! Lumberjacks! when I stop the faces stop, when I move the faces move and stop.

Good one (I recover my breath) not bad at all my friends, you are seven lumberjacks, and you are all right. You, er, work all day and you sleep all night. You, um, chop down trees, and, so on.

They're lit only by faint lamplight from the road, enough to see they all are sporting different pale-and-black check shirts. How did they know I'd make my way to the churchyard? I mean I *would*, but how did they know? Because I – said I – wanted to be scared...

I start guessing on my fingers – Mimi, Jacob, Syrie, Blanche, Yvette? – you donned old plaster heads from some bygone end-of-term show – and I feel like saying so but I've *my* part to play. Scare *me*, I will be scared, mime, dumb-show, play it out, play it through to some denouement over brandies in the Coach House, Mimi, Jacob, Syrie, Blanche? Roy Ford, Ali K? Yvette, I step, the faces move. I stop, the faces look. Make them laugh! Spoil it! You must be hot in there guys! Sweating like pigs am I right?

No don't, no don't, there's been effort. Mimi gathered them together in the week while I was away, she said *we're going to scare the shit out of Max, ideas, team, ideas...* maybe in the Keys this was, or the tables outside Benson, in the daytime, in the sunshine.

There's an old green outer door moulded shut at one end of the workshop room and I see it's been forced ajar. The seven Paul Bunyans suddenly stride from the window as if on cue and cluster, seated, round one end of the table, the end furthest from the green door. I could go in, they want me to, there'd be distance between us, I'll be nearer the door than them. And someone will break, someone will snort, crease, corpse, wreck it, scream now it's over! I store some cold white cemetery breath and take a step towards these people.

And, somehow, what I learn from that deep intake is solemn, rightful, grave: *I am going to teach my Night Class.*

Bunyan   Bunyan

Bunyan   Bunyan

Bunyan   Bunyan

Bunyan

me

Good evening, Night Class.

Mind if I sit?

Good then. I'll sit.

Look I don't really know how to handle this except to – tell you a story. A dark tale's best for autumn. Would that work for you – you – um, wood-*persons*?

Right. I'll take silence for assent. I can only think of two. So:

There was a man dwelt by a churchyard.

That's that done. Then there's, there's – this one. Oh my God

Bunyan

Bunyan

Bunyan   Bunyan

Bunyan   me   Bunyan

Bunyan

Right. O-kay. You gathered round me. On we go. It's the greatest of Poe's stories. It's about a man who believes something dreadful will befall him. He doesn't know what it is, all he knows is it's coming.

If you stay here, I will spoil it for you. You will find out the ending. I don't want that. Don't listen.

I MEAN IT, DON'T HEAR IT! It's the greatest of Poe's stories. It's so great he didn't write it, Henry James wrote it. Skip this!

I don't want you to hear it. That's what the woman tells the man in the story (too late) the man's called John, she says *John I don't want you to hear it,* because she's worked out what it is. She's worked out the ending. She's understood what's coming, the terrible thing he fears, the thing he's spent his life afraid of, waiting for, being ready for. Years go by, she knows, grows ill loving him, she withers and dies, never told him what it was. At her grave, now elderly, in mourning for the lady, he finally cracks it.

He has wasted his life waiting. Unfulfilled, unseen, unmarked, unknown to love. He was simply the man *to whom nothing would happen*. Nothing happened because he was waiting. I told you not to listen.

*

Six Bunyans turn their great gleaming heads towards the one at the top of the table, and she (he?) produces a small brown bottle from the pocket of his (her?) checked shirt, from which slowly and deliberately the Head Bunyan shakes out some pale-and-dark capsules.

A reward for a dark story? (I repeat) I told you not to listen. (Round it comes towards me, are we all taking capsules?) Are we all – I think we are – taking this together are we?

I don't mind. I'm in a coma, dead, dreaming or in heaven, I'm more or less untouchable, and I don't do Friday mornings.

Should you be taking this? Haven't you trees to cut down somewhere? (if I can just make one of them *giggle*, bloody actors, they never break that way) it's a health-and-safety question!

I'm taking my brown capsule, friends. It breaks in two halves. 2P and 3P, but I'll take it all at once! Will I grow a face like yours? Can I get the shirt at least?

(As I swallow the thing, go ha! there comes a rustle through the Bunyans and a couple of them seem to wobble out of character – why, because a *Prof* is getting high with them yay? – no it's something else, it's someone, faint light's spilling from the village hall, there are footsteps) er, someone's in the hall. Shit (and the door opens)

'What the blummin heck is this.'

Bunyan   Head Bunyan

Bunyan   Bunyan

Bunyan Bunyan

Bunyan

CAT!   me

A little black human cat is here, has stepped through the dark cold hall with a torch and her perfume makes the air go rosy. The Paul Bunyans face her, grouped untidily and she waggles the torch-beam along their scowling grins.

'Are those heads from the wardrobe department?'

Hey Tina (I go) it's Night Class!

'Oh for pete's sake.'

(Ambushed by this accident, the hitherto creepy Bunyans have quite lost their drilled wooden poise, and are distinctly beginning to resemble seven students arsing about, but Tina Yeager, cheap costume notwithstanding, has priorities) 'No candles please, people, that's a no-no and I'm going to switch the main light on.'

This appals all seven Bunyans, and while some frantically wave their arms in protest, others make for the door, sod this for a game of woodmen, and are out before Tina makes her move. Two or three of them loom with menace over the little indignant cat – *Minnaloushe!* they seem to hiss – then they quit the scene and she simply stands her ground with folded arms: 'I hope you signed those heads out.'

The last to leave, the top-of-the-table Head Bunyan, comes via me, looms its flaky plaster head towards me, exposed in its fading am-dram crumble, and murmurs under breath: 'Don't be alone. Top floor of Benson.'

'And close the door behind you please!'

I hear them striding sprinting through the hall and out, not doing what she asked.

'Hm. Charming. What did she tell you?'

Now accustomed to the darkness, nocturnal after all, Minnaloushe marches around, double-bolts the green door shut, blows out the perilous candles, one, two, 'there!' then stands up silhouetted, wire whiskers, little cat ears, wells for eyes.

'Honestly, you. I turn my back for a minute.'

*

We go out through the village hall, and she padlocks it behind us. I play the sullen reprobate as she witters on about regulations. I'm wondering why I didn't run off with the Bunyans. It never entered my mind to. I hope they have another plan. Then again, I hope they don't. I am led down the lane like a fool.

'I was actually singing your praises for once, small wonders never cease, I was saying what a cool show he put on, Mr Poe, I was saying to my assistant, and how maybe Maxwell was right and some poets *are* great readers! You see? I can learn, professor, I can compromise! can *you* though.'

Nevermore.

'Very funny. Nevermore! I expect he's a terrible wretch that Poe, he's really in his cups, so what happened was: I said to my assistant I'm going to find this Maxwell and make, you know, make a suggestion, and I thought you'd be in the Cross Keys pub, seeing as you are always!'

Nevermore.

'But one of your students said he saw you opening the churchyard gate and you know what I said I said Halloween shenanigans! and lo and behold.'

You saw a cat coming out of the mist
'Are you alright?'

Did you just say something about a cat and the mist?
'Um, no. But I am one, I *am* a cat in the mist, meow! so are we going to have our peace-making drinks or just stand here in the cold.'

It was like, a voice.
It is a voice, it's your voice
'Very creepy. Come on.'

You see the red sign of the bar down the street, it's the moon for you, the red moon you ordered, rival people want this. You turn, there are people singing your name, foxes, smoking and drinking foxes: professsssor, professsssor .

Yeager.

'Yes. Maxwell.'

Yeager. Tina Yeager. There's a voice commenting on this.

'So you say.'

It comes and goes, it's saying what I'm doing. In the second person.

What are you doing

'Um. Perhaps you need to sit down.'

Is it you who's doing that. The voice, it said What are you doing.

'No, there's no one, it's Halloween, come on. Nevermore, nevermore, croaked the raven! you do it better.'

*

'Barman, show me the whiskies. I wouldn't usually, but I think in the circumstances. Do you know about whiskies Maxwell.'

You don't know anything at all

'Glen-*morran*-jee. Glenma-*ran*-jee.'

You will sling your hook tonight

'Glenma-*rang*-ghee? Oh is it?'

Do you dance Minnaloushe do you dance

'It's Glen-*morran*-jee with a J, the barman's informed me, you know I think I rescued you from a fate worse than death!'

You know this isn't real

'Cheers then! Clink glasses. You have to catch my eye though.'

You can do it she's a dream

'Or not, hmm that's good, is that a peaty flavour is it, I caught your eye but you didn't catch mine, is that even possible?

Ask her to come home

'What's funny now Maxwell.'

Nothing.

'You giggled. What a mess you are.'

You will ask her to come home

Where's the whisky.
'Pardon?'

Ask her to come home
Someone's commenting on everything.
'What do you mean commenting?'
Yes, what do you mean commenting

Like a third voice. In the second person.
Hello
Coming out of that portrait.
Top o'the morning to ye
Leave me the hell alone.
Leave ye the hell alone
That's really childish that is.
'Um: time out. Who are you looking at?'
Whom
Shut up.
'Charming. You're in a state you are.'
Not you. There's a voice over there, from the, the picture.
'Pardon me?'
There's a voice coming out of the portrait.
'Is there really, there's a word for that.'

You are going to ask her to come home with you
No. It's not home, I'm not home.
'Pardon? You're not home? No one's home, professor. You think you're the only one who's not home? I'm not home. I miss my little flat, I miss Baxter. Poppy and Steve are feeding him. At least I hope they are. They had one thing to remember!'
Ask her to come back to your digs
No.
'No what?'
I'm not doing that.
'Not doing what?'

I think I'm going for a walk now.
'I see. And am I just going to wait here am I?'

I'm just going for a walk. I may be, six minutes.

'Very precise you are! Off you go then. I will guard your Glenma-*ran*-jee. No I've got that wrong again. Barman – pardon? Claude, I need a refill, and a pronounciation lesson.'

*

The cold air hit him
Shut up
And the fog was in his bones
No it's not
And no one knew him any more
You do, you're talking to me
The light of the last friendly house receded like the land's end
Whatever
Her gentle soul was the last of the souls
Leave her out of it asshole
This lamp was the last of the lamps of the world
Depends which way one's walking squire
And all about him was the sea
Look I get it it's quite dark

There was nothing to be done now
Yeah except narration
He tried to make light of it
He did, he does, he does what he likes
But we all come to the Third Person
I don't, I'm I, I am here, I am now
We all come to the Third Person
I don't know where I am but I am walking where I am

His words lie still on the sunlit pages
Words can do what they like

The reader closed her book and rose from that place she had forgotten his words
Well sod her frankly
And life was without him

Without me it's not life
Life was without him
Sod what was written, I can hear my breathing
No one could hear him
Bloody *I* can hear him I mean *me* can hear *me*
He was coming at last to the Third Person
I was I am I I I I
He seemed to be climbing, the ground was getting steeper
Is is is is
He was stumbling up the hill, turned back to see the dwindling lights
Turning turning
His words mere whispers
Just getting my freakin breath here
He was unaccustomed to the effort
Will you shut the fuck up
The lights down there were like a fairy bracelet, the great black shire of
the lagoon in the distance, the wooded isle upon it even blacker than that
A-minus english language
He looked so small on the hillside
I'm the same size I always was
He looked so forlorn
I'm not forlorn I'm alive
His words faded on the wind
No
His words faded on the cold night wind

And he was heard no more

The entrance to the railway tunnel began faintly to glow, and from
its lip could be seen by now, several hundred yards inside, a zigging
and zagging upright stick-man, a dot of a child in a spotlight, a spot
on a sun, a mote on an eye, upon a bright beam growing, widening,
whistling, howling, rendering whatsoever creature that was as a black
star, limbs outspread like the Leonardo sketch, then it was whited out
by thundering noise and no one on earth was watching.

•

Week Seven – November 7th

In our lives we are blessed
On the day we love best,
In the north, and the south, and
The east, and the west!

He was woken by the sound of a school choir singing out like bells in a long bright school hall

There is only one day
We are blessed in this way,
Only one soul to sing to,
Only one tune to play!

The melody was familiar to him, but he looked in vain for the source of the angelic sound

Though we dwell far and wide,
Through the darkness we ride
On the highways and byways
To be here by your side!

He looked in vain – you looked in vain – nobody's here but you and you are not at school at all

We arrive on your shore,
Take the road to your door,
And we waltz by the moonlight
As in evenings of yore!

You are waking from a dream and dream and waking are both real

When the time is just right
We will turn out the light,
Light the dear little candles
See them burning so bright!

You are alive, have survived, am hungry, and what's more: I have, there's no you, there's only this song

We have known you for years
Through the hopes and the fears,
Through the good times and bad times,
Through the laughter and tears!

I am lying in my clothes on the jumbled tartan bedspread. I am agitated by an as-yet-inexplicable joy. I see the sky's pure empty blue and that must be the cause.

Through the sun and the rain,
Through the joy and the pain,
We have sung this song gladly,
Now we sing it again!

But it isn't the cause. It's the effect. Because it's only my freaking birthday.

Happy Birthday to you,
Happy Birthday to you,
Happy Birthday, dear Glyh-hin,
Happy Birthday to you!

It's only my freaking birthday, and I wrote this poem about it. It cannot be said hereafter that I've done no creative work this term.

*

So you think November's icy and dreary – not me, *you* think that, *you* – but I remember some brilliant blue sevenths.

On one I was still at school, all by myself in the Upper Upper Sixth, moody layabout tilting at Oxbridge. A term like a dream: sunlit, quiet, edgeless, ranging. I had three teachers one-to-one and no classmates. All my friends had left. I signed in and out as I pleased, tea-time with my Chaucer books, lunchtime with my files on *Lear*, go home, to the shops, to the woods, to the fields. Those free empty afternoons with the new world beginning…

Then on one bright Saturday morning I was picked for the first team. The lads wondered why I was still around. And I was normally a reserve but that bright day I scored twice like in a comic. After the match my cheery mud-streaked teammates were asking me which birthday? *Nineteenth*, I said, and I remember our beaten opponents looking up suspiciously from the far end of the changing-rooms, as if we'd cheated, fielded someone with a superpower.

On another glorious cold blue-sky birthday I saw a game going on in the distance. I hurried over a car-park to watch. This was Western Massachusetts and football was soccer. I was in my late thirties. The players turned out to be college girls, skilled, determined, brave, fair. I was too old to be some boyfriend, and too vain to admit I could be some father. This made me *what* exactly? I fled. This stuff comes up on birthdays.

Well. Here I am where I was, and the sky is blue, the sun low, the colourful village is stock-still and nordic, the distant meadows sheened with first frost. And did I mention I don't have class?

Before I came to this village to teach – I stop at my wash-basin and examine that clause but it holds up fine as I floss my teeth – before I came to this village to teach I *did* have a superpower: I rose so early in the morning I could almost catch Time out. *Who is that sitting there with his little candles burning? What's his name again? Is he on the list?* I am at my work already, while Time is stretching and cussing, throwing on a robe, not *him* again, not *this* again…

I say *almost* catch Time out. It's only after short deep sleeps in the early afternoon that I wake and find it gone. It gone, all gone, Earth gone. Find myself to be, in all honesty, a heartbeat in space. Accede with a wry smile that there's nothing else anywhere, so be it, amen, we rise again – *reviresco*, motto of the lowland Maxwell clan – rise groggily, diplomatically quiet, to make a further coffee.

But waking on my birthday is the opposite of that. Every move feels right, applauded, focused, minded, cherished. See me choosing socks as if my choice profoundly matters. Watch me magic-marking the calendar, inching another day towards Christmas, another happy hour towards home-time. Look out through my slanting windows at blue sky. The day of gifts begins with the sweet obstinate sense that – gifts presume a giver, and it's making an appearance.

So between these two great termini, *Alles* und *Nichts,* I ride my holy train.

*

I don't have class because today there's a 'Field Trip'. No one has explained this to me. It does sound like the kind of thing I'd schedule without planning, so maybe that's what's happened. I did mean to ask questions but I kind of got caught up. As I stroll in the sun to Saddlers I'm remembering last week and yes, I think you could safely say that one thing rather led to another. My last reliable memory has me stumbling down into nettles on a hillside – *field – trip* – oops there we go, the language finds me out. All the stings have faded.

The Saddlers is closed. Still inside, no trace of Nathan or Mr Ridley or any guest, gingham tables set expertly for no one. No sign it's opening later.

Student Services is closed. Kerri's indoor plants look dry and deserted, indignant plaintiffs I turn my back on. And as I do I remember more – *whisky with Tina Yeager… a portrait on a wall. Face-masks? Scare me…* The dimwit supernatural. Edgar in excelsis.

The Village Hall is locked. VHB is bolted, the Cross Keys is shut, the whole place seems abandoned.

On my birthday.

Hmm, I relay to the cosmos, hmm. I include you in this. Whatever made me come here. Whatever sent me to sleep or knocked me out or turned my life so merrily improbable, I include you in the following contention: this does not seem fair on my birthday.

Field Trip could have waited. Was there no one to say 'Hang on a minute!' 'Where's chief'? 'Can't leave without him!' 'Fetch Max he's dead again,' 'Someone go and wake him, he wanted to come on this!' Their voices ring the chimes until I shake my head silent. This does not seem fair on my birthday. As if my birthday includes in its embrace some bright enthroned Presence wielding Her scales.

Yes well, I think, by the crimson bolted door of The Coach House, that's *Libra* that, that's Libra for you and you would insist on hanging back for Scorpio...

At Z for Zodiac and fast running out of ideas, I set off along the residential lanes, with the college blocks looming behind their tidy red roofs. If all the students are gone somewhere... *Mrs Kerr. Bob Tomlin. The McCloud children. Jessie...* No one's lonely when the bell rings...

And here of course it comes, silently turning at the end of the road.

*

Rowena who drives the milk-float also rides a wheelchair, but she's usually left the village by breakfast, so you don't get to see that often. This is the first time I've really looked at her, when the milk-float clinks to a halt, full of empties, all delivered. She's white-haired and rake-thin, with dark eyes, fine cheekbones. She wears dark blue and a bucket hat and only speaks when it's worth it. But it's Barry who told me that.

'Fancy seein' you here!' greets that big friendly passenger.

Whatever it was today, Barry, I've – missed, I think.

'No class today, señor, and there's nothing wrong with the old lie-in!'

Am I not (my heart heaves up but I do have to say this) am I not included in the Field Trip?

'We'll take you where you're going,' says Rowena, adjusting the windscreen mirror.

Right. Right. It's just it's my – it's the Field Trip and I suppose they've all gone there.

Barry gets out of the cabin, lumbers round to the back of the float where I meet him. He's carrying various dusty brown and orange cushions.

'Don't know about no Field Trip, was it on the Reading Series?'
It was.

'Hmm,' and he's clearing a space between crates of bottles,

thumping the cushions into it, patting them down for comfort, 'well you heard the lady say it!'

You'll take me where I'm going.

'She will do just that, old son, and most likely bring you back again!'

Thanks Barry, thank you guys.

And so we trundle along at first, with the bottles clanking and jingling till we're past the last of the buildings, then to the north we leave the village, past the fence where I met Keats and on, out, off, away into country. Soon we're moving along quite steadily through still-frosty silver fields and meadows, and I'm dispatching cherries, grapes and tangerines they gave me.

Take me into the distance, I cry.

'What's that you say?' calls Barry.

I cry take me into the distance!

They are silent for a long while then they talk, the pair of them, Barry in an unfamiliar, lower, private tone, Rowena lighter, musical, but I don't pick out a single word. I listen to their sounds of sense rising and falling and watch the frost on the fields twinkle in the scope and reach of the sunlight.

No one knows it's my birthday and I'm taken where I'm going. I look for signs of habitation, signs of life, I look for *road*-signs, any sign but the existence of the road itself, but our milk-float chugs its way through how heaven looks on days like this, as I grow older and younger but not a whit the wiser.

*

The first sign is a long field we're suddenly passing by. It has a fence instead of hedges, so someone must have fenced it. We're also slowing down and at last make a right turn down a driveway, or the beginnings of a driveway. It curves and bends through the rippling trees for ages, and through them over the fields I glimpse some little buildings, sheds, cottages, outhouses. I think of asking Barry if we're here but why should I, it's my birthday.

Presently through a gap in the trees, downhill a ways I see what must be the destination, a large white country mansion with several smaller wings, paths radiating from it, lawns and walks and water-features, worth the hours it took to drive here – worth the minutes it took, seconds it took? I have no idea how long.

Worthy of my birthday!

'What's that you say, señor?'

Nothing. Come a long way today!

'Fine day for it, señor!'

*

Our journey ended at the front of the house, where we parked in a small oval of gravel. Finally there were people, some men chatting by the stone steps, some all in white, dressed for jogging. Lawns seemed to stretch away in all directions, bordered with elms or limes or poplars. A few stately oaks stood far off in solitude, mighty, misted.

Right by where we'd parked there was a fellow leaning on an ornamental lion. He was tall, old-fashioned handsome, his hair dark and parted, he wore a favourite suit and a white shirt undone at the neck. He smiled as Barry greeted him with: 'Jimmy!' and Jimmy pointed at my friend: 'Barry Wilby! *By* the left, give 'em a hand, Ted, step *to* it!'

Another man, similarly at ease, helped Rowena out of the front of the milk-float and down into her wheelchair, chatting with her all the while, to which she answered 'beat you to it,' and steered the wheels in the gravel.

I jumped down at the back, stretched, taking the scene in, and Barry called me over.

'This is me teacher, Jimmy, better mind ya p's and q's!'

'Right you are,' Jimmy grins, and declares in a timbre sort of well-to-do with a soft Cheshire edge, 'for Reading, Writing and Gazinta!'

I shook hands gladly with whatever he meant, and Barry expanded on his introduction: 'Poetry's his field, you got some poets here, ness-par?'

'Jawohl,' said Jimmy, 'I daresay somewhere. Spot of grub first, eh?'

Barry leaves me in this man's care, and starts wheeling Rowena away along a kind of cloistered walkway, saying loudly without turning back: 'We always do the walks, señor, some lovely walks they've got here...'

'Go right at the well,' says Rowena.

'Right at the well it is!'

And so Jimmy took me to breakfast.

*

There are fifty men or so in here, place-settings for hundreds. Five or six women too, at a round table by the long bright window looking out over the grounds. On the opposite wall four or five tables of breakfast fully laden. Jimmy waves to the women, who are laughing too hard to notice.

'The early birds,' says Jimmy, 'we'll get the onslaught later. Let's find you a tray, professor…'

I settle for Full English, grapefruit juice and a mug of coffee, and plunge in gladly at the end of a ten-man table. Jimmy's naming every bloke he can see, as if testing his memory: 'Burdon, Cobb, O'Driscoll, Fell, Ullerton, Pye, Race, Hapgood, Brassey, not many poets in *that* lot, no wait, hang about, here comes the Rajah…'

This is a fair yawning fellow in a striped silk dressing-gown, who seats himself grandly alone at a new table that's soon settled by chortling pals.

Jimmy spears a half-sausage and relaxes, having found what he was seeking: 'We'll take our lead from the Rajah. He'll be hitting the Pavilion, now *there* we might run into the odd *artiste*…'

*

Which is how we come to be sitting in a brilliant spacious glasshouse, which we reached by way of a colonnade, then a cream marble bathroom where my open-mouthed reflection just stared and shook its head, then a long quiet corridor with pictures of winning teams.

Their Pavilion is set all around with sofas, low tables and exotic plants, it feels like one of the warm havens of Kew, for the air seems tropic-green with all the sunlight through the glass. Except that on three of the walls are bookshelves, and on all of the shelves are books.

'Poets?' says the Rajah, getting comfortable among pillows, and what looks like a small volume of verses in his right hand, 'I met a group of young poets, in London. Extremely poor. They talk cockney. And they write – some are good, some bad – as they talk.'

'Howzat then, Raj?' Jimmy prompts him.

'They allow for *ow* being *aow*. Their love-poems begin: *If yew would come agin to me!*'

We snort at his mimicry, but the Rajah wags his finger, 'That's healthy. That way is life. They were so nice. Very simple, very good-hearted. I felt I'd like – almost – to live with them, protect them,' and with this he subsides into his book, but not before waving us vaguely into nearby seating.

'Wotcher got ya nose in, Raj,' Jimmy wants to know – though I felt the poet wanted us all to be quietly reading too – now he lifted his book to show us:

'Browning's suffered from Browning-*ites.*'

Browning you're reading Browning? (I find my high embarrassing voice at last) oh we've invited Browning! I mean, I think, or both the Brownings...

The Rajah sniffs: 'Browning's not a very good poet. Blake is,' but then he riffles through the pages trying to find a thing he likes: 'It's – *Oh to be in England, now the spring is here* – I've probably quoted it wrong and spoilt it. Read it, it's worth it. Quite short.'

Jimmy nods as if he'll do this, and I feel free to up and explore the Pavilion. It feels like wading through a sea-world it's so warm and green and pungent. I thought the place was empty when we entered, but almost hidden by an old scratched upright piano, a thin-faced man in a collarless shirt is sketching something he can see in the gardens.

Briefly glancing at me he asks politely if I've seen 'the Blakes in the Tate,' a formulation which, out of context, is bemusing, until the artist clarifies: 'England turned out one man second to none. The drawings are finer than his poems, much clearer – but it's unfortunate he – didn't live when a better tradition of drawing ruled.'

'This poet's got questions, Slade,' says Jimmy breezily, joining us, 'what do *you* reckon to the *arts poetical?*'

No it's okay (I splutter) really, you're sketching, do, do sketch! (my mumbling plight compounded by what the thin fellow seems to think of his nickname) Jimmy pipes up: 'Slade's his college o' knowledge!'

Slade ponders the poetry question: 'Definite thought. Clear – expression, however subtle. I don't think there should be any vagueness at all, but a sense of something – *hidden,* felt to be there…'

'Blimey,' notes Jimmy, 'not a walk in the park, is it?'

The artist reddens and defers: 'I'm a very bad talker. I find it – difficult – to make myself intelligible at times, can't remember the exact word. Think I leave the impression of being a, a rambling idiot – '

No no! (I cry)

'Pardoo too,' Jimmy protests, but the Rajah booms an observation from the far end of the glassy realm, from which I can make out only 'Slade' and 'rhythm'.

Slade shifts back in his chair, eyeing his work. Then he nods as if concurring and resumes his sketching.

'Regular rhythms I don't like much – but of course it depends where the stress and accent are laid.'

It *totally* does (I say but softly, not to involve the Rajah)

'There's nothing finer than the opening of Lycidas for music – yet it's regular.'

Once more, ye laurels, O ye myrtle groves! (I begin, with Jimmy blankly beaming 'Ah, great stuff!' and me hoping someone will interrupt before I forget the next bit) with ivy never sere, etcetera!

Slade is thinking it through: 'Now if Marvell had broken up his rhythms more…' He pauses, lowers his eyes: 'I like his poem urging his mistress to love – because they've not a thousand years to love – and he can't afford to wait, I forget the name of the poem – '

You mean Coy Mistress? (I all but yell in triumph)

'Well,' and Slade goes quietly back to work, 'I like it more than Lycidas.'

Jimmy nods and shrugs politely as if he rates the poems about equal – though my guess is he's heard of neither – and we leave Slade to his work, flop happily down on a couple of sofas in the neighbourhood of the Rajah. We can hear him turning pages, one, then many, sighing and yawning. We could see Slade squinting at his sketch if we looked. But we don't look. Except the one time I do look he's staring right at me.

> *what do you see in our eyes*
> *at the shrieking iron and flame*
> *hurled through still heavens*
> *what quaver   what heart aghast*

'How d'you write a poem then,' Jimmy asks me when it's been too long, and before I can answer the Rajah answers from the depths of his pillows, crisp voice emerging from a luxurious yawn:

'Get an idea – opium, or any of the conventional methods – (b) write in as luscious, intricate, scarlet, hothouse, polyphonous verse as possible – perfectly easy – then (c) translate the result of (b) into rough simple verse, making the whole as rural, balladic and unaffected as you can – the result combines all the virtues of all the styles ever – *Ghost!*'

A matinee idol has drifted in, smoking, in shirt-sleeves, with an illustrated magazine. He descends into an armchair. By now it feels like noon or so, a couple of men in pink-grey waistcoats are taking luncheon orders. Ghost asks the Rajah what he's drinking and the Rajah lifts his pewter tankard: 'Stout, it's the only way.'

Jimmy knows the new man too: 'You look a bit worse for wear, Ghost, out on the tiles last night, were we?'

'We got excited,' Ghost chuckles (and the Rajah quaffs again as if minded to catch up) 'Jumped about, sang praises, looked in at half-doors, blessed the people inside...'

'Unutterably fantastic,' murmured the Rajah.

'Saw Shakespeare in a lantern, saw Italy in a balcony – strange way of getting drunk!'

Jimmy and I joined in the laughter. I saw Ghost noticing Slade quietly sketching by the window, and nodded as if to say *we shan't disturb you Slade.*

Jimmy ventures: 'Got another poet for your collection, Ghost,' and Ghost glances, turns, reaches out his hand to mine.

I'm I'm Glyn (I hear myself say, shaking)

'I'm Wilfred,' says Ghost, 'and I follow the gleam.'

'Lad's got some questions for ya, feller,' Jimmy smiles.

I really don't, I'm just sort of passing through and saying hi, it's really –

'*Name?* Ghost demands abruptly of himself, 'words to that effect. *Address?* unfixed. *Health?* quite restored. *Mood?* highest variety of jinks. *Religion?* primitive Christian. *Aim in life?* pearls before swine. *Favourite colour?* sky-violet. *Favourite animal?* children. *Pet aversion?* pets.'

A piano starts to play, as if the pianist had been waiting politely for this list to conclude, and I assume it's Slade but no, there he is still sketching and looking doubtful. He's moved away from us a little but has turned his chair around and may well now be trying to capture our group with his charcoal. The pianist is hidden by the upright piano, and is playing a song I know but can't place.

Ghost and the Rajah settle back to read, and a great trolley squeaks into view, wheeled by an aged man in a tailcoat. The trolley is stacked with plates of food, glasses, cups and saucers. Jimmy sorts me what he calls 'sarnies' – ham, or cheddar, or some pale brown paste of the ages, and a welcome pint of cloudy beer.

Ghost leans forward to see what's on the trolley, fades back empty-handed and winces like his bones ache: 'Refereed a football match yesterday. Calves are still suffering.'

'I saw Peter Pan,' the Rajah says, nibbling a stick of celery, 'it's perfect. The incarnation of all one's childish dreams… Wonderfully refreshing. Never silly.'

The pianist plays a lively tune and the amiable Jimmy tries to spread a smile at that. Ghost blows smoke instead: 'Preserve me from all rag-time. Preserve me from billiards, whist, and football.'

Out on the lawn are more people than before. Most of them seem to be either taking boxes somewhere or coming back without them. Off behind some trees I see tennis-courts where four women in white are merrily contesting. But just about every other soul I see is carrying boxes and crates away from the house. The mood seems good-humoured, but whatever they are doing appears to be quite urgent.

I ask Jimmy what it is and he's struck by all the kerfuffle: 'Blimey O'Riley it's all go today!'

I want to joke it's for my birthday! but think better of it, and in any case, Ghost now saunters up to the window, trailing his sweet old smoke and grinning: 'Nothing can keep *him* from his morning's golf.'

Jimmy and I join him there and look for what he means. I see four men, two tall players striding away from two burdened little caddies, all proceeding across the wide lawn. 'Siegfried,' says Ghost.

The taller of the two faraway figures seems to touch his mouth every few moments till a little puff of blue smoke indicates a pipe. He's the first to reach the last gate and instead of opening it climbs it, leaps, lands, springs along on his majestic progress.

Ghost takes a brisk drag on his ciggie and turns a quarter-turn my way: 'He says *Sweat your guts out writing poetry!* Eh? says I. *Sweat your guts out, I say!* Looks under twenty-five. Admires Thomas Hardy. Condemned some of my poems, amended others. Rejoiced over a few, read me his last works – which are superb. I don't tell him so, or that I'm not worthy to light his pipe. I simply sit tight and tell him where I think he goes wrong.'

From the sofas the Rajah grunts in approval.

We watch the second golfer reaching the gate in the distance. A big fair man, he opens it and waits for the caddies to catch up.

'Graves's technique is perfect,' says Ghost softly in his honour.

He leads us back to our sofas, having gazed his fill of outdoors: 'Eat, drink, and be merry, for tomorrow we live, and the day after tomorrow live, live, live!'

As if inscrutably responding to this, the hidden pianist starts to bash out a tune we all know, but we all take a while, as we settle down in our places again, to identify it, it's – *God Rest Ye Merry, Gentlemen!* all together now,

God rest ye merry, gentlemen,
Let nothing you dismay,
Remember, Christ our Saviour
Was born on Christmas Day
To save us all from Satan's power
When we were gone astray

The pianist pounds away like billy-o in response to our rising volume. Slade's not singing but smiling faintly as he loops a great page over his easel, and the Rajah's drained his tankard and is ordering more stout.

> O tidings of comfort and joy,
>   Comfort and joy,
> O tidings of comfort and joy!

The crescendo echoes and the last chord fades. I hear the creak of the piano-stool as the player sits back in his corner.

'Gor blimey charlie, in *November*?' Jimmy cries with scorn, but he'd been booming his share with the best of 'em.

Ghost sighs, lights another cigarette: 'Christmas has lost its savour. Stare at a sprig of holly – mistletoe – they mean nothing! Father Christmas, Charles Dickens, Scrooge, Bob Cratchit, Plum Pudding, Tiny Tim,' – we all join in – 'Mince Pie, Christmas Tree – '

Silent Night? I wonder,

'No use! Can't get the atmosphere…'

I smile at Ghost in sorrow for his plight and he smiles back at me for mine.

> *I knew you in this dark   for so you frowned*
>   *yesterday through me as you jabbed and killed*
> *I parried   but my hands were loth and cold*

'That was a pretty good concert,' Ghost calls towards the piano, from which a soulful minor chord chimes back as if to say you're welcome.

I'm looking out at the day again, a long bank of shade on the lawn now. Off to the far end stands a group by a little white gazebo, turning to greet someone who's just come into view. My eyes follow where they've turned and I see it's Barry and Rowena, Rowena being wheeled by Barry, everybody knows them! I want to cry out but how would they hear me through the glass? I can't get home without them – I even miss my class and start to wonder what they're up to, I'm leafing through a book, I see who's sitting where, I'm about to teach some poems I know –

'Hey Bartholomew!'

This wakes me from my light doze: the lunch, the murmur of conversation, the comfort of the sofa and the strangeness of the morning had taken their gentle toll. It feels like hours later, a day later, within a further frame of gold.

'Oi, Paderewski!'

Jimmy's gone round behind the piano to take his praise to the accompanist. Yawning and blinking and following him round I see who's there on a piano-stool, a pale stocky fellow in wire-frame glasses, something of Chaplin about him, writing something on a music score.

'They're good sorts,' he says, crossing it out again.

'What you scribblin', maestro,' Jimmy wonders.

'Yesterday,' says the fellow steadily, 'I – felt I – talked to the spirit of Beethoven.' He darts a look at us both: 'I'm serious – something *happened*. I was playing the slow movement of the D Major – felt the presence of a wise – *friendly* spirit, it was old Ludwig Van all right.'

He plays a sprinkling of the master, breaks off, returns to his vision: 'when I finished he said: *Yes, but there's a better thing than that...* Turned me to the E flat sonata. Said he was fond of me, I was like himself as a young man. That – I'd started much too late. Still he – he allowed me to hope much more – '

'This feller's a poet, Bart,' says Jimmy brightly, shrugging off the oddball spirit stuff, 'he's got some poetical questions!'

I stutter one out to which, again without breaking his attention on the score, Bartholomew responds: 'Walt Whitman's my latest. Taken me like a flood.'

I can hear the Rajah muttering from his lair across the room, while Slade sits back from his sketching close by and ponders mildly: 'Can't quite get the – *delight* in Whitman, from one poem of his I know – Captain, My Captain – *Emerson* is America's poet, paved the way for Whitman.'

'He's *democracy's* poet, Whitman,' Bartholomew dissents, playing a complex chord, 'on death he says the supreme word, on the making of men, on the open air and its revelations. This line on the sea – '

But the Rajah booms from his base-camp: 'People who want everyone to write like Whitman are deaf, mad, or wicked.'

Bartholomew presses on, reciting: '*Where the fierce old mother endlessly cries for her castaways…*'

'Whitman's justified,' the Rajah pronounces, 'because he produces good states of mind – which is more than his imitators do.'

The piano player scoffs and sounds a loud bass discord but 'Fellers, let's be havin' yer!' is Jimmy's cordial intervention, 'time for a cup o' cha, eh?'

And before that works its primordial magic, Bartholomew closes the leather black covers of his music book and gently fingering its printed golden title says:

'I should like some verse not yet known to me.'

He looks up, at me maybe, his little round glasses make it hard to be sure.

> *nothing but chance of death   after tearing of clothes*
> *kept flat   and watched the darkness   hearing bullets whizzing –*
> *and thought of music*

'*If yew were the Aownly Girl in the wowld, and I was the Aownly Bor-hoy*,' Jimmy sings in terrible cod-cockney as he takes the teapot from one of the ancient servants, '*a-nuffin else would a-matter in the wowld to-die, a-we would go on a-lavin' in the syme old why…*'

Something in Jimmy's manner hits the spot for all the men. To the Rajah he's amusing in a low way, to Ghost he's one of the lads, and to quiet awkward Slade and the musical Bartholomew, the two now treading our way for tea, he's one of those genial souls who buzz about with the power to call them from chosen solitude to gather, pressed, for the greater good. And to me – well, he's my one link to Barry, who is, now I think about it, my one way home to what I know – or what I've grown used to dreaming of knowing. And now out on the lawn the group by the gazebo has dispersed. I don't see Barry or Rowena and the shudder goes right through me: even in delight I find I've strayed too far from home.

But it's tea and I was England-born. We gather near the Rajah's sofa, the old men in tailcoats make a fuss, and Jimmy checks we got everything we ordered.

'Tray bong,' proclaims Bartholomew, stirring his tea with his pencil.

Slade calls shyly across to the Rajah: 'Thanks very much for the book, you're very kind to think of me,' and the Rajah both nods at the courtesy and waves away the compliment. Then he counsels one and all:

'If you've not read *Tess of the D'Urbervilles* do so.'

'Hardy's a marvel,' Bartholomew says blowing on his tea, 'but he spoilt *The Return of the Native* with sins against art and, and, probability. The book's perverse.'

A voice rings out clearly from the sideboard along the wall, where there's a tall fair-haired fellow in a long green coat with his back to us, sorting himself some lunch: 'I heard he was annoyed by my article in *Poetry and Drama*.'

Jimmy gives me a nudge and whispers: 'They call that chap the Ambic.'

'*I*-ambic,' the sharp-eared Rajah corrects him loudly.

'On account of he always meets you same pub same time, right?' Jimmy nudges Ghost who smokes and smiles in confirmation.

'Said he was a peasant,' chuckles the Iambic, turning his long tanned face towards us, then past us towards the congregations on the lawn. I turn to see what he's seeing because I realize who he is.

'*Under the Greenwood Tree* is perfectly charming,' Bartholomew avers, going back to Hardy, 'Shakespearean in feeling.'

Slade is sitting beside me with his teacup, a yellow wafer-biscuit half-eaten in the saucer, and returns to our old conversation as if no time had passed: 'Nobody told me what to read. Don't think I knew what real poetry was till I read Keats.'

Interesting (I say so he might say more, and I see Ghost turn his handsome face in approval) – Me I started out with Byron (I plough on) well Edward Lear when I was little, but Byron later! (I find it hard not to exclaim every word I say)

'I, I, *galloped* through Byron when I's about fourteen,' Slade stammers, 'but – more for the story...'

'I'm deciphering *Salammbo*,' Ghost offers, 'not that it's difficult reading, but every syllable deserves attention. Flaubert has my vote.'

Since we seem to be voting, the Rajah makes his pronouncement as he rearranges cushions: 'The best story ever written is *Other Kingdom*, by Forster – very charming person.'

'I think Hardy's a better poet than novelist,' says Slade quietly.

Bartholomew peers around at us all, adjusts his spectacles and suddenly breaks out into a pleasant grin: 'Tea-drinking and smoking, with a piano and book-talk!' Simply sounding the chord of the moment.

'*Room With A View*'s very good,' the Rajah added, 'Forster, charming person.'

An assortment of biscuits adorns the Rajah's plate, and he's perched on the very edge of his sofa, trying to choose where on earth to begin – the shortbread? the Rich Tea, the Royal Scot, the Bourbon? – but the task seems too delightful to complete, and he grins when he looks up and finds me watching him, because he knows I know it is. He frowns at me, chuckles to himself. Simply can't decide.

> *if I should die   think only this of me*
> *that there's some corner of a foreign field*
> *that is for ever England*

The Iambic saunters past our group, great walking-boots on the green-and-white tiles, to watch the crowds from the window. Jimmy taps me on the knee, gestures to say let's meet him, and we join him where he watches. He glances at me when Jimmy tells him my first name.

Three-quarters Welsh! (I sort of gasp) and my parents tried to bring us up bilingual in Hertfordshire but no one else spoke Welsh in our town! So – *un dau tri pedwar pump chwech!*

The Iambic sniffs and sorts in his coat pockets, delves, brings out a pipe: 'If you can discover a possible Celtic great-grandmother, you're at once among the chosen.'

Ha! True! We did climb Cader Idris once, on holiday at Barmouth!

He raises his eyebrows, allows this: 'Remember the proverb: if a man goes up Cader Idris at night, by dawn he's dead, or mad, or a poet.'

'This feller's a poet,' Jimmy explains, and the Iambic nods politely. You know the Frosts? (I babble like *I* do)

He gives a wry smile: 'They're rather incalculable.'

Then he draws something out of his other deep pocket, a book, his little worn red copy, ROBERT FROST, MOUNTAIN INTERVAL.

'Every day I read a sonnet or two.'

Two roads diverged in a yellow wood! (I start and fade, and in the silence I wait to wake up, fall down, die, be born, I see the sun is only cloud-light over hilltops now and the sky's not blue it's yellow-pink, and nor is The Road Not Taken a sonnet oh god)

'Great stuff,' goes Jimmy, happy to fill space.

'I'm glad you like Frost,' the Iambic says simply.

'Ella Wheeler Wilcox?' Jimmy wonders, '*By* the left that's fine stuff!'

'The most widely-read poet of the day,' grimly states the Iambic, and Jimmy quotes her with delight: 'Laugh, and the world laughs with you!'

'She can't ever stir an inch beyond what's being said,' runs the Iambic's critical opinion, and Jimmy looks downcast.

I feel sad for my guide, who's been so kind all day, but the Iambic's way ahead of me, his hand is clapped on Jimmy's shoulder: 'Today's been perfect. We must sit in a pub or two,' and all is healed. The Iambic takes in the whole company:

'Had a strange dream last night. Began with me crouching, with a great fear of something – which I knew to be – *dragonish* – behind me, about to grip me by the, the nape of the neck. Then someone I knew but couldn't see – and I don't know who – bent down and whispered *HE is in the orchard!* Then he bent and whispered still lower: *there IS no orchard...*'

The others shiver and murmur approval.

'This is my copyright,' stresses the Iambic, drawing tobacco from a pouch.

The Rajah stands tall, he's stretching, he's leaving:

'I once dreamt I was in the gardens of Heaven, walking between great odorous beds of helichrys and asphodel... Turning a corner I met the Headmaster of Rugby digging up all the flowers. I hit him on the nose, and asked what he was doing. He said he was planting vegetables for food instead. He began to swell as I gazed... he blotted out the sky.'

And soon he was gone, a fond hand-clasp with Ghost, a nod to Slade and Bartholomew, and a murmur to Jimmy and me as he brushes past the Iambic: 'I leave the muses of England in his keeping...'

Slade had trotted back to his easel, we saw him folding away his sketchbooks. Bartholomew was gone too, lowered down the piano lid in silence, his footsteps still echoed down the Pavilion. Ghost went on leafing and frowning through his magazine. But the Iambic had a place to be, informing us briskly 'I've an utterly uncongenial crowd of books to review.'

And soon we saw him walking fast across the gardens, turning a circle once with his arms out as if to say, nonetheless, what a place this is.

> *that I forgot my friend*
> *and neither saw nor sought him till the end*
> *when I awoke from waters unto men*
> *saying   I shall be here some day again*

We – had better find Barry, eh?

'Wossat?' Jimmy jumps.

To take me home again. I saw them walking that way. There must be something happening out there beyond the lawn.

'Blimey. All them crowds, where the blinkin' heck they all gone now?'

I don't know. Don't *you* know?

'Me? You must be jestin'!'

We readied ourselves to go. I began to rather panic. But without the Rajah and the rest of our odd little reading-circle all sense of company had drained away, so Ghost wasn't listening to whatever we were doing. I felt I should do *something* to mark our departure, but all I had was –

All right Wilfred?

He turned a page of his magazine and said without looking up again, à propos of what he was reading: 'I quite see the origin of Theosophy. It's the same as that of Heaven: desperate desire.'

*

…Courage was mine, and I had mystery,
Wisdom was mine, and I had mastery:
To miss the march of this retreating world
Into vain citadels that are not walled.
Then, when much blood had clogged their chariot-wheels,
I would go up and wash them from sweet wells,
Even with truths that lie too deep for taint.
I would have poured my spirit without stint
But not through wounds; not on the cess of war.
Foreheads of men have bled where no wounds were.
I am the enemy you killed, my friend.
I knew you in this dark: for so you frowned
Yesterday through me as you jabbed and killed.
I parried, but my hands were loth and cold.
Let us sleep now…

from **'Strange Meeting', Wilfred Owen (1893–1918)**

*

Jimmy led me down the tiled colonnade, down some steps on to the lawn, which by now was a cool shadowy blue. There were still some folks about, but those that were were still making their way in the sole direction: to the far end of the great lawn, through the gate and over the crest and on into the twilit fields.

We, we meeting Barry up there are we Jimmy? Barry? Rowena?

'Howzat,' my guide said sadly, keeping some thought to himself.

Big Barry, Barry Wilby who brought me here, he's going to take me home –

'Ah we'll snag the feller somewhere.'

And on we go in silence.

*

Over known fields with an old friend in dream
I walked, but came sudden to a strange stream.
Its dark waters were bursting out most bright
From a great mountain's heart into the light.
They ran a short course under the sun, then back
Into a pit they plunged, once more as black
As at their birth; and I stood thinking there
How white, had the day shone on them, they were,
Heaving and coiling. So by the roar and hiss
And by the mighty motion of the abyss
I was bemused, that I forgot my friend
And neither saw nor sought him till the end,
When I awoke from waters unto men
Saying: 'I shall be here some day again.'

'A Dream', Edward Thomas (1878–1917)

*

There was a great crowd out there in the last of the light. Jimmy suggested we skirt around the crowd to one side, along a line of trees and so we do, passing by young men, young women, shoving and chattering company, I can't quite see what's at the centre of what these hundreds – thousands? – have assembled for, but I see most heads are turned one way.

I glance at Jimmy and he's frowning. I say:

We will *find* Barry, won't we Jimmy, I don't know how I got here, and it is, it's it's, my birthday.

'Your *birthday*? *Gordon* Bennett! Put *years* on me you do.'

What?

'*a-Happy Birthday to a-Yew, a-Happy Birthday to a-Yew –* '

Please don't do that (But of course he does, and those we're passing through join in as they always will) Thank you, thanks, yep, ta, – what are they all waiting for, Jimmy?

His long friendly face looks down at me with a grin:

'*Lord* knows, lad, but they'd better bloody start soon!'

And as if on cue they do. With a deafening *whoosh* a black trace
of rocket zooms high into the rosy dusk –
'*Gott in Himmel!*' cries Jimmy –
And the whole crowd draws its breath like a child –

*

The darkness crumbles away.
It is the same old druid Time as ever,
Only a living thing leaps my hand,
A queer sardonic rat,
As I pull the parapet's poppy
To stick behind my ear.
Droll rat, they would shoot you if they knew
Your cosmopolitan sympathies.
Now you have touched this English hand
You will do the same to a German
Soon, no doubt, if it be your pleasure
To cross the sleeping green between.
It seems you inwardly grin as you pass
Strong eyes, fine limbs, haughty athletes,
Less chanced than you for life,
Bonds to the whims of murder,
Sprawled in the bowels of the earth,
The torn fields of France.
What do you see in our eyes
At the shrieking iron and flame
Hurled through still heavens?
What quaver – what heart aghast?
Poppies whose roots are in man's veins
Drop, and are ever dropping;
But mine in my ear is safe –
Just a little white with the dust.

'Break Of Day In the Trenches', Isaac Rosenberg (1890–1918)

*

BANG!

'Remember, remember, the Fifth of November!' Jimmy roars in celebration,

It's not the fifth it's the seventh, Jim!

'Ah well, close enough eh? Happy Returns!'

Red, yellow, green and pink explosions make the sky amazing. Wherever we are it's Firework Night, and I can glimpse at the glowing heart of this enormous sloping meadow the wooden pyre these people built all day is now staggeringly lit, flames gusting and cowering, wagging and raging.

I scan the crowds for the few I might know here, and see one man watching the fireworks, standing apart by a little tree. I only think it's Bartholomew because when he tilts his head to look up at all the fabulous detonations, the two tiny lenses of his spectacles go green, go dark, go red, go dark…

*

Who died on the wires, and hung there, one of two –
Who for his hours of life had chattered through
Infinite lovely chatter of Bucks accent:
Yet faced unbroken wires; stepped over, and went
A noble fool, faithful to his stripes – and ended.
But I weak, hungry, and willing only for the chance
Of line – to fight in the line, lay down under unbroken
Wires, and saw the flashes and kept unshaken,
Till the politest voice – a finicking accent, said:
'Do you think you might crawl through there: there's a hole.'
Darkness, shot at: I smiled, as politely replied –
'I'm afraid not, Sir.' There was no hole no way to be seen,
Nothing but chance of death, after tearing of clothes.
Kept flat, and watched the darkness, hearing bullets whizzing –
And thought of music – and swore deep heart's deep oaths
(Polite to God) and retreated and came on again,
Again retreated – and a second time faced the screen.

'The Silent One', Ivor Gurney (1890–1937)

*

All faces green, all faces amber, the noise is incredible! Jimmy's hustling me along now and I don't know what's the hurry. We have to push the wrong way through the crowds, our backs to the vast bonfire, and I have to watch the sky because it's red now, red and golden, green and golden, bangs and crackles and screeching and sighing – I stumble and trip because the gradient's rising, *field trip, field trip* – Jimmy helps me up and on we go –

Where the fu – where the blazes are we going, Jimmy?

'Higher up,' he's panting, 'better view, better grub!'

I'm done with strangers for the day, man, it's my birthday –

'Strangers ain't done with you!' he's laughing –

I want to go home, Jimmy!

'Don't we blummin' well all!'

Home to where I'm from, also, also, home to the village, home to where I woke this morning, home to where I work –

'Blimey, how many 'omes you got, lad? Don't be down in the mouth, not long now!'

Bangs and crackles and cracks and showers, all faces pink, white, blue – *SURPRISE!!!*

*

If I should die, think only this of me:
     That there's some corner of a foreign field
That is forever England. There shall be
     In that rich earth a richer dust concealed;
A dust whom England bore, shaped, made aware,
     Gave, once, her flowers to love, her ways to roam,
A body of England's, breathing English air,
     Washed by the rivers, blessed by suns of home.
And think, this heart, all evil shed away,
     A pulse in the eternal mind, no less
         Gives somewhere back the thoughts by England given;

Her sights and sounds, dreams happy as her day;
        And laughter, learnt of friends; and gentleness,
                In hearts at peace, under an English heaven.

'The Soldier', Rupert Brooke (1887–1915)

*

And it's everyone, of course it is it's my birthday what did you effing *think* would happen, young men and women in winter coats and jumpers, with their baked potatoes all swathed in crinkly foil, their mugs of steaming wine and chocolate, cold strangers whose faces turn dear in the glow – turn to *Ollie*, has to be, yes *Iona* with her trusty woollen scarf, to Wayne and Roy Ford, to Molly and Jake and Syrie and Blanche and Mimi sodding Bevan, lit sweet faces flickering orange, to Lily and Sami each with a hand kept warm in the other's coat, to Bella and Kornelia, Peter Grain in his West Ham bobble-hat, there's Nathan in his mad sunspecs, Caroline in her dufflecoat applauding, there's Kerri Bedward with six sparklers all dazzling her at once, and Niall and Heath shrieking, stumbling, banging together tankards, Rowena blinking at the galaxy unconvinced from her silver chair, and Barry beaming at me as ever, half-blockhead half-angel, for it's all gone off as planned, and the fiction lot and the drama lot and the god knows who and the who cares what, they're all singing Happy Birthday and they know every last damn verse I taught them.

*

And the rest is rather a blur. They mostly wanted me to drink as much as them, and very soon I probably had. The fireworks blazed away on high, but every girl and boy and lady and gent smiled up at them and slowly was accustoming to awe, going on with conversations, and the display must have ended while I was chatting at the mulled-wine stall with a couple of the suits in anoraks, admin types from the Academy. 'The mauve form!' this guy was imploring, 'you *know* the future is mauve!' At some point Barry rocked up with a fat envelope and said he'd collected all my birthday cards! I do remember parting from Jimmy, he'd bumped into some ladies who knew him, they insisted he went dancing, and the last I saw of him he was pretending to be dragged away, 'blimey here we go' – there are gaps then – I do remember there were people I thought I knew, from long ago, from not that long and we all kept making the same old joke – that we'd all be 'home for Christmas!' – and someone *promised* me this, I can't remember who, saying 'we *do* know you'll be back! We *do* know you'll be back!' then I think I got upset because I heard that Barry and Rowena had gone in the milk-float and I kept shouting (I'm told) 'How the hell do I get home now?' and this must have been annoying because it truly wasn't a problem, it was organized, I had my own seat near the back of the dimly-lit warm coach – 'No one wants to sit with you, Max,' said Mimi, swaying in the aisle so I could swig from her hipflask, 'we decided you're no fun' and I'm saying you fucking drugged me, and she's saying 'what did you think they were tic-tacs? you said to scare you Max,' and Syrie and Blanche were turned round from the seats in front of me, saying '3P is the *bomb*, man, we were *out*, we watched ourselves in The Sound of Music,' and then – I think the coach had to stop and reverse itself laboriously in the dark, there was a great communal groan at that, and I remember being woken up by someone sliding in next to me: 'It's not a lot to ask to be waited for. I'm not blaming you Maxwell,' and later, with the coach dark, rumbling, warm, silent, the one solitary light I could see was Tina Yeager beside me, she had a tiny bulb clamped to her clipboard and was working away on some schedule while everyone else was whispering or snoring, she was scribbling numbers with a blue pen, putting it back between her teeth so she could write some words with a black pen. She didn't look, she just said through clenched teeth: 'Not a lot to ask to be waited for, when you've gone to so much bother.'

*

Somehow I still had the packet of birthday cards, as I remember them all tumbling out on to my doormat when at last I staggered in. I even remember saying distinctly: 'Not my birthday any more!' to no one, but I did crouch down to gather up the cards, I even filled out my mantelpiece with the cards, which were bright or sweet or funny or whatever – the only exception being Barry's, whose birthday greetings were scribbled on the back of some old postcard. But I only know this because I found it on the day I left, it had fallen behind my bookcase, and even then I didn't bother to read the back of it, I didn't read the back till long after, long ago, when I was home again and *that* – that is Time's last word on my birthday.

POST CARD

FROM:

Pte. 2493 Maxwell   Victoria Stn, 6 a.m.

6th batt. King's Lancashire reg. C coy.

5th June, 1916

Dear Ma, Arrived Euston at 4 am. Have not seen Ted yet – no doubt he will come here to see us off. We had Eggs & Bacon at the YMCA so feel a trifle refreshed – but nevertheless feel pretty down in the mouth – I will be glad when the journey's over.   Love to all   Jimmy

THE ADDRESS ONLY TO BE WRITTEN HERE.

Mr & Mrs Maxwell, 2 Hereford Lane, Wavertree, Liverpool, England

---

*   *   *

Week Eight – November 14th

Summer pleasures they are gone, like to visions every one,
And the cloudy days of autumn and of winter cometh on:
I tried to call them back, but unbidden they are gone
Far away from heart and eye and for ever far away,
Dear heart, and can it be that such raptures meet decay?
I thought them all eternal when by Langley Bush I lay;
I thought them joys eternal when I used to shout and play
On its bank at 'clink and bandy', 'chock' and 'taw' and ducking-stone,
Where silence sitteth now on the wild heath as her own
Like a ruin of the past, all alone

*

Back to work, at a new age.

As I heard, then saw, that it was grey and dull and dutifully raining, I renewed my dialogue with the transformations of the sky and accepted the point this one was trying to make: that the last two weeks had swung me wildly hither and thither from where I'd settled in my merry world, and it was high time I returned to the work it had assigned me.

This pendulum was heavy, solemn, centred, holding to whatever cord came down through the low cloud from whatever the cords are roped to. Today I would tick and tock quite soberly and strictly, at least while there was daylight. It was this austere intent that made me rise from horizontal, stand tall, walk, stoop, open the books on the desk, breathe in, put away my birthday cards – I lost one down the back of the shelves and resolved to retrieve it later – then I sang a song as I dressed, *Corinna Corinna, girl where you been so long?* impulsively grabbed some papers from the floor, folded them into my leather satchel, got the hell out, and shared with the wet deserted lane the mysterious words I had to hand: *Not a lot to ask to be waited for, when you've gone to so much bother.*

*

When I used to lie and sing by old Eastwell's boiling spring,
When I used to tie the willow-boughs together for a 'swing'
And fish with crooked pins and thread and never catch a thing,
With heart just like a feather – now as heavy as a stone.
When beneath old Lea Close Oak I the bottom branches broke
To make our harvest cart, like so many working folk,
And then to cut a straw at the brook to have a soak,
O I never dreamed of parting or that trouble had a sting
Or that pleasures like a flock of birds would ever take to wing
Leaving nothing but a little naked spring

*

I must provide evidence to demonstrate how I meet the criteria for
the grade in which I wish to obtain employment, Nathan.

'Say what?'

It's not expected that I should present all types of evidence listed
for my selected categories, Nathan.

'You applying for something?'

Doing it, man, going mauve, I'm going official, I thought it
would be fun but it's just turning into – *words*.

'That can happen, that's for sure. Am I fixing you your usual?'

Eggs in a way never known before and a shedload of coffee.

'You know it, professor.'

*

I know it. Why can't I do it if I know it?

'Pardon?'

Kerri you gotta help me.

But Kerri goes on battling the photocopier 'it's really not complex,
not like *this* is complex,' she hits it and it hums indignantly,

Am I Academic with Research or Research with Education?

'You're I dunno, *work*, sod you, stupid machine – '

And what's Knowledge Exchange?

'Not a clue, it's maybe teaching, it says *clear* I *did* clear!'

You can help me in your sleep Kerri, then you won't know you did.
'I see someone coming up the road who can. I reckon it's teaching.'

*

'Glenn Glenn Glenn…'

Sorry do I know you?

'Nice one! Mike, from your birthday bash! How about some coffee, Kezza?'

'No thanks.'

'Nice one. You were pretty *cheerful* on your birthday, weren't you.'

It was – my birthday.

'That's his story and he's sticking to it!'

What?

'Let's see what we have here…'

(Mike is in Human Resources. They wear anoraks indoors. He sits on Kerri's desk and flicks through my mauve form with amusement.)

'Fail,' he grins, 'Start *agin*, buffalo girls, start *agin*!'

It's blank Mike, I've not filled it in, how's that a fail?

'Oh you *are* one new contestant! It's a fail if it's the wrong form.'

It's – the mauve form.

'Does that look mauve to you?'

Yes.

'It's the lilac form. The lilac form's for Permanency or Promotion, *you* need First-Time Employment and that form's clearly mauve. We sang about the mauve form, you said the future was mauve!

'We were rockin' the night away, my friend. You shouldn't have been given this. Kezza Kezza Kezza…'

'How about some tea Mike.'

'No thanks! little in-joke…'

Look I've been employed all over the place.

'Not here you haven't!'

When I first got here, *Mike*, in September, there was a Reading List with my name printed on it. I was allocated a room, a dump I grant you, but a room to teach in and no one gave a damn.

'A dump with a working kettle,' Kerri reminds me, 'and a table and chairs. What else do poets need? Especially if it's a dream.'

'Well we're still working out how that happened,' Mike informs us, looking along the shelves for the correct pale-purple document.

Also, *guys*, Kerri talked to the agents who talked to the visiting poets.

'Talking of which,' says Kerri, 'your man John is going to be walking here, you have to watch the fields between four and five o'clock.'

Which fields, it's going to be dark.

'I don't know which fields,' she says, 'you can use this torch.'

(This doesn't sit with Mike) 'I hate to rain on said parade but if Glenn's not affiliated this so-called walking man called John is not a Visiting Lecturer. In fact technically he's a trespasser. And that's an Academy flashlight.'

'I *am* still talking to the agents,' says Kerri stoutly, 'so it's official.'

'Does Tina know you are?'

'We have contracts with them, Mike, whether he teaches them or not.'

'His name can't be on the contracts, Kerri, till he's affiliated. Tina said.'

'His name isn't on the contracts. Mike.'

'*He* says it was. Kerri.'

'He's Glyn, Mike, he's got no idea, he thinks he's dreaming.'

'It's not Glyn it's Glenn – oh maybe it's *Glynn*, two *n*'s, where's his form,'

I am actually here, you know.

'Glynn! Help us! Hand down a ruling!'

*

I am actually not here, as I've decided to get some mint tea for Kerri and a moccachino for Mike. It sounds like they need it. Kerri had me sign the mauve form, said I could fill in the rest when I'd done my one-to-ones. She'd do the difficult stuff. I said *Don't go to too much bother*, just to feel what it would be like to choose to say *bother* rather than *trouble*. It felt vaguely concerning, it alerted my cells. One cell sitting by a radar-screen in baleful blue light said: *guys, you wanna see this…*

Mike said as I was going that he wished it could be my birthday every day.

I forgot her tea and his coffee.

*

When jumping time away on old Crossberry Way
And eating 'awes like sugar-plums ere they had lost the may,
And skipping like a leveret before the peep of day
On the roly-poly up and downs of pleasant Swordy Well.
When in Round Oak's narrow lane as the south got black again
We sought the hollow ash that was shelter from the rain
With our pockets full of peas we had stolen from the grain,
How delicious was the dinner time on such a showery day –
O words are poor receipts for what time hath stole away,
The ancient pulpit trees and the play

*

Iona looked sad. Not when she saw me coming to her table at the Keys – at that she smiled her one bright social smile – but I'd seen her first, and she'd looked unusually downcast. I need to believe some people always cope, can always help, will sail through life looking out for ways they can bestow their cheerful care. It's probably always the same proportion of my acquaintance, and probably isn't quite true of anyone, but she was one of those, and she oughtn't to look so sad. *Somebody* must be coping.

I assumed she was homesick. I didn't have it so bad that morning – with Halloween and my birthday out of the way I had my annual lamplit view downhill to Christmas *I am going home at Christmas!* – so I did my level best.

Missing Mr Iona? (I regretted it already)

'Sorry?'

How's long-distance wedding planning? (I was on the opposite of a roll –)

'Aye, well.'

Right (maybe shut up)

'Long distance,' said Iona.

Oh? Okay.

'I've brought a poem. Are we still in the business of that, professor?'

We are. Normal service. Resumed. What you got.

She had a poem about herself as a child in Fife. But somehow the child was also herself now, grown-up and walking by fishing-boats in the snow unrecognized – it wasn't clear, I thought she might bring in stanza-breaks to let the transitions happen, the white space could be the ice around her, or perhaps –

'Wedding's off.'

What?

'We regret to say.'

Shit. Elegant sad Iona McNair shook the dark hair from her eyes, took a sip of her Coke, looked askance through the almost empty pub, gazed her way through the walls, stared all the way home.

How my heart sagged for her. The legendary Alastair, whom all of us had joked about – Lily and Sami and Heath and Ollie, even Niall used to do it – tales of upright gingery Ally in his fictional tweeds shooting fictional grouse with his fictional soft Morningside accent, waiting for his bride to return from down along the glen – no, Over. He'd abandoned our thoughtful gentle queenly Iona: she was far from home, her wedding was off, her hopes destroyed. I hated him.

Hey (said I),

'I don't think I'm cut out for poetry, really.'

You write such lovely phrases, you've a good ear, these are stronger every time!

She took her poem back, didn't want to go on, 'but I like it here. I'll do something else in the spring. Are you teaching in the spring? They say you're teaching in the spring.'

I don't know, maybe, I *am* joining the Academy, I'm filling in the lilac form!

'You *are* grown-up,' she smiled, I wished her so well.

Don't stop writing poems. Please, McNair, for me.

'Och…'

You only say *och* for my benefit, don't you.

'Mm-hm. Has your Mr Clare arrived? I've been reading what you said to.'

I went and got us drinks, Marys Bloody and Virgin with straws for old times' sake, and when I got back Orlando had slid in next to her with a beer. He was her only rival in the field of cheery companionship, though I did have to concede that he'd been a little bit off with me lately, and I suspected there was nothing left of his on-and-off deal with Mimi. *That* I could understand, but he looked jolly enough right now, and I hoped he was doing okay.

Cheers, santé, sláinte, and it was as we all were sipping that the picture unravelled.

Now my admiration for those blessed souls who can write in the Third Person is authentic and profound. Yet, on the earth *I* live on, no one knows the slightest thing. There's only love and guesswork, and I try my best at both.

Ollie and Iona were holding hands, were quite evidently *one*, and my eyes went brightly, innocently from her happy face to his, Iona (love and guesswork) exhilarated yet distressed by what her heart had made her do to her poor fiancé, sadly birdying alone on some rain-swept green, and Orlando (love and guesswork) proud and young again, over the moon, *Mimi who?* and most delighted I'm at hand to savour the happy ending.

When Peter Grain steps in with his poems and his pencil-case I buy all four of us a lunch of beer and ploughmans, as if they've married with two witnesses who happened to be passing. Now we are four good toasting friends. We look at Peter's clumsy sonnets in a cheerful little class of our own, and I part from the trio joyfully, watch them set off over the wet green, a very jovial crew.

Norman.

'Small or large.'

I don't know anything, Norman.

*

Under the twigs the blackcap hangs in <u>vain</u>
With snow-white patch streaked over either <u>eye</u>.
This way and that he turns, and peeps <u>again</u>
As wont where silk-cased insects used to <u>lie</u>,
But summer leaves are gone: the day is <u>bye</u>

For happy holidays, and now he <u>fares</u>
But cloudy like the weather, yet to <u>view</u>
He flirts a happy wing and inly <u>wears</u>
Content in gleaning what the orchard <u>spares</u>,
And like his little cousin capped in <u>blue</u>
Domesticates the lonely winter <u>through</u>
In homestead plots and gardens, where he <u>wears</u>
Familiar pertness – yet he seldom <u>comes</u>
With the tame robin to the door for <u>crumbs</u>.

Heath

Samira	Lily
Peter	Iona
Niall	Ollie
Barry	

moi

John Clare's 'The Blackcap'. Look at the rhymes.

'Highlighters?' Ollie and Heath say in unison but only Ollie enjoys this.

Hush. Underline the last word of every line.

'More mysterious instructions,' muses Barry, getting down to it.

'It should look like this!' Ollie holds up his paper.

What are you Faraday, magic? when did you do that?

'The old class, Maxwell, don't you remember?'

'Ha!' cries Lily, 'dementia, I just knew it.'

'It's a, fascinating rhyme-scheme he's got,' says Peter, underlining with the flat edge of his protractor, 'in fact it's not – quite one at all.'

Rock on, squire. It's not quite one at all. If the Keepers of the Sonnet were watching they would utterly lose their (I'm not affiliated) shit. The poem *starts* like it's in uniform, four pentameters rhymed ABAB (*ain-eye-ain-eye*), then the fifth *bye* suggests we'll stay and play a while in those two sounds – maybe he wants to mash the two famous sonnet-forms together, the two forms being Lily?

'Shakespearean and the other one.'

'Petrarchan,' Peter gets there (bloke works harder than the lot of 'em)

Right, the one that tends to go ABAB-CDCD and the one that tends to go ABBA-ABBA. 'The Blackcap' rhymes this way: ABAB-BCDC-CDDC-EE. This literally isn't the done thing.

But what if John Clare regards the demands of traditional verse-form as something more like guidance, remembrance of a path? So you *might* rhyme or not, you might suddenly *repeat,* the point being *you won't know until you get there.* Now it's not his usual practice to improvise like this, but he does it where I like him best, so I listen, and I pass it on.

Too many of us, of you, of me, think Form an edict to obey like a soldier or scorn like a refusenik. But aren't your passing days more or less like old forms you think you know? Yet they carry shocks and joys within, stuff that jolts you from your expectations. Encounters might do it, the weather might do it. You should respond to what just happened, not what was meant to happen. So not strict Form. But *never* no-Form. That isn't even daylight.

What else. Clare's couplet doesn't arrive or conclude like say Frost or Milton, or go balancing into silence like the infinite custom of Mr Bard of Avon – it goes on describing, while lines are still left to work with. The poet doesn't look away from the object and tell *why I've told you this.* He's no more interested in our feeding intellectually than the bird is. The way Clare uses closing couplets is not as a destination, an expansion or conclusion, but as a stamp on the memory when the bird has flown away. They're the edges of fields that shouldn't be having edges.

'Remembrances'. Eight stanzas, each ten lines, but every fourth line is fantastically *rogue.* AAAXBBBCCC, where X is a rhyme that *does anything.* But always for a reason. There are no couplets in the poem because all the rhymes are in triplets. In the first stanza, X rhymes with B to make up a four, but in the other seven it stands alone, and an unrhymed word among triplets is *very alone,* a notable intruder.

The seven lonely Xs are *stone, Swordy Well, name, Hilly Snow, stone, prey, stay.* Either proper nouns of threatened places, or the implacable *stone,* or *prey* (what the places are), *stay* (what they're not going to do), or *name* (all that's going to be left). In every case there is a *reason* for the loud isolation of the rogue rhyme X.

General point: poets who have no use for rhyme have thrown a great big key-ring into the Thames, and with it went their ingress through hundreds of doors.

More animals in daylight:

The schoolboys still their morning rambles take
To neighbouring village school with playing speed,
Loitering with pastimes' leisure till they quake,
Oft looking up the wild geese droves to heed,
Watching the letters which their journeys make,
Or plucking 'awes on which the fieldfares feed,
And hips and sloes – and on each shallow lake
Making glib slides where they like shadows go
Till some fresh pastimes in their minds awake
And off they start anew and hasty blow
Their numbed and clumpsing fingers till they glow,
Then races with their shadows wildly run
That stride, huge giants, o'er the shining snow
In the pale splendour of the winter sun.

'Schoolboys in Winter'. When I first saw this I noticed all the line-ending vowels were long except *run/sun*, and felt this was about boys going unwillingly to school and in cheery desperation trying to prolong the time before the bell. It *is* about that – how about that line 13, *That stride, huge giants, o'er the shining snow,* six long vowels, the poor line's trying to last forever! – but in fact this listening poet *loves* long vowels at the ends of lines, which is I think an act of relish, a love of the sound as it flies away, a heat to help him across the gaps. And look at the descending scale of the last line – day passing in vowels of the *Alphabet*, the first thing children learn in school. Why wouldn't it sound a deep-down chord?

So, cussedly eccentric, but eccentric control. Find an old English word for the *chutzpah* it takes to rhyme a sonnet ABAB-ABAC-ACCD-CD. That to me is – riding the force of the ancient till you feel – *God, why don't I add MY force to ITS?*

Samira has her hand up: 'What's the meaning of clumpsing.'

'*Clumpsing*, Sash!' Lily storms in disbelief, 'like *this!*' How d'ya not *know* that?'

*

When for school o'er 'Little Field' with its brook and wooden brig
Where I swaggered like a man though I was not half as big,
While I held my little plough though 'twas but a willow twig,
And drove my team along made of nothing but a name –
'Gee hep' and 'hoit' and 'woi' – O I never call to mind
Those pleasant names of places but I leave a sigh behind,
While I see the little mouldywarps hang sweeing to the wind
On the only aged willow that in all the field remains,
And nature hides her face while they're sweeing in their chains
And in a silent murmuring complains

*

So I watch the fields for John Clare, who wrote 'The Fallen Elm' and 'The Mores' and 'The Lamentation of Swordy Well' and 'The Lamentations of Round-Oak Waters' and 'Remembrances' with the dead moles hung in chains from a willow and many other poems because the powerful and wealthy had begun in earnest carving England up for profit, which would threaten and then obliterate the England he knew. As it does, and probably will, and mostly has, the one I know.

Knew. I watch the north-east field by which I met Keats all those weeks ago, as the rain fizzles out and weak sunlight deigns to put in an appearance, and I walk and I trot and I scamper and stride through chill drizzle till I'm watching the south-west field where we had the Hopkins picnic in a dream of late late summer, and I catch the silly old orb as it sinks in dark grey-lemon clouds.

Not a lot to ask to be waited for, when you've gone to so much bother.

Moving between these vigils I find myself stopping to sit on a bench by the lagoon to the west, looking out to that lonely wooded island like a fool, till I realize he's not going to come wandering over the dark rolling water is he you twat, whatever his initials.

Because this is not a *fantasy*, I state aloud for the record.

As I'm skirting between the various watch-points, trudging through mud behind a lane of terraced houses with tiny gardens of scruffy washing-lines and rusty bikes, I think I hear a woman's voice calling, but can't see who or where. I'm about to reach the farmer's fields to the south, beyond the railway station (*it's in the last place you look!* my mother used to prophesy) when I'm called again, and there's Samira walking thisaway in her shiny chocolate raincoat down the length of the station platform.

'We have a crisis, professor,' she calls, though this is slightly belied by the fact she doesn't break into a run, or into much more than a brisk walk, but then she doesn't really strain herself in the course of student life.

What's wrong, Samira.

'Bronzo's pride and joy,' she says as she walks up, sighing at being the one to have to tell me: 'her grand poetry slam. She's having a meltdown. That bitch from Admin's cancelled it.'

You mean Yeager? Yeager cancelled the poetry slam?

'She thinks we tried to dump her on that Field Trip last week.'

You did try to dump her. In fact you succeeded.

'No one *meant* to. They just forgot about her.'

She *says* that's why she pulled it?

'Of course not, but we know that's why.'

Er, what do you think *I* can do?

'*You*? Nothing. But Bronzo has you down for a man on a white charger.'

The Academy Presents

THE FACULTY
AUTUMN POETRY READING

AT
THE VILLAGE HALL

Pamela BANGLER *('The Pond of Disavowal')*
format *('bye bye bye cell cell cell')*
Suzi JUDAS *('Unintelligibilities 5')*
Dr Clyde W. MAPPING *('A History of Hesitation')*
Jeff OLOROSO *('Angels & Arseholes: New & Selected Poems')*
Nikki PHAPPS *('i'm melting')*
Gough SLURMAN *('The Virus Speaks')*
Delphine WICKER *('Cleopatra: The Lost Selfies')*

7pm, November 14th   Sushi and sake

---

*

It's fair to say I don't know how this happened. At the bright end of the darkened village hall someone's reading to the faculty. It's clearly not Lily's poetry slam, The Night of the Living Living, which would probably have come with red lights and heckles and drunken whoops from the audience – most of whom would be on the bill sooner or later, we've all been there – but there's a murmurous consternation, an undertow of protest. Eight professors are seated on the stage, clinging to or sort of climbing in their chairs, two now standing up, one sat back there grinning till it's over – that's Wayne aka *format* relishing the chaos – because in had walked John Clare, flushed and muddy from his endless walk, and now he's planted there bolt upright in his rags very loudly reciting –

> 'Here was commons for their hills where they seek for freedom still,
> Though every common's gone and though traps are set to kill
> The little homeless miners – O it turns my bosom chill
> When I think of old 'Sneap Green', Paddock's Nook and Hilly Snow,
> Where bramble bushes grew and the daisy gemmed in dew
> And the hills of silken grass like to cushions to the view,
> Where we threw the pismire crumbs when we'd nothing else to do –
> All levelled like a desert by the never-weary plough,
> All banished like the sun where that cloud is passing now,
> And settled here for ever on its brow…'

As Lily Bronzo would tell me later at the haven of the Cross Keys bar, 'Titmouse stuck her reading on an *hour* before mine, chief right, Kerri says bitch said she knew nothing about it, but there's like a shitload of flyers everywhere so she's lying through her perfect little teeth right, anyhow I go looking for my poets to tell them it's off, so I don't see him coming, and you didn't see him in the fields chief did you (you had One Job etc) so the bloke must've just seen the lamps and gone right in. He was speaking some poem aloud when he came through the door, he just went clumpsing up to the stage and went on speaking. And those wankers didn't know how to stop him.'

They didn't, nor did I. And I wasn't about to though most likely I'm one too.

I saw Jeff Oloroso rise up in the stanza-break and make a gentle move towards John Clare but he wasn't fast enough and on went the lamentation:

'O I never thought that joys would run away from boys
Or that boys should change their minds and forsake such summer joys,
But alack I never dreamed that the world had other toys
To petrify first feelings like the fable into stone,
Till I found the pleasure past and the winter come at last –
Then the fields were sudden bare and the sky got overcast
And boyhood's pleasing haunts like a blossom in the blast
Was shrivelled to a withered weed and trampled down and done,
Till vanished was the morning spring and set the summer sun
And winter fought her battle-strife and won…'

Once this stanza had begun Jeff's smile steadied into place, and he raised his hands as if to say 'why not', then made his slow beaming way along the side of the hall, doing an odd little rhythmic dance with his arms, as if dancing to the beat of the poem, towards me and Samira.

'Oompa oompa, one of your special guests, Glyn?' he didn't whisper.

Uh-huh. Is there a problem.

'Excuse me,' Samira began,

'No problem on earth,' said Jeff, 'he'll be out by midnight though right? we've got a good few to get through!'

'Excuse me when will you reschedule Night of the Living Living?' demanded Sami fiercely but Jeff enquired of me as if Samira wasn't there: 'We hear you'll be joining us next term?'

That's John Clare there (was all I could think to say)

Jeff glanced at the situation, turned back to me, weirdly put his hand on my shoulder and said, as if I saw this life like he did, 'now *he'd* be good in a slam!'

This observation lost him his chance to intercede in the stanza-break, during which John Clare had to pause to catch his breath and mop his brow, but now three stood up on the front row. One was Tina Yeager in a pale pink frock and a blue wrap, one a young man in a blazer saying 'bravo, bravo, nice one to end on,' but Clare wasn't ending *jack*, he was gathering speed over sporadic heckling:

'By Langley Bush I roam, but the bush hath left its hill;
On Cowper Green I stray, 'tis a desert strange and chill;
And spreading Lea Close Oak, ere decay had penned its will,
To the axe of the spoiler and self-interest fell a prey;
And Crossberry Way and old Round Oak's narrow lane
With its hollow trees like pulpits, I shall never see again:
Enclosure like a Bonaparte let not a thing remain,
It levelled every bush and tree and levelled every hill
And hung the moles for traitors – though the brook is running still,
It runs a naked stream, cold and chill…'

During this stanza they tried all sorts – slow-hand clapping, loudly joking, strolling to the buffet to chat about sashimi – and when the break came I saw Mike, my new pal from Human Resources, whom I saw now was one of the three who'd risen from the front row, move to stand there almost blocking Clare from view, more than happy to bring things to a helpful close.

But the third who'd risen up I recognized too – not at first, as I hadn't expected to see him here – but when he intervened, seemed almost to bump Mike back to his seat, muttering 'Sit the fuck down, mate, free speech,' it transformed into Heath Bannen. He must have gone there because he's *format*'s student. Mike simply grinned and obeyed, smiling 'very well said, exactly,' and Tina, left standing in her pink dress, had no choice but to sit down too, folding her arms to wait it out.

'O had I known as then joy had left the paths of men,
I had watched her night and day, be sure, and never slept again,
And when she turned to go, O I'd caught her mantle then
And wooed her like a lover by my lonely side to stay,
Ay, knelt and worshipped on as love in beauty's bower,
And clung upon her smiles as a bee upon a flower,
And gave her heart my poesies all cropped in a sunny hour
As keepsakes and pledges all to never fade away –
But love never heeded to treasure up the may,
So it went the common road with decay.'

Now Tina pounced, like she was counting lines for the break. She couldn't know he'd actually finished the poem – only he and I knew that – but she'd gone quickly to the upright piano, canvas-draped in its shabby corner, smartly plucked the ageing flowers from the vase there, and had thrust them into the arms of John Clare before another word was spoken. Not just a pretty face.

'That was such a sweet poem, give it up for our surprise guest!'

Jeff went clapping to the stage to make sure: 'As Tina says, a lovely surprise, that was fab, my friend, you're like a rapper with all your rhyming, well done!'

'I think we're thoroughly warmed up now!' Tina declared.

He'd finished anyway (I hissed at her childishly as I reached the scene)

'Any more up your sleeve, Maxwell?'

Come to the pub, John, come to the pub,

John was nodding at the applause because he took it for applause, but he also looked curiously at Heath and Mike and back at Heath and said to them together, though I don't think either one could hear, 'All have liberty to think as they please,' and then up came Lily and Roy Ford from wherever they'd been sitting, and Sami and Heath close by to help me walk him out of there.

*

This squad of doughty rescuers made a beeline for the Cross Keys, and though I began trying to explain the confusion I thought better of it, and made the best of where we'd got to:

Brilliant reading, John, but these are the ones I want you to meet!

He was frowning and glancing back at the hall as we crossed the road towards the green lamplight of the Cross Keys. Lily, still bristling at the loss of her main event, spoke up for the gang we were now: 'Tossers in there, mate, you stick with us!'

'Could see it in their faces,' John said to her, or possibly to her cropped scarlet hair he was trying to make sense of, 'Didn't like his looks from the first.'

'Which one, can you narrow it down,' said Sami drily.

'I'm a good physiognomist,' he said more to himself, still holding the dead flowers to his chest.

We got him through the door into the welcome heat, to the snug with the plum-upholstered armchairs, sat him down in the best one by a merrily raving fire, spread ourselves round in the others. Roy and I went for drinks, Lily perched on the arm of his armchair. When we brought our laden trays to the group it had been augmented by Niall Prester, deep in a fisherman's blue jumper, and Caroline Jellicoe, whom we hadn't seen all day. Lily was sharing her woes with Clare because they were woes and there he was:

'And you'da been totally welcome mate, you'da totally *headlined* right,'

John (I began, presenting him with two foaming pints so I could stay there for a while) a lot of my friends here are just starting out on, you know, the journey, so – d'you remember writing your first poems? Can you tell us about that at all?

He drank and stared at me, sporting a foam moustache, as if sizing up why I was asking. I hoped my face met his physiognomical standards, and began to assume it didn't when he suddenly spoke up:

'I was very timid. Very timid disposition.' He wiped his mouth.

Yes? (The others went silent and leaned in to hear)

'Had, two or three, haunted spots to pass. Impossible to go half a mile anywhere where nothing'd been seen by these, these old women…'

When you were a boy, you mean? You were frightened by – local stories?

He made a little grimace.

'Best remedy to keep such things out of my head, I – muttered over tales of my own fancy, contriving 'em into rhymes as well as I were able… romantic wanderings of sailors, soldiers, step by step…'

Right, right, to take your mind off the ghostly places you were walking through at night? You made up poems to take your mind off –

'Will-with-a-whisp, Jimmy Whisk, Jack-with-a-lanthorn… this November month they're often out in the dark misty nights. Rotten Moor, Dead Moor…'

That's my birthday month for you!

'Melancholy season,' he confided to the girls close by.

November, yup, but you – you cheered yourself up?

'I – loved to see a tale end happy. Intrigues, meeting always good fortune and marrying ladies.'

Lily cackled with joy and her woes were done: 'Were *you* in the stories though Mr Clare?'

'We was not without loves,' he mused to her delight, 'we had our favourites in the village. When a face pleased me I scribbled a song or so in her praise, tried to get in her company.'

He glanced around, but again his eyes fixed on Lily's dyed hair and he seemed very slightly to shake his head, as if processing the peculiar. Then he just as slightly nodded, perhaps thinking some sprite was present and he was noting the phenomenon. I pressed on:

I see this lot writing in the pub, in the café, sometimes walking down the high street, where do *you* like writing, John?

His finger travelled the dust of the table, it seemed to cheer him to remember: 'Always wrote my poems in the fields. Particular spots I's fond of, from the beauty or the secrecy… It's common in villages to pass judgment on a lover of books as – indication of laziness. I was drove to – hide in woods, dingles of thorns in the fields. 'Stead of going out on the green at the town end on winter Sundays to play football, I stuck to my corner, poring over a book… Feelings stirred into praise, and my, my promises muttered in prose or rhyme – grew into quantity. Indulged my vanity in thinking how they'd look in print. Selected what I thought best. Hid the others out of shame's way – laughing-stocks!'

We laughed with him, except for Caroline, who had her own notebook, her own questions: 'John, it was such a privilege to hear your poetry. What was it like when you first saw a poem of yours in print?'

He frowned, closed his eyes as if to see it better, opened them again.

'Scarcely knew it in its new dress.'

It's quite a feeling (said I, having decided to remind my class every three weeks or so that I'm actually a writer too) I remember the first time I –

Caroline said: 'D'you remember how you felt, John?'

'My highest ambition was gratified.'

'To see your poem published?'

He shook his head slowly. 'To let my parents see a printed copy of my poems. That pleasure I've witnessed. It is – thrilling – to hear a crippled father seated in his easy chair, comparing the past with the present – *Boy, who could have thought... when we was threshing together... you'd be noticed by thousands of friends... names of great distinction... enabled to make us happy!'*

Quiet descends on all as we see through our minds' eyes. He drinks at peace for a while.

Was your family at all – literary, John?

'Illiterate to the last degree. The Fens're not a literary part of England.'

Roy Ford says: 'Loved your reading, mate. First book you ever read?'

'*Robinson Crusoe.* Borrowed it off a boy at school who said it was his uncle's. Very loath to lend it me...'

'Oh shit!' cries Lily, 'do you know Byron?'

'Hey you stole Madam Bella's question,' Roy points out and they all laugh, but the question sets John thinking:

'First publication of my poems brought many – visitors to my house. Mere curiosity – son of a thresher – finding me a vulgar fellow that spoke in the rough ways – a thoroughbred clown – they soon turned to the door, dropping their heads in a – in a *good morning* attitude. Many of 'em left promises. I had the works of Lord Byron promised by six different people. Never got them from none of 'em.'

He drinks and sighs, and we prowl in his anger, then he meditates on Byron: 'The common people felt his merits and his power. They're the – prophecy of futurity. They're the veins and arteries.'

'Yeah well he's coming at the end of term,' says Lily proudly, 'innit chief,' and our glasses lightly clink.

Caroline says softly: 'You have a lovely speaking voice, John, can you remember the first public reading you ever gave?'

He thinks and he chuckles, he tells us: 'Imitations of my father's songs! floating among the vulgar at the markets and fairs... they laughed and told me I need never hope to make songs like them! Mortified me, almost made me desist.'

You're saying your first poems got heckled, John?

He grins: 'I hit upon a harmless deception, by repeating my poems over a book, as though I was reading it…'

Hang on you *pretended* to be reading published poems from a book?

'Had the desired effect! They praised 'em, said I could write! I hugged myself over the deception!'

Our laughter hugs him too. By this time he's got through his beers and I go with Heath to get him more.

For some reason I think Heath's help at the faculty reading means we're vaguely friends these days, so I test the water:

Good stuff eh, man. Politics in the house.

'Bit, y'know…'

No, bit what.

'Bit sing-song.'

Well. You heard him, he used to write to ward off being cold and seeing ghosts. Sing-song's how you do that.

'Is it.'

Sing-song keeps you walking. Sing-song gets remembered.

'Maybe for him. I wouldn't've done it like that.'

Heigh-friggin-ho. I like your pamphlet mate.

Heath's eyes meet mine for what I believe is the first time, then he shrugs away and seems to redden, almost halve in years.

'Just some – dunno – probably shit.'

Grow up, it isn't shit.

'Excuse me?'

I said Grow up, it isn't shit.

'Yeah. Well. Alright. There's the blurb sorted.'

And we each sniggered, a moment apart.

*

'Eliza now the summer tells
Of spots where love and beauty dwells…'

At the third or fourth time I went to the bar for replenishment –
this time with Lily, who'd gone back to ranting on the numberless
crimes of Tina Yeager – John Clare stood up swaying, steadying
himself, and began tremblingly to sing.

'Come and spend a day with me
Underneath the forest tree…'

Lots had joined us now, those who'd felt they couldn't leave the
faculty reading but hadn't stayed for the sushi and sake – I saw Bella,
Peter, Nathan, Ollie and Iona, I saw Molly and Blanche, I even saw
Mrs Gantry at a table with some other ladies, and nearby them that
portly bearded man was cooing his own harmonies. Norman was
impressed for the first time ever by someone I'd brought into his
pub. He leaned heavily by his cash-till, nodding his rare approval,
while behind him students crowed their orders in vain from the
other bar. On went the old song:

'And where love and freedom dwells
With orchis flowers and fox glove bells
Come dear Eliza set me free
And o'er the forest roam with me…'

*

At the end I wanted him to myself, if only for a while, so in the
freezing cold along the lane I waited for them all to go. By the
edge of the north-east field, the mist luminous with moonlight, he
mumbled a request to touch Lily's odd hair, now glossy and dark,
and Sami snipped a strand as a keepsake for him, using clippers
from her bag. Iona embraced him and her scarf clung to his coat.
Heath shook hands with him brusquely, nodding, as if untold stuff
passed between two men of verse. Roy clapped him on the back and
told him not be a stranger.

Then the students set off on their blessed way home towards the lights of where they live, and he and I stood there.

'I was in earnest always,' he said abruptly, 'I know I'm full of faults.'

You were brilliant, John. They loved you. You affected them. They won't forget you.

He was looking into the mist.

'We – used to go on Sundays to the Flower Pot, a little pub at Tikencoat. First saw Patty going across the fields.'

Ah, John.

'I've been no one's enemy but my own.'

John.

He looked at me strangely, as if not to say his name any more. Took a deep breath of the cold night air.

'Saw three fellows at the end of Royce Wood, laying out the plan for an *Iron Rail Way*. They'll – despoil a boggy place that's famous for orchises, at Royce Wood end.'

The moon was blurred with cloud. He took his first step into the field.

'All my favourite places've met with misfortune… old Ivy Tree cut down, and my bower was destroyed.'

We're so happy you came – sir, just – so lucky to hear your work.

I had nothing left. A short way into the field he turned and said quite fiercely: 'I recant nothing!'

I'm sorry?

'A cart met me! A cart met me. A man and woman and a boy. Woman jumped out and caught fast hold of my hands. Wished me to get in the cart,'

Right,

'Wished me to get in the cart but I refused!'

You refused, and this was,

'I thought her – drunk or mad!'

Sounds like it!

'I's told it was my second wife Patty.'

Oh? Did you not – that's that's Patty, who, whom you, met at the pub, the Flower-Pot is that right?

His answer was: 'I am Jack Randall, the champion of the ring.'

He stared, his fists were clenched, he sucked in moonlit air, then at once he seemed to ease up and his hands just hung.

'I'm Jack Randall.'

John there's no one to fight now John, there's –

'I'm Jack Randall now. I was Byron and Shakespeare formerly.'

I began to nod so slowly that I didn't move at all.

'Can't forget – her – her little playful fairy form,'

And that's – ?

'Her witching smile.'

Patty?

'Thus runs the world away.'

He looked for one last time at the lights of the village, then off into the mist towards wherever he was heading. Then he set off into the damp grass that was lit with the mist. I called after him:

Lots of ghosts out tonight, lots more poems to compose!

But he showed no sign of hearing, walked on, still stooping to look in the grasses now and then for whatever it was, something down there catching his eye, but he righted himself and stumbled on till just a figure against the mist, inside the mist, only the mist.

*

Here I see the morning sun
Among the beech-tree's shadows run
That into gold the short sward turns
Where each bright yellow blossom burns
With hues that would his beams outshine
Yet naught can match those smiles of thine,
I try to find them all the day
But none are nigh when thou'rt away
Though flowers bloom now on every hill
Eliza is the fairest still

*

'You owe me whisky, Maxwell.'

I knew she'd be there, and she was there. The faculty group had been dining late in a private room in the Coach House but I sat tucked around the bar reading my Yeats, eavesdropping on their chatter. They debated the bill and settled for something, paid their shares and filed out through the door, Jeff, Nikki Phapps in her leather, Gough Slurman, Dr Mapping, Suzi and Delphine, none close enough to notice me unless they looked across this way. Tina did that, clocked me, rolled her eyes as if to say *of course he'd be in a bar*, and then I saw her gesture to someone already gone out into the cold night, saw her turn, still in her big black fake-fur coat, and come to join me, businesslike with scorn: 'Explain.'

My drink was spiked (I said) I was out of it.

'Sure you were, sure it was. *Mind* if I join you? or are you saving this for another midnight lesson.'

She'd already perched on the stool beside me, kicking her silky black legs to get comfortable, plucking out her sparkly purse.

'And you owe me for standing me up.'

I told you, someone drugged me, *fainites,* it was Halloween.

'I don't mean then, I mean today, our brunch meeting.'

What brunch meeting.

'Claude, I want – what are you drinking there – '

Nothing, I'm researching for the poetry class I teach.

'*Poems of Yeats,* hmm sure you were, the cabernet? Two glasses.'

If you're that thirsty get a bottle, it's cheaper.

'You said, on the coach, you said you'd meet me in the café by the Ferry Boat Tavern at ten next Thursday. Which was today, in my world.'

I'm not in your world. I really said that on the coach?

'You don't even remember.'

It was my birthday. Too much bother.

'It's always too much bother with you Maxwell.'

(Claude filled our glasses and she raised hers for a toast. I ignored it. She'd let my students down and I was being aggrieved on their behalves.)

'Stands me up twice and now gives *me* the cold shoulder.' She drank. 'We were going to talk about making you formal.'

I don't want to be formal. I don't like the way you do things.

'Good. Fine. Next item. Can you stop these weird vagabonds of yours wandering round the village?'

He isn't a weird vagabond.

'He looked like one to me.'

He's a weird vagabond to you because you've filled in all the forms. But he didn't, and I haven't.

'I'm fine that you haven't. It's sweet having you roam about in your colourful style, but I don't quite see what you'd add to what we've got.'

You're saying you don't want me to be one of you.

'Affiliated, no. It's what I was going to inform you of at our meeting.'

And now you have. *Sláinte*, Ms Yeager. Did you listen to his poem?

'Pardon?'

It was about enclosure. It was about how English landowners and politicians passed Acts of Parliament that destroyed his world.

'I did *do* History, I got a B.'

Then you know.

'Sure, I remember every word from school, that's what got me where I am.'

Behind a desk in the middle of nowhere.

'I have *heard* of sarcasm.'

D'you get a B in that too?

'Such a smart-aleck.'

Enclosure's where it starts.

'Where what starts, you're so rude, Claude, refills please…'

Enclosure's where the end starts. Enclosure's where an Englishman first spies a piece of land and can't see Englishmen.

'Or Englishwomen – '

English children, English *souls*, can't see anyone at all. Can't see anything but money. Can't see anything at all but calculable value. That's where it starts for England. Where it starts for me.

'Oh brill, it's the life-story,'

It is. Government came in when I was young. Shrunk all life to the selfsame thing like a virus made them do it. Calculable value. Same process.

'Are we talking Gladstone or Disraeli, see I did do History. Claude's saying we should buy the bottle. I vote we maybe should, though of course I don't see a bottle, I just see calculable values, point being that Claude is closing.'

Cowardice broke out. Filthy gibbering cringe in the face of light, blindness to human eyes, *to a pair of human eyes,*

'Is that right Maxwell, I think that's a yes, Claude, we're in for a seminar,'

Enclosure makes a few rich, turns the numbers black on a national scale,

'Make it two bottles, there's a faculty thing tomorrow, I'll claim them,'

As if that's the same as common good,

'Receipt, Claude, oh is it? thanks,'

When in fact it's the murder of common good,

'Oh I know, I *know*, let's go, professor.'

I haven't paid,

'Yes you have, let's go so where *were* we…'

The digital and the analogue,

'Up we get, that sounds so *interesting*, up we get,'

Life is analogue, this is *quite like* that. Memory, mystery, mercy, failure, forgiveness, not this *equals* that in value, but this is *quite like* this, this is *quite like* that,

'Is this lecture printed somewhere, just thinking ahead for Christmas,'

We can never know another, we can only say *quite like*,

'You just held this door for me while thinking *at the same time*, you're quite like a Renaissance man aren't you Maxwell *crikey* it's cold,'

It's love and guesswork,

'Love? no he's lost me,'

The analogue imagines, forgives, is – ineffable,

'I'm putting my effing gloves on, don't know about you,'

The digital sees only 1 or 0, sees yes or no, profit or loss, buy or sell,

'Snakes and ladders I *get* it Maxwell,'

The cowardice of being blind to complexity,

'Is this a new sentence starting? Oh look there goes your vagabond…'

Where?

'Over the field there, bye-bye…'

That's not him, that's Barry Wilby doing his rounds, case in point,

'Well it's *someone's* vagabond, see they're everywhere these days.'

The cowardice of calculation, the gutlessness of letting *numbers* make the case. Market force, mere profit turned to some holy power. Drives the strong to do to the weak what thugs and conmen do – rob them, fool them, scam them, leave them starving or frozen, ignorant, sick, crippled. Price them out of homes, turn their hearts against the helpless, stab the skyline with investments,

'I think we'll take the short cut,'

Write filth about them, blacken names, disrobe, dishonour, tap the phone-calls of the dead and call it free speech… market force the yardstick, dead stake in a wilderness, withered hearts all shrinking from the glories. Self-serving dogma, all's blessed or damned, let the old caveman urges force the law, same black-or-white morality when nature's freakin rainbow, my England is in fucking *hiding*.

'I'm steering you home in case you don't yet know the way,'

That's the churchyard, it isn't the churchyard,

'Yes it's the scenic route,'

I don't live in this churchyard Tina I *dwell by it*,

'Ah my actual name, am I cats or dogs, am I analogue?'

You're analogue Minnaloushe,

'Ah a *pet*-name, that's forward,'

On a field that's been enclosed

'Oh I see we've jumped back there,'

The common man's a vagabond,

'Is it this house or the next one?'

Digital makes him look a fool, world of one-and-zero makes the fives and sixes and nine-and-a-halves *look* like vagabonds – makes those who do the work that makes life *bearable* – guiding, caring, consoling, healing – makes them seem like fools and wastrels, it wolfs down their time on earth, pays them nothing for it –

'And to think I was there when the Truth was revealed!'
Pays its ones and zeroes to the One-and-Zero people,
'This sounds like Dr Who now, do you actually have a key it's hard to believe you live somewhere, how did *that* slip through the system?'
I don't know how anything happened,
'Where's the light, do you *have* a light?'
We have to go up the stairs now,
'Did I say I was coming with you?'
I need guidance
'Glynn Maxwell, first man ever to get lost on a staircase,'
Twelve stairs from here
'Twelve stairs?'
Eight stairs, six stairs
'Look you left your light on,'
Yes beauty it is the light of the world
'You don't even lock it, moron, oh my god he's got CDs how *sweet*,'
Where was I where was I
'Not a clue, do you have any Bowie though,'
Probably actually yes
'I'm taking my boots off, but only coz they're hurting, it's your place you pour the wine,'
I have no idea how we got here
'*Officer*, sure – does this have Sound and Vision?'
It should do, it's a Best of
'Heroes, Golden Years… Sound and Vision!'
Disaster I might dance to that
'Disaster doesn't cover it, why won't it play, the red light's on'
It's on radio
'Why, there's no signal here'
I listen to the white noise Tina
'That's cos you're a vagabond!'
What? CAN'T HEAR
'I SAID THAT'S COS YOU'RE A *VAGABOND!*'

*   *   *

Week Nine – November 21st

I wander by the edge
Of this desolate lake
Where wind cries in the sedge:
Until the axle break
That keeps the stars in their round,
And hands hurl in the deep
The banners of East and West,
And the girdle of light is unbound,
Your breast will not lie by the breast
Of your beloved in sleep.

And there she is, whatever this is. The light is barely blue outside but blue it is, and I'm at my desk where I discover four books open.

Three written books as ever, one empty book I mean to fill and one day you'll find empty, I sit here with them, hauled towards them, jolted up and out for the purpose but nothing comes and there she is, there's Miss Christine Sara Yeager in pale and puzzled half-sleep, dignified in dreaming, soft breath without opinion or a care in the turning world.

I had beaten Time to my desk again, had outrun *myself* for I was there before I knew it, blank and staring like a creature on every day remaining, but I can't write a word, I can only gaze at her curved back in its bunched grey jersey, in her sighing fitful peace, I can summon up some fragments.

It's very early on the Thursday, on the one day. These are the physics of the place I reached and I'm reconciled to that, but there are memories – she and I on a brisk walk in fog by the lagoon, a fierce little handshake, her Moominland umbrella she's brought in case we need, a lazy brunch in a brazen café window, she and I avoiding the Coach House, she with her po-faced hiss, proceeding on tiptoe, a quiz-night somewhere no one knows us, we came third and got rosettes I kept – days that can't be Thursdays at all, nights I can't begin to place…

I don't recall the moment this couldn't help but happen.

'But it isn't official…'

Her back's been turned but now she turns this way and speaks in sleep and I can dimly see her features through her tumbled hair. In my own half-sleep she was someone else and I shivered with our warm backs touching, hers arched, mine straight. I detached and rose and looked and was calm. Now she's her, serene, her busy daily *doing* self laid down to rest for a set time. On my rug her pale underthings are perched on her overthings.

The grey jersey's mine but there's other stuff of hers in my quiet attic room. There's a pink hold-all pushed under this desk, that plump thriller she likes face-down on the rug by her little snow-white sneakers, her long dark coat on a hook by the door, like her minder cast the old blind eye.

Last night, once more, was nights ago.

Is this how I get Fridays, Saturdays, *Tuesdays*? Is this all I had to do?

But it's Thursday now so I can't tell. I may have imagined it. I may have remembered it, but those flickering lights in the brain light one cavern-realm between them:

A memory cries at the threshold *But I happened!* Gatekeeper – *That's what they all say squire.* Memory – *But I REALLY happened!* Dream says *Ah come and join us then!*

> The wind is old and still at play
> While I must hurry upon my way,
> For I am running to Paradise

I have to be somewhere. Before dawn there's a place to be. I would dearly like to be here, but I have to be elsewhere, do my work like she does hers. I leaf the diaphanous pages of the book for an apposite exit-whisper:

> I must be gone – there is a grave
> Where daffodil and lily wave,
> And I would please the hapless faun,
> Buried under the sleepy ground,
> With mirthful songs before the dawn –

'Maxwell?'

(I'm actually halfway out the door) What?

'Tell me you're not affiliated.'

I'm not affiliated. I promised my class we'd go on this Walk at dawn.

'Walk what walk…'

The Compass Walk, I told you.

'It's not official…'

(But this was said in the settling down again, the dozing away, the last word muffled in the blankets, and I said *see you later* and went creaking on downstairs.)

*

I imagine I'm late but I'm almost the first. Three small shadowy figures are huddled along the frozen lane in the fog by the Keats fence. One is hopping from boot to boot, bashing his/her mitts together – his, that's Ollie Faraday – another, Iona? is wrapped around a thermos of salvation, and a third has to be Molly Dunn in a hood and her misted specs. Ollie declares: 'Time is blue for the early ones,' as he knows about the Compass Walk, knows what you have to say when you're where. He and Iona have helped me set it up, the invites and the handouts, but Molly says: 'Sorry blue's not an abstraction, Oll,' as Iona lifts a lid of scalding onion soup my way, warning me 'blow, blow,' and some new arrivals come chattering, stamping through the fog.

Here's Blanche and Isabella in their great big Barboury coats, and then all grumbling happily at the hour and the oddity come Roy Ford, Kornelia and Peter Grain, well-equipped as always, then bare-headed Heath in his bomber jacket, both steaming *and* smoking, 'knocked for Niall, got no answer,' – it being too cold for pronouns – *brrr,* dashes too, it's freezing, and here's C Jellicoe playing mother with a paper-bag of pastries, finally Lily in an elongated bumble-bee mad jersey and Samira in full make-up behind the green dot of her e-cig, each one blaming the other for making them late.

(I shout till they all pipe down) no one's late, there is no time here!

'We're thirteen,' Orlando tallies and reports.

You may be thirteen, but I'm one and you're twelve.

'Apostles eh,' suggests Peter,

Coincidence,

'Of course!'

'So does one of us have to betray you?' cries Isabella, giddy and bright and back on a school trip,

Not until you've kissed me (I reason from scripture)

'Get *you* all sharp in the morning,' goes Lily, sipping the lid of soup till Samira's prised it from her.

Heath fist-bumps with Roy Ford and asks ''sup man, is Mimi coming?'

Blanche turns in her waxen jacket, 'what are you *high*,' while Caroline finally offers me that last croissant I'd prayed for.

Saddlers is open? (I wonder with a smile)

'It doesn't come from Saddlers,' she informs me without one,

'They don't taste very abstract,' Molly's munching and let's start:

WELCOME TO THE COMPASS WALK.

IN THE NORTH it is cold, blue, and almost silent. You've been here before, you've never been here, you'll be here again. It is late and early, outside of Time. It's the midnight before and the midnight after. It's the shortest coldest day of the year, it is winter, it is dawn, it is mist and snow and ice and stone, it is death, it is new life.

All we can speak while we dwell in the North is abstract, theoretical, intangible, thin air.

*

They're all looking at my pebble-blue handout. Weird. Mental. Excellent. Don't Get It.

'*In*...teresting...' Roy begins, warily, and they start to join in:

'What we do,' Isabella says solemnly, 'is not what we always do...'

It's *before* all things (I help them along)

'And after all things,' Heath grunts, which sets him off coughing.

'Time is with us and against us,' states Peter, glancing at me for approval.

'Is *things* abstract?' Molly demands through crumbs, and with a nod of the north I adjudicate it is.

I will do new things today (I only say to keep it going)

'That's more *East*, isn't it?' Ollie argues, 'saying what you *mean* to do?'

'This boy's the authority,' Iona apologizes.

He's absolutely right. I know nothing of today.

*

One of the many poets I don't know how to teach this term is William Butler Yeats. Who'll be reading here tonight, remember. You're not excused coming to that just because you came to this. I don't care if you're not in my class, I'm not a proper class I'm elective, I'm –

'You're saying you don't *understand* Yeats?'

I can do the line-by-line stuff, I could tell you how the sounds work, I could reference the politics or myths or heritage, I can do that till the cows evolve and *put their hooves up asking questions*, Samira, there's plenty I *could* do in William's green enchanted garden, but all I *want* from him, *for you*, is what I drew from him, and I could draw from nowhere else: his systems.

I encountered Yeats's systems of everything in my first summer at Oxford. His systems are fantastically intricate and complex, his twenty-eight terrible phases of the Moon, his types and temperaments that fit within each phase, and then the whole cosmic kaboodle super-imposed on the ages of humanity. This culminates in astounding poems like 'The Second Coming', where the gyres are spirals of world history, and it's his *System* – not some metaphor conjured on the run – that sprouts the appalling vision at the end. This isn't a North poem at all, his North poems are fairyland, pattern and song, but this is to warm us up for the great man young and old, and all I want from us in the North is hushed contemplation: how is a monstrous miracle like this poem ever *reached?* Now be quiet.

Turning and turning in the widening gyre
The falcon cannot hear the falconer;
Things fall apart; the centre cannot hold;
Mere anarchy is loosed upon the world,
The blood-dimmed tide is loosed, and everywhere
The ceremony of innocence is drowned;
The best lack all conviction, while the worst
Are full of passionate intensity.

Surely some revelation is at hand;
Surely the Second Coming is at hand.
The Second Coming! Hardly are those words out
When a vast image out of *Spiritus Mundi*
Troubles my sight: somewhere in sands of the desert
A shape with lion body and the head of a man,
A gaze blank and pitiless as the sun,
Is moving its slow thighs, while all about it
Reel shadows of the indignant desert birds.
The darkness drops again; but now I know
That twenty centuries of stony sleep
Were vexed to nightmare by a rocking cradle,
And what rough beast, its hour come round at last,
Slouches towards Bethlehem to be born?

We have come to give you metaphors for poetry... This rough beast is generated by the poet's own private system. Which decrees that two thousand years after the birth of Christ some god-awful *Diametric Opposite* will hatch. Well yes your attitude to this depends how central or special the Christ-figure is to you, whether you think time counts in thousands, what good you think faith does us, what it means if the Good Book is a gospel and what it means if it's, well, a good book. For we jumped through the hoops of 2000 and nothing really ended, unless you maintain it did, and you can catch that cowardly end-of-days horseshit on a million screens on Sundays in America, most anywhere really, so don't go thinking mine is the majority viewpoint. Anyhow this poem was written in 1919, with Europe a gibbering smoking wreck. What poet worth his salt wouldn't roam the chaos in search of legible pattern? *Poor old Michael Finnegan begin again.*

But I'm not talking about what it is, I'm talking about *how one poet found it.* How he got to write poems that have the force of flaming *scripture.* Perhaps the world trying to tell you all that scripture *is?* but let's not go there.

I was twenty, a young twenty, doing my own slouching thank you, but I was *transfixed* by Yeats's systems. That you could make them with – *you* could make them, Mr Grain, with your compass and protractor, now I know why you always have them! you could draw a circle on the page and explain the whole wide world inside it. I was all Magic Markers, rainbow labels, tracing paper, because I thought I'd do my own. My own system. And my own is very simple, a child could and in fact did do it, we could cover it in a page. We are, we're covering it in a day, on our Compass Walk, in our village. And *I do not* want it mentioned to our visitor tonight! I don't want to see his gaze blank and pitiless as the sun. For it's my humble little system, and it's served me for a thousand years…

Now we'll walk. We walk from midnight on the clock-face, we walk clockwise round the 1 and 2 towards the 3, and yes I know it's not *really* 3, throw your watches overboard, don't get literal on me now, we're walking January February March towards our leafy Library in silence, then I'll read a poem when I'm ready, then we arrive in the East, we clear?

'Clear,' say one or two as we set off down the lane, 'clear as light,' 'is light abstract?' 'clear as abstract light,' 'light means light,' 'no means no,' 'ha! coming from you,' 'what's *that* when it's at home,' 'home's not abstract,' 'fucking well is to *me* guys,' 'language, language,' 'fairy down, need back-up,' 'language isn't abstract either,' 'fairies are,' 'you calling me abstract?' 'if the cap fits,' 'cap's not abstract, mate,' 'mine is, check it out,' okay gang how about we walk east in silence?

*

Where the wave of moonlight glosses
    The dim gray sands with light,
Far off by furthest Rosses
    We foot it all the night,
Weaving olden dances,
Mingling hands and mingling glances
    Till the moon has taken flight;
To and fro we leap
    And chase the frothy bubbles,
    While the world is full of troubles
And is anxious in its sleep.
Come away, O human child!
To the waters and the wild
With a faery, hand in hand,
For the world's more full of weeping than you can understand…

*

IN THE EAST it is temperate, green, and we hear birdsong. All you can see is growing, and your mind is full of hopes. It is early, it is spring, it is youth, apprenticeship. It's young love, first kiss, first heartbreak, the dream of The One. It's innocence and guilt and both gone by noon. It's high cloud and sun through showers, it's soon, it's coming.

    All we can speak while we dwell in the East is hopeful and foreseeing, making plans, dreams.

*

The Library really is to the east of the village, by a wide road that bends through the brown trees either shedding or bereft, the large houses sunken back down wooden steps on both sides in restless leaf-cascades, then a brook is suddenly audible, splashing away in the early light, and it's here, the set-back clearing we come to, some giggling, some chatting, some reading aloud the next page which is lime-green in colour.

'*We hear birdsong*, I *do* hear birdsong!' cries Isabella.

Seek poems of the East – *I will arise and go now, Had I the heavens' embroidered cloths, Had we but world enough and time, Let us go then You and I*…

'I shall find a poem that changes me!' Ollie declares, grave and glad in the rules of the game.

'Good luck with that,' says Iona, effortlessly right.

'I'm gonna be famous when we hit the south,' yawns Lily now she gets it, shaking her bee-long sleeves which must have hands somewhere inside them.

And listen (I call out over them now they're starting to enjoy it) the one-to-ones will take place now – I mean soon – in the Borrowing Hut, whoever's this week, Caroline, Lily, who?

'It is I!' cries Ollie, turning archaic, 'I hope it shall go well for me!'

'What are you, six-and-a-half?' Heath mutters.

'Soon I shall be grown!'

*

So they spread out among the stalls, to hunt for Eastern lines and poems, pulling back the canvas covers, bashing off the dust, and I head for the little Borrowing Hut in the trees to switch the heater on. Caroline's got that done already, and I renew my efforts to be friends. It doesn't start that well.

'What did you just say?'

Write him a love-poem.

'That's what I thought you said,' (we're either side of the tiny table, the columns of our white breaths engage and retire)

Write Ronald a love-poem.

'Any particular reason?'

You're in the west about this man, west going on north again, like he never existed, so why not write like it's the east going on south?

'What to serve this system of yours?'

Yes to serve this system of mine. No. To write a love-poem with the voice of innocence but the breath of experience. To write the east from the west, or the west from the south, Yeats does it all the time.

'Have you ever done it?'

Good question but the wrong one. Write the man you hate a love-poem.

She doubts it, then dismisses it: 'I'm afraid it's too late for the book.'

By the book she means her putative collection, which she's designed herself and glossily printed in Kerri's office and which she now with reverence holds in her yellow wool-gloved hands: 'These are the thirty poems.'

Write it. If it's good it goes in, and something drops out. One of your fairies dies, right? Have thirty and always thirty.

'What if I improve, I mean by *your* lights, what if I get better? Then I might have thirty-one.'

If you're better you'll have twenty-nine.

'I see, and do *you* have thirty?'

I'm lucky if I've got five. I used to have five hundred.

'Why don't *you* write a love poem?'

(Bad question but the right one, I feel like saying but I say) Excuse me?

She tenderly lays her stapled collection back in her bag and does a smile which costs her nothing: 'Seeing as you've a subject.'

I – it's not about having a subject (and she's standing up now in the process of leaving) and I don't have a subject (but I do and don't know what to say)

'Well I don't have a dog in the fight, *squire*, but there's no fools in this village.'

(As she leaves I'm actually forcing a grin as if clinging to what I have) Send Orlando in will you, if it isn't too much *bother*.

*

(I tell him to write a song)

'Like a lyric?'

Words for music. Perhaps. Call it what you like.

'Something for the midnight slam?'

What midnight slam.

'You don't know? Bitchstock!'

Oh god, go on.

'It's rearranged, that gig the Titmouse cancelled. It's in the hall tonight at midnight, *totally* off-piste and Lily's calling it *Bitchstock!*'

Is she, well there you go.

'So I could write a song for that I suppose.'

I haven't told you what yet.

'Wait! Notebook, notebook,'

Write a lullaby, Orlando.

'O…kay?'

Write four lines to the tune of Brahms's Lullaby.

'Right. I can – do that.'

Because I sat with my baby daughter awake for *so* many nights, listening over and over to that melody. In the end I helplessly had four lines: north, east, south, west. Do that. Because I did that, do that.

'A lullaby doesn't sound like slam material!'

Everything's slam material. If it isn't, nothing is. You're in the east, Ollie, you've a sweetheart in your life, write a lullaby for nothing.

(He shuts his mouth and writes it down, he nods, he's back on assignment)

And sing it till she's sleeping…

(Done, he looks up, and I stare at him for a moment. Then I stop)

You haven't asked me, man.

'Eh? Haven't asked you what? – Oh your four lines!'

Nah,

'What were they?'

Too late, Ollie,

'No *please*, Bach's Lullaby!'

Brahms's. Go and get me some of Iona's soup. Have children. Write songs.

*

I told Lily it was time.

'Time for what.'

Time to write a play.

'I don't know jack about writing plays.'

You're a born heckler, you won't let shit lie, there's where you start. In a poem a voice tries mastering time, it duels with silence.

In a play what stops the voice is another voice. Mr X can speak till
Miss Y interrupts.

'Miss Y? Fuck her.'

Bad example, Miss A speaks till Dr B breaks in, then Captain
C makes a point – so you animate the part of your brain that sees
things from the north, and let it run till the east rears up *that's
not quite how I see it,* or the south *that's total crap you guys!* or the
west *shall we have some tea now?* hey presto Chekhov, the world's
crowded, have children, write plays.

'So is that you teaching drama?'

Uh-huh.

'You doing that next term?'

No. I'm not affiliated, I'm going home to my life.

'Lucky you.'

They don't want me in this place.

'They've a weird way of showing it.'

What?

'I heard Pete say you were one of them now, that's why I ain't told
you jack about the slam.'

I know about the slam and I'm not one of them.

'Midnight slam, you can come if that's true.'

You're one of them, Lily, you study at the place.

'Yeah but you know what I mean, I don't have to think like
Titmouse do I.'

You could argue she's doing her job.

'Yeah you could if you were an arsehole.'

*

There's excitement at the little modern stall, the one closest to the
road. Bella's found a book of mine and is reading from it to Molly
and Blanche and Kornelia: '*made east and west of nowhere. North
and south it left itself, whichever way one looked* see? It's all his system,
see it's all your system!'

It is, yes.

'*Hard to remember, now there is nothing here, that there was once
nothing here…* Is this mysticism?'

Realism, Bella. Think of the blank page.

'He's published,' Blanche observes, 'he kept that quiet.'

(I don't really know what to say to that) I don't really know what to say to that.

'We're supposed to be talking about future plans,' Molly points out, 'so, professor, are you going to write more books in the future?'

Well I hope so, Molly, and what do *you* intend to do in the time to come?

(But Blanche is still open-mouthed) 'Were you aware this was here?' she wonders, '*Pluto*, by Glyn Maxwell. That's you.'

Let's walk eh, Blanche, and I'll tell you all about it. Put the covers back, team, we're heading south! The Coach House! (and a great cheer goes up, because word has got round that the South is going to be special.)

*

If like me you come from nowhere you kind of *need* a system. My home-town was a rail-track through a meadow in 1920, the place is light on history. I fell back on geography. We lived in the west of town and the sun went down in our garden, so the west had to be home. There were woods to the north – darkness, mystery, isolation – and London to the south – people, parties, noise, work. The east was on the far side of the railway where all the factory chimneys were so it was daunting and alien and I didn't have friends there. To a child that's adulthood. I had – have, actually – a magical spot in the north (a glade in the wood) and a magical spot in the south (a small hill beside the A1(M)). Dead-centre of our town there is an ornamental fountain in a foamy pond. Every time I pass it, on the way to or back from shopping, I look north to the wood, south towards the capital, east to the factories, west towards home, I think *here I am on earth again* and then I'm gone. That's it for the autobio. Why am I telling you this...

I was struck by how naturally the circle of the hours, the months, the four seasons and Seven Ages of Man interlocked and echoed each another. How this might play out in a space, a room, a town, a nation. I wondered at the patterns, the temperate climate, the four walls and ways there are, the grand calibrated stillness of *writing in England*. A day as a year, a year as a lifetime. Writing a poem was not so much a solitary walk beside a rail-track through a meadow as a voice that, even as it speaks, ignites its 180-degree opposite – the young man v the old, memory v daydream, bliss v bereavement – or, 90 degrees to one side or the other – its origin and consequence. That the language having been there recalls there, remembers past, imagines future. That walking this circle was loyal submission to Lord Time, but *running it* – or *whacking it and watching it spin* – was like Marvell's virtuoso lust –

> …Though we cannot make our sun
> Stand still, yet we will make him run…

And what if these compass-points were also *temperaments*… Years later when I came to write a version of old *Wind in the Willows* there they were: Badger wise, grave, dwelling deep in a wood, Moley innocent and hopeful, peeking out into sunlight, Toad dizzy in his mansion, sated with his *goods*, Ratty wry and nostalgic, watching the river flow. What if character was nothing but *relationship to time*?

Look, the idea that spring and autumn sigh for opposite things isn't news to any poet in Palgrave's Golden Treasury, but at least I arrived there blank as paper, found the place myself, or found it with a little push from William Butler Yeats.

We have come to give you metaphors for poetry…

It's about eleven, we are thirteen in number and we're walking round the clockface 4, 5, on the way to 6. This section of the Compass Walk is April, May, and June. Imagine the past, remember the future.

*

IN THE SOUTH it is warm, still, pungent, fertile. All is grown to full height, full colour, you are sated, and dazed. It is noon, orange-red, it is summer, it is adult. It is sex and sport and dancing, it's eating, drinking, sweating. It's the five senses revelling, what we wanted, what we'll miss. It's sunshine or humidity, warm rain and storm and rainbows.

All we can speak while we dwell in the South? Nothing but what's happening NOW.

*

Being neither warm nor sunny, nor summer, nor yet noon, we'd make do with a Mighty Brunch.

For a small fee Claude had agreed to open the Coach House privately, and let us sit – which we will, through bruncheon, elevenses, luncheon, thirteenses – on a long table by the fire. In we proceeded, and the sight was sweet and lavish, grand and cosy, candlelit, unlikely, but before we sat down I told them to put away the rose-pink page in the handout and recite the lines they should have learned –

All Together Now! and it went a bit like this…

'That is no that is no country for old men old men the young young in one another's arms others arms birds in the skies trees trees! trees those dying generations at their song at their song their song song the salmon? the salmon-falls salmon the mackerel-crowded seas seas flesh seas fish fish flesh or fowl fish commend all summer long summer long whatever is begotten dies born and is dies dies dies…'

Abysmal. And be seated.

*

Kornelia	Peter	moi	Isabella	Blanche
Roy				Lily
Heath				Sami
Caroline	Orlando		Iona	Molly

*

Claude emerges gleefully with laminated menus and they set to it with gusto or in certain quarters shrugging indulgence, while Molly and Isabella police our conversation so that nothing but the passing second can ever be addressed.

'I like smoked salmon,' 'How do you *know* you like smoked salmon,' 'I just do, I want it, I want it now!' 'I want beer now!'

'I want sex now!' 'Go on then,' 'Can't, it's in the future,' 'In your dreams it's the future,' 'What are dreams?' 'What's the future?' and so on, and I say *let's everyone touch your neighbor in some way* just to see what happens – all sorts, Sami and Lily mutually grimacing and strangling, Blanche's head in Bella's lap, Heath and Caroline awkwardly high-fiving – and all the while I think of Tina sleeping, still, and I say grinning to my neighbour Peter, with whom I heartily shook hands as Bella tidied my hair by way of touching:

So, Peter, Lillian said you said I'm, you know, affiliated?

'What's that? I do not discuss the past, professor!'

Good man, uh-huh, that I'm *one of them,* am I *one of them?*

(He tries to get it right for the South) 'I know you, you are Professor Maxwell, newly affiliated! No, not *newly,* that implies a past – '

It's not true though, Peter, about the Academy,

'What I need now is apple juice!'

Yep okay who says I'm affiliated, I'm not yet, and you work there,

'And the pear and walnut salad!'

Whatever. Starters come and starters go, toasts are made – to me, to Yeats, to Claude, to Ollie and Iona for helping me out with this, no that's the past – to Ollie and Iona for *Being An Item,* for Lily and Sami for *Being An Item* (Sami winces, starts writing on the tablecloth), to passers-by for passing by, to the sun for making the wet lane sparkle out there, and I drink my drinks in the spirit of Mrs Georgie Yeats *née* Hyde-Lees, the wife of the poet William, who on their honeymoon in 1917 told him *something was to be written through her,* and what it was was this:

with the bird all is well at heart. Your action was right for both but in

London you mistook its meaning

Which may well have sprung from the spirit-world, as Yeats with no hesitation accepted it did, but may, just possibly, just sayin', have been the ingenious attempt of an anxious twenty-five-year-old newly-wed to convince her fifty-two-year-old famous husband that he'd done the right thing by marrying her – only a few weeks after his rejection by the even younger Iseult Gonne (the 'bird' or 'hare') about whom he was still brooding –

what you have done is right for both the cat and the hare

– and also not long after his recent rejection by Iseult's mother Maud, whom Yeats had adored or pursued for years.

Anyway nine days after these first occult 'communications' via Georgie Yeats *née* Hyde-Lees, *a.k.a.* 'the cat', Yeats was writing to his old friend Lady Gregory: 'within half an hour… of this message my rheumatic pains and my neuralgia and my fatigue had gone and I was very happy… This sense has lasted ever since…'

you will neither regret nor repine

Georgie said the Voices said. Women eh. Men eh.

They did this for three years, automatic writing, *she said They said*, husband and wife. They did it in Oxford, London and the Hundred-Acre Wood, in Dublin, Sligo, Galway and Coole Park, Portland OR, Pasadena CA, on a train from Cleveland to New York City and on the SS Megantic they did it sailing home. Their marriage, such as it was, lasted. Read it up.

'I'm going to,' cries Bella, prodding at her sea-bass, 'I *totally* believe in those kinds of voices, this is good but it's quite bony…'

'And he used that for his poems?' Iona leans across the table puzzled.

'We don't care, it's the past!' says someone confusing the game with the lesson, and I ominously intone as I pour my one-and-umpteenth glass:

we have come to give you metaphors for poetry

'Thomas of Dorlowicz', 'Ameritus', 'Apple', that's what *They* told Georgie to tell her husband. Soon he's writing 'Easter 1916', 'Demon and Beast', 'The Second Coming' and then *A Vision,* his vast compendium of *four hundred and sixty sessions of automatic writing* – 'I dare say I delude myself in thinking this book my book of books' he rumbles to his publisher – ladies and gentlemen I give you Georgie Hyde-Lees, the immortal co-creator!

'Georgie Hyde-Lees!'

We drank, and she is sleeping, she is talking in her sleep, and the gossipy sloshed students changed their places all around me, and one or two tottered off to where? to *classes* of all things, good luck with that, I remember Samira not being there any more, or Caroline, or Kornelia, but word must have got around, as we now had the acting students Jacob and Yvette at the loud end of the table ordering vodka shots with some guys I didn't know at all, plus we briefly had *format* who sat down opposite, opened out a foil-wrapped raisin bagel of his own and began to eat it, informing me with his mouth full:

'You went out to the hazel wood.'

I'm sorry?

'You went out to the hazel wood, I noticed. Any reason?'

Oh, oh yes – well it was actually because a fire was in my head,

'And what did you do there, professor?'

I cut and peeled a hazel wand, then, um, wait,

'I think you'll find you hooked a berry to a thread.'

I did just that, Wayne, and when white moths were on the wing, um,

'I'm listening,'

And something something flickering out –

'You dropped something in the stream, can you tell us what it was?'

A berry!

'Which resulted in what exactly?'

I CAUGHT A LITTLE SILVER TROUT! (half the table joining in)

'It's *moth-like stars*,' said Wayne, 'and you a poetry professor.'

When I looked up in the jovial aftermath of that, there was Mimi sitting at the loud end in her suede black jacket, with Roy Ford and JPJ, stirring a Bloody Mary and it's suddenly gone quite quiet.

'It's a wind-up, right?' says Bella, 'as per normal.'

'Straight up, Bell.'

'What's going on?' demands Lily from the other end of the table and Peter Grain says slowly, frowning to absorb it, 'She's gone. Left town.'

'Who's gone?'

'Yeager. This morning. She resigned. Apparently.'

I look at Mimi and she looks away, telling the nearest person 'The words *witch* and *ding-dong* spring to mind,' then she asks Claude for a menu.

*

To the tune of Brahms's Lullaby…

> *On a day when I lay where I used to forever*
> *And the voices I was watering were in flower as I rose*
> *Then I in the fields with the clouds in my fingers*
> *Could sing till the sun was a road on the sea*

*

It *couldn't* have gone through.

'It did.'

I didn't do the form, Kerri.

(She's sorting through a drawer) 'It passed with flying colours! we all thought you'd be pleased.'

Who the hell is *we all*? You mean Mike?

'What happened to your big walking thing? Someone said you were in the Coach House having a wild shindig!'

I was, are you saying someone made my application *for* me?

'Well you signed the lilac form for me, remember, and you did seem all like keen. So Mike said let's just fill in the rest from his CV on file.'

Did he. And when did Mike do that?

'Last week. And it went through on Monday.'

I've been on the staff three days. Did Tina know that three days ago?

'Well not unless Mike told her.'

Not unless Mike told her. And where is Mike?

'He was here this morning, he and Tina had a meet at nine.'

And then she –

'Then she resigned. Still can't believe it. Jeff's Interim Dean.'

What?

'Jeff Oloroso. Interim Dean. It's not my fault, frankly, that you're never here on Mondays. Oh and Mike's gone on that course now.'

*

I only went there to argue against a fate accomplished. I thought if I made a good enough case then her few things would still be at my flat, or she would, but she wasn't and they weren't. There was no note, neither there nor at the office. Kerri wouldn't or couldn't tell me where she'd gone, the map just fades into words and space and symbols, 'she said she had to feed her goldfish.'

*

IN THE WEST it is oh write it yourself, christ. I scrunched the amber page up and tossed it at the bin and missed.

'Good shot,' called the landlord of the Ferry Boat Tavern.

I put that right, and he bought me a cider and I bought him one too. No one else was there. It was the middle of the afternoon, time had stopped for a breather. Out through the window were the grey waters of the lagoon, the short-lived crests of white to and fro, and out there the island, a dark tuft of evergreens.

The landlord of the Ferry Boat Tavern – where West was meant to have been on the Walk, and now *was*, if a few hours prematurely – did some landlord things with glasses and grubby towels and then stood behind the bar, near the till, not leaning, slouching, swaying, just *standing*, doing nothing at all.

Excuse me (I said) are we square, Louis, did I – I paid up, right?

He smiled. He stood there, upright, hands down by his sides, a blank, doing nothing. No one ever stands like that.

Are you – expecting someone?

Louis smiled and waved and his gesture took in all the empty room.

Are you – expecting someone? – here? – at the – the Tavern?

Then he mouthed the name of the pub right back at me: *F – B – T –*

At the *Ferry – Boat –* Tavern, did there used to be a –

Then he rolled his eyes: who knows?

(There's a ferry –) There's a ferry is there a ferry, there's a ferry-*man*?

And Louis *sighed*, like he'd been hoarding breath, and fell against the bar delighted.

*

You know Barry I should fail you, shouldn't I?

'I was failed long ago, señor, I'm only here on sufferance!'

He rowed me on the lake with his back to the dark island, the water was rougher than it looked from the shore, the spray sprayed me which was heavenly, and he told me the day's story.

'Master Nathan from the Saddlers said the Irish gentleman arrived early, and he asked about the sights to see, and Master Nathan said go see the lagoon, go sail to the wooded island, and he sent me a note by little McCloud to get down there quick-quick, sort the boat and so on, I ain't used this boat since August, out of shape!'

There's an August, is there.

'You and your funny comments! So I rowed the gentleman, and two other parties in addition, little McCloud and my right royal highness, to show the feller round and that, and I said I'd come for 'em all by six as I believe he has a performance?'

What.

'The Irish feller.'

Whatever. I've resigned, the ghosts can do what the hell they please.

'Ooh ghosts never do that, ghosts try to please *us!*'

Well you'd *know*, Mr Wilby.

'You don't half stink of booze you do. Not far now. Heave-ho!'

*

Barry tied up the bobbing boat on an old threadbare jetty, helped me out and off we trod down the muddy path through the shivering pines. He had his trusty torch at the ready, but enough light was filtering down through the high branches from a mild hour in the weather. When the path ceased to curve around to the right we spied the lanterns of the hut down a narrow way which brightened as we gained the clearing.

Ten paces took us over churned ground to the wooden cabin, and through the front window we saw the company at tea, at the moment they saw us:

Rowena sat on a wooden throne-like seat at the far edge of a round table – had Barry carried her that whole way? – to her right a slender girl of ten or twelve with straight long silvery hair was playing with a clockwork ballerina, and on her left was seated the man of the hour, striking, grey and stately in middle-age, sipping at a willow-pattern teacup. He glanced at us through the foggy window, set down his tea as Barry led me towards the door, and soon we made a sociable five in the room, our chair-legs planted in the lumpy brown old carpet. A bar-heater blazed from a corner, there was a camp-bed under a frosted porthole, and there were old books everywhere, the place reeked like ancient book itself, like the place that scent will always take you.

The poet had been telling them something and having paused he resumed, while Rowena poured us tea in the blue teacups, 'One troop of the creatures carried berries in their hands,' he was saying matter-of-factly, 'my cousin saw them very plainly.'

'*Fairies…*' breathed little McCloud in awe, and Yeats put a finger to his lips.

She wondered, 'What did they write on the sand again?'

He leaned forward and lowered his voice: '*Be careful. Do not seek to know too much about us…*' nodding at her amazement as he sat back. I expected him to look away from the girl now, smile in kindly jest at one of the adults, but he did no such thing.

Rowena coughed, 'We've been speaking of childhood days,' and passed the child the platter of cakes, meaning her to move it on to Barry and me – though McCloud started carefully choosing one instead.

Oh yes have you? (I rather blurted, still accustoming to the tone of it)

'I'm *having* childhood days,' McCloud mumbled with her mouth full, to Yeats's deep nod of approval, and Rowena moved things on in every way:

'Earliest memories, Mr Yeats? (You pass them *round*, Fiona),'

The big plate orbited his way and he pondered and selected:

'Fragmentary, isolated, as though one remembered vaguely some – some early day of the Seven Days…' he peeled the wrapping off his cake then raised his hand as if he'd just seen something, 'I… remember sitting on somebody's knee, looking out of a window at a, a *wall*, covered with cracked plaster,' and his eyes were bright seeing only that, 'Sligo,' he noted.

McCloud fumbled her toy with a squeal and Rowena hushed her.

'I'm… sitting on the ground looking at a, a, a *mastless toy boat*, with the paint scratched, and I, I say to myself – in great melancholy,' he smiled and proffered this to McCloud who again was listening open-mouthed, 'I say in great melancholy: *It is further away than it used to be…*'

We sat back, liking that, and I tried again, more calmly:

Early books, d'you remember, sir, first poems or stories?

'We're poets too, you see,' confided Barry, 'wanna know where you get your ideas!'

No we don't I mean yes we do I mean no, oh god –

'We're only beginners, though, teacherman and me.'

Yes, sir (I said directly to Yeats) we are, we are beginners, do you remember when you were that too?

'He'll pinch 'em all, I warn you!' Barry teased and Rowena stilled him very gently.

'My father read to me,' Yeats said upon reflection, 'when I was – eight or nine. Between Sligo and Rosses Point there's a, a tongue of land, covered with coarse grass that runs out into the sea – or the mud, according to the state of the tide.' Now he leaned and whispered to McCloud, as if for her ears only, '*It's where dead horses are buried…*' and the child gaped and stared at Rowena who did it right back at her like a looking-glass – like a young girl old – and Yeats carried on: 'sitting there, my father read me The Lays of Ancient Rome. First poetry that moved me.'

'*Sligo…*' Barry re-echoed to his own satisfaction.

'There used to be two dogs there,' said Yeats, bringing this tenderly back to McCloud, 'one smooth-haired, one curly-haired. I used to follow them all day long.'

'Like Stanley and Jep!' the girl reminded Rowena who shushed her in agreement as Yeats went on, 'I knew all their occupations, when they hunted for rats and when they went to the rabbit warren, they taught me to dream maybe. Since then I follow my thoughts as I followed the two dogs – the smooth and the curly – wherever they lead me!'

'Which one was smooth and which one was curly?' wondered McCloud, and he wrinkled with a smile of *who knows?* 'the very *feel* of Sligo earth puts me in good spirits.'

My mouth was full of lemon cake but I went for it anyway:

D'you remember the very first thing you ever wrote?

He sat back, spreading out to muse on this, and McCloud suddenly jumped in her chair: '*Ugh* – ants!'

We saw three pioneers setting out in file for a cone of spilt sugar.

Yeats said in the warm voice he was using with the child, 'What religion do the ants have? They must have some notion of the making of the world?'

Rowena gasped theatrically to show McCloud the gravity of the question. It did seem quite to take the little girl's mind off disgust and deep into theodicy, as she peered at the tiny things.

McCloud thus preoccupied, Yeats politely remembered what I'd asked him.

'My father suggested I should write a story. In London I wrote *Dhoya* – a fantastic tale of the heroic age. He said he meant a story with real people! and I began *John Sherman*, putting into it my memory of Sligo – my longing for it.'

He paused and I readied my breath for my next of three next questions, but he recollected more: 'While writing it I was going along the Strand – '

As in the seashore, right,

'No no the Strand, *The Strand*, passing a shop window where there was a – a little ball, kept dancing by a jet of water, I – I remembered waters about Sligo – '

So right this was *prose* rather than –

'That shaped itself into The Lake Isle of Innisfree.'

I choked and spluttered my cake to hear that, and Rowena sent the girl to fetch me some water, she also quoted softly:

'I shall arise, and go now, and go to Innisfree…'

The poet grinned and made the best of the here-we-go-again: 'I grow a little jealous of the Lake Isle,' he sighed, 'puts the noses of all my other children out of joint!'

Is it a real place (I asked him, knowing it was)

'In Lough Gill,'

'Sligo!' Barry sang.

'Sligo. A little rocky island with a legended past. In my story I make one of the characters, whenever he's in trouble, long to go away and live alone on that island. Old – daydream of my own.'

Does *this* island have a name (I aimed this at Rowena)

'Presumably,' she said.

And, unsettled by her brusque reply, thrown back on my romantic sorrow and oceanically homesick, I asked William Butler Yeats what he was up to these days.

He looked at me and sniffed, a little dismissive, as if this wouldn't be interesting for the child, but said: 'I spend my days correcting proofs. Just finished the first volume – all my lyric poetry. I'm – I'm greatly astonished at myself.'

How so, sir?

'I keep saying – what man is this? What man is this who says the same thing in so many different ways?'

Oh that's harsh on yourself!

'My first denunciation of old age I made before I was twenty. The same denunciation comes in the last pages of the book.'

Early and late, it's a totally different style, sir!

'Style's – almost unconscious. I know what I've tried to do.'

Yes. Yes? …Mr Yeats?

He breathed deeply, framed it: 'Tried to make the language of poetry coincide with – with passionate, normal speech. To write in whatever language comes most naturally when we *soliloquize* – as I do all day long – on the events of our own lives – or any lives where we can see ourselves for a moment. It was a long time before I'd made a language to my liking.'

McCloud dropped her toy with a cry again but Rowena let her be.

'Because I need a – a passionate *syntax* for passionate subject-matter – I compel myself to accept those – *traditional* meters that developed with the language.'

'Sonnets and the like,' said Barry glumly, Yeats was helping himself to milk:

'Pound, Lawrence – wrote admirable free verse – I couldn't. I'd lose myself, become joyless…'

'The sugar, Wilby,' said Rowena.

'If I wrote of personal love or sorrow in free verse – or in any rhythm that, left it *unchanged* – I'd be full of self-contempt, because of my egotism and, and indiscretion – foresee the boredom of my reader.' He stirred his tea. 'I must choose a traditional stanza,'

But wouldn't that, that kind of, *colloquial* thing, with traditional stanzas kind of, wouldn't that be, like, really original?

He said quietly, knocking his spoon on the cup: 'Talk to me of originality and I'll turn on you with rage. I'm a crowd, I'm a lonely man, I'm nothing. Ancient salt is best packing.'

And there was a salt edge to the air. Then he gave a short laugh, recalling something –

'Once when I was in delirium from pneumonia I dictated a letter to George Moore, telling him to eat salt. Symbol of eternity. The delirium passed, I had no memory of that letter…'

He shrugged it off and began to stand up, as Rowena pointed out through the door to a small decrepit hut on the far side of the clearing. He finished the thought as he went out, 'I must have meant what I now mean.'

When he'd gone, McCloud looked across to me and said stolidly 'he has arised now, and gone to Innisfree,' which set me off coughing with laughter, Barry hastily correcting her, 'I think you mean the bathroom!'

I had quotes at the ready too:

Love has pitched his mansion in the place of excrement…

Rowena had something better: 'Go on, Fiona, say it now.'

'He'll come back, I don't wanna.'

'Say it quickly, you've time, Fiona's learned one of the poems, what's it called Fiona.'

'The poem is *entitled*… Girl's Song, by W. B. Yeats. Him!' she hissed, looking warily at the door in case he was returning but the coast was clear, so she clattered down from her chair and stood beside it. She took a deep crackly breath, looked afraid but proved word-perfect, though she wasn't keen on line-break and the punctuations were all her own:

'I went out alone to sing a song or two. My fancy on a man and you know who. Another came in sight that on a stick relied to hold himself upright. I sat and cried and that was all my song. When everything is told, saw I an old man young? or young man old.'

Rowena and Wilby and Maxwell applauded, and so did the author, who came clapping back inside, bowed, stooping to shake her little hand like a good king in exile, and told us as we settled back down:

'Crazy Jane is more or less founded on an old woman who lives in a little cottage, near Gort. She loves her flower-garden – and has an amazing power of audacious speech.'

Wait Crazy Jane is a real person?

He adjusted his wonky chair and chuckled, an old man young: 'One of her great performances is a description of how the meanness of a Gort shopkeeper's wife – over the price of a glass of porter – made her *so despair* of the human race that she got drunk,'

'Oh lordy!' cried Barry, but Yeats didn't mean just drunk, he put one hand on Barry's broad shoulder, raised the other like an orator, and spoke gravely, comprehensively, to one and all:

'The incidents of that drunkenness are of… an *epic magnificence*.'

*

Well what, well this. When you're spat out by time find the timeless things, the writing you love, the place you always meant to go, the complexities of children, the simplicities of wisdom. Find north afresh, begin again. I would spend the night on the island.

Yeats didn't know who I was, so it didn't strike him as strange when I told Barry I was staying, there's a heater, there's a camp-bed, and I never struck Barry as anything but a puzzle passing through. He offered to row back later in case I changed my mind, but I didn't think I would, so he promised me he'd be back again at ten tomorrow morning. Rowena had showed me some little snacks in the cupboards, and a star-chart, and a dream-catcher.

Once the farewells had been said and the dusk was coming down they were little more than shadows: Barry with Rowena hoisted on piggyback, their bulky silhouette some kind of gentle quarrelsome giant, the poet on their right, arms akimbo, gazing up at the violet sky and breathing out the constellations, and little McCloud between them, scolding her ballerina.

And when my hold on all of it slipped again I muttered to their departing shades:

In the deserts of the heart
Let the healing fountain start,
In the prison of his days
Teach the free man how to praise.

I heard a scuffling sound: the old poet had halted by the pathway at the far edge of the clearing. He turned and called back steadily though he scarcely could have heard me: 'I admire Auden, more than I said in the anthology.'

Then he turned and they were soon gone, the last image to recede the silver hair of the little girl, bobbing along between them on the disappearing path.

I breathed out for an age. I was alone with everyone, it was much like any night. I lifted the old brass lantern and in three steps was home.

*   *   *

Week Ten – November 28th

~~Dear Walt Whitman,~~
~~I find myself alone. I~~

~~Dear Mr Walt Whitman~~
~~I seem to find myself all alone. This was a day on which I hoped~~
~~to meet you for the first time, and now that this is most unlikely to~~
~~happen, I feel I ought to exp~~

~~Dear Walt,~~
~~My name is Glyn Maxwell, a poet of the Old World. I sit alone~~
~~in a small deserted chamber off a dusty old village hall where I have~~
~~recently been giving classes in the craft of poetry, and can think of~~
~~no better use of my time than~~

I scrunched that one up too and threw it at the bin and scored.
I'm leaving.

There's no class left, no Whitman visiting, no reading in the
village hall, no Q and A, no pub, I'm going to drink myself pink
at Café Maureen, going to climb the hill not turning round, going
to walk right up to that tunnel entrance and this time I'll keep
on going, till the white light's an approaching train or the white
light's the other side. I guess they're the same thing if you're keen on
metaphor. I'm not really, not these days, so I see two outcomes only.

One: it all goes dark, and this was a dream, or a coma, or the
grandest *mal* there ever was, and I'm safely returned to Angel and
I see my daughter again, my kith and kin, old friends and new, my
Atlantic amigo, my play-reading gang, and I tell them what happened
– I met famous poets who are dead now! we all went to the pub! I
briefly had a girlfriend! – and they look at me kindly over pasta and
pinot grigio, for nothing I'm saying is a radical departure from how
I've always sounded.

Two: I find myself back here, because whatever it is that put me here won't let me go till the term is taught. But Two doesn't make any sense! It wasn't me who cancelled class, wasn't me who ordered my students to quit, wasn't me who called the agent and said *Mr Walter Whiteman needn't come here thank you.* I would have stuck it out to the very end of my gilded Reading Series. Week Twelve is the Christmas party, I'm told, I'd have met Lord flaming Byron, who *wouldn't* hang on in there?

*

~~My Honoured Friend, a poet of the Old World greets a Poet of the New!~~
~~When the dawn broke and I awoke in my attic digs today, I had every expectation of meeting you this evening, and of hearing you read your wonderful~~

*

That one hits the floor too and here I sit, the very visual cliché of a writer at work, scrunched-up sheets around my ankles, in the bin, beyond the bin, short of the bin, all's silent, all's over for this particular Old World Man of Letters.

How did I get here?

*

I was rowed, obviously, rowed home from the wooded island but I have no recollection, the spray on my cheeks? no that was the outward voyage. Again there were traces in my mind of that candy-apple swirl of a week before, the one I must have passed with Tina, but I couldn't work out where they fitted on my calendar. In my dozing she was hard at work at the desk, trying to figure it out with coloured pens and her little book-light. *You've forgotten the afternoons,* she said, *typical Maxwell...*

I woke up this Thursday morning like I do each Thursday morning. There were books open on the desk, *Leaves of Grass, Drum-Taps, Specimen Days,* it was white and windy and cloudy outside, and I suddenly had a good idea.

And, as often happens, that one good idea, which would make the whole class make sense today, gladdened and fixed me so utterly that I slid back into bed and dozed and dreamed, and dozed until the sacred question reared up *What is the POINT of you, asshole?* and in two shakes I was back at the desk.

*

I believe a leaf of grass is no less than the journeywork of the stars,
And the pismire is equally perfect, and a grain of sand, and the
      egg of the wren,
And the tree-toad is a chef-d'oeuvre for the highest,
And the running blackberry would adorn the parlors of heaven,
And the narrowest hinge in my hand puts to scorn all machinery,
And the cow crunching with depressed head surpasses any statue,
And a mouse is miracle enough to stagger sextillions of infidels,
And I could come every afternoon of my life to look at the farmer's girl
      boiling her iron kettle and baking shortcake…

*

~~I have been reading your magnificent poetry, sir. My life in art~~
~~comes a long time after your life in art, and there's so much to tell~~
~~you that I don't know where to begin, so instead I will count the~~
~~ways in which your example has illuminated my journey.~~
~~However, the chances of my finishing this letter without crossing~~
~~it all out are pretty remote = it's about the twentieth I've begun = and~~
~~the chances of my placing it in the hands of one who can place it in~~
~~yours are so remote as to be beyond all compass. Having said that~~

*

Back in the cold white morning of Thursday the 28th, when I was going to teach my class – I tried to teach my class – and I was going to meet Walt Whitman – I will not be meeting Whitman – I worked at my desk a while, had a further two-and-a-half ideas of what to try in class, swung by the bathroom, flossed and gargled, messed up my hair, shocked my unshockable mirror-self, went out.

You've forgotten the afternoons, Maxwell.
Go on then, You: fill them in for me.

I sat alone in the Saddlers, head down and unavailable, and the only soul deemed welcome was Nathan Perlman to take my order.

You've lost your shades, Nathan, you're all smart.

'I'm dressed for the occasion, look.'

What occasion.

'You don't know? You been here too long, man!'

No shit. Did you hear Yeats read last week.

'He was awesome.'

I was ill last week, what poems did he read.

'You know, foul rag-and-bone shop, that one.'

The Circus Animals' Desertion.

'Cool, and the one about the swan, and that tower of his and what was it, – do ya dance Minnaloushe?'

Don't know that one.

'We asked for the Lake Isle of Innisfree, but he said he's just come from there. Kinda mystical.'

Mm-hm.

'Peter says it would have been Whitman today. That sucks.'

It is Whitman today. He'll be on the 6.19.

'Truly? Hm. You ought to check that, professor. Let me get you a refill.'

*

Vague disquiet encroaching on my gut, I went next to Mrs Gantry's, who looked up from her stock-taking, wished me good morning and watched me placidly sorting through the toys of the ages.

The homeward bound and the outward bound,
The beautiful lost swimmer, the ennuyee, the onanist, the female
    that loves unrequited, the money-maker,
The actor and actress, those through with their parts and those
    waiting to commence,
The affectionate boy, the husband and wife, the voter, the nominee

'Anything take your fancy, professor?'

Not today, Mrs Gantry.

'We had some zombies in on Monday, they got snapped up pretty sharpish.'

Shame, don't have any zombies.

'There's a robot left.'

Fuck him. Sorry, Mrs G.

'I'm used to it, professor.'

What I need is a pack of cards.

'Aisle two in the yellow box. Everything's in its right place.'

It was, but I didn't mean cards, I meant blank cards and I found some. The lady had everything. With an hour to go before the Cross Keys and my one-to-ones – I'd no idea whose turn it was and felt too low to be of any use – I headed up the east road to the Library. No one was there as usual, though a thoughtful soul had left behind one last smudged soaking handout from the Compass Walk last week, which *Spiritus Mundi* soon had me forlornly leafing to the crumpled amber:

IN THE WEST it is always autumn, and we hear a lost stream running. All you can see is fading, and your mind is full of memories. It's afternoon, it's middle age, it's knowing all and nothing. It's love ended, it's perspective, the fallen leaves, the last light. It's wry and philosophical, caves in to tearful grins, smiling sorrow. It's dusk, it's the wind, both forgiveness and forgetting.

All we can speak while we dwell in the West are memories of what was, or dreams of it, and the soft crumbling of the difference.

I had to read it to the end, it would seem a heresy not to, time being Lord and so on, but I drew weird consolation that I was somehow netted in my own contraption. I would leave the damn thing in the Borrowing Hut, but when I opened the door to do so – there's that bearded portly man in a hat I always see, he's drawing a little picture.

Sorry, man, didn't see you there.

'What is the difference between a hen and a kitchen maid?' the fellow enquires without looking up. He's actually drawing a hen, now I see. His brown beard dabs the page as he works.

I, well, no what *is* the difference between a hen and a kitchen maid.
'One is a domestic fowl, the other a foul domestic.'
Yep, I'll just – leave this colourful leaflet here. In the, the bin. There.
'I'm a sad fellow for disliking parties.'
No you're not, sir. I don't like them either.
'There's no help for it. Goodbye.'
Goodbye, sir. See you later.

*

I tramp a perpetual journey,
My signs are a rain-proof coat and good shoes and a staff cut
    from the woods,
No friend of mine takes his ease in my chair,
I have no chair, nor church nor philosophy,
I lead no man to a dinner-table or library or exchange,
But each man and each woman of you I lead upon a knoll,
My left hand hooking you round the waist,
My right hand pointing to landscapes of continents, and the
    public road.

*

I met Samira on her way out of the Cross Keys, clipping up her
briefcase.
    Am I late? (I wasn't)
    'It's pure hell in there.'
    (It was, we stood there at the dark door of the pub and rock was
playing loud enough to dement every bunny in the neighbouring fields.)
    Where do you want to go then? Saddlers? Maureen?
    Samira looked away down the lane, west towards the Green and
the student halls, 'I'm afraid I'm double-booked.'
    You are? Okay (off she went) another time (she nodded as she
walked).
    Fine. I backed into the pub and turned, it was loud and dark
in there. Low-lit, crimson, as if for some club night, yet it was
lunchtime on a Thursday. Odd no? Anyway skipping Samira meant
a precious deafening half hour to myself.

'Small or large.'

SURPRISE ME. ACTUALLY DON'T. WHY'S THE MUSIC
SO LOUD?

'Not bloody likely.'

WHAT? WHY'S IT – forget it. Thanks, Norman.

What was odd was there was no one there. I went with my wine
and peered round into the red booths expecting Kornelia or Niall
or Molly Dunn, all of whom would sometimes sit there reading,
but this time there was no one. It was only when whatever deathless
string of soft-rock oldies had subsided in the juke-box, that three
young men emerged in mid-trivia from the other bar and hung
around the silvery nickelodeon till the same chain of songs began
again, again.

ON A DARK DESERT HIGHWAY

This is absolutely dreadful (I cried, lost in the volume)

They must have heard something from me, they all turned and
grinned together as if on cue. None of them was Mike, but I thought
I'd seen them with him. The tall one was called Lance, the blonde
one I call Blondy, and the one in the parka was called Parker or he
fucking well is now.

Sorry, Mrs Gantry. Sorry Norman. Sorry fairies.

Evil re-engendered, they went sniggering back to the small bar
and I went on waiting, to the tune of *Piano Man, Hold The Line,
The Final Countdown, In The Air Tonight* and *I Want To Know What
Love Is*.

I tried to remember who I was waiting for. *Whom,* I whispered
from the bottom of the ocean.

*

Dear Walt, it is said that you are the father of free verse. But I
think you are above all a formalist, sir! In fact I think you

If poetry is formed from the body in space and time – which is all
I learned on my journey – you are a formal poet too, Mr Whitman.
I mean

*

It was Niall I was waiting for, but he didn't come for me. He came to dance, he was suddenly there, he'd stolen in so quietly I missed it, he had wended his way to the dead centre of the saloon bar and simply started dancing.

Christ.

You couldn't call it dancing. It wasn't dancing to the music. It was dancing despite music. It was making the most of it being too loud to think. They were steady jolting spasms, he meant it all, I sat there, I was too alarmed to stop him.

IF YOU WANT MY BODY
AND YOU THINK I M SEXY

Norman watched him gloomily from the till, hope gone for civilization, and soon the jukebox guys were into it, gathering at the bar-stools, grinning and shouting in each other's ears.

When the trio ventured on to the floor and started idiotically doing what Niall did I was quickly in there too, arm around him, saying stop, stop, no more, no more, withdrawing him from view.

I sat him down in my booth, and went up to the bar. I asked Norman to switch the jukebox off and he said he wasn't allowed to by the leasing company.

I turned to the three young men and asked them to quit putting songs on.

'IT'S A PUB NOT A LIBRARY,' said Parker.

I TEACH HERE, MAN, EVERY THURSDAY, RIGHT HERE.

'YOU DON'T,' said Lance, 'YOU NEED TO TALK TO THE DEAN.'

I DON'T HAVE A DEAN.

'YOU NEED TO TALK TO THE DEAN,' the blond one stated, as if a blond man saying exactly the same was what would do the trick.

YOU'RE NOTHING BUT A PACK OF CARDS (was all I could come up with. Pig-ignorant of Wonderland they trotted to the bar) 'IT'S THE DEAN YOU NEED TO TALK TO,' Parker turned, trying out this ingenious new syntax – only then, as chance would have it, the last of their rock songs faded.

I looked at the machine, they looked at the machine.

It stood there guiltily beaming *Not my fault guys, obeying orders here.*

I had absolutely no idea how this was going to go.

I felt that if they put more songs on I was going to pretty well lose it, outnumbered or not, but instead I summoned up that cheek-turning meekness that's half cowardice half strength.

Put some Tom Waits on at least.

They didn't, but they didn't put anything else on either, they just huddled and chortled like it was all part of the plan.

In the red-vinyl booth Niall was dancing where he sat.

Man, slow down, slow down,

'Can you see me?'

Yes, slow down (I actually put my hands on his arms and tried to look him in the eye) are you taking something? have you come off something?

'It won't find me here,'

What?

'It's on the other side of town,'

What is (I suddenly felt I knew) you mean the white space, you mean the thing that's eating your lines away,

'All gone, yum yum,' he said, looking pleased, 'it's for the best, it's for the best that's yet to come,' (now a familiar intro came from the jukebox, but I couldn't place it, the guys were there again in the silver glow, giggling at their deed)

ON A DARK DESERT HIGHWAY

Lance and Parker and Blondy smugly glancing in red light, it made them seem both brazen and blushing, like it was the most aggressive thing they'd ever done in their dumb lives.

YOU'RE PIECES OF SHIT (was all this Oxonian could summon) NIALL, NIALL MATE,

'I'VE COMPLETED THE COURSEWORK!'
GOOD GOOD, SO NOW RELAX, TERM'S ALMOST
OVER, ENJOY YOURSELF EH,
'DISTRIBUTED HANDOUTS!'
THAT'S THE WAY TO GO, MAN,
'THEY'RE SILVER HANDOUTS!'
WHAT?
'THEY'RE VERY BRIGHT SILVER SO NOBODY CAN
READ THEM!'
NIALL MATE,

I HEARD THE MISSION BELL·

AND I WAS THINKING TO MYSELF

THIS COULD BE HEAVEN OR

Heath Bannen had walked in during this verse. He'd gone to the
bar, said something to Norman, heard something back, strode over
to the jukebox and yanked the wire right out of the wall. It reared
like a snake and expired on the carpet.

Silence. Then he said what you'd expect him to say to the three
young aficionados and they did what he requested of them really
pretty sharpish. As he sighed and muttered and led the beaming
Niall from the place the only loud sound left was slow hand-
clapping. Then that stopped too: Norman closed his eyes and
basked in glorious peace and quiet.

*

In terms of what you say = love everyone and everything, *all, any,
every, all* = you rise beyond all other poets, writers, statesmen and
philosophers, and you leave the zealots of your day and mine all
babbling from their mill-ponds. You leave the

*

What?

'Talk of the devil!'

Jeff Oloroso was standing by Student Services, zipping up his brown leather jacket. But he was on his own, so his comment made no sense. Then again it was cheerfully made, and he was holding the door open, so in we went together.

Kerri was typing silently at her desk. Someone had splashed out on a slimline laptop for her, and she wore pink tiny earphones which were probably advising her to *Ignore Professor Maxwell*, for ignore him she very capably did.

Jeff eased behind the desk and said: 'Pull up a chair, my friend,' then, as I was doing so, his friend, he sought in his hard black briefcase, 'I haven't really had a chance to say that I very much do like your work, that formal technique of yours!'

Formal technique of mine, okay, you ever read the stuff out loud?

'Now now, are you giving me homework?' he grinned, 'I'll make a note. Didn't really have you down for a performance poet.'

I didn't say I was, I said read the stuff out loud. I don't come to your house and do it for you. The poetry's in the voice, on the body, in the echo,

'Indeed, indeed, now we're going to make this easy, we're all of us very busy, you can't teach here any more, we all like you, we admire the work, New Formalists do dwell among us! but, shall I just run through it all, shall I?'

Knock yourself out, Jeff, I'm only dreaming anyway, it's my New Form,

'Ah now I've *heard* that said about you,' and he implicated Kerri without looking at her, 'can I call you Glynn?'

If I can call you Jefff.

'You see, as it goes *I'm* only dreaming too…'

Are you, go on,

'In my dream I teach Contemporary Literature at a fine Academy, I teach all my favourite texts, and everything goes swimmingly but for one intractable visitor who sets up his *gatherings* so they clash with ours,'

Is that right.

'And whose coursework is playing-cards, felt pens and toy soldiers, and who uses our support staff to summon various eccentrics from the fields hereabouts, and who gets them intoxicated, and his students moreover, on Academy property, who sends them all out intoxicated to their classes just last week, and who demands that they, where is it, here, all "touch one another", and who, having successfully applied for an Adjunct Position in the Academy, proceeds to, well, do we know where this is going?'

Some adjunct position, I suppose,

'On Academy property. Were you aware the person in question is married?'

No, mate. Was the person aware she was?

'The person was very much aware she was.'

Is this in your dream or mine?

'In my dream, *mate*, letters are going out to your students this afternoon. If they wish to continue attending your – *events* – they'll be required to cease their studies in the Academy. We've also informed the readings agent that we do not need a visit from Mr, where is it, Mr Walter Whiteman,'

In my dreams you'd know his name. In fact you'd sit in on my classes.

'In our dreams we're *all* happy, the whole *world* sits in on our classes...'

Well. You got me there.

'No hard feelings.'

Absolutely none.

'Then we're good here.'

What?

'Then we're good here.'

I think your dream got stuck.

'Maybe *your* dream got stuck.'

*

~~Walt Whitman sir, your lines are the utmost reach of your breath as it praises all it finds, recalls, imagines. You rise to what's there, you say it till it's song, you sing it till it's gasping, you gasp it to its final ebb. Then the breath is over and the white space washes in, and~~

~~the hush is dumbstruck wonder, as the next surge of praise begins to
form, *because it can do no other.*~~

~~There's more Life than there is Art, your poems seem to say, and
the glory is in the reach, the stretch, the straining ever upwards, like
plant-life in the sunshine. Your ecstasies won't wait in the shade to
get themselves in order. Order is not theirs to bestow. There's too
much light to meet, there's too much warmth to~~ oh in the bin we
go, my friend…

*

There'd been two hours to kill before class. I decided I would go
to class as if nothing had happened, that was a skill I was skilled
in, I would go at the appointed time, I would see if anyone came.
Perhaps they hadn't received their letters yet. Perhaps there'd be
farewells to say. I'd want to be ready for those.

In the meantime I went home. I stood in the dead centre of
my humble digs. *Contained multitudes, contradicted myself,* decided
not to pack. No one had told me to leave. They could stop me
teaching but I was free to dream a fortnight's holiday. I made a pile
of Browning and Byron books why not, I read for pleasure, then I
went for a long walk.

On my long walk I said *hi man* to Jake Polar-Jones in his huge
gold headphones crossing the road by Saddlers – Saddlers looked
closed for something, the blinds were all down –

I said *¡hola amigos!* to Heath and *format* sipping coffees outside
Benson –

And *hello there* to the little girl McCloud as she wheeled her bike
along the lakeshore. I was reciting,

The smoke of my own breath,
Echoes, ripples, and buzzed whispers, love-root, silk-thread,
    crotch and vine,
My respiration and inspiration, the beating of my heart,
    the passing of blood
and air through my lungs…

'Is that by W B Yeats?'
No Fiona, it's by W Whitman.
'I didn't say to stop.'
Thank you. I won't.
'I have to go home now. O revoir then!'

*

The sniff of green leaves and dry leaves, and of the shore and
    dark-coloured sea-rocks, and of hay in the barn,
The sound of the belched words of my voice, words loosed to the
    eddies of the wind,
A few light kisses, a few embraces, a reaching around of arms...

Peter Grain was walking trimly along by the village green in a
suit. I saw him see me, I saw him blanch and veer into the first shop
– Mrs Gantry's – and decided I'd mess with him by following him
in. Bells jingled for him, bells jangled for me, and there he was all
downcast in his three-piece suit.

Hey Peter, got a promotion did we.
'I – no, oh the outfit, well – no.'
Come on man, think of something, jeez.
'I – kind of a whim.'
Yeah really. So, my term is over, but then, you knew that.
'I – no I didn't. It's, a pity.'
Yeah right. Those Academy guys don't half know a lot about my
private life.
'I – don't know anything about that, professor.'
Okay. Fair enough. Do your shopping, mate. She's out of zombies
but you might snag the last robot.

*

The play of shine and shade on the trees as the supple boughs wag,
The delight alone or in the rush of the streets, or along the fields
    and hillsides...

'Is this how you teach now Max, sort of shouting in the road.'

(Mimi Bevan and Roy Ford were sitting on two lopsided swings in a ragged garden near the halls. They both had glasses of red wine, like they'd spilled from an all-day party. Roy doffed his trilby. Some bloke was crashed out on the grass.)

No. I'm teaching later.

'Not what I heard, Max.'

What did you hear.

'Heard you were quitting.'

'Hey no!' said Roy, 'that true?'

No it's not. I'm not going anywhere. Not till the end of term.

(Roy raised a genial fist in approval. Mimi shrugged.)

That alright with you, Ms Bevan?

'Not my circus,'

Not your monkeys. Thanks for caring.

'Who's caring.'

My mistake.

'No harm done.'

*

~~It's prose because it's to hand, and it's verse because it rises and falls in the meadows of the lungs. The rhyming/metrical/stanzaic poet is formal, yes, balancing the freedom of imagination with the constrictions of breath and pulse and synapses and footfall – but you are too, you are no less, it's just that there's nothing set between your heart and the sky.~~

~~Now I see what Father Gerard saw. You are the great unstinting protestant to his gauging catholic splendour – catholic, small c for a poet, I'm rowing my heart out too in that little painted coracle with all the well-intentioned schemers. Yours, his, both are praise of life. Both are cries of vivid loss, lovelorn black upon speechless white, but the white of all the lasting poets is what in the end? – awe, gratitude, thanks that pass all understanding, for *we don't know who we're thanking*...~~

*

They came, they all came, as the bell was chiming three.

They all did except Peter Grain.

Heath

Niall   Caroline

Barry

Samira   Ollie

Lily   Iona

moi

You okay Niall? (he's giving two thumbs up)

'He's cool,' Heath said, 'right mate?'

'I've had a chemical reaction.'

Don't have it again, all right?

'No. It's finished.'

I'm glad, I have an exercise for you. Yes! Please, please, control yourselves, your spontaneous outpouring of joy is overwhelming, it's – touching, I'm here, you're here, wherever we are, I have an exercise for you,

'Hell yes,' said Lily sadly, pulling out her notebook.

Put away all your notebooks.

'For fuck's sake,' sighed my London friend.

This is the Postures exercise. Put away everything. Hello Peter, very smart.

'I've been asked to distribute these letters, if I may, just,'

Bit late for my birthday, man. Bit keen for Christmas eh? (nevertheless I let him, it was his day-job in this galaxy, they went round and they were opened. Read, re-read, folded, stared at, put away, frowned at, filed and I listen to all of 'em breathing. I decided not to be stopped) So! The Postures Exercise…

Caroline Jellicoe rose first: 'It's been an interesting class, lots to get your mind round,' and she tucked her chair in with a scrape and was gone through the open door.

At the count of three, I want you all to assume a posture. It doesn't matter what kind of posture, as long as it's something relatively comfortable that you can hold for a few seconds…

(They were staring either at each other or the table.)

It doesn't have to be natural to you, for example. Do you have another clash, Samira?

'I do, I'm sorry, it's my funding, it's been memorable. Good luck though.'

(Samira left, Lily glared at her but she didn't look back, Peter had backed out discreetly at some point, and now Orlando somehow sagged upwards: 'Look they kind of have us over a barrel, man,')

Oh you can fold your arms, put your head in your hands, you can lie back and look at the ceiling. You can lean forward open-mouthed, you can put your hands behind your head, you can bow your head, you can shut your eyes, you can stroke your chin, you can hold your nose,

(Ollie shrugged a doleful shrug and Iona said softly 'Thank you for everything, Glyn,' then they were gone, heads bowed, and Heath was stirring)

So remember, my friends, at the count of three,

'Time's up, mate,' Heath went, 'it's been real,' and he took Niall Prester with him, Niall raising a V for peace,

At the count of three you assume a posture, I won't tell yet you why,

'Laters at the Keys, chief?' said Lily, not beating them joining them, but I just ploughed on:

You can pray with your hands, you can lock your hands, you can hide your eyes, you can plug your ears,

'We'll be there, chief, oh and look this belongs to you,' Lily said, pressing a plastic toy into my palm, 'adios, Baggs the Monkey,' (and she was gone with a wave while Barry sat there troubled),

'It's like musical chairs, señor,' he said, 'but more like the other way round in a way.'

One, Two… Three! Assume the posture!

Barry

Baggs

moi

Er. What's your posture, Barry?
'It's just sort of, well now, it's like this.'
That's – just how you were sitting.
'Well I liked how I was sitting.'

O-kay… What's *your* posture, Baggs?

Don't be shy, Baggs. Take care, Barry.
'*You* take care, teacherman, you take *good* care.'

I'm waiting, Baggs. You just gonna sit there like that all day –
what's that? Sorry *what* did you say, Baggs?
Not my shircush, not my humansh.
Very sharp, Baggs, very sharp. Let me give you your money's worth.

The Posture Exercise

One, two, three. Assume the Adjunct Position!
That's good, Baggs. You're seated, cross-legged, on the table,
looking quite comfortable, with your right hand curled around
your knee, and your left hand outstretched as if to make a point,
and yet resting its elbow on the left knee. Your expression is mild,
civilized, open-eyed, you are weighing up opinions. Dare I say –
cautiously optimistic?

All the rest of the creatures would have their own. Were they
present.

We would all look around at everyone's posture. We'd go clockwise
round the room, discussing the meaning of each one. How relaxed
or how tense? How engaged or disengaged? How conscious how
unconscious? How thoughtful or observant or focused or vague?
What does it mean to be sitting in that shape? At the start, in the
middle, at the end of an emotion? of a mood? a thought?

We would each of us choose *three* of the postures.

And we would seek the three that tell a story.

Let's start with mine. I have my head in my hands, or rather it's resting on four fingers, the index and middle of each hand, with the thumbs at my cheekbones. It's not despair, it's more like thinking through anxiety. Posture One.

Let's say in Posture Two I sit back like this – watch me, Baggs – now I'm draped backwards looking skywards and my arms flop down beside me to the earth.

I have disconnected from thought. My body has called time on it, and now I'm slung back disinclined to go on. I hold this second posture like you're still holding yours.

Ask yourself: what grew the second posture from the first?

Ask yourself: what grows a second line from a first line?

What if I do yours next? Yours is my third and final posture, Baggs, I'll sit cross-legged on the table like you, look I'm climbing up and doing it, I open my eyes and engage with the world, I rest one arm and hold the other one out. A half-smile comes to me. I'm one thoughtful monkey.

In those three postures I've journeyed from – let's say – anguished thought to wry resignation to renewal of hope. Do you understand me, brother?

We would write three lines that do that, three lines with breaks between them, for example, top-of-the-head (I mean *really* top-of-the-head)

There was now no moment left he could foresee   [sit there]

so he ceased to see, he let go all the moments   [lie back]

until time set them ticking like old toys it found   [sit up again]

Whatever. Lines, or stanzas, two-line, three-line, it's all about the progress *between* them and *through* them.

Do it yourself, Baggs the monkey, you fail too, fail better. I'm going to sit here on this table and write a letter to Walt Whitman, if it's all the same to you, and then I'm going home.

*

Listener up there! what have you to confide to me?
Look in my face while I snuff the sidle of evening,
Talk honestly, for no one else hears you, and I stay only a minute
    longer.

Do I contradict myself?
Very well then, I contradict myself.
I am large – I contain multitudes.

I concentrate towards them that are nigh – I wait on the door-slab.

Who has done his day's work and will soonest be through with
    his supper?
Who wishes to walk with me?

*

Walt Whitman, old captain, I am so happy you will never see
this letter.

It's about my fortieth effort! I'm at peace with that oblivion.

And sir, I am so happy you can't see your poor country at this
moment in its history, because I love and revere the nation you
describe, the land you exalt, the beautiful high bar you raised for
it. No god is its hope, no law – *you* are, my captain, your work
is its hope – what it says, not *how it says it,* but *what it says, what
your poetry actually SAYS* – love everyone and everything, *love ANY,
EVERY, ALL!*

You tried to sound America to the bottom of its soul.

But don't look now, my dear – Look away, you rolling river –

Most who followed, they fell for how you said it. As if your
freedom were freedom from praising, freedom from the heart and
the face of the sky, whether one infers a kind attendant Magus or a
blind spiralling Nature – what can pertain but praise?

What one can hope is Heaven – what one can see through
Hubble – what can pertain but praise?

274

~~But they will scuffle to their freedom. As if your freedom were freedom from oxygen, blood, skin, hair, spit, bone, enamel. As if it were freedom from time. As if the space between your lines were anything but *Intake*, the common trembling inhalation of humankind.~~

~~The obscurantists of my day have no time for praise. And yet they leave the gaps for us to flounder in, wondering *What's meant here? Am I good enough to get it? Can I give up my breath to a thing that's got its back turned?* But isn't that just what the dead gods made us bleat out loud? Is it not what the lost white Lord insisted on our howling? WHAT'S MEANT HERE? AM I GOOD ENOUGH TO GET IT? CAN I GIVE UP MY BREATH TO A THING THAT'S GOT ITS BACK TURNED?~~

~~To steal away from human form, to back away from questions, to hide out in The Book, how the children love that game these days, oh, zealots all, disciples…~~

~~Sir, my captain, my friend, my brother, your poetry is no less than a blueprint for earthly survival. And it gets studied for style options. I myself oh~~ sod this my hand's tired

Something just slid under the door, Baggs.
Thash jolly intreshting profesher.
Go and see what it is.
Not my shircush profesher.
Tosser. Fine I'll go.

*

Dear chief, change of plan, swing by
the saddler's so we can buy you drink's
and give you your thank-you gift etc

peace & love   Lillian ☺ xxx

*

I walk, gladly, I see the pale sun battling westward home through clouds. I see the flat far grey of the lagoon between the houses, I think of the wooded island and the hut and McCloud's little blue bike and Rowena. I turn my face to the south and think of the Coach House, I think of that girl and another girl, and all the girls and one girl, I turn to the east and think of that lone portly fellow at work on his hen with his worn old pastel crayons, I turn to the north and my bed and its tartan blanket and its books re-reading themselves on the desk.

Most things aren't there, or there any more, and now I think – the Saddlers was closed for something, there'll have to be some other place, some other place to say goodbye –

But no one's waiting outside on the pavement. No one is anywhere.

Till I reach the front of the Inn and there's no mystery on earth – for –

There's the church and there's the steeple, open the door and there's the people, standing, sitting, laughing, getting jokes, sharing secrets, listening and explaining and insisting and demurring, over candles being touched alight on three great long tables.

Look if you've no truck with sweet endings just don't follow me in here, friend, you go home and sketch a cool ironic take on your general disenchantment while I stumble through this door into memory and fantasy, made lovely and inexorable by all that I've forgotten – that it was the last Thursday in November in our village, and Nathan Perlman hailed from Massachusetts and was dressed up to the nines, with Peter Grain beside him, suits matching very proudly, and plates and drinks were everywhere and over reception they'd hung a huge great banner in reds and blues and whites that said

HAPPY THANKSGIVING
WALT WHITMAN!

Because why, because of Peter.

Peter didn't think it was right, when he heard it all from Kerri. He thought it wrong that Tina had had to go, and wrong that my students should be barred from my classes. Perhaps it was pure selfishness, as he did enjoy my classes. And because he was an employee he knew the number of the readings agent, and when they cancelled the invitation he went in after hours to the village's locked-away landline and he dialled and invited Mr Whitman after all, but not to read or perform or lecture, just to join some forty strangers for Thanksgiving, which he and his new Yankee partner Nathan proposed to host at the Saddlers Inn. And the readings agent listened a while and agreed why not, sounds crazy.

Of course the thing grew as word got around (this all came out over the butternut squash soup and the pumpkin bread and this New World white with its tones of passion-fruit) Peter had seen the letter to my students on the system, so they all knew about it the day before my class. They didn't like being told what classes they could go to.

Lily said let's make a game of it, let's agree, let's pretend to be that *lame*, let's see what that would feel like, guys, they can't chuck us all out!

And so, one by one, they opened their letters and play-acted the thing, taking up their bags, walking bleakly from my class…

Steps quickening round to the Saddlers, to dress up, Gentlemen and Ladies, in pristine guest-rooms, Bluebell and Oleander, to glide downstairs arm-in-arm to the tables, seek and spot their names on the great Seating Plan, and wait for their professor to get with the programme…

And to think how Nathan had nearly blown the secret this morning, looking so smart in the Saddlers at breakfast – he couldn't help it! *habit* he said, but I'd not bothered to ask him more, being so taken then with the arc of my sorrows.

Oh and Peter had lost his job, he was helping out at Mrs Gantry's.

I was the second shabbiest man there. The shabbiest was in a long coat and hat, he was entering conversation, tearing off bread, I heard his brimming and barrelling laughter at some crack somebody made, I saw the crust-crumbs sprinkling the grand white beard. I took my seat right opposite, shyly, couldn't speak a word. I'd written so many to him that day, not one of which he'd ever see. I didn't know where to start. Except not to start. And instead to range my eyes about the crowing and chattering multitude, at all the ones I knew and loved or loved and didn't, it all felt the same, friends and strangers, the various helpers who'd been summoned from all the hostelries and halls of the place to cook and carry, uncork and uncover, to set down and serve, and the mostly elderly puzzled ones Barry must have swept up on his lonely rounds towards the great hearth-fire of the autumn.

*

	Blanche	Mimi	Molly	Nikki P	Gough	
Roy						Claude
	Bella	Syrie	JPJ	Kornelia	*format*	

	Ollie	Iona	moi	Lilly	Niall	
Caroline						Heath
	Kerri	Peter	Walt	Nathan	Sami	

	small girl	old lady	portly man	old bloke	Mrs Gantry	
Rowena						Barry
	McCloud	small boy	Maureen	Mrs that	Mrs this	

*

Before the much-trumpeted turkeys arrived there was the not-insignificant matter of the Iroquois Thanksgiving Address, which Nathan and Peter did from memory, and in which all living things were thanked – in person, it felt like after a while – and everyone chanted *Now Our Minds Are One* whenever there was a gap, until it seemed as if they were, though not in a good way. And when it was done and everyone turned to bless a neighbour – 'Sorry, chief, our minds are one,' Lily warned me – Mr Whitman set his napkin aside, then rose and took the floor.

'Thanksgiving!' he began and there was hush. 'Thanksgiving goes probably far deeper than you folks suppose,' and he turned a wide angle to include the lot of us attendant limeys: 'I'm not sure but it's the source of highest poetry. As in parts of the Bible. Ruskin makes the, the *central* source of all great art to be – praise to the Almighty for life. And the universe, with its, its *objects* and its play of action.'

There was a whole lot of nodding going on, whatever we believed, I was nodding for Old England.

'We Americans devote an official day to it every year,' said Whitman with brisk pride, and he clapped his hand on Nathan's shoulder, which turned the young man gold, 'yet I – I sometimes fear the real article is almost dead or dying in our self-sufficient, independent Republic…'

'U-S-A,' ventured someone in a cautious English voice,

'Gratitude,' he went on solemnly, 'has never been made half enough of by the moralists. Gratitude,' he said again, 'is indispensable to a complete character – man's or woman's – the disposition to be – to be appreciative, *thankful*.'

A starting ripple of applause and 'That's the main matter!' he called out over it till it subsided, 'the element, inclination – what geologists call the, the, the *trend*. Of my own life and writings I estimate the – *giving thanks part*,' now he beamed all around, 'with what it infers, as, essentially the best item…'

I was nodding so hard he looked down at me, so I calmed into it a vague accord directed at my soup.

'The *best* item. I should say the, the quality of gratitude – *rounds* the whole emotional nature. I should say love and faith would quite lack vitality without it. There are people,' and his eye sort of twinkled at this, 'there are people – shall I call them, even, *religious* people, as things go? – who have no such – such *trend* to their disposition.'

'Hear hear!' said someone and I resumed my rapid nodding.

Whitman lifted his glass and beseeched, 'Keep your face always toward the sunshine – and shadows will fall behind you!'

We were all so hungry we buried this in clapping and cheering, and he sat back down, a shabby ancient in his might, to our tumultuous acclaim.

I raised my glass to his, and he clinked with Iona and Peter and me and my old pal Ollie Faraday and with everyone else in reach, and then everyone out of reach, for here came Heath Bannen and Roy Ford and Kornelia Nowak and Barry Wilby bringing one of his old gents with a large dog-eared volume to be signed...

And there young Nathan Perlman stands, toasting the perfected thing in fire-lit splendour, because now here come the silver trays with the golden glistening birds upon them, and I hear the young man helplessly cry out, as if a moment only dreamed of has come true in every detail. I watch him staring now it's passing by, I watch him look down a moment, as on life goes, with the lord knows what revealed to him hereafter.

*

And the rest of that November day? Is what I can remember of what Walter could remember.

I don't recall his ever moving from his central station in that flickering firelit hall made so rich for one night only, but I do remember the slow piecemeal westward movement of the rest of us, the polite villagey scrape of chairs, the waving at waiters to serve me now I'm moving here, as we settled and formed our hemisphere of listeners.

Fair Isabella always seemed to reach the seat she wanted, and there she soon was beside him pouring elderflower, getting him started on the old days.

'Living in Brooklyn I went every week – in the mild seasons – to Coney Island – at that time a long, bare shore – which I had all to myself! Loved to race up and down the hard sand, declaim Homer and Shakespeare to the seagulls...'

'Did you see plays in New York, sir?' Nathan asked and Whitman smiled: 'As a boy I'd seen all Shakespeare's dramas, reading them carefully the day before... One of my big treats was *The Tempest* in *musical* version, at the old Park. Castle Garden, Battery, splendid seasons of the Havana musical troupe, the fine band, the cool sea-breezes... It was there I heard Jenny Lind,' he told beaming Iona, who could listen like a child. I found my voice at last:

What did you read when you were young, Mr Whitman?

'Everything I could get,' of course, but the poet had still more to say about the old dream-city we both adored, the mention of which will always cast a spell: 'I should say – an appreciative study of the current humanity of New York – gives the directest proof yet of successful democracy.'

'The friendliest place I ever was,' I offered from the heart.

'Not only the New World's but the *world's* city,' he proclaimed, to general satisfaction.

'Did you see famous people in New York?' Lily demanded, jerking her thumb at Ollie next to her, 'this guy wants to know,' and Ollie gaped and spluttered as the old man thought about it,

'Andrew Jackson, Van Buren, the Prince of Wales, Charles Dickens, the first *Japanese* ambassadors, lots of other – *celebrities* of the time. Remember seeing Fenimore Cooper in a court-room in Chambers Street, carrying on a law case.'

'*Last of the Mohicans*,' I said helpfully, and my drunken soul flitted far to a library long ago – in an old boarding-school where we had some summer holidays – the scent of polish and the bygone – twelve years old? I would turn the ochre pages and breathe the illustrations – Sykes and his dog at the end of *Oliver Twist* – *the eyes again!* – frightful *Strüwelpeter*, poor joyous Edward Lear – I could smell the ancient soil of the books, I was moonstruck then as now. Some journey had begun there and here I was still marching through the fields, how could that *be?* The length of my life had so gently disarmed each moment of its strangeness.

Walt proceeded with his memories: 'I remember seeing Poe – having a short interview with him in his office, second storey of a corner building – Duane? or Pearl Street?'

'Poe's crazy!' Bella cried, 'did you like him?'

'He was – very cordial, in a quiet way. I've a – *pleasing* remembrance of his looks, voice, manner, matter – very kindly and human. Subdued.'

'*Drunk!*' hissed Molly Dunn and he indulged her: 'Perhaps a little – jaded.'

'Do you admire Lord Byron?' Bella wondered, merrily ignored the groans.

'A vehement – *dash*,' said Whitman, 'plenty of impatient democracy,'

'But?' she anticipated, rightly,

'Lurid and introverted! amid all its magnetism...'

'Hey Bell, you can tell him yourself,' Mimi jabbed from the next table.

'What d'you reckon to Poe's *work*, Mr Whitman,' Heath questioned, flushed with wine and ha! starstruck.

Whitman smoothed his unsmoothable beard: 'An – incorrigible propensity to... *nocturnal* themes. A demoniac undertone,'

'Tell us about it!' yelled Molly,

'I want for poetry,' Walt said, 'the clear sun shining, fresh air blowing. The strength and power of health, not delirium...'

'But what if you're, y'know, delirious?' Heath tried.

'Even among the stormiest passions,' said the old man firmly.

I wondered if Heath was thinking of Niall, whom I noticed was long gone.

From the other end of our table Caroline with her notebook open queried the poet on Form. He turned, responding simply and firmly:

'The day of conventional rhyme is ended.'

'Tell that to *him*,' Heath muttered my way, but when I glanced up he was grinning, not quite *at* me, but still.

'The truest and greatest poetry,' Whitman proclaimed, 'can never again, in English, be expressed in arbitrary and rhyming metre.'

He said more but I was murmuring beneath, as if I thought this might get relayed somehow to Master Bannen:

I'm allowed to *think* beyond what I *wrote*, you know…

Nathan was raising up his *Leaves of Grass* for signature, 'Would you do the honours, sir?'

'My chief book,' cried its creator, 'unrhymed and unmetrical, has as its aim… to utter the same old – *human critter!*'

Jubilant Lily cried 'Our teacher says poetry should be *creaturely* but now it can be *critterly* okay guys?'

She raised her pint of cider to 'All critters small or large!' as the old poet scrawled his name and Nathan's, blew on the drying ink, checked it, closed the volume.

'The song of a great, composite, *democratic* individual – male or female. The poem of average identity – yours, whoever you are,' which in fact he said to me, as I was in his eyeline, whoever I was…

And he'd caught me at the strangest moment, thinking life could be strange no more…

I was at my place of work, it seemed, in Angel, long ago, or soon or now, or once again. I was sitting at my small black desk in the utterly quiet hours of the night.

Seven candles I've lit, as I do when I begin, and out there on the dark canal I see the green lamps under the bridge, they'll go blue next, then maroon, I see the single amber streetlight above, below I see a soft dwelling glow emanating from a houseboat, and behind me in the long dark room I've coffee burbling on the hob…

Was I wishing for this or remembering this? The poet's voice roared and rippled, he was riding horse-drawn taxis down the spine of Manhattan,

'Night-times, June or July, in cooler air, riding the whole length of Broadway listening to some yarn. I knew all the drivers then, Broadway Jack, George Storms, Pop Rice, Yellow Joe…'

Then he was hearing the news of Abraham Lincoln – 'that dark and dripping Saturday, that chilly April day. Little was said. We got every newspaper. Not a mouthful was eaten.'

Then he was telling us of his place of work, perhaps it was *that* that had set me dreaming of mine, or am I stationed now at mine, helplessly recalling his? What was beginning – the end of term was beginning. Was I beginning to depart?

'The upper storey of a little wooden house near the Delaware,' he's saying, 'rather large, low-ceilinged, like an old ship's cabin. A deep litter of books, papers, manuscripts, memoranda, two or three venerable scrap-books. Two large tables – one of St Domingo mahogany with immense leaves... Several glass and china vessels, some with cologne-water, some with honey, a large bunch of yellow chrysanthemums... Many books, some maps, the Bible, Homer, Shakespeare, Walter Scott, Emerson, John Carlyle's Dante... A strew of printer's proofs and slips, and the daily papers. Several trunks backed up at the walls... Three windows in front. At one side's the stove, with a cheerful fire of oak wood, a good supply of fresh sticks, faint aroma... On another side – the bed, white coverlid, woollen blankets. A huge arm-chair, yellow, polished, ample, rattan-woven seat and back, and over the latter a great wide wolfskin of hairy black and silver, spread to guard against cold, and draught. A time-worn look – and scent of old oak – attach to the chair... And the person occupying it!' he roars and raises his palms to the happy company, and it's only then, as twenty faces dip back and forth, candlelit, unlit, in and out of laughter, that I realize I spent the entire length of that account staring at someone who is staring right back.

Patiently, blankly, like a game she's never lost at. Then irritably *what? what?* then as I muddle to respond to that she's sparking up her roll-up, cheeks colouring, *whatever*.

*   *   *

Week Eleven – December 5th

I was wrestling with *Wolfskin*, I was evidently losing, I was cold, I need a *wolfskin*, and Walt's got one in his big room, bastard, trade me your hairy silver *wolfskin* it's draped across that armchair look, I would ask if I could borrow it, the black Delaware ran moonlit past the window, and as I woke his last words to us all were fading away with the last of the night, we were on the railway platform each looking at the moon coming over the hillside and he said of the moon 'A true woman by her tact – knows the charm of being seldom seen, coming by surprise and staying a while…'

Soon he was gone on his train, seldom seen, and here I am still in my attic, staying a while.

*

I knew it was Thursday morning. When you know Thursday like I do, you know when it's Thursday morning. Books open on your desk. The fun's both over and not started yet. You feel you're in the wings, but the wings of what, who knows.

In my next dream – not so much dream as a fancy that got hold of the reins a while – the other six days of the week were hiding out in a hole-in-the-wall like a slapstick frontier gang. Monday was prowling at the threshold exhorting them to saddle up and fight back, Tuesday and Wednesday were hunched round the billycan, *not our circus, not our monkey,* Friday was turned to the cave-wall in gloom *She always said she'd stand by me* – Saturday was murmuring *Who needs her I've got plans…* Not a peep out of Sunday, all but entombed in wolfskins.

The gang faded, Thursday reigns. Outside the sky was low with cloud and *whatever,* I need a wolfskin. Then I'll be fit for teaching.

*

How do I love you? Let me count the ways! –
I love you to the depth & breadth & height
My soul can reach, when feeling out of sight
For the ends of Being and Ideal Grace.
I love you to the level of everyday's
Most quiet need by sun and candlelight –
I love you freely, as men strive for Right, –
I love you purely, as they turn from Praise;
I love you with the passion, put to use
In my old griefs... and with my childhood's faith:
I love you with the love I seemed to lose
With my lost Saints, – I love you with the breath,
Smiles, tears, of all my life! – and, if God choose,
I shall but love you better after my death.

I didn't know what to tell my class about gracious stricken Elizabeth Barrett of Wimpole Street, who seized happiness from oppression, except she didn't write that poem. I thought I'd substitute *you* for all her *thous* and *thees,* so they'd hear her voice more clearly.

How is that better than paraphrasing Shakespeare? It isn't, but most Romantic or Victorian poetry could do with salvage from the waters of archaism, the veiling sea-changes. Why. Because unlike Shakespeare those Victorians wrote in settled forms, forms that had set like, well, stone. It becomes a problem. Cushions on stone. They were comfy with tradition.

It's why, for example, their verse-plays don't work. It's why T. S. Eliot, sharp thinker on tradition, eschewed the pentameter when he came to write his. Why I *uneschewed* it when I came to write mine I'd have told them in spring term, in the Paradigms of Drama class I would have taught (the official form for that is a shade of bird's-egg green, you know) but I don't think I'm invited.

Then again, I *did* know how to tell my class the avant-garde has been comfy for a century. More cushions on stone. You don't need to *like* tradition to *be* tradition. If you don't know when you're comfy you'll be a problem too one day. We'll think you're an old snapshot.

No one's listening, I'm in bed.

How do I love thee? Let me count the ways! What to say about Elizabeth…

First of all, love conquered. Some lives ring clear like bells, they beckon us somewhere. Their empty space is love, like in lullabies or gardens.

I wasn't sure what to say about her husband either. My old teacher, when I was his young student, and he wasn't that old, nor I that young, went around our class on Bay State Road, and asked us each to name a poet we didn't get.

Though I wouldn't say Robert Browning now, I did then. My teacher nodded, was not surprised, but asked why and I don't know what I said but I suppose I found Browning messy, bric-a-brac, full of Italian names I had to look up – in the days that this meant leaving the desk – it was lords and lovers trailing pricey costumes on elaborate stage-sets.

I get it now. Voices in stories, stories in voices. Maybe the playwright in me was still too shy to put his hand up. How is a poet to find that mythical chimaera His Own Voice if his mind is cacophonous with disputatious folks, quarrelling norths and souths, bantering easts and wests?

So, that from Robert, genially setting voices free, and this from Robert too: voice riding the moment, telling its hapless truth between the centrifugal forces of rainy black-and-white Then (heritage, habit, order, pentameter) and misty rainbow Now (chaos, impulse, wonder, chat) – for what flashes in that friction is character, is relationship with the turning world, the authentic voice of one's deal with Time.

Meet his murderous Duke:

> …She had
> A heart – how shall I say? – too soon made glad,
> Too easily impressed; she liked whate'er
> She looked on, and her looks went everywhere.
> Sir, 't was all one!

Meet his painter Lippo Lippi, red-faced and red-handed in the red-light district, babbling to the cops:

> …Who am I?
> Why, one, sir, who is lodging with a friend
> Three streets off – he's a certain… how d'ye call?
> Master – a… Cosimo of the Medici,
> I'the house that caps the corner. Boh! You were best!

And here's an earthly bishop expiring, clocking who exactly has showed up at his deathbed:

> Vanity, saith the preacher, vanity!
> Draw round my bed: is Anselm keeping back?
> Nephews, sons mine… ah God, I know not! Well –

The onward impulse of form plays the onward impulse of life. Right. That would take me six minutes. What to do with the other one hundred and fourteen…

Boh! I've remembered, given the circumstances, given the *non grata* of my *persona*, I would probably do nothing.

I got out of bed and started packing. Whether I'd leave or not today, or in a week, or never, my soul now took the lead and I was standing at my wardrobe, counting the number of shirts left to wear, *two*, one blue one black, taking the rest off hangers, folding jerseys into the enormous suitcase that had sat there all this time. I didn't remember arriving. I was undoing the work of another. I would leave my books behind. I looked at the open page on the desk. The real thing:

> How do I love thee? Let me count the ways.
> I love thee to the depth & breadth & height
> My soul can reach, when feeling out of sight
> For the ends of Being and Ideal Grace.…

Sickly housebound 'Ba', who would have to leave her life behind – her bed, her room, the Barretts, Wimpole Street, London, England – when love came calling in the form of Mr Browning. But she did, she fled with Robert – though her father threatened she'd be dead to him forever, and the wretched man meant it – they travelled and settled, they loved and were happy at the Casa Guidi, Firenze, they loved and were happy at the Casa Alberti, Siena.

This voice is one at peace with Time (I'd tell my class, wherever I may find them) and it's love that made it so. We don't do that in footnotes. I don't teach a complex subject.

I mean, this is how poetry sounds when the white space is love. One lets the other be. Subject, object, one lets the other be.

*

As it happened, I wouldn't teach a class that day, not Elizabeth nor Robert, for the day was zipping up its own dark coat, stone-deaf to all our plans.

It was the day I learned that one of us was gone. Gone, it was generally felt, for keeps.

I got ready and went out not knowing that yet, but as I neared the crossroads, hands in pockets, I saw a small group huddling and hugging in the numb white morning, quite a large and soon familiar group gathered at the rusty open gates of the church.

*

...lo, as they reached the mountain's side,
A wondrous portal opened wide,
As if a cavern was suddenly hollowed;
And the Piper advanced and the children followed,
And when all were in to the very last,
The door in the mountain-side shut fast.
Did I say, all? No! One was lame,
And could not dance the whole of the way;
And in after years, if you would blame
His sadness, he was used to say, –
'It's dull in our town since my playmates left!
I can't forget that I'm bereft
Of all the pleasant sights they see,
Which the Piper also promised me.

For he led us, he said, to a joyous land,
Joining the town and just at hand,
Where waters gushed and fruit-trees grew,
And flowers put forth a fairer hue,
And everything was strange and new;
The sparrows were brighter than peacocks here,
And their dogs outran our fallow deer,
And honey-bees had lost their stings,
And horses were born with eagles' wings:
And just as I became assured
My lame foot would be speedily cured,
The music stopped and I stood still,
And found myself outside the Hill,
Left alone against my will,
To go now limping as before,
And never hear of that country more!'

*

Alas for Hamelin, Niall was gone.

His things were still in his room, but he hadn't been seen since Sunday morning. Most everyone had congregated sadly, but it wasn't quite clear why.

'We were going to the Keys on Sunday night,' Heath said as he lit up, 'me him and Roy and Claude to play pool right, but he wasn't in his room. We left a note on his door, still nothing. Monday morning we got the warden guy to open up and he's gone. All his things are there.'

So come on Heath he's – met someone.

'Who there's no one, we're all here. They looked everywhere.'

The wooded isle!

'I said everywhere.'

He's met someone you don't know, man.

'Nah he left everything.'

He's Niall, he's wandered off, like John Clare, he liked John, he's just – he's – walking through the fields.

'Yeah without his shoes. Like you know him.'

Fine. Look. Why d'you not think he'll come back? it's not like you found – you know –

'Well we found this,' said Caroline, easing gravely into the group with a slim script of some kind in her woollen yellow gloves, 'his collection. It was on his desk.'

What?

'He left it on his desk,' said Ollie, arm in arm with Iona McNair, setting his other hand on my shoulder as if to bring me into the place they had reached, 'It is finished.'

The formal diction alerted me. Most of my class were gathered around now, in close, waiting for me to get it.

He's, hasn't he, he's called it *It Is Finished* (I said, to show them I'd arrived) – it's – going to all be blank (I was suddenly weak in all my limbs)

'No,' said Ollie, 'weirder.'

'That's why we're here,' Iona sighed, 'we're going to read the – work.'

'Read one will you, old chief?' said Lily taking my arm, 'we waited for you to get back. Couldn't do this shit without you. Mrs Finbow said this one.'

She passed me a folded sheet and as I reached for it I saw behind her, stationed by the railings, white-haired Rowena in her wheelchair looking at me. I went, and the students stayed behind me, closing into a ring that kept opening, smilingly, to incorporate new arrivals in their big warm frozen huddle, and from which I heard Lily cry out 'Niallstock!' like their talented young captain, and the others send it skywards in staggered voices weak and strong.

Hey Rowena.

'Monsieur. What do you think of it?'

What.

'The poem.'

I haven't read it yet, I want to be alone to.

'Fair enough.'

Rowena, why don't they think Niall will come back?

(She looked away through the iron bars at all the illegible dumb mossy graves, breathed in and out, her breath the not-a-colour of her long lank hair) 'Why don't you ask *them* that?'

They think – because of that manuscript? Look, think it through, he handed in his work, he was proud of it, it was done, then he got homesick, he left Thanksgiving early I remember, Niall, yes, he was homesick he went home to wherever he was from, Home Counties or somewhere, he got that train that comes sometimes…

Rowena, it took him home, right? It took him home, to his, whatever he has, Home Counties, for Christmas, early Christmas, Sunday was what, the first, home for Advent, to open the first window on the calendar, the first window for his, his, his, little *niece* they have a bond, she missed him…

Uncle Niall you're home! she was opening number 1, there was a Quality Street behind it, yay the red one, the strawberry-creme, she opened it, she's eaten it, they've opened five by now! She's eaten five by now and Niall's sitting in the sitting-room, looking out at the frosty lawn, silly Christmas fairy-lights blinking in the arch of the window, he's thinking about white space, answering daft questions from his friends from home, questions about his term here, his term studying poetry, you know he's actually missing us, wished he hadn't left so soon, but look there's his little niece playing on the carpet christ or *something*, I'm not saying that's where he is, that's just – like – where *I* see him, but why can't he be somewhere?

Rowena why can't he be somewhere?
'I know.'
What what what what what do you *mean you know*, you and Barry, jesus, what *do* you know?
'I know you don't accept it.'
Look *Tina* left. Come on. Tina left and I wanted her to stay.
'Tina – Yeager?'
Ha! something you *didn't* know, at last! I was sad, it made me sad she left. But I don't think she's – *no more*.
'Where did I say I thought Niall was no more?'
We've gathered by a church, Rowena.
'We've gathered by a village hall. And you ought to prepare your reading.'

*

'*It is finished.* By Niall Prester.'

Caroline Jellicoe breathes at the lectern. No one's on the front row. We're all on the second and third rows. I'm at the side because I'm one of the readers.

'The poem is in square brackets. I suppose that means it's not really the poem, or maybe it does, I never could remember, that, type of nonsense… the punctuation's a bit, well, that was Niall, that's Niall…'

She smiles apologetically. It's freezing in here. We breathe white breath, despite a little bar-heater seething red in the corner.

I notice flowers in the vase on the sheeted piano and am wondering who replaced them when Caroline begins:

```
[something punchy to get us started
something to pretend Im here
Ill show I know my way round line-break
and stanza break

and note to self I better keep it short
so Ill knock off in a second
with something that really makes you think
go on then think]
```

*

Tall Iona leaves her coat with Orlando, who folds it sadly in his bliss. She's wearing a dark blue dress with a flower. Civilized sweet woman. She pauses at the breaks like I taught her, and won't say the bad word, as if we really were in church.

```
[its probably about time
I showed you I can rhyme
if I want to I just dont
so I wont I could also show you
my
short lines and my long lines but Ill only do that
```

```
once to show I can
cos its also about time
I left this poem hanging
like theres some really important ('s-word,' she grins)
I dont think Ill tell you yet]
```

*

Lily's up next. Her eyes are red. I mean pink, her hair is red. She says she's reading this one cos it reminds her of a chat she and Prester once had in the middle of the night on the banks of the lagoon. Heath was there, she says.

'Right, Catford?'

'Right, Camden,' he says in a low voice from the row behind me.

```
[then at this point I would probably
stick in a poem I only wrote
because it was my homework
though Im not home and it isnt work
but no one needs to know that yet
and it fills the space and takes the time
so anyway here goes ASSIGNMENT
write a poem in which
you love me nevermore
also you hate me nevermore
thats cos you envy me nevermore
same time you pity me nevermore
mind you you fear me nevermore
you have the hots for me evermore
whoops misprint my bad you have the
hots for me nevermore]
```

*

I'm up, here I go, my steps resound through all the times I've passed through here, I realize I've not looked at the poem, my eyes read it as I reach the lectern, my voice catches it as it falls.

[then the next page should be nothing
but space like the man said
because make no mistake its winning
hands down mate

and this blank page would tell a tale
about how the white space one day
smelt someone scared of it
and said aye aye

theres my way in theres my chance
chance to make my mark
and it came in through the window
blanking the dark

and there was no one in the room
the white space swanned about
where is the one hes out is he
suppose Ill just what

kick my shoes off all alone
da dum da dum da dum
cos I miss the one whos scared of me
I do I miss him]

*

Walking back I'm blinking. Everyone's crazily jagged and aslant in
the fresh blur of my eyesight. I wipe that away and they're in their
rows like in some bygone school. I see Heath rising from his seat.

Mimi is cross-legged in her black suede jacket and skirt on the
seat next to his. She looks at me calmly, no shrug, no frown, no
joke. She's never looked at me that way but she is now. I turn away
defeated, can't win, too late, you got me.

Heath is last, he does nothing for a while.

Then 'I fucking love this poem,' he says, glances up defiantly, as if
he, in his own way, like Iona in hers, has a sense the place is sacred.

[Id save a good one for the end
as if I knew how anything ended

it would also be quite thankful
as old walter says be thankful

and it would touch on all the brilliant themes
weve already pretty much covered

and it would choose some pointless detail
to leave you with so in the pub

you can say you love that bit at the end
where he's got that pointless detail]

*

They all smoked in the churchyard, even those who don't, all sniffed and hugged and yawned in the cold, recounting, retelling, reminiscing themselves free. It was like any group in a churchyard, whether christening, wedding, or funeral, no one wants to be the first to go, the next page of life seemed a bit of a stretch from here. Not a stretch for me – from my spot I could see the crooked chimney of the Cross Keys and my soul was being asked *small or large* – but a stretch for the broad assembly.

Caroline was promising anyone who asked her she'd get Niall's collection copied. 'For personal use only,' she stipulated pointlessly each time.

Gough Slurman, Academy prof, came up with two big take-out coffees, neither of which he gave me: 'Well *read*, bro, did him proud,' as I heard Barry bothering the hipflask-ready Heath 'where on earth did he get his *ideas* d'you reckon,' and Ollie, save the mark, just wanted to know what happens next.

What do you mean what happens next.

'I mean is class on? Are there one-to-ones? Is there a reading?'

Well, no, I don't think so (I was piecing last week together and concluding there'd be nothing) I mean, it was Peter who brought Mr Whitman here, me I'm out of the picture, I don't have, like, *support*, you know? I'd've done a class on the Brownings for anyone interested, but not now this has happened.

'We *need* a class,' was Iona's plea, 'we feel like being together, I vote for the Brownings!'

'That's my last duchess painted on the wall,' Ollie went forlornly,

Be together in the pub (I said, more brusquely than intended, I meant let's all be there) I mean all of us,

'He won't be in the pub,' she lamented, meaning Niall, 'but he would be in our little room.'

'They locked your little room,' said Mimi, stalking by with Syrie and Jake Polar-Jones on their exit from the scene, 'we just tried the door. No soul, that lot,' (and they left not turning round).

Ollie watched her going too, and his eyes met mine on the way back, 'Pub it is then,' he said to me blankly, then softly to Iona: 'he'll be there, Mac, he'll be there.'

*

What is it about snow?

Only a week later, a *week,* I heard folk say it started snowing then, in the churchyard, on the carvings and the graves like it was Hardy, or *The Dead*, but it didn't, it's fiction, I remember, I was present.

Does snow spread out in the memory and claim the empty days, like rain does with Mondays, like sunshine does with Saturdays?

It didn't snow till later.

Oh yes it was going to, plainly, the sky was numbly conceding as much, it was lilac-white and hushed and frozen, it was stony, it had *no other course*, but it didn't happen yet, we were in the pub when it happened, we didn't even notice, the green lanterns were lit, there was mulled wine coming, we'd threatened Norman with a riot if he didn't start mulling *it's December it's December Norman mull some freakin WINE!!!* they all swarmed behind the bar to help him – Roy, Jake, Bella, Lily, Blanche, Syrie, Molly, Mimi – 'no no! not her, not her!' he growled – but no one gave a damn what he growled, he didn't really mean it, he muttered and bore it and tasted and sugared and mulled the dear day away by the gallon.

*

O little town of Bethlehem,
How still we see thee lie!
Above your deep and dreamless sleep,
The silent stars go by,
Yet in thy dark streets shineth
The everlasting light,
The hopes and fears
Of all the years
Are met in Thee tonight…

Once in Royal David's city
Stood a lowly cattle-shed…

Good King Wenceslas looked out
On the Feast of Stephen…

Now that's what I call a jukebox.

Last days of summer, first days of school, Halloween and Bonfire Night… the birth of *moi*, Remembrance Sunday… Thanksgiving, Advent, home by Christmas… Here at the threshold, early December, this little crock of silver, is a spell of childish innocence wrenched back from age, fatigue, and the infections of the market. For a handful of hours the old music, old flavours, dark berries, red candles, little gifts, lit windows…

By the middle of the month we'll be back at our stations, wandering through malls blinking ruefully at children.

Right now we revere *something*. Something came again.

Plus we'd all be gone in a week so we would have our Christmas *NOW!*

O tidings of comfort and joy,
Comfort and joy,
O tidings of comfort and joy!

Glor-or-or-or-or-or-or, or-or-or-or-or-or, or-or-or-or-or-orrrrrr-i-AH
Hosanna in excelsis!

Arbitrary, miraculous, implausible, mundane. Badges I collected from the cradle to the what, to the snug at the Cross Keys, with my students who were friends somehow, dear intimate strangers, ever coming and going as the bottles stood and emptied, jokes were told and retold, gossip, rumour cooled to fact.

In that deafening warm atmosphere, with the lavender sky outside gone dark blue in the length of an in-joke, cheap decorations magicked up in here at staggering time-lapse speed – the gang had begged or borrowed or swiped all the tinsel from Peter at Mrs Gantry's – I felt once more it was beginning to be over.

So I tried what had nearly – but never – worked in childhood. Sitting there so aware of the seconds they'd slow down into my hands and I might – I might signal them to stop now, stop it with their *passing* –

In the main saloon, standing on a table, Blanche tangled up in hundreds of fairy-lights, seeing me seeing her, softly mouthing *Help!*

By the bar Kornelia Nowak primly garlanding Norman with a chain of frosted baubles…

A trio of guys in Santa caps are checking out the jukebox…

'Y'alright there?' Roy Ford is bustling towards me along the red couch.

Yeah mate, good, just getting through it.

'Yeah you decided on next term yet?'

I don't decide on anything, Roy. Got a feeling I'm done here.

'Been thinking of choosing my options for Spring.'

Aren't we all. Look, I've been meaning to ask you, Roy, how can I put this,

'Go on,'

Yeah I suppose, like, well. Yes. My question being: where *is* this.

'What's that?'

Where: *is* this. Like – I mean – in terms of the world, I mean – I don't –

ON A DARK DESERT HIGHWAY,

Oh for fuck's sake
'Man what happened to the carols?'
What always happens,
'Mimi says you'll come back and teach Drama,'
What?
'You know Mimi, she says you'll come back and teach Drama in
the Spring,'
I know Mimi, *she* doesn't know,
'Lady tells it like she does!'
Yeah right,
'You being her special subject,'
What –
'Cheers!' (he clinks me)
What did you just say
'How can he teach Drama?' Molly Dunn demands from the
other side of him, 'when he isn't even a playwright,'
'He *is* in fact,' says Roy as he drinks,
Yeah I'm also *here* (say I) if you look, going *back* a second, Roy,
'Right,' says Molly, filling our tin goblets from the mulled wine
jug then spilling it all, 'but he's not had any hits has he oh bollocks
look was that me…'
Shall I have a hit at Christmas, Molly?
'Yeah you better!'
Just for you then.
It's right about now that the Brownings show up.

*

Term-time, autumn-time, Michaelmas, fall, *term*… things that sound
absurd make perfect sense near the end of *term*. Back in September
I'd have thought what I first thought about Keats – that some kid had
dressed the part, why *not* dress the part? – but as it happens it was him,
John Keats, we met him, and the others were the *others*, Emily, Gerard,
Walt, Sam, John Clare – week in week out they *were*.

So when a short dark lady in ringlets, in a black snow-dusted cloak, and a lavishly-bearded gent in a similarly sprinkled fur-collared cape, appeared, politely puzzled, in the blue- and green-lit arch of the doorway, I knew they hadn't stepped off the side of the Quality Street box – it was obvious who they were. Whatever I'm undergoing it ain't costume drama.

What was surprising wasn't that two poets from the nineteenth century had ambled into our pub – to this event I've grown accustomed, what's a term *for* but advancing in experience? – it was that I'd been sure the Academy had ended my classes and stopped my Reading Series. I was vaguely packed for home.

Indeed my first responses to setting eyes on Elizabeth and Robert were two realizations and one plan: *Oh christ no one cancelled the Brownings – Crikey look it's snowing* – and *Let's get them some mulled wine.*

The one plan was swiftly accomplished, by Bella and Blanche and Ollie, the second realization sent a few students out for a while to be dizzy wet kids in wonderland, and the first was later explained away at the bar, by one of Santa's sloshed elves in a mini-skirt:

'They didn't tell you? *Unbelievable!*' Kerri blurted, 'they didn't tell you, Dean Jeff said cos Niall had, you know, gone away and you were sad, he said they'd let you finish your term right, your little series, but it was probably cos you all kicked up a stink last week but he couldn't say that was why, could he, so he said for the other reason, the Niall reason but in a way he should have told you your vagabonds were still coming, not made it a surprise, and what was the other thing oh yeah, they offered Peter his job back but he said no thanks he likes the toy-shop, and the *other* other thing was could you maybe, once you've done your class next week, *Glyn*, with one n, not two n's, *note*, and it's *not* me saying, it's them lot right, could you maybe sort of, not-me-saying-them-saying, sort of never like come back?'

*

Lily, Roy, Molly, Mimi, Blanche, Caroline

R. Browning   E. B. Browning

Ollie, Iona, Heath, moi, Kornelia, Bella

      '...yet I find some good
    In earth's green herbs, and streams that bubble up
    Clear from the darkling ground, – content until
    I sit with angels before better food:
    Dear Christ! when Thy new vintage fills my cup,
    This hand shall shake no more, nor that wine spill.'

We applauded, we mooed, we mumbled approbation as Elizabeth beamed and bowed her head in return, by *god* we did our best. We none of us thought they'd *be* here, we'd been off on the warm sweet wine all afternoon, yuletide fever had turned the Keys to *kindergarten*, we'd done no preparation, we'd quit on the day, we were plastered, we had *headaches!*

And apart from such a crew of wassailing eejits having suddenly to become one mannerly sober audience, I also had to take some kind of lead, *me*, make it look like it was planned this way.

Easy enough to announce we'd do the reading in here. The village hall would be *arctic*, here it was vivid and cheery and thronged. Easy to get my class into the snug – no Samira, who'd been gone since Niallstock, no Peter, who was at the shop dealing with the surge of seasonal demand, no Barry of course, he'd gone out on his rounds in the snow – but the others were here, add to that Bella, Blanche and Kornelia, Mimi, Roy and Molly, we made a dozen, and the rest kept the noise down in the main saloon. Heath had done what he does to the jukebox.

We got the Brownings warm and dry, draped their magnificent cloaks near the heaters, and settled them down in the two best armchairs, so they could face one another from their ends of the table, with my rabble ranged along the sides.

I welcomed them and wondered if they might read us a little?

'I don't mind, indeed,' said Elizabeth, and her soft voice silenced all, 'what d'you say, Robert?'

He spread his arms out, raised his eyebrows, as if inviting her to begin.

Having blushed and acceded, and read 'Past and Future' while we all in secret pulled ourselves together, she then read four of her *Sonnets* from a cloth-bound book, very steadily and clearly. I guessed she knew them off by heart and was trying not to look at him.

'I love thee with the love I seemed to lose
With my lost Saints, – I love thee with the breath,
Smiles, tears, of all my life! – and, if God choose,
I shall but love thee better after my death.

'Didn't mean to strike a tragic chord!' she laughed, and seemed ready to finish. But as the applause peaked Robert gestured for more.

'I've done, Robert!' she said and sent the gesture back.

He considered and sighed, meanwhile she turned to her nearest neighbours, saying with a grin, 'Wouldn't do to vex him!'

But he still seemed disinclined to read aloud, and only consented to after Caroline, who'd been gone all afternoon, and whom I saw now had been in tears throughout Elizabeth's poems, murmured well-nigh inaudibly:

'The year's at the spring…'

Robert heard her words. He glanced at her like I had, must have seen what shone from her cheek. He leaned forward, swallowed, touched a knuckle to his lips, and rendered this in a loud melodious bass:

'The year's at the spring,
And day's at the morn;
Morning's at seven;
The hill-side's dew-pearled;
The lark's on the wing;
The snail's on the thorn;
God's in His heaven –
All's right with the world.'

That done, he sat back inside the sigh emitted by many, but as the clapping came I felt it marked the end of the readings. I stood up with my drink, harvested one more round of applause for the famous couple, and said, carefully sounding sober,

'We are all like, the beginners here, the beginners as it goes, in the poetry, art, and we would like to know from you, either of you perhaps, we would like, to know how you, *you*, began,' and I sat. 'How you began in it. The poetry.'

'Good speech Max,' I heard murmured close by.

Elizabeth looked down at her cloth-bound book and Robert made that gesture towards her again: *you* tell, *you*.

She had one hand on her book, she put the other to her brow which had lined in thought, so I took it upon myself to remind her:

'You do not have to do any thing,' I said, 'Mrs Browning, er Barrett Browning, Barrett, miss, if you don't choose to, it won't be held against you etc, I mean, officer, whatever, up to you, both you, both *of* you.'

I ceased, I desisted, Time disavowed me with a cough and on we went. Elizabeth Barrett Browning drew a deep breath, sat back, took us in, and began:

'I grew up in the country. No – social opportunities. Had my heart in books and poetry. It was a lonely life, books and dreams were what I lived in. Time passed and passed… When my illness came,'

Robert's mouth opened slightly, audibly, and his hand was raised as if to dissuade her from more, but she caught his eye, paused to sip water, shook her head softly and went on:

'When my illness came I seemed to – stand at the edge of the world, with all done, no prospect of ever passing the threshold of one room again,'

'Ba,' he said softly, but without compulsion.

'Seen no human nature, beheld no – great mountain or river. Nothing in fact. I'd not read Shakespeare and it was too late d'you understand?'

Robert seemed about to try harder to stop her, but now the questions came gently from my group, bless them, and I saw him sigh, try the beer we'd chosen for him, seem to come to terms with the candour of his wife's talk, the way the thing was going…

'Mrs Browning when you were young,' (fair Isabella) 'who inspired you?'

'I was precocious!' cried the lady, inspired right there by having a smile to smile at, 'used to make rhymes over my bread and milk… At nine I wrote an epic! – what I called an epic. We used to act in the nursery.'

'Yeah we did that,' Molly confirmed to her goblet.

'Were your parents encouraging?' asked Caroline.

'Not really,' said Molly,

'Not *you*,' said Caroline, 'for heaven's sake.'

Elizabeth laughed at a memory:

'Papa used to say – Don't read Gibbon's history, it's not a proper book. Don't read *Tom Jones* – and none of the books on *this* side! So I was very obedient – never touched the books on *that* side. Only read Tom Paine, Voltaire, Hume, Rousseau, Mary Wollstonecraft. Which were *not* on that side!'

The women near her chortled with her, some approved her choices. In this pause the dynamic subtly changed. Bella, Blanche, Kornelia, Caroline, all leaned in closer, and when Robert began answering the same question, he directed it to his own neighbours – Ollie, Roy, Iona, Lily, Heath – as if, for her benefit, he preferred the talk divided, the limelight parted, the tension somehow calmed that way. Sitting midway down the table I could choose to listen to either poet, and, noticing that Elizabeth seemed more comfortable with the women, I turned to begin with Robert. Mimi, opposite me, looked the other way. Molly Dunn scrutinized her hands and made occasional observations.

'I was allowed to live my own life,' Robert was now responding, 'choose my own course in it. All sorts of books, in a well-stocked, very – *miscellaneous* library.'

Any major influences? (I pushed in, and he pondered)

'My parents' taste for whatever was – highest and best,' he admitted, 'but I found out for myself many forgotten fields, which proved the richest pastures… So far as preference of a *style* is concerned… I believe mine was the same first as last. I can't name any author who exclusively influenced me…'

Tennyson! (I thought – then heard my voice say it aloud) I mean are you close at all to Tennyson?

'Face to face,' he said, 'no more than that.'

Elizabeth heard this from the other end and broke off what she was saying to the women with a gasp of amusement, 'Robert, he spent two *days* with us! Dined with us, smoked with us, opened his heart to us (and the second bottle of port) – going away at half-past two in the morning – read *Maud* through from end to end, stopping every now and then,' and she put on a lordly, laureately voice, '*There's a wonderful touch! How beautiful that is!*' –

Uproarious laughter at that, and even Robert cracked a smile, caught out being discreet. Elizabeth's chuckling turned to coughing, 'wasn't made to – live in England,' she uttered hoarsely, but before Robert could address this in any helpful way, she had downed her water, waved him off, restored herself, and Lily was touching Robert's elbow:

'So Robert, in like Last Duchess right, when you say you *gave commands*, though it's not you giving commands I know, but the *guy*, whatever, the Duke right? when he says that, *I gave commands*, does he mean like he had her wasted?'

Browning looked at her, seemed about to respond, then sought safety in his beer, which he lifted and drained. I began to offer another but he indicated no. I felt he was uncomfortable, would be trying to cut this short soon,

'It's a brilliant poem!' Lily nonetheless proclaimed, Ollie harmonizing: 'a superb dramatic monologue,'

Browning sat there, doubtful, the empty glass in his hand. Then he grinned and told her mildly, 'I meant that the commands were that she should be put to death,'

'*Yesss!*' Lily cried but he went on, undecided,

'Or he might have had her shut up in a convent?'

Lily stopped, mouth open. Briefly she ran this by in her mind, then firmly rejected it, 'Nah, nah, he definitely *offed* her,' she concluded, which phrasing – along with her certainty – puzzled the poet away from the subject. So he rose, a shade nonplussed, gazing over at his Ba, who was back in lively chat with the girls at the far end. She glanced up of course – her eyes knew his were looking – but she wrinkled her nose at him and with her fingerless-gloved right hand gently shooed him away, to the delight of her new friends.

Then that excellent gentleman offered to buy a round. Ollie wrote our various orders down on a napkin, and off they went to the bar.

*

'Robert has a sort of mania about shops,' she's saying loudly, this is later, and he's listening politely to the students at his end, but clearly she hopes he might overhear her charming indiscretions. He obviously can, you can see his straight face trying not to grin, and he doesn't seem to mind as she sings on: 'He won't buy his own gloves! He bought a pair of boots the other day – because I went down on my *knees* to ask him, and the water was running in through the soles – and he won't soon get over it… he'd rather leap down among the lions after your glove – as the knight of old – than walk into a shop for you!'

'Yeah that's like me,' Molly notes for the record, and meanwhile Mimi, catching my eye as she mimics Bella's posh voice – though Bella's out of earshot – enquires of Robert 'perchance d'ye know *Lord Byron?*'

The poet sipped at his third, fourth beer,

'Leigh Hunt tells a story he had from Byron. A Jew who was surprised by a thunderstorm, while he's dining on *bacon*… tried to eat, but the flashes were – *pertinacious!* At last he pushed his plate away, remarking with a shrug, *All this fuss about a piece of pork!*'

People got that or they didn't, but everyone laughed. Our tipsy company had clearly formed a consensus that the Brownings would only stay as long as Robert was enjoying himself. Elizabeth, at her end, seemed delighted with it all, whether it was Blanche or Bella probing for gossip, or Kornelia or Caroline putting their solemn questions. Caroline asked her one that had them all quite still, flickering, clustered to the lady's flame.

'While my poems are full of faults, they've my heart and life in them. Poetry's been as serious a thing to me as life itself – life's been a *very* serious thing – there's been no playing at skittles for me in either.'

*

When I go with Mimi to get more wine for their end of the table, she biffs my sleeve with her fist.

'There's something,' she says, 'something weird like, *between* them,'

I dunno (I didn't) – you mean love? maybe that's what it looks like,

'What are you Max some expert,'

No, but – no, what do you mean *between* them?

'It's like – they're – not in the same place.'

Not in the same place? don't get it,

'Like they're, I dunno, shot with different film-stock. The way he looks at her. Makes *her* read poems, makes *her* take questions, doesn't say much, I dunno, forget it, pour the wine, it's your freakin party, we just live here,'

Can I cry if I want to?

'Your circus,'

My monkeys,

As we get back to the women there's a peal of laughter, and Elizabeth cries joyfully, 'Women *adore* him! Far too much for decency!'

I saw Robert turn his polite puzzled face to the clamour, and tried to see what Mimi meant: some distance in his eyes, maybe sadness, maybe something recollected? Maybe they somehow – *weren't together?* But he went back to listening to whatever urgent monologue Lily was slurring at him from the arm of his chair.

Now *spiritualism* had come up with Elizabeth's women.

'We did a séance in our halls of residence,' Bella was saying, 'we *totally* felt something didn't we Blanche,'

'Investigation is all I desire,' Elizabeth said, 'Robert's heart softens to the point of letting me have the *Spiritual Magazine*. Edwin Landseer's received the faith.'

Landseer the painter? (quoth I, at the outer rim of the conversation)

'Did everything possible to get Dickens to investigate. Dickens *refused...*'

'Dickens the writer?' quoth Mimi, taking the piss.

Bella was dazzled: 'Omigod they know *Dickens...*'

Elizabeth nodded, saying of Dickens: 'Afraid of the truth, of course, having deeply committed himself to negatives. Dickens! So fond of ghost-stories, as long as they're impossible…'

'Yeah that's Charlie for ya,' went Mimi, whom I tried to kick but missed.

Kornelia, who's religious, didn't want to hear about spiritualism: 'Mrs Browning,'

'Elizabeth,'

'Elizabeth! was it difficult being a woman to write your poems?' She clasped her little hands together.

'Grumbling's a vile thing…'

'But?' said Blanche, coaxing her to say more,

'You'd smile,' said she, 'the – the persecution I've been subjected to by the people who call themselves *The Faculty…*'

TELL ME ABOUT IT! (I roared but no one got it so I straightened up quickly) you mean what, medical people?

She sipped her wine and nodded.

'I had a doctor once who thought he'd done everything because he'd carried the *inkstand* out of the room – the *inkstand! Now,* he said, you'll have a pulse tomorrow. He thought poetry a sort of disease – a sort of fungus of the brain! – for women it was a mortal malady!' – now she was having to top all the shrieks of the gleefully aghast – 'He'd never known a system approaching mine in, in, in – *excitability!*'

She rode the crescendo, and their five glasses clinked with the toast:

'To *EXCITABILITY!*'

'I'm really very quiet!' she giggled, 'and not difficult!'

Poor Robert at the far end glanced over, his face all worry, and yet went on being polite because Lily was explaining something. He saw his Ba shooing him away again with her bright eyes glistening, as Caroline chose this moment to ask her what were her favourite novels.

'*Villette's* a strong book,' she said, over the sound of the other women still chuckling at that idiot doctor, 'Balzac,'

'What about Austen?' Caroline wanted to know, ever keen to meet a new Sister-in-Jane. Elizabeth shrugged.

'Miss Austen… her people struck me as wanting souls,' – *that* shut them up – 'the novels are perfect as far as they go, but they don't go far, I think.' She put her hand on astonished Caroline's, allowing 'it may be *my* fault…'

There were other surprises before the time was done. Robert noticed an old neglected piano in the corner, the lost twin of the one in the village hall:

'If it won't disturb you,' he announced, 'I'll play.'

And he did! He played tunes and he played songs, he played *Jeanie With the Light-Brown Hair,* he played *Beautiful Dreamer* and *The Rose of Tralee,* he played *Silent Night* and then *Skip To My Lou* with a grin as folks came and stayed and boozed and roared the bits they knew.

But Elizabeth's company remained constant. I craned my neck to hear her better, as I sat alone on the edge of the group.

'I know Florence Nightingale slightly,' she told them to a ripple of awe, 'she came to see me in London. I remember her face and her graceful manner, flowers she sent me afterwards.'

But as we lulled ourselves in the vague saintliness of the legend, Elizabeth, catching my eye for the first time – she would have caught me thinking how pretty she was – snapped us out of it:

'Every man's on his knees before ladies carrying lint – calling them *angelic* – whereas if they stir an inch as thinkers and artists from the beaten line – the very same men curse the impudence and stop there. I don't consider the best use to which we can put a gifted woman is to make her a – hospital nurse.'

As I tried to beam my accord with this, she looked past me towards Robert, who gazed back at her as he played *Liebestraum,* he played *Für Elise,* he played freakin *Jingle Bells* – which I didn't expect him to know – and he also played this, which I'd forgotten *I* knew…

Who would not happy be
Sailing in sight of thee?
Santa Lucia
Santa Lucia

*

When it was nearly time, and we could see their black horse and carriage out there trembling in the snow – somehow avoiding the worst of the snowball fight that had broken out between the *Scribblers* and the *Thesps* – all those who'd been sitting near Robert, or had gathered to his little recital, now descended on Elizabeth, though her quartet of new friends had no intention of giving up their ringside places. I went over to the bar just in time to stop Robert paying for the whisky I now paid for, ordering one myself.

'Single or double.'

Octuple, Norman.

'What's that then, a malt?'

Just a large one, Norman.

It was quiet now, no jukebox, no piano, and most people who were left were clustered round our legendary table in the snug. Lily had barged in loudly with a question about London, so the poet was telling of her trip to the Abbey:

'We were there at the wrong hour, the service was to begin – I was frightened of the organ! I hurried my companions out of the door! Frightened of the organ... you *may* laugh a little, they did! People can't help their nerves,' she smiled, looking out from the group at Robert: 'I don't cry easily, either.'

Browning dutifully chinked his glass with mine, didn't look at me as we drank. Now I looked at him looking at her. I both – saw what Mimi meant, yet was unable to explain it. He looked – far away.

Elizabeth was still talking, her dark eyes flitting from face to face, as she spoke of Poets' Corner: 'How grand, how solemn... Time itself seemed turned to stone.' Alarmingly she looked right over at *me* and I froze – 'Remember what's written on Spenser's monument?'

I beamed as if to say Oh it's okay we know *nothing* in our world! so she told us: '*Here lyeth Edmund Spenser, having given proof of his divine spirit in his poems...* something to that effect. It struck me as – *earnest*, and beautiful, as if the writer believed in him.' Then she said quietly, to no one in particular, 'Michael Drayton's inscription has crept back into the brown heart of the stone. All but the name and a date.'

'That name being *Michael Drayton*,' a deep voice confirmed from the rear of the group: Barry was in the building.

A whisper at my ear:

'Ask him where he lives,' – Mimi had elbowed up beside me, shiny, soaking, breathless from some fooling out in the snow, 'what his day's like, see if he mentions her. It's like you told me, with the Yorkshire girls.'

And I decided I *would* – though I wasn't sure quite why –

What's your day like, Mr Browning?

This time he did turn, turned the whole way round, his palms flattened on to the bar, his back to all the company. I remember thinking it was the only time he'd let her from his sight. Then he answered my question.

'Every morning at six I see the sun rise. My bedroom window commands a perfect view. The still, grey lagoon – few seagulls flying – the isle of San Giorgio in deep shadow… The clouds in a long purple rack, behind which – a sort of – *spirit of rose* burns up, till presently all the rims are, are – on fire with gold… and last of all the orb sends before it a long – *column* of its own essence. So my day begins.'

You *live* there (I said, and then I said) you live *there?*

Robert looked at me. I noticed Mimi had drifted away and was sitting at the table, at the edge of the company, she was sitting right next to Barry. But Barry was trying to peer past her at us, looked like he needed badly to join us at the bar – if it weren't for Mimi being playful, dodging her maddening face into his eyeline, flirting, poking, stopping him from rising –

So there was time enough –

Robert seemed to beckon me in close, so we were both stooped together at the bar, agéd agéd men, but I could also see over his shoulder his thrilled, enchanting, graceful, hopeful young Miss Elizabeth Barrett in her glory, lit green and blue and gold, surrounded by the friends she'd made of strangers, in the precious last moments of an evening to treasure.

'She suffered very little,' Robert said suddenly, and love held its course. 'Had no – presentiment. Assuring me she was better – comfortable – if I'd come to bed. To within a few minutes of the last. Slept heavily, brokenly – that was the bad sign – then she'd sit up, take her medicine, say unrepeatable things to me! and sleep again. Face like a girl's,' – the man was saying what I could plainly see from here – 'smiling, happy, in my arms, head on my cheek. Her last word – '

And Barry was in agony trying to ease himself past Mimi – *you're too nice to be an angel, mate*, I'd tell him one day – and though he finally shouldered his way to my side he couldn't stop me hearing –

' – was when I asked – *How do you feel?*'

'You lads!' Barry cried as he reached us, 'you renegades you!'

'*Beautiful,*' said Robert, turning away.

*

Term-time, autumn-time, Michaelmas, fall, *term*… things that sound absurd make perfect sense near the end of term.

What made little sense in October, in a meadow, when Father Hopkins had said it of the Northern Lights, did seem to make some now, so much so that it came back to me and I told it to my friend big Barry Wilby, as the wine-dark staggering last of us watched the Brownings' carriage, lit by lanterns, clip-clopping away northward from our still white wonderland:

A strain of time not reckoned by our days and years, Barry. But simpler, correcting the preoccupation of the world.

And 'That's as may be,' he answered with a sigh, one arm round Mimi Bevan and the other arm round me.

*　　*　　*

Week Twelve – December 12th

So, we'll go no more a-roving
    So late into the night,
Though the heart be still as loving,
    And the moon be still as bright.

For the sword outwears its sheath,
    And the soul wears out the breast,
And the heart must pause to breathe,
    And love itself have rest.

Though the night was made for loving,
    And the day returns too soon,
Yet we'll go no more a-roving
    By the light of the moon.

*

I sit up and it's late.

There's a moon on dark blue heaven, hence the music, lonely music, I'm wide, wide awake in the sky…

*

I sit up and the moon has moved. I'm going to start my packing. No I've done my packing, I must have done it last thing last night, I even zipped the suitcase, and look an empty gesturing shirt and moonlit jeans are draped on top of it, new clothes for my victim chalked on the floor, or my self before I'm there? they *do* know I'll be back, they're saying, I turn, I've time, I've time to turn, rejoin them in the dream…

*

I sit up and it's early.

Night has gone and it's morning, time lost, time still to lose, clouds in motion over the blue, the helpless brightness rising and falling. There's the daylight moon look, faint, somehow you wandered over there…

O you, the moon, the reader, you're gone, you're there, you're unlit, lit, what *are* you to this world? The loved one by the bedside as on drags my coma? The spotlight being adjusted for eleventh-hour surgery? Porthole, portal, eye? The beaming, mourning star of the next of kin? I won't hear you if you judge me, but I'll love by your light.

As I reach the slanting windows, encumbered beast in my tartan blankets, I see still snow upon the village. Between the nearest lamps on my lane are some tattered chains of lights, a couple of Christmas trees flash weakly at bedroom windows, all-of-them, some-of-them, these-ones, those-ones, tinsel flutters from a porch. People walking on that distant inch of lane I see, too distant to know whom, I realize at last it's that little cobbled short-cut to the village green, it leads there from the Coach House. *I'll pretend I didn't hear that.* I open the window wide to the precious cold, and off towards the heart of town can hear a brass band playing carols. Soon an amateurish choir joins in, and I wedge the window open.

*

Today and Memory team up matily on the coffee, but begin very quickly to go their separate ways.

Today boils the kettle, spoons instant from the jar, does everything, let's not miss a second, last day, time to take your leave…

Memory's sod-all help with the coffee frankly, just slouched there seeing out of the window, setting off through the dark again, the lanterns on its mind…

A company of six or seven staggering over violet snow arm-in-arm, we're going to play a poker game, we're going to deal till dawn…

Today reasons: that was last week. Memory wonders: was it?

Today adds: also you didn't. Memory: right, I didn't.

Today's pouring: you saw reason, called it a night. Memory says nothing.

Today milks and sugars and stirs and sips the only coffee.

Memory sulks, whines: *I* wanted one. Didn't I?

Today says no, there was only me, hears Memory sniff. It's fuming.

MRS. GANTRY'S POETICAL FIGURINES.

> *"The Assyrian came down like the wolf on the fold,*
> *And his cohorts were gleaming in purple and gold;*
> *And the sheen of their spears was like stars on the sea,*
> *When the blue wave rolls nightly on deep Galilee."*

Blimey, that's impressive.

This calligraphy is on silver card and glued to the base of a warrior, a fearsome armoured infidel-smiter with a shield and jagged scimitar. Peter Grain has arranged a line of ten toy figures on a plinth in Mrs Gantry's stall, which is the first stall I've reached at the Christmas Market on the green.

Are they all Byron-related?

'They are! in celebration of his visit.'

Do I get a discount?

'Oh – well, yes, of course, I – '

I'm kidding Peter, I want to buy one. I want to buy her, the witchy one in the black robe.

'Oh, good choice!'

> *"She walks in beauty, like the night*
> *Of cloudless climes and starry skies;*
> *And all that's best of dark and bright*
> *Meet in her aspect and her eyes."*

'Bastard! Beat me to it!' says Jeff Oloroso cheerfully, coming up beside me, blowing on his foamy drink.

Sorry, Jeff. Peter have you got an Interim-Dean figure? He might *well* have, Jeff, he's got zombies.

'*Interim?*' cries Jeff, 'bollocks to that. Real thing, mate.'

'Sold out of zombies,' sighs Peter, sorting my change in his woollen mittens.

What does Byron have about zombies Peter?

'Oh, wait, yes, *With curses cast them down upon the dust,/And gnash'd their teeth and howl'd...*'

That's 'Darkness'. Man you *so* pass my course.

'The chap is bloody gold,' Jeff says, 'we lost him! Fly away Peter! We'll have to hire Paul. Look, can I have a word...'

I'm still browsing Jeff.

'At the glühwein stall over there...?'

Goodbye Peter.

'Is there class at three, professor?'

VHB, Peter. Unless it's locked, is it locked, Dean Jeff?

'It's even heated, Poet Glynn. Feel free to call me Santa.'

NORMAN'S HOT YULETIDE BEVERAGES. SMALL (£5) OR LARGE (£7).

'Cheers.'

Cheers. Can I ask you something Jeff.

'Fire away.'

Was Tina married to you?

'Oh another life. I think we separated. I hope we did. Nikki hopes we did!'

So okay, so, what did it matter?

'To me personally, zilch. She was always a stickler for rules, though. I guess she felt caught out.'

I didn't do that to her.

'Me neither, squire, look, moving on: during the three days you were technically an employee you did show pretty good numbers,'

That's nice.

'Shall we give it another go, eh,'

Here?

'Spring term, Drama, word is you're interested.'

Drama? I've never had a hit, Jeff.

'Well, I've never won the big one.'

O…kay. I'll think about it. Norman?

'Small or large.'

I know why you say *small or large*. Normally we'd say *large or small*, right, it's a trick, isn't it Norman.

'Alright then large or small.'

Ooh, large I think. Dean Jeff?

DR MAPPING'S ACADEMY PRINTWORKS.

Alright Clyde?

'Morning. Can I interest you in any recent publications?'

I'll take an Oloroso, and… a Slurman and this Phapps here.

'Excellent choices. I *presume* you possess the Mapping already…?'

I do, Clyde, it's excellent.

'Hm. What's your favourite poem in it.'

What.

'What's your favourite poem in the book of mine you purchased.'

'Favourite poem, professor.'

I –

'Ha! Only joking!'

Good one,

'Yay,'

And what's this card…

'It's a link.'

A link to what.

'I'm not sure. There's no signal. But it would link you to *format*. Then you buy up units in a future text created by *format*.'

Why would you do that, Clyde.

'Well an investment, I suppose.'

I have birthed a monster. What's this?

'Oh, do you not have one? There's one in your pigeonhole.'

I don't have a pigeonhole.

'That's where you'll find it.'

Just when you thought it was safe
to play in the snow…

IT'S THE FACULTY CHRISTMAS PARTY!

ON THE TWELFTH OF THE TWELFTH!

TILL MIDNIGHT AT THE MAPPINGS!

31 East Cross Lane

*

You coming, Baggs?

Baggs, you okay mate, you coming to class now?

Baggs what's wrong.

Do I have to do them poshchurs.
No you don't have to do the postures Baggs.
Don't wanna do them poshchurs.
We won't be doing the postures!

*

George Gordon, Lord Byron…
　　Shortest lesson of all. First poet I read who made me want to do it myself. Because he mastered forms till they sounded like thought. Because he lodged in my mind. Because he made me laugh out loud. Because he pretended not to care and yet he cared so much it hurt. Because he lived so fast that in his last poem he could say his 'days were in the yellow leaf', pure song of the west, and the kid was thirty-three. He taught me to love it, savour it, give and not give a shit about it at the very same time, *and,* moreover, *call* a shit a shit – be that shit the King of England:

He died! – his death made no great stir on earth;
His burial made some pomp; there was profusion

Of velvet, gilding, brass, and no great dearth
Of aught but tears – save those shed by collusion;
For these things may be bought at their true worth:
Of elegy there was the due infusion –
Bought also; and the torches, cloaks, and banners,
Heralds, and relics of old Gothic manners,

Form'd a sepulchral melodrame. Of all
The fools who flock'd to swell or see the show,
Who cared about the corpse? The funeral
Made the attraction, and the black the woe.
There throbb'd not there a thought which pierced the pall;
And when the gorgeous coffin was laid low,
It seem'd the mockery of hell to fold
The rottenness of eighty years in gold.

The Vision of Judgment. Ottava rima – or 'eighth rhyme' – an Italian form. Easy to do in Italian, everything rhymes, but in English you have to really work the lexicon to make your trio of pairs. That's why it's great for comedy – the contortions are part of the fun, the feel of figuring life in it – and our lordship mines it to the utmost, in this and his masterpiece *Don Juan.*

The Vision of Judgment is eight hundred lines of wit and scorn and vitriol heaped on the grave of the recently deceased George III – and on the Poet Laureate Southey, whose poem of the same name had mindlessly praised the monarch like – well, like the English mindlessly praise monarchs. Byron wrote it in Ravenna and would never go home. It was published anonymously and the publisher was fined, the poet's name – they knew who it was, ffs – shredded in the press. But Byron's name could take it. Southey's has never recovered. Yet something always struck me. When push came to shove – and where his satirical hero Pope would have fried such a man as George forever – Byron nudged the old king into heaven, not hell: with a sigh he folded what he most despised into life's wider comedy.

As for the rest, to come to the conclusion
Of this true dream, the telescope is gone
Which kept my optics free from all delusion,
And show'd me what I in my turn have shown:
All I saw further in the last confusion,
Was, that King George slipp'd into heaven for one;
And when the tumult dwindled to a calm,
I left him practising the hundredth psalm.

Oh I loved Byron for the clichéd reasons too – what's not to like at seventeen? he drank, he shagged, he took a bear to Cambridge – but this outlasted those, this compassionate, humane, low chuckle at the world. Not morally *low* like they thought him then – low as in deep, profound, like a well.

Heath

Samira   Caroline

Peter   Barry

Lily   Ollie

Baggs   Iona

moi

I don't know who you are, and I don't know where you come from. I know some names of your towns and so on, I hear places in your voices, and I can see you all sitting here, I can extrapolate sweet long lives for you all like maybe you can for me – feel free to do for me – but none of it's anything like your truth, or your facts, or, if such a thing can govern in this mist, your fates.

I don't know why you came to my class, I don't know why I came to this place. I've told you the three, seven, twelve things I know. I don't know how I know them. Tomorrow we'll all be somewhere else. But we had good times, and we met great poets, you should keep this, look, look, keep this yellow – this *golden* souvenir, I'm going to be keeping mine…

READING SERIES.

Elective 711: Poetry/Maxwell   Thursday, Village Hall, times TBC.

26th Sept.	Mr. J. Keats.
3rd Oct.	Miss. E. Dickinson.
10th Oct.	Fr. Hopkins SJ.
17th Oct.	The Misses Brontë.
24th Oct.	Mr. S. T. Coleridge.
31st Oct.	Mr. E. A. Poe.
7th Nov.	Field Trip.
14th Nov.	Mr. J. Clare.
21st Nov.	Mr. W. B. Yeats.
28th Nov.	Mr. W. Whitman.
5th Dec.	Mrs. E. B. Browning and Mr. R. Browning.
12th Dec.	Lord Byron.

Now let's do this…

The white space. The nothing, the element you work in. It's been good to us, it's canvas, it's sheet, it's bed, it's soil, it's,

It's brought sorrow too. Our friend went somewhere and we don't know where. I – too lost someone to it. It may be a busier place than this, more fun, less fun I've no idea, it won't say, but – let's – face it one last time, shall we?

Let's face it, mis amigos, let's *face it down*. Let's hear it out and *take it out – waste* it, right? *Off* it, yes? One last minute and then let's fill it with the lines we learned this term, or the lines we wrote this term, or the lines each other wrote, or Niall Prester wrote, we'll blacken it, pepper it, riddle it with lines! Find poems in your minds, your hearts, your notebooks, push them into the middle of our table for the last time, your minute's starting *NOW!*

*

Now speak.

And so they do. Iona plucks something from the pile and begins reading softly, Ollie blurts out random lines from his brimming notebook, Barry shuts his eyes and summons up some nursery rhyme from his planet *where the cats have spats and the dogs have clogs* and Caroline sighs aloud to the ceiling *and I shall have some peace there for peace comes dropping slow* and Heath growls the lines of Niall *I'd save a good one for the end as if I knew how anything ended* and Peter and Samira lean together politely to read from each other's poems, Lily grabs and rips at sheets in a random fractured medley, then as I rise I hear she's tearfully speaking *Clare* in the plaintive voice of Baggs – *my friendsh forshake me like a mem'ry losht, I am the shelf-conshumer of my woes,* and as I contemplate them all in their beautiful tumult, and seek some lines of mine to free into the sound, I hear the voice of my once and future teacher, without whom which, without whom this, and without remembering I am simply reciting *Then all the nations of birds lifted together the huge net of the shadows of this earth, in multitudinous dialects, twittering tongues, stitching and crossing it* and in came sunlight, in and throughout, along and across like the day I came, and it lit their hair and lit the arms of their coats as they read and read, and it didn't stay long, it sunk behind the church now, because a winter's day was ending, and by the time their unfathomable roar petered out their teacher was gone too and walking down the lane with an ordinary white sheet of paper in his hand –

READING LIST for Elective Poetry Module
3pm, Thurs, V.H.B.   *Prof. Maxwell.*

– Reading *List*, not Reading *Series*, because his term was over, like last autumn is over, and the poets he'd taught are dead and gone, the poets he taught he'd never met, the poets he'd met he never will, and it was time to go now.

*

The spell is broke, the charm is flown!
    Thus is it with life's fitful fever:
We madly smile when we should grown:
    Delirium is our

'Where the hell are *you* going in such a hurry.'

I stopped dead on my frozen beeline to the pub. I turned and winced my eyes to make her out. Mimi sat smoking on a slanting gravestone in the gloom of the little churchyard. I could still hear the droning passion of my class from the room inside the village hall.

I'm done, that's it, that's my last class.

'They'll ask for their money back, *I* would.'

No you wouldn't. What are you doing here?

'Waiting for you. I don't mean *you*, I mean you lot. Couldn't take any more.'

More of what.

'The Keys. Chap's getting the *Bell* treatment, sensurround, stereo Bella,'

Who – what chap,

'Who d'you think, your freakin Byron.'

He's here

'You okay Max? you look like you've seen a ghost. You look like you did on Halloween when you fucked off with whatshername,'

Yes I – I – Lord Byron, is, is in the pub there,

'No Max fucking *Dale* Byron, fucking *Darren* Byron, get a grip, what the hell are you *on* these days?'

*

'Know me? Everyone knows me, I'm deformed.'

'Omigod I don't *believe* him!' Bella shrieks,

'I'd have shot myself last year, had I not recollected that all the old women in England would've been delighted.'

In the blazing laughter of the girls my eyes accustom to the winter heat, the Christmas light, the reality: he's ensconced, *enthroned* in the snug, with wine and a cigar, in the place we place our visiting poets.

'Truth is I'm too lazy to shoot myself, and it would annoy Augusta.'

Ecstatic Bella waves to me from her armchair by his side – I see Blanche, Kornelia, Molly, Roy, Kerri all close by, women I don't know, Nikki and Delphine from the Academy, and I realize I'm no longer essential to the passage of events.

Not sure I ever was, you know.

'Small or large.'

Infinite, Norman, *endless.*

'I'll take a Savoy Corpse Reviver, barman, straight up, that's brandy, crème de menthe,'

'Mulled wine or sod off, miss.'

'Go on then.'

We gaze on the wild assembly as we wait.

'He doesn't remember her,' Mimi says, as we see Isabella lolling and drooping against him, 'you know, from that wedding. She thinks he does.'

(I watch, I don't know what she's on about)

'Same action, same result,' she mutters, 'definition of madness, Bell.'

*

'I'm the very worst companion for young people in the world,' George Gordon Lord Byron's saying as he accepts the bottle I bring to the table, spares me not a glance, thus reducing me to a waiter, and Isabella, who's giddily running the show here, gets someone to drag up a stool for me:

'This is our poetry professor, Noel!'

Hey Noel. *(Noel?)*

'He's also a poet,' yells Blanche, 'but he keeps that pretty quiet!'

Actually I don't (I shout cheerily) but they're my students so they've no idea!

'I don't draw well with literary men,' says Byron, faintly acknowledging me with a nod, 'never know what to say to 'em after I've praised their last publication,'

'His is called *Pluto*,' Isabella shouts in his ear, and he looks about as interested as he'd be in a night on that lost planet,

'There are exceptions,' he goes on, 'but they've either been men of the world, such as Scott or Moore – or visionaries out of it, such as Shelley,'

What's Shelley like! (the waiter hollers in the din)

Byron shrugs, fills the available air with cigar: 'the mildest of men,' he goes, 'the least selfish. But I've nothing in common with his *speculative* opinions,'

'We had Keats here!' cries Bella,

'Who?'

'*Keats!*'

'Jack Keats?'

'*JOHN KEATS!!!*' all but hysterical,

'Keats, Ketch, or whatever his names are,'

'His real name is Bains,' Mimi murmurs from nearby, and the acolytes ignore her, goth bitch, no respect etc,

'Little Johnny Keats,' says Byron, 'took the wrong line as a poet,' What? Keats? How?

'Cockneyfying, *suburbing*…'

You know what, Noel, I (what, I come *this* close to telling him where I come from, but) I come from Pluto,

'Ah, just like your *book*…' Blanche is nodding, as if the mystery makes sense now, but Bella's spreading into his Noelship's eyeline, 'I thought you were all of the Romantic School!' at which he quite convulses with contempt,

'School, *schools*, a word never introduced till the – *decay* of the art has increased with the number of its *professors*,' (this last word a glancing swipe at me, like it's my bloody fault the word's the same) 'There've sprung up two sorts of *Naturals* – the Lakers, who whine about Nature 'cause they live in Cumberland, and the Cockneys, who are enthusiastic for the country 'cause they live in London.'

(The squeals of laughter that greet this practised crystal rather grate on me, as does his use of me as one of *They*, a *professor*, a prop to him, so I call out)

This is because Keats doesn't rate Pope, right? (and *man* that hits the mark, he's placing his right hand over his glass, he's taking a moment…)

'Pope, Pope, the most beautiful of poets,' he says, and all have quietened with him, he seems soothed by the very name: 'his poetry is the book of life.'

Look I love Pope (I say, ready for anything) but I love Wordsworth and Coleridge and Keats and Shelley and Blake too. Christ I even love *Byron*.

'You shabby fellow,' he grins, raising his glass for me to raise mine, 'don't be afraid of praising me too highly, I'll pocket my blushes,'

Well *now* you've done it! (I begin on my praises, but he hasn't finished with schools,)

'Wordsworth and Coleridge have rambled over half Europe, but what on earth have the others *seen*? When they've really seen life – when they've felt it – when they've travelled beyond the far distant boundaries of Middlesex, when they've overpassed the Alps of Highgate – then, and not till then, can it be permitted to them to despise Pope.'

*

Twas the season to be jolly, and twas the season to forget how precisely one thing led to another. My class arrived of course, indignant to have missed what they'd missed, and I seemed to be saying over and over *this is nothing to do with me any more*, as Lily and Heath and Ollie and the others shouldered into the group where they could, so that each stool sat two folks at least, and the armchairs either side of Byron seemed to bear about a dozen.

'Is there anything in the future that can possibly console us for not being always twenty-five?' the poet wondered, and Ollie exclaimed: 'I *am!* I always will be!'

At one point there was a poem in Byron's hands, I think it came from Caroline, who was kneeling on the floor by the fire.

'Second thoughts in everything are best,' I heard him counsel her, 'but in rhyme – third or fourth don't come amiss.'

At another time Nathan Perlman crouches beside him with a *Selected Poems* to sign, and Byron softly punches his shoulder: 'When an *American* requests, I comply,' he says, 'these transatlantic visits make me feel as if talking with – *posterity*, from the other side of the Styx.'

'I'll be sure to wave, sir,' Nathan beams, and now here came Isabella's poem – she'd been furiously doing last-minute revisions without conceding an inch of her seat – Byron took the paper with a flourish, 'Ah, my goddess of the armchair…'

Isabella blushed the colour of the light, as the poet scanned and mouthed the poem. Then he stopped and looked steadily at his wine.

'I wrote one sonnet before, but not in earnest, and many years ago. As an exercise,' he said and was giving it back, and I feared for her, 'I'll never write another. They're the most puling, petrifying, stupidly platonic compositions.'

By the time he got this far, Bella had turned her back and was rising, escorted by Blanche and Molly, away, and he addressed what followed to a girl I didn't know, brown-skinned, hair golden-dyed, who had rotated to the neighbouring chair and nodded and sighed as if she understood his yawning explanation:

'I detest the Petrarch *soooo* much, that I wouldn't be the man even to have obtained his Laura – which the whining dotard never could,'

And yet then, with Bella gone, he looked at the chair she'd left behind, grinned and told us: 'I'll be in love if I don't take care. *Ça ira, ça ira…*'

*

'And on that cheek, and o'er that brow,
    So soft, so calm, yet eloquent,
The smiles that win, the tints that glow,
    But tell of days in goodness spent,
A mind at peace with all below,
    A heart whose love is innocent!'

Because yes there was a reading too, in the heated and lamp-lit, hollied-and-ivied, mistletoed village hall, the flock had truly wandered clear of my drunken shepherdry, and as Byron stood and bowed and bowed, and the full house thundered riotous approval, I heard him wonder 'Where's my goddess of the armchair?' and there she was, Isabella Marsh, bravely revived in the third row, reassessing her new-found hatred of her horrid former idol, meeting his dark eyes with hers, and as the applause was fading, and no one seemed to be rising to the moment, I had a role left after all, here's me ambling to the stage –

Sir, that was magnificent! George Noel Gordon Lord Noel Byron!

'Child of Harrow's Pilgrimage,' he sniffs, 'me and my damnable works...'

There wasn't a chair to be had, so, as he retired to the seat on the stage and fuelled his tankard with dark claret, I stood uneasily to one side, vaguely directing questions his way, but the thing went well enough. We were both buoyed up by the size of the crowd, and the spell in the pub had loosened all tongues.

Ollie was quickest off the mark: 'Is it true, man, you took a bear to uni?'

'A *tame* bear,' Byron specified, like it was, well, no thing, 'they asked me what I meant to do with him, and my reply was he should sit for a fellowship.'

Ollie tried to follow up through the laughter, but 'The answer delighted them not,' Byron added, and Caroline pounced at the right time:

'Sir, can you speak about the night at *Gernsheim*...'

He pouted, looked blank, so she prodded:

'The ghost-story night?'

Then he got it, shrugged, 'Ah, the ghost books... Mary Godwin – Mrs Shelley,'

'Frankenstein!' shrieked Lily, 'were you like shit-scared when she told you that story?'

He looked nonplussed, drank, set down his glass.

'Wonderful work for a girl of nineteen.'

Some of the women did some affable boo-hiss, but he'd no idea what their issue was, and corrected himself instead – '*not* nineteen, indeed, at the time,'

'Why haven't we heard of *your* story?' Lily demanded, and for once I was thankful for the enquiry of a recent arrival – 'Where d'you get your *ideas*, Lord?' which I gladly transformed as I helped it along,

Yes, what *is* poetry to you. Noel.

'What *is* poetry?' He sipped his wine and said, rather quietly after thought:

'The feeling of – a former world and future.'

*

We were a great barnstorming gatecrashing horde on our way out into the patchy snow. I mean, *I* was invited, the Academy profs were, but someone had told Byron there was to be Yuletide tomfoolery at the Mappings, and nothing was going to stop him, as long as he could rail against the very *idea* of parties while the company crossed the green:

'I don't talk, can't flatter, and won't listen – except to a pretty or a foolish woman,'

'Oh we got shitloads of them!' cried Lily, and I was aware of Bella and her mannerly friends all grimly embarrassed right behind us but hook or crook it was Glyn's bloody turn:

'Don Juan, mate, I'm telling you, funniest poem in the language,' and the effect of praise proved yet again timeless:

'Is it not good English? Confess, you dog, is it not good English!' He hugged me and shoved me away and turned so he was walking backwards, five young women giggling in his wake as he roared for a joy that was equally timeless – 'Is it not life? Is it not the thing? Could any man have written it who hasn't lived in the world?' Then he stopped, they almost fell against him, and he clasped them, cast them off again, one by one by one – Blanche – 'Fooled in a post-chaise?' – Molly – 'In a gondola?' – Bella – 'Against a wall?' – Blanche again – 'In a carriage? On a table? *Under* it?'

*

Clyde Mapping and Angela Wilbery Mapping broke out into twin grimacing smiles of welcome as they opened the door to two dozen of us. I was one of the few who was actually invited, but once Lord Byron, in his black fur cloak, cried 'Better late than never, pal!' and the students started flooding past him, *force majeure* and Christmas spirit were bound to carry the day.

'I am amazingly inclined,' he now informed all those in earshot, 'to be seriously enamoured.'

And soon Mr Noelship, charming most of those he passed, and his company of falling angels – who took the pained English politeness of the hosts for a free ride on anything – had overrun their splendid kitchen, blaring out thanks whenever they eased past, shouting whatever was coming to mind. I just kept on walking down the hallway to a door. I opted for the great outside, on a tiled patio under the heavens, with Orlando Faraday and Iona McNair, a centering couple for a centrifugal evening, to await whoever else might stumble on us here.

*

And now that we were sitting down, and the mayhem raved and babbled on in the bright house through the glass partition, we began to feel time quickening, term rolling to its end.

They were leaving tomorrow too, they said, on the last of three trains that would come throughout the day.

When? *8.17, 12.17, 4.17,* Ollie was reading from a scribbled note. What would happen after those? How would they know? They hadn't been here either. They'd spend the Christmas nonsense up in Fife and the New Year nonsense in London. The sound of these plans was so soothing I felt no need to ask my thousand things. Life here, now I think of it, had been better than my questions. They'd be coming back for spring, would *I* be? Don't know, all depends.

We three stayed where we were. Heath and Roy and Mimi came. We saw Lily and Caroline head out to the back garden, perch on a snowy bench like birds, huddle and drink from a bottle, talking.

'Poor Lily,' said Iona,

'It's the sauce,' said Roy Ford, 'Sami's told her she got to quit.'

'It's not just that,' Heath said, 'it's the whole lifestyle deal, all the meet-the-family shit.'

What, are they finished?

No one knew.

From inside we heard a peal of Academy laughter. Then, in the lull that followed, elsewhere, close by, the conversation of two smoking silhouettes: 'I can promise you good wine,' drawled the one we recognized, 'and if you like shooting, a manor of four thousand acres, fires, books, your own free will, and my indifferent company…'

'Fuckin' Guardian Soulmates,' was Heath's take on this.

*

The Mappings were too polite to kick us out, we'd have grown old sitting there, remembering our term together, the high times, the troubles. It was Noel who broke the thing up. When he joined us out on the patio with his entourage, all the fiction girls hysterical with tinsel in their hair, Ollie stupidly asked him about that time he swam the Hellespont?

'I *plume* myself on this achievement!' he bellowed, 'hour and ten minutes! – in humble imitation of Leander – though no Hero to receive me on the other side…'

And so it was that one of the fiction girls, one of these several auditioning Heros, started yelling about the lagoon, the Ferry Boat Inn that might be open late, the wooded isle out there with the huts, and what do you think, two hundred yards? Three hundred? No way! *LET'S SWIM OUT THERE AND PARTY!*

*

It was one of those suggestions there was no one to gainsay. He wanted to see it, they wanted to show him, he wanted to do it, and the rest of us, kind of, wanted to leave the stoical Mappings alone to their Christmas clearing up. So those of them who were up for it hurried on ahead, along the East Cross Lane that would wind us back towards the village. I hung behind with the same crowd who'd sat the party out on the patio. On either side of us the large houses were lit or very dark, two or three ludicrously strung with Christmas lights: Santas, reindeer, elves, the works. In a gap between houses I saw the pitch-dark space of our library, the canvas covers gleaming darkly from the thaw, I wondered what state the books were in.

Barry was there somehow. I hadn't seen him at the party, but there he was, arm-in-arm with all-singing all-dancing Lily, and when she took a break to dance in a ring with Heath and Roy and Ollie and inevitably all fall in a pile in the shuvelled roadside snow, I thought I'd ask him something:

Barry.

'Señor…'

Why do you always ask where poets get their ideas? It's like – your only question.

'Why? because well, why now, because: because I don't know where people – *get* – ideas. Where they go to, sort of thing. I don't, myself, have them.'

That's because you're holy. You visit lonely people. That's a better idea than I've ever had. Or will ever have.

'Ooh, still time to have it, teacherman!'

Don't think so, feller, don't think so.

*

When we reached the Cross, where the pub was desolate and silent, and the village hall well-nigh unbearably deceased, we saw a clump of someone on the bench by the churchyard wall. Lord Byron and his swimming-crew were yelling and clamouring far beyond the village green by now, on their way between the college buildings down towards the lagoon, but we'd seen whatever it was, so we had to do something.

We stepped nervously to the bench. The bearded portly man! – the sketching fellow – had fallen asleep, was snoring and burbling, his coat pulled up around him, his face in his beard and his beard on his chest. His bowler hat had rolled clear onto the ground. Ollie picked it up and brushed it, put it on himself.

'Poor guy'll freeze, where does he live?'

No one knew. Barry thought his name might be Eddie, that's all he knew.

I thought you knew all the lonely people (I said)

'You don't know if he's lonely,' Barry reasoned in response.

Then I remembered the first-floor room at my digs, the one that was always empty. It took five of us to lift the chap up from the bench, and as he stood he seemed to revive, mumbling softly to himself:

'Most beautiful, nice people, no life is ever lost.'

'We're going to find you a bed, Mr Eddie,' said Ollie, setting the hat back on his head, 'you can't stay out in the snow now, can you,'

'You'll catch your death, love,' Iona yawned.

'So thankful for a change,' he said, and as the odd fellow could more or less walk, Ollie and Iona and Roy were enough to help him down the lane towards my digs.

It's unlocked! (I called out after them) the first-floor room, it's empty.

'Don't wait for us,' Ollie called back from their good deed, 'we're calling it a night, man.'

'Likewise,' said Roy, turning with a grin, 'my people don't do swimming.'

'Mine don't either in fucking December,' Mimi observed, finally getting her roll-up lit.

*

If, in the month of dark December,
    Leander, who was nightly wont
(What maid will not the tale remember?)
    To cross thy stream, broad Hellespont!

Just do it, as they say.

And off they ludicrously shiveringly go, plunging in screaming in their underwear at one? two? in the morning, Lord Byron, Bella Marsh and Blanche and Syrie, Kerri Bedward and Delphine, while Barry Wilby gathers their clothes with a chuckle and sets sail in their wake in his rusty bobbing boat, to help them out if they get into difficulty. Heath's climbed in too, hauling Lily down beside him wrapped in Caroline's dufflecoat: nobody thinks she's capable of swimming it. Caroline's long gone.

I can't remember the last thing our Noel said that night, or cried out joyfully from the rolling deeps – there was certainly some howl of articulate pleasure accompanied by a great plurality of shrieking and splashing – because Mimi, abandoned on the shore with me, chose that exact same moment to assert: 'This is lame, Max, let's do something else.'

*

We walked, or rather, we went for a walk. Planned it, chose a route, started out. It was gone the middle of the night, clouded over, nearly starless. The only light was street-lamps here and there in the distance, and the snow gazing back the great grey-orange of the sky. Along the lakeside southwards we went, behind the college houses over icy trails and bike-paths, seeing the looming silent blocks of Benson, Cartwright and De Vere, then on along beside the meadow where once we had our picnic, on we went, round the side of frozen tennis courts towards the railway station, from where we saw, away on the dark white hillside, the mouth of the railway tunnel.

What train you getting tomorrow d'you think.
'Dunno. You?'
The first one.
'You'll never make the first one.'
I'm not going to sleep tonight.
'Is that something you control, Max.'
Not really no.
'Let's do it.'

It being what.
'Y'know, hang out till the sunrise.'

Agreed, we walked in silence up from the station back towards the Cross. There isn't far to walk in our little village.

It's here.
'What's here.'
This is the place.
'What place.'
It's here where I – where I – began *being here.*
'Mm-hm what you just, materialized.'
Yes Mimi I just materialized.
'Okay. I was gonna say let's do some 2P-3P, but it sounds like you started early.'
I don't need anything. I don't do anything. Oh I do get plot ideas from inhaling amyl nitrite,

335

'Do you. Moving on,'
The weirdest things develop, you can't imagine,
'Can't I, what star d'you think that is.'

*

It's not twinkling, it's a planet.
   'It's a star. It's twinkling *twinkling* Max, you know the song, jesus.'
   It isn't twinkling, it's moving, it's a plane. It's a plane, oh my god there are planes in the sky, there are *OTHER PLACES ON EARTH!*
   'It isn't moving, Max.'
   Oh. No. I guess not. I just wanted – it to.
   'Cor, *another* thing you control, I better stick with you eh.'

*

I could go another lap.
   'I *beg* your pardon.'
A circuit, round the village, we've not been everywhere.
   'I ain't going everywhere. I ain't goin nowhere.'
Tomorrow's the day when my bride's a-gonna come…
   'Excuse me?'
Nothing. Dylan. If I stand still I'll fall asleep. Like a horse.
   'Let's go to yours and play music.'
Really?
   'I think it's almost dawn. Listen.'

Listen?
   'I mean breathe.'

   'Go on, breathe.'
I am breathing.
   'Breathe.'
   'Good boy, keep breathing, top tip from Bevan there. Go on, where we going, lead the way,'
We're right here, you know we are.
   'What? no I don't.'
This is my digs, where I've lived all term, that room lit up at the top there. You didn't know that?

336

'I'm supposed to know where you live now?'
No. Just saying.
'*I* don't care where you live.'
Why should you, hell, not your circus, is it,
'Not my bonobos Max look there's something on your front door.'
What?

Glyn hiya!

That first-floor room was locked, sorry! Did what we had to!

O x

PS – semester was ace, see you in spring for drama!!! ☺

---

*

We could hear him as soon as we got inside the house.

'Is that snoring or like, the Apocalypse.'
Have you got a light?
'You don't smoke, you just materialize.'
To see our way.
'It's a fucking staircase Max.'
Yep, first man ever,
'Also there's a light here.'
It doesn't work.

*

'So it doesn't. Well. I'd say – follow the sound of marching bears.'
I think Ollie and Roy put the drunk bloke in my room.
'No shit Sherlock.'
Heath says that.
'Never heard of him. Hey Max am I going to prick my finger on a spindle and *die?*'
Probably, why?

337

'Come on, it's *so* like Sleeping Beauty right?'

Sleeping Beauty didn't snore like that. Ending would've been different.

'Arm-in-arm, Max, scared now.'

It's like I've – been seeing him everywhere.

'Who-which-what-where-why?'

The snoring guy, I keep seeing him, he's – familiar in some way –

'Probably *you*, in the future, *woo…*'

Anyway. Er. Welcome. Max's lodgings.

'*Such* a romantic idea. Get a girl up to your room, most guys would go that whole candlelit thing, table set for two, cheap pasta dish from a TV chef, five bottles of wine cos *you never can tell*, but no, none o' that crap, instead a fat old snoring man on the only bed I *like* it, I *like* that style!'

He was writing something look…

'*Do* you have any wine…'

It's the last page of a letter…

'Fridge yes, wine no. What's this rosette on the wall?'

What? pub quiz

'That's classy. I think we should do my drugs.'

No look, look:

I confess that a little more society would sometimes be pleasant – for painting, Greek, music, reading and penning drawings are all used up by the end of the day. Various friends, however, write and come – so I don't complain.

If you let me know – shall I send out and gather toadstools in hampers for you? You can sit and pick them in the large hall.

O! that I could get back to Jerusalem this spring!

Goodbye. Yours,

Edward

'D'you like, know him, Max?'

Uh-huh.

'Is he like – your dad, is this your subtle way of – '

He's the first poet I ever read. As a child. That's Edward Lear.

'Oh. Right. The nonsense guy.'

I've a nonsense poet in my bed.

'No change there then.'

I'm – dreaming after all. Oh no, oh god,

'Hey hey, I'm not, I'm not, shut up. I got your back, okay, okay Max? Been a long term etcetera,'

Hang out till sunrise, can we,

'Etcetera, gather toadstools while ye may,'

I know one of his poems by heart,

'Not going to cost me, is it,'

No Mimi, I'm an elective, you can take me or leave me,

'Is *both* an option maybe?'

What

'Nothing, read your nonsense, you know you want to…'

*

> *When awful darkness and silence reign*
> *Over the great Gromboolian plain,*
> > *Through the long, long wintry nights;*
> *When the angry breakers roar*
> *As they beat on the rocky shore;*
> > *When Storm-clouds brood on the towering heights*
> *Of the Hills of the Chankly Bore…*

*

And this is how the term ends, me sitting cross-legged with Mimi Bevan on the faded carpet of my attic in the small hours, reciting The Dong With A Luminous Nose while its author snores above us on the bed,

'The *what?*'

The Dong,

'That's what I thought you said,'

And waiting for the sunrise.

*

Then, through the vast and gloomy dark,
There moves what seems a fiery spark,
A lonely spark with silvery rays
     Piercing the coal-black night –

'You'll never make that first train,' she murmured where she lay over there with her back turned, in my tartan blanket, under the window.
I'll get the second one then, 12.17, you want to catch it with me?

Mimi?
'Yeah alright go on.'
You'll meet me at the station, twelve noon?
'Copy that.'
Where was I...

     A lonely spark with silvery rays
          Piercing the coal-black night –
          A Meteor strange and bright:
     Hither and thither the vision strays,
          A single lurid light.

     Slowly it wanders, pauses, creeps,
     Anon it sparkles, flashes and leaps;
     And ever as onward it gleaming goes
     A light on the Bong-tree stem it throws –

'The *what* tree?'
The Bong-tree,
'For fuck's sake...'

     And those who watch at that midnight hour
     From Hall or Terrace, or lofty Tower,
     Cry, as the wild light passes along,
          'The Dong! – the Dong!
               The wandering Dong through the forest goes!
          The Dong! the Dong!
               The Dong with a luminous Nose!'

*

By the time the Dong had fallen for the Jumbly Girl who would
break his heart, Mimi Bevan was fast asleep. I eased the last of her
roll-up out of her fingers before it burned her, and by now the light
outside was – light, not morning yet but light, and I had seen myself
through Thursday.

Edward snored, Mimi sniffed and shuffled and turned in her
blanket, and I stretched out on my back, with my palms behind my
head, the way as a child I thought would always make me stay awake
if I needed to, and my eyes began to close on the growing light,

> *Far and few, far and few,*
> *Are the lands where the Jumblies live;*
> *Their heads are green, and their hands are blue,*
> *And they went to sea in a sieve…*

*

They were both gone when I woke. The bedclothes were neat but
the tartan blanket lay crumpled under the window. The earth was
foggy but the sky a blinding blue, and out of the window I could see
all the way to the wooded isle to the west, blue pines poking out of
the mist, for mist was all I could see of the water.

I bade the view farewell and was out of that room with my bag
and my case in less than a minute.

I left my books behind, but I took my birthday cards, even one I
remembered had gone behind the bookcase.

The village was very quiet. I made the station for noon. The
platform was deserted but for a tall lad in uniform.

I'm waiting for the 12.17. Is there one?
'Heavens yes. You're early.'
Well yes. I'm expecting someone.
'I see.'
A companion for the journey.
'I see.'

Good I'll. Just stand here then. And wait for seventeen minutes. Sixteen minutes. (I waited for two.) Watch my things will ya mate, I'm going to find my companion.

*

The Keys was full to the rafters, it was doing a roaring trade, I could see that through a frosted window, in fact –

It was nice through a frosted window. I could see it was steamy and crowded in there, with the Christmas lights all blazing away, the tree in its glory, the fire going in the corner over there, but the window blurred the many faces, so there was no one I could put a name to. Just like the day I arrived, I thought.

But I hadn't time to savour this smear of gold and crimson light: I went round to the next window, where the panes offered a clearer view.

There they all were, at the tables they favoured. Ollie and Iona, with Caroline, Roy, Heath all toasting and who was in that reindeer jumper? Claude, from the Coach House. Suitcases, hold-alls, packed bags were heaped all round the place. Lily was in there with Molly Dunn at the bar, they both wore dark glasses and were prattling and shouting. Rowena Finbow was there, reading the menu in her wheelchair, McCloud was there kneeling down on the floor, with a smaller boy and girl who both looked pretty much like her. They were piling wrapped-up gifts round the base of the tree. Peter Grain and Nathan were there, in a booth, heads and hands together. My ghastly jukebox trio were in there, banging their tankards for some idiot reason. Jeff Oloroso, Nikki Phapps, Gough Slurman, Delphine! ah, one of the ones who'd gone swimming was there, so maybe they hadn't all drowned or frozen. But I couldn't see Bella or her friends from fiction. Barry was in there, ambling round on his merry way, being tapped on the shoulder and asked something by *format*, who wore a white coat and stethoscope, like a doctor, let's have a listen to heart-rates today. Norman was stooped at the bar with a magazine, straightening up to serve someone, oh flippin heck not her.

Mimi was in a red tee-shirt, a green elf-cap, black jeans, she was ordering a round, she kept looking back and pointing, demanding what they wanted – Jake Polar-Jones, Syrie, Ali K, Yvette, all the gang from Theatre Studies – it was 12.07. She had better make that order quick.

A window I was staring through, and a window of time passing. If I didn't go inside now, into that rich warm brimming tableau, just a matter of yards inside – it was the walk away to the station for me, and the train and goodbye. 12.07, 08…

Except – I could get the later train, there was still one departure left, I could get the 4.17!

Go – back down to the station, collect my bags, come back up to the pub, enjoy myself, drink drinks, eat three-course lunch at length, say adieu to those who stay here, go staggering back to the station at four with all the folks who are leaving today, take the long ride home with them all, chat, play word-games, look out of the window, sleep, sleep, sleep…

12.10, seven minutes – Mimi was ordering food, they were all there, leafing through the menus, reading the specials scrawled on a blackboard, oh and here came Bella and Blanche and Kornelia, bursting out of the Ladies together, all in the clothes of the night before, shrieking at something, laughing and weeping, now *format* was listening to Mimi's chest, breathe *in* and she did, breathe *out* and she's doing so…

If I go in now, it will all be hurry, haste, stress, no time for proper farewells at all –

When I left that window I was set to go inside.

But now I find myself walking, footsteps clocking away south in the bright cold wind, and there on the snowy hillside with a hoot the distant train glides out of the tunnel, I guess it's 12.12, so I look – it's 12.14…

*

Is that the 12.17?

'Yes, sir. That's the one you mean to catch.'

Well-remembered, mate.

'It's my job, sir. Here are your bags.'

I know, man. I'm in fact, I'm going to take them, change of plan,

'Is there a problem, sir?'

There's a 4.17, isn't there,

'There's a 16.17, sir.'

Wow even better.

'That's not for four hours though, sir, four hours and two minutes.'

What?

'THAT'S NOT FOR FOUR HOURS, THOUGH, SIR, FOUR HOURS AND ONE MINUTE!'

WHY IS NO ONE ELSE TAKING THIS TRAIN?

'ONCE MORE, SIR?'

WHY IS NO ONE ELSE TAKING THIS TRAIN?

Lad didn't mind, or know, and here it came why not, the 12.17, rumbling emptily down to a jolting juddering halt here at the buffers, hissing and done. I could go now. I can go.

'Can I help you with your bags, sir?'

No, mate, thank you, I got it.

'Are you awaiting your companion?'

What?

'Mind the gap there sir.'

I got it, thank you. What did you say?

'Merry Christmas to you, professor!'

And to you – to you and – yours –

To tell you the truth I was so stunned to have suddenly got on the train, I almost forgot to watch my own departure. I was just sitting there, staring forwards, letting the world turn under me.

I was moving! I sat up with a gasp – I'd even sat down on the wrong side – I almost fell against the opposite window in time to see the dear old place beginning to recede. Way over there I saw the roofs of the student halls, I saw the spire of the tiny church, the village hall beside it where I'd taught the three, seven, twelve things I know, I saw a white flash of the village green and the lampposts there, I glimpsed the pub and it was gone, I saw the field from my first day, the woods where we'd gone walking that green dark afternoon in the rain, the meadow on the other side where I said let's make it summer, I saw the little winding road on the opposite hills, curving off between the fields, the road which took me on the Field Trip with Barry on my birthday – blackness slams it away, the tunnel, now I stare at my own self in shock in the hammering streaming window.

I sat, the tunnel was long, I must have slept, I must have dreamed.

I dreamed I was going downhill on a sleigh, sleigh-bells were ringing and ringing and ringing, and then I was in the village hall and I could hear bells chiming but it was still dark tunnelling black when I woke, and then all at once it wasn't – I was thumped back into different daylight, rainy fields and houses and trees, and something in my bag was chiming, *that* was the chiming from the village hall, it was a flat canary-yellow oblong of metal, it wouldn't stop chiming, a *phone* it was, it was my own phone chiming, and when I turned it over to see it was chiming and blinking with names and questions, sad face, smiley face, holly, heart, dad, snowman, xmas, text after text after text after text

WWW.OBERONBOOKS.COM